Praise

"One of the most exciting and disturbing voices in extreme horror in quite some time. His stuff hurts so good."

— Brian Keene, author of *Earthworm Gods*

"Whatever style or mode Triana is writing in, the voice matches it unfailingly."

— *Cemetery Dance*

"Triana is without question one of the very best of the new breed of horror writers."

— Bryan Smith, author of *Depraved*

"*Full Brutal* is the most evil thing I have ever read. Each book I read by this guy only further convinces me that he's one of the names to watch, an extreme horror superstar in the making."

— Christine Morgan, author of *Lakehouse Infernal*

"(*Gone to See the River Man* is) such an impressive piece of writing it will rank amongst the best of 2020. You're unlikely to come across a better example of how to build dread over a relatively short page-count."

— *Horror DNA*

"Jesus! And I thought *I* was sick!"

— Edward Lee, author of *Header*

THE THIRTEENTH KOYOTE

Kristopher Triana

BAD DREAM BOOKS

ISBN: 978-1-961758-06-3

BAD DREAM BOOKS

for Bear

forever my pack's right paw

PART ONE

THE ONES WHO RUN
AT NIGHT

CHAPTER I

THE COFFIN CAME OPEN.

Vern put the bandanna over his nose and mouth like a bandit, squinting against the rising dust, his brow damp from exertion. This was no cheap coffin, not a pauper's grave like so many others in the lot. This damned box was sturdy as a stagecoach. Vern, on the other hand, had a build like a scarecrow. It'd taken the pickax to get the danged coffin to give up the goods inside.

"Sweet gallnippers!"

As he pulled away the scraps of wood, the corpse was presented to him in a haze. He lifted his lantern and the orange glow revealed the decayed flesh and hollowed out eyes, the long, gray sideburns like tumbleweeds.

Vern tipped his hat. "Salutations." He chuckled at his own joke and wondered if all these late nights in graveyards were starting to wear on his sanity. "Sorry to disturb your slumber, friend, but you've gone up the flume, so I doubt you'll mind me pilfering a thing or two you won't be needing."

He opened the man's coat, finding a silver pocket watch. He put it to his ear, hearing nothing, but if it were wound, it'd be mighty fine. The coat was too far-gone to salvage. From the looks of him,

1

this fellow had been in the ground for years. No way to tell his true date of death; few tombstones remained in these ruins. Unlike the good, Christian cemetery at the chapel, this graveyard was a forgotten lot deep in the woods beyond Hope's Hill. Possibly a family plot, judging by the many smaller graves, or an improvised burial sight for pikes or pioneers who'd perished along the trail. Simple, wooden crosses, green with moss and rot, were all that marked the graves. He'd only stumbled upon it by chance while buck hunting atop Black Mountain, returning to it after nightfall with excavating tools.

The dried flesh crackled as Vern slipped the man's rings from his skeletal hands. They left the bones in gray puffs. He ripped the man's blouse open, hoping to find a necklace, maybe a sterling silver crucifix or a bejeweled medallion, anything to make this excavation worth the work he'd put in. The corpse was too old to make any money off the body. Whatever the dead man had on him was all Vern would get. The buttons popped from the body's clothing as Vern tore it free, revealing the withered ribcage. Vern glowered when he saw it was bare of jewelry.

"Consarn it."

The lamplight bounced off of something. Vern leaned in, expecting reflective rock, but as he dusted away more of the man's flesh he saw a golden capsule in the shape of a large egg.

"Well, I'll be…"

The capsule was beneath the corpse's ribs. Had it fallen into him as his body decayed, or had it been shoved into his chest upon burial in some surgical procedure? As an undertaker, Vern had manipulated flesh enough to not be surprised by what dead bodies could do, what they could withstand. He had to dig into this one now. Pushing his hand into the mummified skin of the dead man's belly, the body crumbled like clumps of dirt around his forearm. Vern dug deeper until his fingertips touched the capsule pressed against the back of the coffin. He expunged it, surprised by its weight. He had to put down the lantern to lift the golden egg with both hands. He turned it over and back again, examining the engravings. Vernon Pipkin was an educated man, but these strange symbols he did not recognize. They might be of Indian origin, but he thought the piece was too elegant to be made by any redskin. There were letters engraved in it too, some sort of Spanish or Italian. A thin line ran around the circumference of the egg, and when Vern pulled on both ends the piece began to separate. These were not merely gold plates. The egg's shell was thicker than two fingers stacked. He pulled a little harder, careful not to break it, and when the top came free Vern gasped at what lay within.

It began to pulse.

CHAPTER II

GLENN COULD SMELL THE CORPSE a mile over the ridge. The blood still held moisture, filling the air with the rich fragrances of copper and salt. His pale flesh quivered. It was a familiar odor to him, one that had burned in his nostrils since boyhood. He'd called The Mexican Cession home then, long before his life in the saddle. Then, like now, the smell of blood made his mouth water. The leg of the bank teller he'd killed in Pope's Rock had begun to spoil, the meat decaying to the point of being nearly inedible. It had kept the pack full as they rode through these mountains, but now they needed fresh meat. He'd been hoping for another kill, but sometimes scavenging would have to do.

He gathered the reins, clacked them.

"Yah!"

Belial rocked between his thighs, the young mustang charged by the same excitement as its master. The men followed, smart enough not to ask questions as their leader ventured off the trail and across the rocky terrain. His spurs of bone clattered and the bullwhip at his side flapped against his thigh. Pebbles crackled like kindling aflame beneath the hooves of the five horses, serenading the black rise of evening, and a cold wind made whispers through trees growing from out the stones in gnarled, defiant coils. When the riders rose to the crest, Glenn scanned the valley basin below. He spit tobacco and waited for his night vision to kick in. Redness brewed in his eyes.

"There," he said, sniffing out the body more than seeing it.

The pack trotted forward. A screeching above them caused Glenn and Hiram to turn their heads to the sky. The buzzard spun alone in the twilight, his brethren feasting somewhere below. Glenn loathed these filthy creatures. It was simple instinct to detest any competition for food.

Being the fastest draw of the gang, Hiram drew his iron and blasted the buzzard off its orbit, sending it tumbling to the earth as the rest of the flock fled into the sky, spooked by the crack of the silver-plated revolver. As they filled the air, Glenn's men drew their pistols, Dillon, Thad, and Web joining Hiram in the sport of bird slaughter. Unless they were ravens, the men had no love for winged creatures. Feathers left the buzzard's bodies as bones snapped and blood spurted.

Hiram smirked. "Only thing they's good for."

The riders holstered their weapons and moved on.

They found the dead man's body tucked behind an assortment of boulders. He was naked and facedown in the dirt and pebbles, a spattering of blood about his head like an Indian headdress. The buzzards had picked his back and buttocks apart. Now the flies were having at him.

Hiram dismounted and crouched beside the body.

"He's been scalped. Musta crossed the wrong chief."

Dillon swung down from his horse's back. The youngest of the company, Dillon Boody seemed to fly in and out of the saddle. He lifted the brim of his Stetson and wiped his brow with the back of his glove.

"Reckon it's the Shoshone?" he asked.

Glenn shook his head. "Doubtful. That tribe's too friendly to white men."

Web laughed, his brown face like granite. "That's mighty foolish if'n you ask me, an Indian trustin' a white."

"If this sucker crossed an Injun," Dillon said, "I don't care what tribe they are, they'd do him in just like this. They're all savages."

Glenn shook his head again, marveling at the irony of Dillon's musings. Just two days prior, Dillon had raped a schoolgirl, no older than fourteen by the smell of her. He broke her arms so she couldn't even try to bat him off, and once he'd satisfied his carnal desires he vivisected her heart and bit into it, sucking down the blood while it was still hot. Yet here he was calling Indians savage.

"They musta robbed him," Hiram said. "Took his clothes on top of his greenbacks, and whatever else he had."

"How long?" Glenn asked.

"How long what, boss?"

Glenn glowered. "How long's he been *dead*, Hiram?"

His second-in-command gulped, realizing he was trying his pack leader's patience. It'd been a long, hard road and Glenn wasn't as young as he used to be. He was saddle-sore and the hide on his mustang's back was wearing down.

"Sorry, boss." Hiram leaned in closer to the corpse, taking a good sniff. He lifted the head in both hands and lapped at the exposed skull. "Shit. Can't be more than an hour."

Dillon drew his iron and glanced around the plains. "Goddamn Injuns could still be here."

"Nah," Hiram said. "They's gone. Simmer down."

"And end up scalped like this sumbitch?"

Glenn silenced them both with a mere rising of his hand. He dismounted Belial and removed his hat, releasing a long shock of black hair. He approached the body and Hiram got out of his way. The pack leader used one foot to turn the dead man over, and then spat the wad of used tobacco into his face. He opened his coat, bypassing the pistol slung at his hip, and reached into the hidden pocket. The steel of the kris dagger's handle was cold to the touch, an arctic sensation so bitter it would burn the flesh of a normal man, but thick, blackened calluses protected Glenn's palms. He drew it from his coat and gazed upon the blade. It was curved back and forth like a snake slithering through desert sands. Where the blade met the handle was an inverted pentagram of fire opal, the same blood red as the eyes of Glenn Amarok, the exalted commander of The Koyotes.

The blade entered the dead man just beneath the ribs, preparing the carcass for evisceration. Glenn tended to discard the guts in favor of the steaks and chops. Hiram, however, was more ghoulish. Glenn removed the liver and tossed it to his sidekick. Hiram devoured it almost instantly. Being the cookie, Web set himself to gathering kindling for a fire to cook with. The other men gathered around, awaiting their portions, whatever pieces Glenn would toss to them once he'd chosen his own. When times were hard they had to settle for his scraps, but tonight there was enough to fill all their bellies.

"This'll hold us over," Glenn said, "until we get to Broken Ridge. We'll hit their bank and snatch us some whores for breakfast."

He pulled free a strand of meat the size and consistency of a strip of hog fat. He rolled it around his finger and bit into it, thinking of the territory and the small town that lay somewhere within it, hidden deep within those azure mountains.

It wouldn't stay hidden very long. Not with Koyotes closing in.

*

Children bounced down the steps of the schoolhouse. It was almost winter now but abundant sunshine made this the warmest day Hope's Hill had seen in a month's time. The wee ones were ecstatic to run along and play now that their studies were over. Grace related to their jubilance. Her students had been trying today. She too was ready to enjoy the rest of the afternoon. She hitched the bottom of her dress over her shoes as she went down the steps and into the street, tilting her head skyward so her bonnet would not keep the sun from her cheeks.

This week marked the one-month anniversary of Grace Cowlin signing on as Hope Hill's schoolmarm, having taken over the position from the late Nanna Buckingham, an ornery woman who'd held tight her vocation some thirty years. The children weren't the only ones relieved to have a younger, more amicable teacher. Even their parents had sighed with relief.

Grace was glad to be here too. Sure, this far north the seasons were a bit colder than Broken Ridge, but it was worth it to gain the sense of peace she'd found here in Hope's Hill. It was a simple mountain town located dead center where three territories met, as if it couldn't decide where it belonged. She related to this too. Such was the nature of the west, she figured. But Grace was not the pioneer her kinfolk had been. The urge to explore did not entice her. She merely hoped to find a husband, 'jump the broom' as her mother often said, and buy a piece of this land while she was still young and teach some children of her own. A simple life. Nothing

7

fancy, but also no trouble.

Passing by the chapel, she spotted Sister Mable walking through the garden. She and the nun exchanged waves and Grace noticed the black gloves the nun always wore. She thought it queer but did not ask about them. When Grace looked back in the direction she was going, she realized she'd nearly bumped into Father Blackwell.

Grace blushed. "Oh, my. I beg your pardon, Father."

Blackwell gave a gentlemanly half bow, revealing the sunburn atop his head where the white hair had thinned. The old preacher's eyes were equally white, plagued as they were by cataracts, and his black suit seemed a size too big for him though he was a healthy weight, the collar loose upon his gizzard neck.

"No forgiveness necessary on my part," he said. "I leave that to the Lord."

His choice of words seemed odd to her, but his smile was pleasant, genuine. She doubted the preacher had meant anything other than praising His name. Reverend Blackwell was one of the earliest settlers of Hope's Hill and claimed to have contributed to the town's name. He was widely accepted as the town's oldest resident, though even he claimed to have lost track of his birthdays. The schoolchildren told tall tales that the preacher was one-hundred-years old. Looking at him close up, Grace could see why.

"Such a nice day," she said.

"Indeed it is, child. I've always fancied the reaping season. Even with winter coming, it makes me mighty grateful for all we've been blessed with."

"Truly."

"I do hope to be seeing you at our harvest festival."

"Of course, Father. I plan to make pies for the giving of thanks."

"That'd be mighty fine."

Grace smiled but clutched her handbag a little tighter. She didn't want to be rude, but she was tired of social interaction, the children having worn her out. She craved some quiet hours alone to read.

"Well," she said, "it is always nice to see you, Father, but I must be—"

They were interrupted by a sudden cry.

Grace turned to see a young man running down the street in bare feet. His coveralls hung by only one strap, the other flapping free upon his chest. Even from this distance, the man's fiery hair revealed him to be of the O'Conner family, a clan of grain farmers from just beyond the town limits. Grace and the preacher watched as he ran up. The boy's younger siblings had just let out of school and stood there dumbstruck as their big brother bypassed them. Alerted by the ruckus, Sister Mable came out of the garden, and when the young man saw the nun and preacher he headed their way, legs hammering the pebbles of the street. Grace looked to Sister Mable, but the nun's face was stoic in its beauty, revealing nothing.

The young O'Conner nearly fell into the nun's arms. He was caterwauling and making little sense. Sister Mable took hold of his shoulder and told him to speak slower.

"Yes ma'am," he managed. "It's Ma and Pa...they...they is..."

The young man hung his head, sobbing, unable to go on.

Father Blackwell stepped in. "Be still, my son. Your parents, are they not well? Shall we fetch Doctor Craven?"

The young man shook his head.

"What's your name, child?" asked Sister Mable. "You are the O'Conner's eldest boy, correct?"

"Cillian O'Conner, ma'am." He sniffed. "My Pa...his farm..."

The boy pointed to the rolling hills on the edge of town.

Blackwell asked, "Where's your horse?"

"Couldn't ride one, Father. Had to run on foot. It's all wrong. Things have all gone...gone *wicked*."

The preacher's face fell gray. "Wicked?"

"The horses won't let us mount. Our cows are giving up sour milk. Now the fields are... *turning*. It's all wrong, Father, all wrong. Pa ain't right. He's got all these black veins standing outta him. He even upchucks black! Mama's spooked something powerful, says we need a gospel, sharp."

The nun shared a glance with Blackwell. They returned their attention to the blubbering O'Conner boy. Grace could not look at Cillian. She'd never seen a boy his age cry publicly. She felt embarrassed for him despite how genuine was the fright in his bloodshot eyes.

The preacher produced a small Bible from his pocket, rosaries wrapped around his wrist like gypsy bracelets. "Sister Mable, have Barley bring the stagecoach around."

The nun turned back into the chapel, calling for the driver. Cillian followed as if afraid to lose sight of her. The other O'Conners

9

approached the chapel, slow and cautious, four freckly children looking not to their religious leaders for guidance, but to their teacher. Grace entered their little circle, touching the children's heads and shoulders, consoling them. Suddenly, relaxing with a book seemed less important.

She turned to Blackwell. "Allow me come with you."

"Come with?"

"They are a large family. Bridget O'Conner has mothered four boys and two girls, including their newborn. If the situation there is as dire as Cillian says, perhaps I can assist by managing the children, keeping them from getting too riled up."

The preacher rubbed his beard, mulling it over. "May be best if you take the children back to the schoolhouse until we know what's going on."

The little O'Conners whined in objection. They'd seen their eldest brother's tears and clearly wanted to go home, wanted their parents

"Cillian claims there is wickedness," Grace said. "What do you think he means?"

"I've known the boy all of his life, Ms. Cowlin. He is a good lad, trustworthy. If Cillian says something wicked has befallen his kin then I believe him."

"Perhaps then we should fetch the constable?"

The preacher shook his head. "Constable Kirby has fallen ill and is bedridden. Besides, we'll have my driver if we need protection, though I doubt we will." The children stirred but the preacher pacified them with a smile and quick clap of his hands. "Who'd like to ride in my buggy?"

*

It was a cramped ride with the O'Conner clan and Sister Mable and Reverend Blackwell piled into the stagecoach, so Grace rode upon the driver's box with Barley Reinhold, a brother whip with broad shoulders and eyes like rivers in wintertime. His handsome features were amplified in the orange sunshine. Beneath the blonde beard, Grace guessed him to be in his late twenties, just a few years older than she. Had he not been married, she may have set her cap for the driver and fancied him a potential gentleman caller.

Autumn leaves fluttered upon the swaying treetops, a myriad of colors adding additional splendor to the mountains. The sun was sinking lower, threatening to hide behind those hills, and Grace drew her overcoat across her bosom, the November chill giving her a shiver.

Reinhold raised the brim of his derby. "Would you like my coat, Ms. Cowlin?"

"I always appreciate a gentleman," she said. "But I'll be fine. I wouldn't want you to catch your death of cold on my account."

"Oh, I'm used to the elements. Fond of 'em, even. I'm a woodsman to the manner born. I like to feel the wind on my cheeks." He reached beneath the dashboard and winked at her as he retrieved his flask. "Besides, this keeps me warm enough. A wee nip of nose paint does the blood good."

He took a drink and passed the flask to her. She politely declined. He took one more pull before tucking it back into its hiding spot. Grace doubted his employers would approve of him drinking while he worked, but it was not her business. His winking implied it was their little secret and she wasn't sure if she should feel honored by his trust or insulted by his assumption she'd want to hit the booze with him.

When the stagecoach reached the edge of the O'Conner farm, the horses slowed, snorting. Reinhold tapped the reins but the animals resisted his command. Clearly embarrassed, he gave them harsher orders and the horses obeyed, but their heads remained turned to the left, their ears and eyes locked on the farmland.

"They're frightened," Grace said.

The driver glowered. "They're just tired is all. Pay 'em no mind."

But Grace knew this was a weak excuse. The horses were breathing heavy—not from exertion but from a sudden disturbance, sensing something the passengers did not. The stagecoach followed the trail deeper into fifteen acres of grain. Though the sky held a tangerine haze the trail was cast in shadow, the sunlight stifled by gray mountain rock. At first she thought it was these shadows that made the grain appear black, but as the field closed around the trail she realized it carried a strange substance. The tips of the wheat appeared dusted with soot, the rye plagued with rot. In the distance, the maze of cornstalks had gone from green to gray, the leaves limp with death.

"My goodness."

"This land is out of sorts," Reinhold said. "Soil must be sour."

Somehow Grace knew it was more than that.

The horses came to a stop and Reinhold helped her down from the driver's box and then opened the stagecoach doors, helping Sister Mable out first, then the reverend. Cillian guided everyone to his homestead and his siblings ran ahead of the adults, eager to see their parents, hoping to find some sort of comfort there. A freckled woman opened the door and they swarmed upon her like army ants. When she saw the reverend she clutched the cross upon her breast and came down the steps in a hurry, her housedress nearly tripping her. She chose to forgo greetings.

"It's Shane," she said. "He's...he's..."

Father Blackwell approached and she all but fell into him.

"God is with you, my child. Tell me what is wrong."

Bridget O'Conner's eyes brimmed with tears. "It's my Shane. He...oh, I am pained most plaguily to tell you, Father. Please, come inside."

The group entered the farmhouse, only Reinhold staying behind with the horses. Bridget led Reverend Blackwell and Sister Mable upstairs and Grace removed her bonnet and tended to the children, gathering them into the kitchen.

Tabby asked, "Why is Ma crying?"

Cillian hushed the little girl. He was trembling. Footsteps on the second floor made the boards creak above them, sounding like rickety gates. Grace heard a door open, then a man's voice, raspy, ornery. Shane O'Conner. Grace couldn't make out what he was saying, but there was no mistaking the venom in his tone. The man was furious.

Tabby went to Grace and wrapped her arms around her waist, burying her face in her hip. Cillian put his head into his hands. When Grace looked at the other youths, they too had covered their faces. It was almost automatic, ritual. Patrick and Isaiah folded their arms on the table and lay their heads upon them as if sleeping. Maurice, the youngest, sat beneath the table with his legs drawn up, his head against his knees. They'd been through something like this before. Grace wondered if their father was a drunk who took to whipping them like mules when he took up too much whiskey. She'd never seen bruises on the O'Conner children, but perhaps Shane placed them were others could not see.

More muffled voices from upstairs—Bridget pleading, Shane hollering. Even Sister Mable had raised her voice.

Grace's skin prickled. "Cillian? What's going on here?"

But the young man wouldn't answer, wouldn't uncover his eyes.

There was a sound like an oncoming locomotive.

The windows exploded.

Grace screamed and the floor shook beneath them, the walls vibrating and knocking knickknacks and pickling jars from the shelving. They shattered as they hit the floor. As strawberry preserves spread across the wood the jam separated, revealing black decay within. The preserves were alive with maggots. The boys cried and Tabby screamed. Grace went to the children, guiding them all under the table with Maurice. They never took their hands away from their faces. Cillian remained standing and Grace called out to him, having to yell over all the noise.

"Cillian! Get low! It's an earthquake!"

He parted his palms away from his mouth. "No, it's no earthquake! It's the curse!"

"What are you talking ab—"

There was a clack like thunder, like a single gunshot, and the spaces between the floorboards grew wider, imbued by a blackness that rose from below like negative rays of light. It was not smoke, but rather shadow beams, unlike anything Grace had ever seen. The sight of them chilled her to her core. How could *light* be *black*? It shot up to the ceiling and spread out in fans, sliding down the walls like lava and blocking out the daylight. It flowed fluidly, the lonely rapids of a merciless darkness.

It was unnatural. It was unexplainable. It was *wicked*.

She heard Father Blackwell shouting from above.

"Deliver us, oh Lord! From all sin, from everlasting death, from the blackest of the black, from the snares of the devil!" The reverend's voice grew louder. "Turn back the evil upon my foes, and in Your faithfulness destroy them!"

Reinhold burst through the front door, spotting Grace crouched under the table, the O'Conner children huddled beneath her arms like hatchlings under a mother bird's wings. A Sharps rifle was in his hands.

"Ms. Cowlin!"

The panic in the man's eyes sprung her into action. They had to get out of this forsaken house. She ushered the children out from under the table as the blackness swarmed. They refused to open their eyes, so she and Reinhold had to wrangle them toward the front door. Grace grabbed Cillian's arm but he would not budge. She would have to come back for him.

"Come on!" Reinhold said.

She came with Tabby and Maurice, one child at either side of her, her hands pressed upon the backs of their necks so not to lose them. Reinhold had left the front door open and the large square of natural light seemed to call to Grace. The glow of early evening was flushed with varying shades of copper and gold. As she ran, her hair began falling in front of her eyes, the bun loosened. The strands were thick with sweat. The children came out first and Grace nearly leapt across the threshold and stumbled when she hit the steps. Reinhold caught her by the elbow and they ran together. Free from the house, the children dropped their hands and opened their eyes. Reinhold yelled at them to get into the stagecoach, but the horses were wet and bucking, necks arched, and the young O'Conners backed away in fear.

Grace heard footsteps behind them. She looked back, half expecting some hoofed demon to be on their tail. From out of the darkness Sister Mable appeared, leading Father Blackwell by the hand. Cillian was with them. Seeing them safe, Grace breathed a sigh of relief, but the looks on their faces dimmed it. The reverend was the color of chalk, the nun's beauty suddenly aged. Their hands were slick with blood and Father Blackwell's Bible was smoldering in his hands. Grace stared at the doorway, waiting—*praying*—to see Bridget O'Conner and her newborn baby.

The mother never appeared.

*

"I say we burn it," Reinhold said. "Burn it to the ground."

He was leaning against the wall, rolling a cigarette. His little wife was beside him, silent as ever. Across from them, Sister Mable was leading the other sisters in a quiet prayer, blessing everyone who'd come to the meeting. The town hall was packed, the residents having gathered to address the strange goings on in Hope's Hill. Some wanted to hear about the O'Conner house firsthand. Some had gossip to spread. Others had strange stories of their own.

"You want to destroy the whole house?" someone asked.

Reinhold shook his head. "Not just the house; the whole farm. Cleanse by fire."

Angry murmurs floated through the gatherers.

"The land has gone to the devil," he said. "It's cursed!"

A man in the back said, "Horseshit. Have another drink, Reinhold."

"I done saw it, you fool! Sister Mable and Father Blackwell saw it too. So did Grace Cowlin and all those poor children who're now orphaned. You think we're all liars? Some of you have seen the grain from the road, haven't you? Seen the rows of corn? It's all as black as the ace of spades."

A man Grace recognized as the shopkeeper of the general store stepped forward. "We don't know the O'Conners are dead. They might be missing but that don't mean they done passed in their chips."

"And what of their bouncing baby girl? What of her, Cassius?"

The shopkeeper looked away.

After the strange encounter at the O'Conner farmhouse, town leader Murphy Hyers, the town's two deputies, and a few of the townspeople had ventured there to investigate. Barley Reinhold had been among them. Constable Kirby's illness had progressed and he was unable to attend or even leave his bedroom. No supernatural darkness was present inside the farmhouse when they arrived, but the fields lay in ruin and all the livestock had fallen dead. They showed no signs of injury, and all of their eyes were wide open, as if still afraid of whatever had taken them. Though the hills were known for troublesome wolves, none had come to dine on the livestock and no buzzards or insects had touched them either. The house was a hollowed out shell of itself. Boards had shaken loose, all the windows were busted out, and the searchers reported a foul odor they'd been unable to identify.

Shane and Bridget O'Conner were nowhere to be found. Neither was the baby.

Being that four respected members of the community and all the O'Conner children told the same story, no foul play on their parts was suspected. The preacher and nun told of an evil presence in that house, something from another world that had swallowed the O'Conners up and then sealed shut like the lid of a deep well. Grace believed him. She'd seen that crawling blackness with her own eyes, felt the horror of it as it had slithered across her very flesh. Their story was so fantastical Grace was surprised anyone would believe it, but when similar reports of sickly livestock and spoiled vegetation started coming in, even those townspeople without faith began to believe in the impossible.

"We've been hexed," Reinhold said.

Murphy Hyers cleared his throat. "That kind of talk won't help matters."

Grace looked to their portly town authority. There were bags under his eyes that told of his burden. He looked wan, exhausted—too weak to lead.

A woman spoke up from the back. "He's right, Mr. Hyers. My chickens are only laying shells filled with blood. When I cut open my squash there's only gravel and worms inside."

"I've had problems on my ranch too," a cowpoke said. "My best bossies gave birth to nothing but acorn calves. They're so weak they can't even suckle. And the horses won't settle or dry. Only takes the buzz of a fly to spook 'em."

Hyers sighed. "That doesn't mean we need to jump to conclusions and call this a hex."

Cassius the shopkeeper agreed. "We don't need folks to—"

"I'm no theologian," Reinhold said, "but I know the signs of a curse. Our livestock, our land—it's all gone sour!" His eyes went hard as he scanned the room. "We've got us a witch in our midst."

Grace wanted to stand up and object, for the sake of the town's collective sanity, but something told her to stay silent. After all, she too had seen things she could not explain.

Murphy Hyers did the objecting for her. "Mr. Reinhold, I'll thank you not to rile up this town with your addle-headed superstitions. We have serious issues to attend to—sickly livestock, poor vegetation, missing people. These things could cripple our good town if we don't take action proper. We can't get distracted by foolery."

"Don't you call me no fool, Murphy!"

"Then by God, sir, don't behave like one. We'd be putting ourselves back two hundred years if we caved to that kind of hysteria. Last thing we need is a witch-hunt!"

Many of the townspeople began speaking at once, shouting over each other. The only one who stayed silent was the undertaker. He was standing with his hat clutched in his hands, staring at the floor. Most of the townspeople seemed to support Hyers, but not all. Reinhold wasn't the only one given to superstition. Grace hugged herself, sensing things would get worse before they got better.

CHAPTER III

THEY CAME TWO NIGHTS LATER.

Grace was preparing class work when there was a knock on the door to the room she rented in the Abercrombie house. She wasn't surprised to hear the housemother's voice on the other side of it. Perhaps she was bringing up a spot of tea.

"Are you decent, dear?" Joyce Abercrombie asked.

"Yes. Do come in."

When the older woman came through the door, Grace stood. The housemother looked paler than usual and the sides of her mouth twitched. Seeing Joyce wasn't alone, Grace pulled her housecoat closer around her. She was decent, but only for the company of another woman. The two men wore hard expressions. They did not do her the courtesy of removing their hats, and this small act made her mouth grow dry.

Joyce said, "These men wish to speak with you, Ms. Cowlin."

The strangers approached Grace and she kept the small table between her and them. She felt intruded upon, disrespected, but she did not make protest. Instead, she waited.

"Ye Grace Cowlin?" the tall one asked.

Half his teeth were gone. The second man stood further back

but Grace could still smell him. Clearly these were wild men of the plains, outlaws barely civilized.

"I am," she said.

Joyce gasped when the tall one snatched Grace's wrist. She tried to squirm away but he had a blacksmith's grip.

"What is the meaning of this?" Grace asked. "Unhand me!"

"People 'round here want us to ask you some questions is all."

"Then do it here and now. Do not accost me."

When she pulled away again the stranger grabbed her by both arms, turning her back against him as he marched her toward the doorway. The second man stepped aside to let them through, and when Joyce tried to plead with him he shoved her back. She stumbled and nearly fell to the floor, catching herself on the windowsill. The strangers escorted Grace out of the room, ignoring her efforts to reason with them. The housemother tried to intervene and was backhanded for it. She fell against the wall and started sliding. Grace's bare feet kicked against the floor as she was carried down the stairwell and dragged out to the front porch where a shadowy stagecoach awaited. Though he wore his derby low upon his brow, Grace recognized the man upon the driver's box.

"Mr. Reinhold! Please, help me!"

But as the strangers brought her closer to the stagecoach, she began to understand. Barley Reinhold did not look at her. His eyes stayed hidden beneath his hat's brim as one of her attackers swung open the door to the coach. They hurried to get Grace inside, sitting her on the edge. She grabbed the sides of the doorway and braced herself there, fear for her life giving her strength, and managed to get in one good kick to the face of the man who'd been holding her. But it wasn't enough to keep her out of the stagecoach. When she turned the second man drew his iron and clacked the butt of it across the back of her neck. Had she not been thrashing, he might have landed the blow directly upon her skull. Once they had her inside, Grace heard Reinhold clack the reins and the coach began to roll, the strangers closing in on either side of her, still manhandling her.

The short one laughed and patted the other man's arm. "She got ye good, Delbert."

The tall man tried to laugh it off, but his tight eyes betrayed any humor. "Silly sage hen kicks like a dang ol' mule."

Grace groaned when she tried to move her head. Stars swam before her eyes and the movement of the coach made her nauseated.

"Where are you taking me?"

"You're a wanted woman," the short man said.

"Pardon?"

He chuckled. "Well, somebody wants ye anyway. Maybe not the law, but folks happy enough to part with their coin in order to see ye brought in."

"Brought in where?"

Delbert grabbed her by her hair. "Enough of your questions, womern."

Bright pain climbed her neck. When her face pinched her captor flashed his shattered grin and the menace Grace saw there made her flesh prickle with chills. Her thighs clenched together beneath her housedress. The danger she was in was becoming all the more visceral. What cruel intentions did these strangers possess? What was a fine citizen like Barley Reinhold doing in their company? He was goodly husband employed by the church, was he not? Why would he be involved in a kidnapping?

There was a gunshot.

It tore the night open, echoing off of the mountains like the hammer of some capricious god. Reinhold's horses bucked and brayed, causing the wagon to halt abruptly. Grace and her captors flew forward, bouncing off the opposing seat, and Delbert landed on top of her and for a horrible moment they were face to face, his foul body pressed upon hers, his breath against her lips. She winced and turned her head away despite the spasm it brought to her neck.

Reinhold shouted. "Sake's alive!"

Then there was another man's voice, clear and deep.

"Best let that woman go."

*

Reinhold hadn't noticed them until the muzzle flashed. The man's rifle was pointed skyward, having only fired a warning shot. Though Reinhold recognized the two deputies that flanked the rifleman, him he knew not. They sat atop their horses in the middle of the road, blocking off the trail leading down to the creek where Reinhold had intended to take the schoolmarm for questioning. She was the newcomer in town, and a woman at that. It only made sense to suspect her of witchery first and foremost.

19

The rifleman was mostly in shadow but Reinhold could make out his Stetson hat and the thick handlebar moustache.

"Let the schoolmarm go, Barley."

Reinhold glanced at his Sharps rifle tucked behind the dashboard. Would the deputies and the rifleman use their iron if he made a cautious move for his own?

"She's done nobody wrong," the rifleman said with a southern accent, "least of all you and those turds you brought on. Three men against one woman seems like the actions of a yellowbellied coward to me, but there's still time to prove you have some semblance of honor. You let her go and I'll let you off easy."

"On whose authority, mister?"

There was a sudden flash. Reinhold tensed before realizing the man had struck a match. He cupped his hand around the flame and lit his pipe, the glow revealing a face like granite.

The rifleman kept the pipe in his mouth and held up his weapon in both hands.

"On my authority," he said.

"You don't look like Constable Kirby to me."

"Don't have to, Barley."

"You know my name but I don't believe I've had the pleasure."

"Oh, well, the pleasure is all mine, I'm sure."

Reinhold sneered, his fingers itching for his Sharps. "Since you ain't offering like a man ought, I'll just ask you straight out: who the bloody hell are you?"

"You can have it your way, Barley." The horse moved forward, bringing the rifleman beneath a blue beam of moonlight. "Name's Henry Russell. But you can just call me Marshal."

Reinhold's face fell slack. "So you're a lawman then, are you?"

"A marshal of these glorious United States. Now if you have some sort of beef with the laws of our great country I suppose you can take it up with me and my men, but I reckon the gentlemanly thing to do would be to let the Cowlin woman go so she might get to safety 'fore I blow your damn fool head off for disobeying my direct order."

Reinhold went rigid, face flushing. Though he gave no instruction, the door to the stagecoach swung open. He turned on his driver's box to see Grace Cowlin stepping out. One of the men he'd hired was even holding the damned door open for her!

"Cowards!" he yelled. "No courage to come to the scratch?"

The hired men exited slowly, their hands in the air. It seemed they hadn't been paid enough to go head to head with the law. Grace hitched her dress almost to her knees and started into a run. Her breath steamed in the autumn air.

Reinhold fumed. "Come back, witch!"

But the schoolmarm kept on running. As far as Reinhold was concerned, this cinched her guilt. A good Christian woman wouldn't flee an accusation of witchery. She'd want to clear her name even if by means of torture. Reinhold hadn't planned on taking things that far, and she should have known that about a man of his high character. He'd just wanted to ask her questions. Well, obviously she didn't want to be caught in her lies. When she reached the lawmen she hid behind them, staring back at Reinhold with devilish eyes. The marshal stepped down from his steed and helped her up and then climbed back into the saddle. Though he had to put his rifle back into the scabbard to do so, he showed no sign of fear. Reinhold clearly didn't worry him, and that just insulted Reinhold all the more.

Marshal Henry Russell tapped the reins and his horse trotted forward again. When he was beside the stagecoach he looked up at Reinhold and puffed his pipe, the glow of the tobacco illuminating his stern expression.

"I want you outta my town 'fore sunup," he said. "Your missus can stay behind if'n she's so inclined, but you and these saddle bums are no longer welcome in Hope's Hill. You show your face 'round here again, you just might find yourself dancing the polka from the end of a rope."

The heat that had been rising in Reinhold's chest drew tight around his heart. A thousand curses bubbled on his tongue and yet he said nothing.

"You understand me, boy?"

Despite his grayed facial hair, Russell could only be a decade older than Reinhold himself. Calling him *boy* was yet another jab at Reinhold's pride. It was no way to talk to another white man.

"I understand you fine," Reinhold said. "But just 'cause you get rid of me doesn't mean this is all over 'n done. I'm not the only one who wants this woman to fess up."

"Then you may see them others joining you shortly, won't you?" Russell leaned in. "I will not have a lynching in my town. Not unless I'm the one tying the noose."

21

"So now it's *your* town, is it? I thought this land belonged to the people living on it."

"As of today that population includes me. I'm the law in Hope's Hill now."

He kicked his heels and the horse moved along. As they passed, Grace glowered at Reinhold, her stare never faltering. The other lawmen followed. As they entered the shadows leading back to town, Russell made one final proclamation.

"Sunup, Barley. Sunup."

*

"I just don't understand. A *witch*? Me?"

Henry Russell sat back in his chair. The office was smaller than the one he'd had in Battlecreek, but it would do.

"You're new in town, Ms. Cowlin. The stranger's always the first scapegoat when things get all catawampus."

"But witchcraft? This is not the 1600s. These are modern times."

"You'll get no argument from me on that, ma'am, but the people of this town, well, many of them are still pilgrims. Superstitions have a way of passing down from one generation to the next. Even I don't whistle when I pass by a cemetery."

Grace sighed, rubbing her sore neck. Russell took her in. Long dark hair and equally dark eyes, a marvel amongst the many blondes and redheads he was used to. Clearly she was no Mexican, but maybe she had some Spanish blood. Her house clothes, while not too revealing, did nothing to hide her fine form. She would have made a good dance hall girl with those looks, but she was too learned for such a profession.

Her eyes locked on his. Though Russell never lost a staring contest with even the vilest outlaw, he found himself going aquiver under the woman's gaze.

"Will you truly hang Barley Reinhold if he does not comply?" she asked.

"Nah, I just wanted to put some fear into him. But if he doesn't do as I say, I'll run him out of town. That or lock him here in my jail."

"How did you get to us so fast?"

"Just had an inkling."

"An inkling they'd kidnap me?"

"Word traveled to my deputies that those two ruffians had come to town. They stopped into The Rusty Nail saloon earlier tonight. We had our eyes on them."

"In that case, could you not have stopped them sooner?"

"Had to wait until they did something. They grabbed you and we cut them off at the pass."

"But you did not arrest them."

"Running them out of town sends a message to all of Hope's Hill."

Her eyebrows raised and she sat back in her chair. "And what of you, Marshal? What has brought you to Hope's Hill? Surely you're not just here on my account."

Russell propped his feet up on his desk, flakes of dried mud falling from his boots. "I was sent down by the council. Constable Kirby has the tuberculosis and is not expected to survive."

"My heavens. I do regret to hear it."

"Murphy Hyers and the rest of the councilmen want to keep this town from turning on itself. So they brought in me."

"What do you mean by *turning on itself*?"

"I mean just what you went through tonight. Bad things are happening all over town from what I've been told. Bad crops, bad cattle. Rotten eggs and barren farmland. The worse things get, the rowdier folks get. They turn on each other 'cause they need somebody to blame. The last thing a nice, little town needs is to fall under mob rule. Mr. Hyers is working with the county to make himself a mayor's office, and I'm here to make sure that happens."

Grace took a deep breath. "I see. Well, Marshal, I'd like to thank you for rescuing me from those bad men. I don't know what came over Mr. Reinhold, but who knows what they might have done had you and your deputies not intervened."

Russell reached for his pipe. The wind had picked up outside and it whistled against the window, the branches of a dying maple scraping the roof like the claw of a bear.

"Unfortunately, ma'am, I know exactly what those scallywags would have done to you. Even a nice, little town can be home to wicked men."

CHAPTER IV

VERN KEPT IT WRAPPED IN sackcloth, tucked away in a drawer. He'd tried to tell himself he'd dreamt what lay inside it, but he still dared not reopen the golden capsule. Once again he wondered if he'd gone off his rocker.

The thing inside the capsule looked like old meat and was coated with some sort of black syrup like molasses. When Vern had reached with a finger, he gasped. The mass was *warm*. He hadn't even touched it but could feel the heat coming off it. The grave he'd expunged it from was witch's tit cold, and yet this thing was a woodstove. It was about the size of a cottontail and oddly shaped— many bulges and divots, a hole in the center. When he'd pressed on it with a stick, it had begun to pulse.

Vern had screamed then. The capsule fell from his hands and bounced upon the mummified corpse in the hole below. The thing inside the capsule inflated and deflated like a lung. Smoke puffed from it as if from a coal stack. Only it didn't behave like smoke. Instead of rising into the air it slithered around the grave in festoons before climbing its walls and pouring across the cemetery beyond in a black miasma. Vern had watched this fog without blinking. Whatever he'd unearthed, it was mighty special. His greed gave him courage normally uncommon to him and he snatched up the capsule and resealed it.

When he'd gone back to town he'd hidden the capsule in the morgue, tucked in his wickerwork desk. He wasn't sure what to do with it yet. The gold alone would bring in significant pay. His profession brought in seventeen dollars a week when business was good, but when nobody was dying he had to fall back on his meager savings. In a small town like Hope's Hill, new deaths could be few and far between, unless something terrible rolled in. It was a shame Constable Kirby's tuberculosis hadn't spread. Vern's debt was piling up. That's why he'd taken to robbing graves in the first place. He wasn't a ghoul. These excavations were merely a fiscal matter.

The same could be said of him selling bodies; not the decayed remains in those old graves but the fresh ones brought to his funeral home. Once a wake was over, the kin of the dead didn't take another look once the coffin was closed. As long as Vern put enough rocks in those pine boxes, it felt like a body was still in there when the time came for pallbearers to carry it to the grave.

This young lady upon his slab was so lithe he'd had only to gather a few stones from the mountainside. Her name was Jane, one of the Hopkins' girls. Such a tragic thing for a young'un to be kicked in the back by a mule, her skull separated from her spine. But she hadn't been decapitated. There'd been no damage to the flesh other than bruises and a few scrapes. More importantly, there was nothing wrong with her organs.

Dr. Uriah Craven pushed his spectacles up the bridge of his nose. He brushed the girl's hair aside and stroked her cheek like a loving father.

"Fine skin," he said.

"Powerful fine. T'was only seventeen."

"I trust she hasn't been *molested*."

Vern frowned. "Consarn it, Uriah, I told you that was just the one time."

Sarah Parks had been a rather beautiful woman, one he'd lusted over long before her demise. She was one of the few corpses he'd done anything like that with and it irked Vern that Uriah knew he'd had his way with Sarah's body, having found fresh semen inside her upon inspection. Vern had never thought the doctor would have looked *in there*.

"Good," Uriah said. "I'd hate to have to treat your pecker for infection."

"It was typhus, Doc, not diphtheria. Wasn't going to catch anything from her."

"Just stay safe, Vern. Stick to the whores down at The Green Lily. Better still, find yourself a goodly woman and marry her."

"For some reason ladies don't fancy undertakers."

"They would be particularly deterred if they found out said undertaker was a necrophile."

"Uriah! I swear—"

The doctor raised his hand. "Undertaking is a respectable profession. That's why I deal with you instead of going to the other resurrectionists."

"Come on now, Uriah. I ain't no necrophile and I ain't no resurrectionist."

"You sell corpses illegally. Call it what you wish."

"You *buy* them illegally. What's that make you?"

"I study them. I'm doing this for the sake of modern medicine."

"Yeah, well I'm doing it for the greenbacks. Now you want to buy this little lady or not?"

Uriah straightened up and reached into his vest pocket. He tossed a small sack and when Vern caught it he looked inside immediately, hungry for his due. When he saw the coins, his lips pressed white.

"This ain't the amount we agreed upon, Doc."

"It's the going rate, Vern. I'd give considerably less to the resurrectionists in Onyx Banks."

The doctor coasted his hand across the dead girl's breast, one finger circling a puffy nipple. His eyes and lips were wet as he cherished his new possession.

Hypocrite, Vern thought.

He put the sack in his pocket. The money was hardly even enough to pay his tab at the general store. Vern knew he shouldn't have put Old Man Harley in the ground. He was elderly, but Craven may have bought him nonetheless. Vern needed more money, much more. He was so behind on his loan. If he couldn't get his finances in order, he risked the bank taking his business away. Then there'd be no money coming in at all.

He glanced at the desk drawer.

"I've got something else," he said, "something that may interest your medical community."

"Is that right?"

"Right as rain. It's not your usual fare. This is something *unique*."

Craven stepped away from the slab. His cherry lips, slicked back hair, and bow tie made him seem somehow perverse to Vern, like a man who'd lay with a colored woman or maybe even another man.

"You have my attention," the doctor said.

Vern went to his desk and slid open the drawer. It creaked as if in warning. When he removed the sackcloth, Craven raised an eyebrow.

"What is that? Some sort of amulet?"

"And solid gold too. Not just plated."

"It's a good find, Vernon. I'm sure it'll go over well with a jeweler but it's hardly of interest to the medical community."

But Vernon could see the curiosity wet upon the doctor's face. He held out the capsule.

"It's not the piece itself, Doc. It's what's inside."

*

The pack had been getting restless. They'd done no killing since the Broken Ridge bank robbery. The teller had given them no trouble, but bloodlust ran like a river through the dreams of Koyotes. Glenn Amarok had more self-control than his subordinates, but he too had been struggling with the instinct to murder, to destroy.

They needed prey.

He gazed to the stars in search of Mars but the clouds were thick tonight and he could not find the red planet. Even the moon was hidden, lying in wait just as Glenn was. He sat Indian-style upon the tarp-covered bedroll, his long, black hair and muttonchops fluttering in the wind like the tails of poltergeists. He'd put a good six feet between himself and the fire, preferring the arctic touch of an autumn breeze to the warmth of flames. There'd be time enough for fire. A whole eternity.

He'd taken off his buckskin and shirt and the hair on his bare chest and back rose like the hackles of an excited dog. It'd been almost five years since he'd felt the presence of Jasper Thurston and now, inexplicably, the elder Koyote's scent drifted upon the wind. Though faint, it was a tantalizing miasma. Glenn's old mentor was dead, but his magic was as infinite as the cosmos and just as black. Glenn could feel the sweetness of it, a tremendous force for evil no longer in thrall. Whatever pinions had imprisoned Jasper's sorcery had finally snapped loose.

So far only Glenn had sensed it. Soon Hiram would sniff it out just as he had, and then the rest of the pack would feel it too, all down the chain of command. Then they'd understand the purpose of this lackluster journey. For, deep in the bowels of these mountains, some small town awaited their wrath.

Glenn would lead his pack to the slaughter.

Jasper's heart would be his.

CHAPTER V

IN THE HOLY PIT, SISTER Mable stood at the top of the ladder beside the altar. It was a stone and mortar sepulcher beneath the chapel, only accessible via a hidden channel that wound beneath the earth. Lanterns and wooden crucifixes lined the tunnel for safe passage. The pit itself was decorated with steel crosses forged by several generations of blacksmiths. They lined the walls and ceiling of the pit, buttresses to bear the load of the earth above. Upon the altar was the largest cross of all, a towering, golden statue of the crucified Savior.

Sister Mable drew the nail from the right hand of the statue, revealing the pipe that ran through the body. She placed the funnel above the hole and looked down at Sister Genevieve. The young nun was holding the pitcher with both hands, overly cautious in her piety. Mable could not blame her for being nervous. On her first night in the pit, nerves had caused Mable to throw up a little. Luckily she'd managed to swallow it and not embarrass herself by soiling such a holy place. Though that night was decades ago, sometimes it felt like mere days. A life in servitude to the Lord was a glorious one, but not without its pains. For all God gave, He also asked, especially of the brides of Christ.

"Hand me the pitcher," she said.

Genevieve offered it up and Mable took care to keep it balanced. She couldn't afford to spill a drop. Not a second of suffering could be in vain, not a smidge of sacrifice disrespected. Sister Evalena knelt before the altar, her rosaries in hand, and Genevieve dropped to her knees beside her, the light of a thousand candles making an army of their shadows.

Evalena began. "I am sure that neither death nor life, nor angels nor rulers, nor things present nor things to come, nor powers, nor height nor depth, nor anything else in all creation, will be able to separate us from the love of God in Christ Jesus our Lord."

Mable raised the pitcher to the lip of the funnel. "Listen Lord, for Your servant is speaking. When I am afraid, I put my trust in You."

The pipe in Christ's hand made a hollow sound, wind whispering through an underpass. Its opening dilated.

The nuns quoted Deuteronomy in unison.

"Because of the dire straits to which you will be reduced when your enemy besieges you, you will eat your own children, the flesh of your sons and daughters who the Lord has given you."

Mable tipped the pitcher. The children's blood sluiced through the funnel and into the statue's piping, running down the Savior's arm and through His torso, then down through His legs. The sisters below brought their cup to Christ's crossed feet and withdrew the nail. The blood of the orphans, now purified and as godly as holy water, poured from the spout and into the cup. Evalena drank first. Though it was her first time, Genevieve showed no hesitation and slurped the blood down. Mable was proud of her. She climbed down the ladder and accepted the cup, swallowing what was left and then licking it clean. Not a second of suffering could be in vain, not a smidge of sacrifice disrespected.

When Mable looked again to Genevieve, the younger sister had tears in her eyes. When Mable placed her hand upon her shoulder, there was a faint blue glow upon both nuns' lips.

"Blessed are the children," Mable said. "Suffering brings them closer to God."

"Yes, Sister."

"With rest, berries, and prayer, the children will return to full health. Bloodletting is not as terrible as it appears."

"Of course, Sister."

When the three sisters fell into formation, Mable cried to heaven.

"Lord, we pray unto You, for in our midst a demon lurks. It prowls around us, a roaring lion hunting for souls to devour. It has poisoned our livestock and salted our earth so that nothing may grow." Mable breathed deep. "This wickedness is no stranger to me, Lord." She could feel her sisters' eyes fall upon her. "Help me, oh Lord. Help me catch this devil by his heels once more so I may banish him to the black abyss forever. We trust in You and the power of Your might. Give unto us the full armor of God, so that we can take our stand against the devil's schemes. For our struggle is not against flesh and blood, but against his sorcery. Give us the belts of truth and the breastplates of righteousness. Let us take up the shield of faith to extinguish all the flaming arrows of evil."

In the center of the Christ statue's chest, the chamber that caught the majority of the blood swirled red, surrounding the thrumming, black stone within.

The nuns crossed themselves and stood. It was time.

"Mister Reinhold has fled town," Mable told them. "We shall need a new stagecoach driver."

*

Russell licked his thumb and smeared away the dirt from his star. The main streets were pebbled but some of the alleys were clay and the dust had risen beneath his horse's hooves as they made their way to the well. Russell dismounted, used the pulley to raise the bucket, and sipped from the gourd. He led the stallion to the trough and let it drink its fill as he leaned against a post. It was a warmer day thanks to the cloudless sky. The sunlight warmed his body and made the black coat of the stallion shine like wet leather.

"Nice day, ain't it, Fury? Real nice, indeed."

When he'd finished watering Fury he led the horse around to The Rusty Nail and tied him to the hitching rail. The inside of the saloon was dim and smoky and it took Russell's eyes a moment to adjust. He bellied up to the bar and the barman nodded to him, eyeing the star on his jacket.

"What'll it be, Marshal?"

"Need an eye-opener. Any bourbon?"

The barman smirked. "You're too far west for that Kentucky

whisky, friend."

"Just straight up whisky then."

The barman returned with a bottle and glass and poured Russell's first drink of the day. He sipped and the combined flavors of burnt sugar, booze, and chewing tobacco danced upon his tongue. It went down like the fires of hell. Russell studied the open barroom. There was a dance floor and a standing, honky-tonk piano. Sitting on the bottom of the staircase was a young girl in a blue dress and petticoat, the only saloon girl in sight. Tables were on the far side of the place, many townsfolk drinking though it was only now reaching noon. Three men were playing faro in a cloud of cigarette smoke.

"Saloonkeepers never starve," Russell said.

The barman leaned on the counter, a skinny man with a gaunt face. "When times are good they come in to celebrate. When times are hard they come in to drown their sorrows. And times are hard in this town now. Ye passing through, Marshal, or are ye here to stay?"

"Staying. Long as I'm needed."

"Reckon we could use a strong arm 'round these parts, things going as they is. Them deputies are too green."

"Jake and Norton are good men."

"T'wasn't saying otherwise. Name's Zeke. Zeke Ottoman."

Russell nodded but did not offer to shake hands. "Henry Russell."

"Whelp, welcome to The Rusty Nail. And welcome to Hope's Hill."

Russell finished his drink. The barman poured another. The saloon doors swung inward and a black cowboy approached the other end of the bar. His chaps were caked in dirt, his cotton shirt stuck to his back by sweat. Three day's worth of beard covered his face. Zeke went off to serve him and three men playing cards in the back eyed the cowboy with sour expressions. Russell watched them from the corner of his eye just in case they made their objections vocal. He wasn't sure if the men knew he was the law or not, but he'd made no effort to conceal the Colt at his hip. The cowboy was a large man, a good six-foot-four with broad shoulders and the musculature of a hard laborer. Not the sort of man one ought to pick a fight with.

Zeke and the cowboy were talking in a friendly manner. It seemed the barman held no prejudices, and Russell respected that.

He heard the cowboy's name was Oscar. The men in back put down their cards and got to their feet. As they stepped away from the table, Russell turned on his stool, pulled back his coat, and placed his hand on the holster of the Colt. One of the men fell back, but the other two approached the bar. Their faces were tanned and worn by too many years toiling under the sun.

The large one looked to Zeke. "Thought this was a white man's drinkin' hole."

The place fell into a hush, the other patrons looking toward the bar now. The saloon girl got to her feet and clutched the railing, ready to run upstairs if things got rowdy.

"Don't start somethin' with me, Earl," the barman said. "This is my establishment and I don't turn away no paying customer."

Earl smirked to his friend. They shared a mean glint of the eyes and then turned toward the cowboy. The cowboy stood up straight, his height astounding. He sipped his drink, still not looking at the men. Earl stepped closer.

"What're ye doing in here, boy?" he asked the cowboy. "Ain't nobody want ye leavin' a trail o' grease all over this here bar. Make the dance floor too slippery for the girls to show us a good time." He looked to the saloon girl on the staircase. "Ain't that right, sugarplum?"

The girl looked at the floor, saying nothing.

The cowboy put his glass on the bar, hard and loud. "Treat the lady with respect. She's a saloon girl, not a whore like your mama."

Earl's neck turned bright pink. Big, yellow teeth sneered. "What'd ye say to me, boy?"

Now the cowboy turned to face Earl and his friend. His dark eyes were sharp as knives and flashed just as brightly. "You call me *boy* again, and you'll be crawling out of here."

"Then I guess I'll just have to call you dead man."

Earl swung but the cowboy was too fast. He grabbed Earl's punching arm and snapped it into the air, then pushed him down into the bar, cracking his face open. His hat fell to the floor. Earl's friend bent over and pulled a straight-backed knife from his boot and Russell drew his iron and placed it so close to the back of the man's head the sound of the Colt cocking made the hairs on his neck stand up.

"Best stay out of this," the marshal said.

The man froze and Russell reached over him and took the knife without any resistance. Earl struggled to regain his balance, blood trickling out of his busted nose and wetting his moustache. He reached for something inside his coat but the cowboy punched him in the gut and Earl's hands grabbed for his wrist with both hands. The big man swung his leg behind Earl and tripped him, and once he was down the cowboy reared back and booted him in the head, then pressed the sole down upon the bloody pulp of Earl's face. He shoved the toe of his boot into Earl's mouth, shifting a loosened tooth.

"Hope you like the taste of cow paddies."

Russell stood. "Alright, now. That's enough."

The cowboy looked to him, sweat dripping down his forehead. Russell pointed to his star and the cowboy stepped off of Earl. Russell nodded to Earl's friend and the man got Earl up, placed his arm over his shoulder, and helped him limp to the door. Russell expected them to shout some promise of retribution but the men stayed silent. Earl was finally keeping his fool mouth shut.

The cowboy went back to the bar and took a stool.

Russell approached him. "Buy you a drink?"

The cowboy was silent. Then he grinned.

"Oscar Shies," he said.

"Henry Russell."

When the door swung open again Russell drew his iron half out of the holster, but when he and Shies turned to look three women were silhouetted against the backdrop of the harsh sunlight. When they stepped into the saloon, Russell saw they were clothed in the livery of the Lord.

Both men stood.

One of the nuns spoke. "Good morning, gentleman. We're looking for the new marshal."

Russell removed his hat. "That'd be me, sister. Can I be of service?"

"My name is Sister Mable." She introduced the other nuns. "We seek safe passage to a sacred place. It's not far from here but lies in the wilderness of Black Mountain. It'd be unwise for women to travel there alone. It was our hope you could lend us one of your deputies to escort us."

Russell put his hands on his hips. "Well, I'd love to oblige such a request but my men have a good deal of work to do here in town. Have you no men in your service who might escort you?"

"You ran him out of town."

Russell cleared his throat. "Well, I am sorry to inconvenience the church, but Barley Reinhold earned his expulsion. He chose lawlessness."

"Be that as it may, you've put us out of a driver and guardian. That is why I have come to you. Your assistance is due service to our nunnery, and to God."

Russell hung his head. Though not a religious man he knew the guilt of denying the sisters would eat at him, especially if they fell harm to Indians, bandits, or wolves. And refusing to lend a helping hand to the church would hinder his efforts to win over the town as their new leading lawman. Helping these nuns directly would put him in everyone's good graces, not just God's.

"Alright then," he said. "I wouldn't be one to shy away from my Christian duty. I'll escort you myself."

Shies stepped beside him. "Black Mountain has a lot of trails that lead to nowhere. I know them mountains like my own hand. I might could get you where you need to go without getting you lost."

Russell nodded. "Much obliged."

Shies turned to Mable. "So, this sacred place?"

*

The deadcart wheeled down the street, the corpses it carried swarming with a fog of flies. Their wings made a hellish racket. The pulling horse hung its head low upon its neck, slouched just like the rider, a raggedy man as pale and foul-looking as the bodies he transported. Glenn watched the deadcart as it rolled by. It was bowed in the belly and the wood was peppered by black rot. It was withering away, much like everything else in Onyx Banks. The town was dirt poor and burdened by the dual anchors of misery and desperation. Its people would be low-hanging fruit.

Hiram pinched one nostril and shot a booger out of the other.

"Even with the stink of that cart," he said, "I can still smell ol' Jasper on the other side of them mountains."

The whole pack had picked up on their old leader's scent. Even Dillon, who was too young to have met Jasper Thurston, was aware of the spirit. A Koyote always sensed when one of his own was not far.

"His presence was always the strongest," Glenn said. "Seems it remains so even in death."

"What do you think they done with him?"

"Buried him somewhere holy, I reckon. Somewhere they thought safe. All these years we've been unable to find him. Now the trail's warm again."

They rode down Main Street in a slow gait. Even in the center of the village lay withering ruins. Like most mining towns the buildings were flimsy and had been placed too close together, causing several to crumble during the previous summer's great fire. Townsfolk moved up and down the walkways like sloths. Most avoided looking at the rough outlanders, but some men made sour faces when they saw Web, him being an octoroon who showed a hint of African descent. Miners shuffled along in black tufts, their backs bent from work. Glenn cocked his head. This pathetic prey was so docile the pack might as well be scavenging. Belial snorted and brayed, sensing his master's annoyance.

Hiram grunted. "This ain't no place to go full split. Killing these pikes would be like swattin' skeeters."

Behind them, Web, Thad, and Dillon grumbled in agreement. The men were hungry, but there had to be some sport in it. They journeyed on, bypassing an apothecary shop and a small café. The townspeople watched them, wary of newcomers. Onyx Banks was hardly a destination for tourists.

"Maybe we ought hit the pharmacy," Thad said. "Get us some laudanum."

Glenn glowered. "Koyotes get their highs from the hunt."

"Right, boss. Just a passing thought."

"They'll be plenty of drink tonight for celebrating, once we have something to celebrate."

Hiram pointed. "Look yonder. Might have found just the thing."

The pack gazed out at the open stretch of land to the east, far from the streets of town. There was a small grove of trees set against the backdrop of a creek lined with black rock. In the center of the clearing was a large, square tent. Rope and metal stakes held down the canvas and at the top of the entryway was a wooden crucifix painted white. A flatbed wagon was pulled up in front. Tied there were multiple horses and a couple of mules, waiting for their masters.

Glenn grinned. "Hell's bells."

"We passed a chapel earlier," Web said. "Why're they out here when they could be up in their church?"

"It's a tent revival," Hiram told him. "A community all its own. Probably Mormons. They've been migrating up here since '48."

"Shit," Thad said. "I hear them boys marry six, seven girls a piece."

Dillon rocked in his saddle. "To hell with laudanum, let's go!"

The men laughed. Glenn clacked the reins and howled. Belial led the other horses in a fury, their hooves like thunderclaps as they rode onto the winding trail, dust spinning about their bodies in dreamy wisps. Blood pumped through Glenn's black heart. The hair on his muscles rose, thickening with anticipation, and a psychedelic redness swirled into his irises.

The hunt was on.

When they reached the tent they swung out of their saddles, landing in squats, their arms hanging down apelike, fingers curled, nails clicking. They drew their hunting knives. Glenn thought of his whip, but decided to be more hands-on this time around. Tied to the hitching post, the churchgoers' pack animals stirred at the presence of the Koyotes. Glenn waved Dillon and Web over to one side of the tent and Hiram and Thad circled the other. Glenn came around the back. He could smell the congregation from here. Inside, a preacher was spouting off yet another interpretation of the Bible, something about sin and damnation and all the things Glenn lived for. Once each of the Koyotes was in place, Glenn clicked his tongue twice. The pack sprung at his signal and sliced through the canvas and tore their way inside. Then they tore their way through the flock.

Glenn charged through the back of the stage and came up on the preacher from behind. He stabbed him in the back, twisting the blade into the man's kidney, and as he barreled over in agony Glenn withdrew the knife and brought it to the preacher's throat and opened it in a red mist. Grabbing the preacher by the hair, Glenn tossed the knife and dug his fingers into the slit in his neck. The preacher tried to scream but it only forced blood bubbles to pop out of his exposed throat. His open arteries gushed crimson. Glenn's elongated nails ripped through the meat, pulling the trachea out in a single lunge, and he sank his canines into it, shaking his head back and forth like a bird dog with a catch. Steaming flesh dripped from his chin. A spattering of blood decorated his whiskers. He pulled at each end of the neck and pried the preacher's head off.

THE THIRTEENTH KOYOTE

The gatherers went for the openings in the tent, some trampling each other in an effort to escape. Mothers clutched their shrieking children. A few of the men fought back against the Koyotes and were instantly murdered for their efforts. One man drew a pistol but Web rushed him and hacked at the man's wrist, separating his gun hand from his body. Screams filled the tent in a sickening cacophony. Thad had opened a young man's stomach and buried his face in the gorge of him, lapping and chewing and snorting in the pool of guts. Hiram threw an old woman to the floor facedown and sat on her while he raked her back with wolfen claws. Skin left her body in fluttering, wet ribbons. Dillon grabbed two teenagers—siblings by the look of them—and bashed their heads together. Their skulls shattered like eggshells and when they dropped to the dirt he tilted his head back and howled. Glenn couldn't even see Web. All he saw was a glorious fog of blood where the giant man-beast danced in another frenzied mutilation. Children cried. Bodies flew. A woman clutched the gushing stump where her leg had been and a small man vomited blood while the teenage boy beside him lay freshly decapitated yet still twitching.

Scanning the terrified crowd, Glenn spotted a man crouched on the floor holding a teen girl in his arms. He sensed they were father and child and that only excited him all the more. He pounced from the stage, spurs of bone clattering as he hit the ground, and his prey cowered back. Glenn snapped his jaws and lunged, ripping the man from his daughter, and when the father tried to fight back Glenn grabbed him by the leg and stomped on his knee until it snapped. He twisted the leg like a corkscrew, tearing it in half, the shattered kneecap popping free from the sinew. The man went pale with shock. He trembled there in the dirt, watching helplessly as Glenn bit into his daughter's dress and tore it free, exposing the budding breasts and pale belly. The girl yelled herself pink as Glenn ripped her undergarments away, his claws raking the insides of her legs, drawing blood. The smell of virgin cunt made his mouth foam. From the scent of her, Glenn knew she had only just reached her menarche. He undid his slacks and pushed down hard on the girl's hips and her pelvis cracked and broke as he entered her. She screamed, but her father was the one who screamed the loudest. The poor bastard wouldn't have to watch much longer. As soon as Glenn was done with the girl he would gouge the man's eyes out and feast upon them like grapes.

Most of the congregation died by their hands, only a few escaping into the woods. The Koyotes feasted and tore away flesh to make jerky and belts. Women and children were molested and raped. Once the Koyotes had had their fill they left the tent and stepped into the cool light of dusk. A simmering, red sun peeked over the horizon as it slipped away, a murder of crows silhouetted in the orange firmament, and Hiram went to his horse and drew his Wesson from the saddle scabbard. He shot the mules first and they brayed in dying, making the congregation's horses buck against their ties.

He killed them too.

CHAPTER VI

THE DISTANT GLOW OF MARS reflected off Luther Byrne's eyes as he gazed into the cosmos. The red planet seemed swollen tonight, weighted by a bad omen. Byrne knew not of this omen's origin, nor did he care to know. Whatever ill fate was coming—be it plague, fire, or famine—it didn't concern him. He sensed Mars even when he could not see it, but tonight it was bright enough to spot with the naked eye; or with his naked eyes, anyway. Not everyone had his heightened vision.

Crouched there in the wheat, he returned his gaze to McMillan's sheep. They stood about the tall grass, ignorant of the danger despite how many of their kind had been slaughtered, struck down by the very beasts Byrne was here to stop. He wondered if Old Man McMillan knew the rifle was all for show, would he have offered up the same amount of money for Byrne's services? He had to bring the Winchester and traps along. No other wolfer in the territory could stop the predators from taking livestock without such tools. But Byrne had tools of his own, ones the farmers who hired him could never understand. They'd just call it witchcraft and, in a way, that might even be right. In his thirty-plus years, Byrne had needed weapons to deal with men, but never with wolves. It simply wasn't necessary.

He ran his hand over his muttonchops, listening, waiting. His shaggy hair brushed off of his neck, exposing the brand he usually kept hidden, a scar from another life. His brown flesh rippled. As the dusk settled in full, the waning moon had appeared, bathing the farmland in a rich, aquatic glow. The cool of evening always brought him back to those nights he'd spent beneath the stars with his mother. Nostalgia was his only solace. These silent moments on the open range were the only peace he'd ever known, and the only kind he could hope for anymore.

There was a rustle in the thicket. Byrne raised his nose and tested the air, sensing the wolves before seeing them. They stepped into the field in a V formation, the huge pack leader at the head, flanked by the younger, faster males with the females not far behind. Their gray coats glimmered like silver in the light of the moon.

Dire wolves, Byrne realized.

When they moved, he moved, masking the sound of his footfalls. Some of the sheep shuffled into the clearing while others remained in the field to graze. The damned things were oblivious. Byrne would have to move fast to get between them and the approaching wolf pack. He shuffled along in a crouch, his body hair rising, pupils dilating as his eyes went red. The pack leader sniffed the ground where Byrne had pissed to mark the territory. The others wolves waited until the leader moved forward again, cautious now but undeterred, closing in on their prey. If the sheep spotted them, they'd run, and then the wolves would give chase. The flock stood no chance of survival if that happened. Byrne had to hope they remained stupid.

He cut through the field now, his hulking form crushing the tall grass, and as he reached the wolves one of the females spotted him and snarled. The rest of the pack turned to back her, their eyes reflecting yellow in the night as they stared at Byrne with hackles raised. The young males inched closer, barking now, and from the corner of his eye Byrne saw the last of the sheep scurry away. The wolves were too focused on him to pursue. And though the young males were closest to him, Byrne focused on the pack leader. He was almost the size of a black bear, his body tough and battle-scarred. Part of his snout was missing, torn free during some long ago conflict, and his ears bore the puncture holes of rival wolves' fangs. His gaze held all the wisdom of the wilderness.

Byrne nodded to this fellow warrior.

"This land's been claimed," he said. "These sheep, they're not yours to annex and feast on."

A low growl escaped the leader. The other wolves fell silent.

"I know you don't like it," Byrne said, "but you can't be hangers-on to farmers. I reckon you're strong enough to make your own way."

The leader titled his head, his growl lowering to a grumble.

"These hay shakers have enough trouble without you slaughtering their livestock, understand? Now, I come to you as a brother. Be a shame if we had to settle this by combat. You leave this farmland and I'll tell you of a better place."

The leader stared at Byrne, his teeth no longer bared. He motioned to the other wolves and they scuttled back into the thicket from which they came, but the leader stayed, waiting.

"Go west over them hills and through the canyon. Follow the wagon trail at a distance. Therein lies a town called Battlecreek, named because it's near a natural spring. You won't have to go into town to enjoy that water. Best you shouldn't, for they employ wolfers who will shoot you dead and skin you for furs. You stay hidden in the low caves of the mountainside and make a home there. The terrain is aplenty with wild asses and other varmints suitable for prey, so your bellies will stay full and you'll have no thirst in summer."

The wolf locked eyes with Byrne. Between them burned an honesty unknown to man. A noble lupicinus, Byrne spoke only truth when it came to other canines, and because he walked on two legs yet communicated with them as if he were one of their own they considered him superior. He was not always met with obedience, but always with respect. As the pack leader turned to go, Byrne drew a strip of tallow from his leather weskit and tossed it the wolf's way. The pack leader caught the strip in midair and scurried away chewing this offering of peace.

*

Pockets heavy with coin, Byrne rode back into the village the following morning. He watered and fed Bo and stabled the horse at the back of the boarding house. He brought his saddle, Winchester, and canteen to his room and ate in the dining hall with an old spinster and a pair of prospectors. The woman spoke politics Byrne had no interest in and kept calling him Mr. Luther, using his first name instead of his surname. He did not correct her. When evening came he made his way to the dance hall, one of the few sources of entertainment Steelbranch had to offer, and paid his seventy-five cents for entry.

The band consisted of a scrawny piano man and a dwarf playing a mandolin while tapping little tambourine cymbals with his boots. The piano was not quite in tune but the music had the patrons feeling jovial. Some of the locals were playing dominoes, others having a hand at cards. Byrne leaned under a lamplight and rolled a cigarette, then opened his matchbox. Through the smoke he spotted a lithe dance hall girl. Long, yellow curls of hair fell across her bare shoulders. She wore a bright ruffled skirt and brighter petticoat that barely reached her knees, and a pair of kid boots. He tested the air with his nose. The girl smelled sweetly of Florida Water, hints of lavender and iris root rising from her cream-colored flesh like steam. Her very youth made Byrne's heart ache, but her beauty made it burst.

"Buy a girl a drink, cowboy?"

Byrne snickered. "Ain't even bought my own yet. 'Sides, I'd rather buy a dance."

"Plenty of time for that. Got a name?"

"Luther."

"Where you hail from? Californy?"

He released a bloat of smoke. "What's your name, girl?"

She titled her head and the lamplight caught her eyes, green as Christmas.

"Sorrow," she said.

"Well, now. In that case, maybe you do need a drink after all."

They approached the bar and Byrne called for two glasses of whiskey.

"And don't just give her no sugar water," he told the barkeep. "I ain't paying a whole dime for that."

The barkeep uncorked the bottle and poured, then went off. Sorrow tipped her drink in toast and they clinked their glasses. She slammed her whisky back as gruffly as a sailor.

"So what brings you to Steelbranch?" she asked.

"I go where the work is."

"And your vocation?"

"I'm a wolfer."

Sorrow smiled, coy. "From the looks of them whiskers, thought you might be a wolf yourself. We've got a house barber if you're in need of grooming."

"They can't be cut."

She raised an eyebrow. "You're mighty attached, I reckon."

He gently took her hand and raised it to his muttonchops. She stroked the hair with her fingertips.

"Lordy," she said. "Be these whiskers or metal shavings? I've felt softer thorn bushes, Luther."

He liked it when she spoke his name. The girl did her job well. He'd always preferred dance hall girls to whores. The soiled doves of bordellos served their purpose but didn't make as good of company as the ladies of the saloon. They were only there to dance, sing, and make the men feel welcome, and they made good money doing it, often more than they would have selling their bodies, and any man who wanted to keep his reputation treated them with decency. Like any road-weary rider, Byrne found their presence worth every ounce of coin.

"How 'bout that dance?" he asked.

They spent fifteen minutes doing schottisches and waltzes, the girl having to guide him at times, and when his time was up Byrne paid Sorrow for another go. Other men were waiting their turn with her but Byrne ignored them and tipped the girl extra to do the same. Her hands were so small in his, the fingerless gloves made of lace softer than a kitten's underbelly. The feel of her skin made his mouth water and he felt the echo of an old hunger he'd worked so hard to suppress. It was just the ghost of a past life, he told himself, a hellish yesteryear he'd buried along with the very man who'd recruited him into that hell to begin with. When they were through dancing, Sorrow brought him back to the bar. He figured she got a cut of every cent a customer spent on drink, but he didn't mind. He kicked back another whisky. It was potent stuff. Already the walls were going fuzzy. His body warmed and his shoulders relaxed.

"Tell me more about you," he said, leaning on the bar.

"What's there to know? I'm just like you, Luther, I go where the work is. I'm just another refugee from the mill. Steelbranch is the same as any other small town in that there's a limited amount of vocations for ladies. I didn't fancy myself a homesteader's wife. Saw a handbill for saloon work and here I am."

"And what about your name? *Sorrow...*"

Her eyes fell away. "I prefer it to the one my folks gave me. Suits me finer."

Luther Byrne wondered, not for the first time, if his father had had any say in what his boy was named, wondered if the Navajo had stuck with Bryne's white mother long enough to even take part.

"Sorrow may suit you," he said, "but you've given me anything but."

"That's 'cause I only exist to take it away."

He leaned into her, noticing for the first time the small blade tucked into her cleavage. The tops of her breasts were the color of newly fallen snow and he struggled to keep his gaze away from them. In the past he'd simply taken whatever he wanted, even women. But he was civilized now, no matter how hard it was to remain so. Once you've drunk deep of the well of total hedonistic sin, it hurts twice as hard to take mere sips.

"You're an angel," he told her, slurring.

"Maybe that's 'cause hell won't have me."

Byrne laughed then. "Darlin', you'd be surprised by the rules of hell."

*

Soused to his gills, Byrne staggered from the saloon with the scent of Sorrow still on his clothes. The galaxy offered a tapestry of starlight and a witch's wind blew down the alleyway behind the courthouse, fluttering the brim of his hat and making his hair writhe and twist. He needed a bath even if it were in day old water. But despite the smell of his own body and the aroma of the saloon girl, Byrne detected another, sharper miasma sailing on the back of that night wind, an odor familiar and yet so far gone he had trouble recalling its origin. It sluiced through the branches of the mountain hemlock, overpowering the rich smell of the woodland and its night creatures. There was something sour about it, rancid and decayed. He thought of milk curdling... and then he remembered. And once he recognized the stench he felt the presence of its source, the shuddering evil he'd thought had been buried deep enough. It sobered him. The stars dimmed in warning and the moonlight faded though there were no clouds. There would be much darkness now, thick and deep and without hope, a blackness so all-encompassing it would

THE THIRTEENTH KOYOTE

pull the sun.

Jasper Thurston was dead.

But his heart had been awakened.

CHAPTER VII

THEY HEADED OUT THE NEXT morning. Russell was atop Fury while Oscar Shies manned the stagecoach full of nuns. The three sisters spoke little, Mable having given the men vague directions to a cemetery she claimed lay deep in the thickets of Black Mountain, tucked behind a wall of pines. Shies was wearing the same clothes as the day before, his chaps and boots just as dusty, his beard a little thicker. He slouched in the driver's box, squinting against the midmorning sunlight as he worked the horses up the trail, an army canteen slung over his shoulder and a wad of tobacco wedged under his lip. Beside him was a worn Whitworth rifle with a hexagon barrel.

Russell spoke just to break the silence. "Good deer up in these parts?"

"Aw yeah. Good spot for hunting. Bucks up in the high ground and wild horses in the valley basin."

"You break horses then?"

"Done broke some for the Union army, and some mules for the grangers. Even when you can't break 'em they make a good eatin'. Not as good as buffalo, but now that they're being slaughtered so greatly a man must take what he can get." He spat a brown wad. "I ain't never seen no cemetery up 'round here, though. Of course I weren't ever looking for one neither."

"These trails—how deep do they run into the mountain?"

"Powerful deep. And too many to count. Some Kiowa trails, others made by white men. Ol' Black Mountain has a lot of history without record. A lot of secrets."

Russell saw the hardness in the cowboy's eyes, the face cracked from hard labor. His hands were heavily callused and he was bulky with muscle and very little fat. Oscar Shies was a man with grit. Russell would remember that later, when times called for men of such caliber.

They carried on for two hours, climbing until they were as high as the trail would take them, and then they took a rest so the men could stretch and get their bearings. Russell packed his pipe. Shies helped Mable out of the stagecoach and she put her hand to her forehead to block the sun as she scanned the western red cedars that burst from the hills.

Russell asked, "Anything 'round these parts seem familiar, sister?"

The nun was silent, her eyelids tight against the glare.

"Sister, you've got to give us some sort of direction or you may as well put a spoke in the wheel of this here coach."

Mable turned to him. "Marshal, I do beg your pardon."

"I ain't aiming to disrespect. I just need you to tell us which way. These trails go in all directions, it seems. If we don't choose correctly, we might'n be up here until we lose light. I doubt any of us want that."

Shies stepped beside Russell, backing him up without having to say a word. Sister Mable looked away, the tail of her wimple fluttering in the breeze. She seemed to be waiting for something, as if the wind would offer directions if only they showed patience. The nun bowed her head and put her hands together. Russell moved back. He was always uncomfortable with prayer. It seemed an act too personal for public display, even from a nun. Mable spoke silent words and when she finished she raised her face to the sky, bathing her cheeks in rich sunlight. Russell admired the woman's features—she could be twenty or forty or anywhere in between. There was a mythic quality to her beauty, like something from a child's fairy book.

Mirror-mirror on the wall...

Russell's wife had liked that one.

Mable said, "We follow the sun."

The men waited for more that never came.

Shies shrugged. "So west, then?"

"West, my good sir. The trail will fork beyond that crag. Take the left hand path where the cedars are plentiful."

Russell put his hands on his hips. "Sister, will all respect intended, why withhold this information 'til now if you had it on the half-shell?"

"I did not have it at the ready, Marshal. The way was spoken to me just now, shared unto me by Lord Jesus."

Russell and Shies shared a glance.

"Well," Russell said. "Did our Savior give you any more instruction?"

She shook her head. "None you need know presently."

*

Mable watched out the window as they eased their way down the crag. The terrain was steep here, less forgiving of error. This path had been deliberately chosen upon the wicked man's burial. Any hindrance, any deterrence, had been utilized. Thwarting the other Koyotes from unearthing Jasper Thurston was a task tantamount to contrition, such as the fasting the nuns endured to hear Christ's voice or the bleeding of the orphans to open the arms of the Lord and make them shimmer with the holy, blue light. Thurston had been the worst of the man-beasts, a seed so bad it had sprung vile roots below the earth and poisoned everything around it. Under the guidance of The Morning Star, the leader of the Koyotes had become the scourge of all that was pure and right and Godly. He'd left a trail of ruin in his wake and it had been nearly impossible to steal the man's life force from him, taking another wolfen to stop him.

Though Mable had failed to remember every twist and turn leading to the burial grounds, she had not forgotten the terrors she'd endured that night. She rubbed her hands together, the deep scars hidden by the gloves. Some ghosts never stopped haunting you, she thought. And some evils, it seemed, would not die, but only rest. Rest and wait.

They ventured low where the mountain's rocky walls rose out of the earth in cracked monoliths. They ascended to the high ground where black cottonwood trees cried to the sun, their bark split into avenues for red carpenter ants. The group followed the sound of a babbling creek and wet the horses. Shies checked his compass. The stagecoach rolled west and when they reached the fork in the trail they followed the left hand path—the hand of unrighteousness, the path of deviltry. Mable held her rosary closer to her breast. Beside her, Sister Evalena shuddered, feeling it too. The sudden cold was not the kind that rippled one's skin, but closed around the soul and squeezed. Sister Genevieve hugged herself and rubbed her arms.

Mable said, "You feel it, don't you?"

"I do, Sister," the young nun said, "it's like an *intrusion.*"

The trees grew denser, blocking out the sun, reminding Sister Mable of another time they'd lost all natural light. The darkness had seemed infinite. To think of it happening again…

She heard the marshal halt his horse and the stagecoach came to a slow stop.

"Sister," Shies called, "I do believe we are nigh unto your location."

Russell trotted back to her window and pointed to the tree line. She peered out, seeing a low basin encircled by briar. Jesus whispered in her brain and she opened the door to the stagecoach and stepped down, not waiting for the men to help her.

She crossed herself. "We have arrived."

Russell dismounted. Shies hopped down from the driver's box and assisted the other nuns out of the cabin. Mable moved forward gingerly, taking the lead, but Russell came up beside her, his coat tucked back behind his iron as they approached the basin. The wild roses of summer had wilted, leaving grayed petal ash scattered across the cemetery, many of them stuck to the splinters of the crosses. A prickly entanglement of sweetbrier surrounded the graveyard like Christ's crown of thorns, another deliberate arrangement by the church, but one section had been hacked away, a passageway just wide enough for a small wagon. Mable swallowed hard, clenching her rosary tight enough to make the old injury in her hand ache.

Stepping upon this holy land, Mable shivered. She remembered every soul beneath her now, the ones who'd died too soon but for the greater good, and she offered up a silent prayer for them as she entered their final resting place.

Russell said, "What is this?"

But she knew not how to explain to a man with such little faith.

The marshal's doubt was clear to her. She could sense it like coming rain. How could she explain a sacred ground designed to seal away an abomination?

Shies and Evalena took in the grim surroundings, Sister Genevieve tailing behind with a harried air about her.

Shies looked at the little plots. "All these graves... they're spaced so close together. Too short for a man."

Russell went gray. "Who're buried here?"

Mable chose to lie. "I couldn't say for—"

Suddenly Genevieve shouted, "Sister!"

They all turned to see where she was looking. At the center of the clearing was the only plot long enough to be Thurston's. All the crosses in the cemetery were tilted in its direction, the one plot without a cross of its own. A mound of dirt was piled beside a large hole in the earth.

Mable gasped. They were too late.

She and Russell approached the unearthed grave and stared down at the sarcophagus. The coffin lid had been split open. Mable's chin trembled as she gazed upon the withered corpse within. She shook her head in denial of what she saw and, worse yet, what she didn't see. Her greatest fear had come to fruition. The golden sphere had been taken.

"You knew this man, Sister?" Russell asked.

Mable's eyes grew wet. "Yes, I knew him. But no, he is not a man."

CHAPTER VIII

AT FIRST DR. URIAH CRAVEN thought it must be a bull's heart. Large and black and dead-looking, and yet it pulsed. It pumped slowly though it had no body to deliver blood to. His morbid curiosity sparked, he immediately made Vern Pipkin an offer. The undertaker had been asking too high a price, so they negotiated it down by allowing Vern to keep the capsule the heart had come in. Craven had little use for the gold. Though it held monetary value, it was not nearly as valuable to him as the scientific anomaly before him. *This could be it*, he thought. This could be the great discovery that made his whole career, one that got him out of this one-horse town and off to one of the prestigious cities back east where modern medicine was revered, perhaps St. Louis or even Boston. Vern was a fool to give up something like this—a dead heart that still *beats*—all for five and a quarter dollars. But Vern Pipkin was an odd man, to put it mercifully.

Craven leaned over his examining table, watching the great heart, his monocle firmly in place. Morphine dulled his vision at times but without it his hands would shake when he investigated the heart's workings. He had to examine it gingerly. The very last thing he wanted was to injure it or cause it to stop beating. Then he'd be left with just a dark chunk of muscle. Hardly worth the good money he'd paid for it. He turned it over slowly with his forceps and listened closely with his stethoscope. The heartbeat was not only slow but also irregular, an Indian drum echoing from a world unseen. It reminded Craven of when he'd been a volunteer solider in Colorado, massacring peaceful Cheyenne and Arapahos and chasing them from their winter campsites. He'd learned to be a medic on those frontlines, and regretted none of his years of service, not even the slaughter of women and children who'd had little means to fight back. It was a necessary evil. These vulgar savages had no place in a white man's country.

The evening sun fell through the room, making the amber bottles glimmer on the shelves of the bookcase. He would have to go through periodicals tonight to find the right doctors and scientists to contact, probably via telegraph to speed up the communication. He had to get this magnificent specimen where men like him could see it with their own eyes. Then there would be the press and the fame and, at last, his legacy.

It was a good thing he had an ample supply of morphine; otherwise he would never be able to sleep tonight. He touched the heart with his fingertips and the warmth surprised him. He placed it in a secret compartment inside a wooden cabinet and secured the lock.

Time to go out and celebrate.

*

The travelers came back to town just as dusk was settling. Encroaching darkness stretched across the low valley, enveloping them in its navy-blue glow. Russell had already pulled Shies aside and told him where they'd be going. The nuns would be returned to their chapel, but not before answering some questions.

Hope's Hill was quiet tonight, only a few lamplights flickering in windows. A collective depression lay heavy upon the townsfolk, their prospects growing dim with the land barren and the livestock withering. Some spoke of a curse—superstitious folk like Barley Reinhold, but also religious ones like Sister Mable. As they'd stood about the exhumed grave, she'd spoken of a creature not quite man and not quite animal, but some terrible hybrid of the two. This had caught Russell off guard. He never would have expected the nun to be one for tall tales... other than the ones she found in the Good

Book, of course. But that holy hogwash was hers to manage. What he needed to know more about was that cemetery and the excavated corpse.

When they arrived at the stationhouse he led the nuns out of the stagecoach and they did not object when they saw where he was taking them. Mable especially showed no surprise. Shies tended to the horses as Russell led the nuns inside. He offered them seating but they chose to stand. Exhausted from the ride, he plopped down in his chair and leaned back, crossing his hands over his belly.

"I need to know the real story," he said.

Sister Mable blinked. "I've already given it to you, Marshal."

"Not about the man in that hole—"

"The *beast* in that hole."

"—about the graveyard."

"We should have reburied him."

"Not until I examine the evidence."

"You found none today." She blushed as Russell gave her a hard look. "Forgive me, Marshal. I mean no disrespect. It's just that time is of the ess—"

"I'll be taking men back there at sunup. Now, you can tell me what else is buried up in them graves, or you can make me wait until we dig 'em up; either way I'll find out. Since I was kind enough to escort you all the way over that mountain, I'd like to believe you'd do me the courtesy of a straight answer. So I'll ask you again, Sister—who else, or *what* else, is buried up there?"

Now Mable did take a seat. She put her hands in her lap and took a long breath.

"Children," she said. "They are the graves of children; seven of them, to be exact."

Russell sighed, his suspicions confirmed. Just as Oscar Shies had said, the graves were too small for anything else.

"And the other crosses?" he asked. "There's more than seven."

"The other crosses mark not graves, but purified land."

"I'm guessing you—or, I mean, the church—built this cemetery?"

Mable looked to the floor, nodding.

"Now why is it this child's graveyard is so far from town? And why was one adult man buried among them?"

When the nun looked up again, her eyes were swelling with tears but she would not let them fall. "Marshal Russell... have you ever heard of The Koyotes?"

Russell leaned forward, his face going grim. "Any lawman worth his salt has heard tell of them boys. Band of outlaws no marshal has yet to bring in. Vicious as all sin."

"So you know the things they've done."

"Crimes so heinous I'd never speak of them to a lady."

"Unfortunately, I am no stranger to their atrocities." Her eyes turned to cold steel. "The man in that grave is Jasper Thurston. He was their leader; the wickedest man since Cain himself. He prided himself on being a servant of Lucifer, and some say he was trying to open the very gates of Hell. It took a miracle to put that man in the ground."

Russell raised his eyebrows. "You're telling me *you* killed him?"

"No. Not exactly."

Russell had to chuckle. "Sister, I—"

"He was slain. Right here, in this town. Hope's Hill holds many secrets, Marshal."

"I reckon so."

"Some people are too new in town or two young to remember, but Jasper Thurston was lynched here in Hope's Hill, killed for his crimes against man. But some of us knew his evil went beyond what lies in this world. A select few buried him high on Black Mountain. The land had to be made holy if there was to be any hope his spirit would not return in another form."

"Sister, please. When it comes to that sort of thing, I'm at sea."

"Please, hear me. He had to be buried in a *holy place*."

"But a children's graveyard?"

"The children weren't there when we buried Thurston. We placed them there on purpose, to seal him in. The land was purified by those innocent souls, children from the orphanage who'd come to us sickly and died young. We unearthed them from the graves and moved the bodies, you see? You must understand we had to."

Russell fell silent but his gaze never faltered. If he stared at the nun long enough he might find some sort of sanity in all of this.

"When?" he asked.

"Fifteen years, nearly."

"And what of the other Koyotes?"

"Some were with him, others weren't. It surely was not the entire clan. But, other than the thirteenth, no Koyote in Hope's Hill that night escaped with their lives."

"The thirteenth? There where that many?"

"Not in the town all at once. Each man of that company has a number on him, numbered like the beast. This man was the thirteenth Koyote, if he can be called a man at all."

"And he escaped?"

"In a manner of speaking."

Russell squinted. "Why's that?"

"He helped us. Helped us more than any normal man could."

"And what of the other Koyotes' bodies? Do they have holy gravesites as well?"

She shook her head. "No. We laid the bodies in a great fire."

"Not even a Christian burial?"

"There was nothing Christian about those creatures."

"So why not toss their leader in that fire too?"

"We did," she said. "But Jasper Thurston would not burn."

CHAPTER IX

THE DAY HAD STARTED WITH sunny skies, only the slightest autumn breeze making long sleeves necessary. Delia was rushing to get the stalks of burley tobacco stacked in shocks before these gathering clouds brought rain. With Papa laid up sick with rheumatism, his only daughter had to tend to the farm on her own, her older brothers having left on cattle drives by the age of eighteen. Mama was busy nursing baby Leonard and caring for her husband, but at least she'd slopped the hogs so Delia wouldn't have to worry it.

Though only seventeen, Delia Van Vracken was tall and made of lean muscle. She knew her way around a straight-peen and anvil, and made quick work chopping wood. She was also a better shot than any other Van Vracken, including her father. In fact, she was a better shot than anybody in Cottonwood. She'd even won a junior tournament two years prior, back when the farm was prospering and the family had more free time. Now it seemed she barely had time to eat her meals and read the latest *Wild West Weekly* before bed. Hopefully she'd get in a few pages tonight after supper.

She adjusted her long, fiery pigtails beneath her woolsey. Silent bolts of lightning tore the gray skies like bone fractures and a witch's wind touched her skin and Delia shivered despite the sweat

57

she'd built up. Mama called from the porch. Delia turned to see her cradling the baby against her shoulder, bouncing him to sleep.

"Delia," she called, "best get inside. Looks like a storm's coming something powerful."

"Yes ma'am. I'll finish this'un and come right in."

Mama went back inside. Delia tossed the last stalk, brushed off her coveralls, and stood up straight. Movement on the horizon caught her eye. She squinted. Black shapes bobbed across the hillside and into the valley, bodies like shadows among the dying trees and briar. They drew closer, five men on horseback, rapidly gaining ground. Delia tensed, thinking they might be unfriendly Indians or Mexicans or a hellish army of the two. But when they drew closer she saw they were white men. Still, something about them made her consider going inside for her repeater rifle, no matter how ornery and unwelcoming it would make her seem, but Mama would never allow her to chase off travelers weary from the trail. She'd deem it unchristian.

The horsemen slowed their steeds as they came upon the farm. Two were riding point, the others tailing just behind. One of these leaders was bony with beady eyes that locked on her like an owl's. The other was burly with hair long and black as midnight. Delia's skin prickled when he grinned at her.

"Hello, muh-lady."

She didn't smile back. "Howdy."

"I 'pologize to disrupt yourn tobacco pickin', but my men 'n I are saddle-sore and these horses need waterin' somethin' powerful. We was hopin' ye might could let us taste of yourn gourd."

Delia glanced in the direction of the well. It was behind the house where they could not see. She returned her attention to the riders.

"Reckon we can offer up some water for you if'n you're passing through."

She added the 'passing through' purposely, to suggest they keep on moving afterward. Her family had too little food to share and not enough beds. Even if they had, she wasn't fool enough to trust five strange men. She wouldn't even let them sleep in the barn.

The skinny one curled his lip. "We'd be mighty grateful, miss."

His folksy accent was not as convincing as that of his dark companion. Delia watched them then, a silent moment passing slowly. The muttonchops men didn't blink. Only their leader smiled. But there was something disingenuous about the smile, a tender predator about to show fangs.

"Alright then," she said. "Foller me."

Leading the men meant turning her back on them. Delia's shoulders went tight and the first flutter of butterflies tickled her stomach. If she made a break for it, they could easily nab her before she made the first porch step. Whether or not she was watching them, she was still vulnerable. She wished for a gun, wished for Papa to appear. Heck, if only Billy and Josiah were still on the farm—the family would stand a chance if these men had come with malicious intent.

"Mighty white of ye to spare us our thirst," the dark one said.

"Wouldn't shy away the needy no matter their color, long as they's peaceful."

Delia eyed the barn, wondering if she could make it there, if need be. Not that it would do her any good. The riders continued to tail her, the clomp of hooves slow and soft, the occasional hot snort of the horse's breath on the back of her neck. When they reached the well, the dark one dismounted and removed his hat. Without its shade Delia could see the thick eyebrows that met at the middle and when he smiled again his gums were black like the jowls of a dog. His upper lip curled when he spoke.

"This tobaccy farm seems like too much work for a little'un to do on 'er own… 'specially a girl."

Delia wheeled the bucket up from the well just to give her something else to look at.

"Ain't just me," she said. "My folks and big brothers here too."

The lie about her siblings gave her some comfort. It wouldn't last.

The dark rider stepped closer and Delia had to force herself not to jump back. She didn't want her suspicions to show. She was still hoping she was wrong. He came upon her gingerly, smelling of sweat and leather and raw meat and smoke. Though dirty and dark, he had a handsome face behind his tenebrous whiskers, but it did nothing to make him less threatening. She was still holding the water bucket as he reached into it for the gourd and the back of his hand grazed hers. His eyes never left Delia as he slurped, dipped, and slurped again.

"I pray ye—if yourn kinfolk be 'round, why ain't they helpin' ye pick these stalks, lil' girl?"

Some of the other riders chuckled at this, but their leader shot them a look like poisoned-tipped arrows and they shut their yappers in a hurry. But for Delia, the message had already been sent. She turned her torso away from the riders, as if to shield it. She neither blinked nor breathed.

"Greetings," Mama said.

She'd stepped off the front porch sneakily enough so not to be noticed until she could come up behind the men with Delia's repeater in her hands. Her words were cordial, but her tone held ice.

"Can I help you gentlemen?"

For a passing moment Delia was relieved to see her mother there to back her up, but almost instantly despaired at what this revealed to the riders. The women were alone in this. If men were present, they'd have been the ones to come to Delia's aid. The brothers she'd spoke of were long gone, her father too crippled to fight. And the strangers did not flinch at the sight of Mama. Delia wondered where her baby brother was stashed. The thought made her swallow hard.

"Howdy, ma'am," the skinny man said, tipping his hat.

But Mama's gaze never left the leader standing right beside her daughter. Her hands were tight enough on the rifle that her knuckles had gone to chalk.

The dark one said, "Yourn daughter was goodly enough to offer us up some water, ma'am."

"You've had your drink now. I'll thank you to be on your way."

The other men had still not dismounted. Their leader took another sip from the gourd, and the ease he expressed packed the menace of a mountain lion. The clouds sunk lower to the earth, swirling black and angry, bending the cedar trees and tearing away orange leaves that had lost their will to live. The last of the hogs trotted through filth to seek the shelter of the pen, as if they knew what was coming.

When the dark one spoke again, all traces of his country accent had gone. His voice was deep now and it boomed though he hadn't raised it.

"And what if there's something more than water that we need?"

Mama stared at Delia, her taut expression speaking for her. But Delia knew if she ran the violence would begin, and Mama, being the only one armed, would take the brunt of these men's wrath.

The skinny rider snorted, shooting a booger into the dirt. "Come on, Glenn. Can't we just get to it?"

Glenn glared and the other man changed his tone.

"Just sayin', boss. We've got a lot of ground to cover. Just sayin' is all."

Glenn took a deep breath, mulling it over. "Well, shit. Reckon you're right at that, Hiram."

He clicked his tongue twice, breaking loose all of hell.

The sound was some sort of signal and the men responded like excited pets. Some stayed atop their steeds while others flew out of their saddles. All drew their guns. Glenn grabbed Delia by the arm and pulled her close to him but she managed to twist away before he could get a good grip. The sleeve of her shirt tore free, sticking to the man's claw-like fingernails. A shot broke the stillness, riling up the horses, making them buck and bray. The youngest rider dropped into the dirt with a yelp and Hiram, still atop his horse, drew a long Wesson from his saddle scabbard and aimed upward where the shot had come from. As Delia ran, she saw her father leaning out the second story window, his Spencer carbine propped against his shoulder. He looked so weak, so small. Hiram fired back and Delia screamed as her father's chest burst in a crimson mist. Mama started shooting, running backward, but she was virtually useless with a weapon and her shots went wild. The young man Papa had dropped was getting up on his haunches. Delia wanted to go to her mother and take the rifle but would never make it through the swarm of men, so she hightailed it to the back of the house where the woodpile lay.

Someone was pursuing her. Delia didn't look back until she'd grabbed the axe. She came up swinging. One of the riders—an older, brown-skinned man—was running at her and just barely saved himself from being chopped in the chest by raising his arms to block her attack. The axe head sank into his left arm and when he screamed into the wind Delia saw he'd sprouted fangs amongst his rotted teeth. The blade of the axe was so deep into his arm that when he fell over it pulled the handle from Delia's grip.

Her mother cried out in desperation.

Delia cried back. "Mama!"

Delia grabbed at the axe handle, placed her foot on the man for leverage, and pulled it free. A spurt of blood rose in the air and the man hollered again but did not give chase when she ran back toward the chaos she'd just escaped, her love for her mother outweighing all fear and good sense. She couldn't let them take Mama. She'd rather die right beside her than abandon her to be murdered or worse. But when she rounded the corner there was a loud snapping sound and suddenly Delia's cheek came open. Pain ruptured her head and ran like rivers down through her body. One eye went blind with blood and she stumbled, struggling to hang on to the axe while regaining her balance.

Glenn stood before her with a bullwhip. It dribbled red.

The other men were circled around her mother, the one called Hiram standing while the other two pinned her to the ground and beat her. Delia came forward but it only brought her another thrashing of Glenn's whip. This time it snaked around one of her legs, sending fire up through her thigh and into her groin. She fell hard but never let go of her only weapon.

"My old man was a cracker," Glenn told her. "Didn't have much for cattle on the plantation, so he whipped niggers. The son of a bitch taught me to do the same before he up and died."

He cracked the whip just above her head. The other riders grew rowdier, guffawing and hooting. Mama's screams fell mute under their fists. Thunder clapped and there was the distant train sound of a mean storm forming in the east, the great, godless sounds of Hades.

"I could kill you with one crack," Glenn said, "take your damn fool head off with this whip faster than you could say *please*."

Blood had trickled into Delia's mouth but she dared not spit. She glanced up only once, but seeing Hiram ripping her mother's breasts free from her housedress made her shut her eyes.

"Stand up," Glenn ordered. "Stand now or I'll kill you graveyard dead."

Delia struggled but complied. She dropped the axe without having to be asked. Glenn came upon her and this time his grip on her arm held true as he marched her toward the veranda. Hiram was suckling breast milk from Delia's mother now, but Glenn clicked his tongue again and the men pulled Mama to her feet, the rags of her dress falling about her. Her face was pulped and her lip was split, nose bent to one side. The men escorted them to the front of the house. Hiram produced a rope and tossed it to the others. He went up the steps and disappeared into the house with one of his silver-plated pistols in his fist. The men spun Mama around and pressed her face first into the decking, then raised her arms and tied her wrists to the railings. The young man Papa had shot withdrew a knife bigger than Delia's forearm and tore away at the rest of her mother's dress, exposing her bare back.

Glenn began whipping.

Anguished screams drowned out the moans of thunder. Delia closed her eyes and put her hands over her ears but could still hear the terrible cracks of the whip as it ripped her mother's flesh away. She tried not to count them but her mind betrayed her. Ten. Fifteen. Twenty. On and on until her mother wasn't screaming anymore. And even then the whipping continued. When at last Glenn grew bored of it, he grabbed Delia by both pigtails and her eyes snapped open in her fright, seeing the slack body of her dead mother hanging by her wrists, her back so shredded Delia could see some of her spine and shoulder blades. Glenn dragged Delia by her hair through the dirt, his men cackling like jackals, and when they reached the body Glenn tore free a long piece of gore and sucked it into his mouth, swallowing the sinew without even chewing. Delia vomited.

Glenn smirked. "Oh? Do I sicken you?"

She was shaking so violently he had to press her into her mother's corpse to keep her in place. His free hand was covered in blackish fur and the nails were now thick and yellow like an eagle's talons. He plunged the hand into Mama's lower back, twisting the fingers up to the wrist, and came back with a chunk of glistening meat. He squatted beside Delia.

"Open," he said.

She wept.

He lifted her chin. "Eat as I eat, little girl. How do you know you won't like it if you never try it?"

She sobbed as he forced her mother's flesh against her lips.

"Chew that up," he said, "and swallow it. Eat your beloved mother, and maybe I'll see to it my men don't eat you. Hell, I'm feeling generous today. I might even let you live, long as you show me respect, the way a woman ought to a man."

He pressed mother's meat against her teeth—*hard*. She opened her mouth with a whimper.

Hiram came out of the house just as she was finishing. In one hand he held a cotton sack filled with whatever belongings he saw fit to steal. In the other squirmed her little brother Leonard, Hiram holding the baby upside down from one ankle. Leonard was pink in the face and screaming like he'd just been born into this horrible, horrible world.

Hiram grinned, all fangs.

"We'll eat good tonight, boys."

CHAPTER X

IT WAS A SUNNY WEEKEND and the open market was swamped with merchants and shoppers, people looking for ointments, medicines, food and drink, and entertainment. Men shouted out of their traveling wagons, pitching snake oils and charms to desperate gatherers while Bible salesmen showcased their fine, leather-bound editions. A man in a stovetop hat was winding up a music box for children. A gypsy woman was hocking crystals. Some of them may have even been real. The townsfolk shopped gaily.

Byrne had only come for one thing, so he followed the flies.

At the meat stalls he was greeted by the pungent stench of hung carcasses, the very ones he'd smelled for blocks. Men from town were haggling with the vendors for prime cuts of bull over a row of flensed animal skulls. Byrne bought sheep viscera and strips of hog fat. He snagged a tough cut of bull before the meat ran out and carried his vittles out of the market, walked into an empty alley, and consumed them raw. It was enough to satiate the hunger that came and went with the phases of the moon. Though no longer a Koyote, he was still wolfen, still *carnivorous*. He had to feed the beast within if he expected to control it.

When he finished gorging he cleaned himself by spitting into his neckerchief and clearing the gore from his chin and neck. He rolled a cigarette and returned to his horse, Bo. The Missouri fox trotter neighed and Byrne ran his hand through its mane.

"We got to go back. I know I said we'd never return to that damned town, but I never thought this would happen." He put his foot into the stirrup. "Sorry, old pal. I can ignore a lot of bad things happening, but, well, I may a bastard but that don't mean I want to see Armageddon."

They trotted down the clay street, bypassing the whorehouse and the general store, and when they reached the saloon Byrne brought Bo to a stop. He hadn't planned on it, but something tugged at him. He stared at the entryway before laughing at his own foolishness. The girl called Sorrow was paid to like him, he reminded himself. Sometimes a man's loneliness could play tricks on him, a woman's purchased company seeming all too real. Women were few and far between out here in the west. You could fall in love at the mere sight of one.

Still, something about his night with her lingered, a soft spot in a heart that had never known the love of a woman. He'd never been with one he didn't purchase or force while in his full wolfen form.

He tapped his heels and the horse went on, and when they reached the edge of town they picked up the pace. Juniper trees welcomed them onto the trail in lush waves and the mountains hulked ahead, all black rock and briar, their caps heavy with snow. Dogs barked in the distance. A lone cock called as if it were dawn. Byrne blew the last bit of smoke from his nostrils, an animal amongst animals.

Onward to Hope's Hill.

He'd heard the place had prospered, that it was no longer the sad manure pile he'd been raised in after being torn away from his mother and placed in the orphanage. At least the nuns had taught him to read and write. Sister Mable had taken the biggest interest in the young, feral boy. Byrne wondered if she were still alive and beautiful. She'd been like a second mother to him, despite all her flaws. And she had many. How much of his blood had gone to her brass Christ? Just a trickle here and there, but it added up. The bleedings were all so medical in nature none of the children ever questioned it. If Mable were still alive, she would no doubt still be in charge of the holy alliance. Reverend Blackwell was important, but merely a figurehead amongst the nuns—hell, Byrne had heard the old preacher was still alive too, which was astonishing if true—but that was always the way with these particular Catholics. The men were not without their value, but it was the sisters who held the power of white magic. It was they who were supposed to utilize it, to hold back evil forces and keep Old Scratch from knocking on the door to their world. The same went for keeping his demons in Hell where they belonged—demons like Jasper Thurston.

How could the nuns have let the dead Koyote's sorcery return, especially after all Byrne had gone through to get that cursed heart entombed?

But he'd been a willing Judas. If his old pack didn't believe Byrne had died alongside Thurston, he'd have been hunted down and skinned long ago. Glenn Amarok would not have rested while Byrne's head was still attached to his neck instead of floating in a jar of mescal inside his saddlebag. And if the Koyotes knew what had gone down in Hope's Hill all those years ago, that little town would be nothing but cinders. It chilled Byrne to know there was still time for it to happen, and now, with Thurston's heart exhumed, the Koyotes would come, and much like the Bible warned, all Hell would follow.

He camped out under the stars and ate cornpone, buffalo jerky, and stale biscuits. He nursed his canteen to make it last until he reached the next town. When he crossed into the mountain range, a storm of freezing rain forced him to spend a day tucked inside a cave that stank of bears long gone. Another night found him in an abandoned mineshaft that squeaked with bats, the ground slick with guano.

He thought of his first nights on the range after he'd run away from the orphanage, back when he'd been just a human. He'd stolen the money from the chapel's poor box and one of the preacher's mules, riding off without a destination, carrying an old breechloader to hunt buffalo, a gunnysack of his meager belongings slung over one shoulder. All that mattered then was that he was a man. How he made his way was insignificant and he felt no shame for his lawlessness when he turned that old rifle to robbing. After four months of lifting from shopkeepers at gunpoint, he joined up with an outlaw.

The stranger had approached Byrne in a dank saloon in some pissant town, saying he needed another man to pull off a bank heist. Said he'd done it before and showed off some greenbacks to prove it, buying Byrne drinks and taking him to the whorehouse where he lost his virginity to a woman ten years his senior.

The man's name was Web Tipton. Said he hailed all the way from Texas.

The third man they'd be hitting the bank with was a black-haired boy not much older than Byrne but hairy like an Italian. Web introduced him as Glenn, and it didn't take Byrne long to realize the younger man was the brains of the operation. Web was all brawn; a lumbering bull of a man with blacksmith's arms and a face always caked in soot. It wasn't until after the bank robbery that Glenn decided this Luther Byrne kid had enough grit to meet the boss.

They rode high through rocky terrain, deeper and deeper into the forest, the mule struggling to keep up with the two men's horses. He was led to a series of caves and a campground where a cast iron Dutch oven sat above the dying embers of a fire. Five men sat on rocks and a fallen log, eating from clay bowls and drinking cactus wine. When the riders approached, another man stepped out from the cave. He was older, like Web, and wore his hair long but slicked back. He was shirtless beneath a black overcoat. Between his teeth was a small cigar and his muttonchops were unruly, the hairs thick as pine needles. His eyes were two different colors.

The man looked to Glenn. "So this be him."

"Yeah, boss."

The man approached Byrne as he dismounted the mule.

"What's yourn name, kid?"

"Luther, sir. Luther Byrne."

"Don't give me that *sir* crap, kid. This ain't the bloody army. The name's Jasper Thurston, but these boys tend to call me boss."

Byrne nodded, not knowing what to say. He'd felt no anxiety while robbing the bank, but standing before this man he felt a nervousness uncommon to him.

"Been long on ya own?" Jasper asked.

Byrne nodded once again.

"This land can be mighty unfriendly to a boy," Jasper said. "I know that from experience. Best not to play a lone hand. Better to travel in packs." He puffed his cigar. "How old are ye?"

"Be thirteen in July."

Jasper smiled but it came off like a sneer. "Well, ain't that a funny coincidence. Thirteen was already gonna be yourn number."

"My *number*?"

Jasper turned his head and brushed his hair away from his neck, showing Byrne the back of it. Deep scar tissue revealed the number one. Byrne looked to Glenn and the young man drew back his long locks, showing the mark seared into his flesh—number seven. The others didn't show off their brands, carvings and tattoos. They didn't have to.

"Ye hungry?" Jasper asked.

"Starved something dreadful."

"Our cookie done whipped up some son of a gun stew."

"Ain't heard of that, but I'd be grateful to have some."

"It's a soup. Made of heart, liver, and tripe."

Byrne shrugged. "I'll eat it."

"Of course ye will."

Byrne realized Jasper hadn't said from what animal these innards came from. Somehow he knew it was best not to ask.

"Sounds good... boss."

When Jasper smiled, Byrne noticed his canines were a little longer than most men's. He clapped Byrne's shoulder and walked him over to the oven and handed him a bowl and wooden spoon.

"Welcome to the pack, kid."

*

She didn't feel safe in the room anymore, not even with the deputy downstairs. The marshal had appointed Hustley to stay at the Abercrombie house, in case any other townsfolk decided to make Grace Cowlin a target, or if, God forbid, Barley Reinhold returned. Norton Hustley seemed like a nice enough man, clean-cut and carrying the star of the law, but Grace remained nervous nonetheless. After what Reinhold and his hired ruffians had done, she doubted she'd see a good night's sleep for a while. She lay in her bed reading Jane Austen, one of her favorite authors, but just couldn't concentrate, reading the same lines over and over, her mind refusing to process them.

The memory of the black radiance in the O'Conner's house flashed through her mind. She could almost hear the family's patriarch roaring as Blackwell had recited some archaic prayer.

A knock at the door made Grace flinch. "Who's there?"

"Ma'am, it's Norton Hustley."

"Do wait, deputy. I am indecent."

"Yes, ma'am. Marshal Russell has come to see you. Seems something's happened."

"Something?"

"Best to let him explain."

"Alright then. I'll be down directly."

She dressed and came downstairs to the house's parlor where Joyce Abercrombie was serving yesterday's coffee to the lawmen. Russell and Hustley rose to their feet when Grace entered the room. They said their greetings and Russell got to it.

"I wanted you to hear from me first, though it is with regret I inform you the O'Conner farmhouse has burned down."

Grace covered her mouth. "My goodness. The whole farm?"

"The house mostly."

"What of the children?"

"They're safe. They've been staying at the orphanage until their aunt and uncle can get here. It's a long trip."

Grace had to sit down. "Do you suspect someone has done the O'Conners ill service?"

Russell sat on the ottoman before her, elbows on his knees, hands clutched.

"Could've been arson, for sure. That's what I've come here to ask you about. You were there when the first... *incident* occurred. You and the preacher and Sister Mable—and Barley Reinhold to boot. Would you be so kind as to tell me why?"

She blinked. "For the sake of the children."

"I see. Reverend Blackwell done told me he was there to do an exorcism on Shane O'Conner 'fore the man and his wife up and disappeared. He and Sister Mable say there was some sort of evil presence on that farm."

Grace looked at the floor. Her face tightened.

"Ms. Cowlin, I'd just like to get your take on what happened that day. All this religious stuff, see, it just leaves me confounded. With all respect to the preacher, he has struck me as a queer fish, what with all this talk of deviltry. I thought you might'n could give me some perspective, seeing as you ain't from the church."

Her eyes flashed. "I am still a Christian woman."

"Apologies, ma'am. T'wasn't suggesting otherwise. I just need to get all the information I can. That day up at the O'Conner farm put this whole mess into motion. Since then, Hope's Hill has been in chaos. One unfortunate event after another blamed on witchcraft and other such tomfoolery. I'm here to civilize this land once again. If I'm gonna find success in these aspirations, I need you to give me every detail of this madness."

And so she did.

She told him of the unholy blackness that had risen from beneath the floorboards of the house—risen from the very earth—and how the sky had turned tornadic and the windows burst and how she'd barely escaped with her life. She told him how the blackness had come for the family and claimed Shane and Bridget O'Conner and their bouncing baby.

"This darkness," Russell said, "you think it's some sort of evil spirit?"

"That I cannot say, but to me it felt not so much like a spirit, but a force."

"A force of nature?"

"No. There was nothing natural about it. I don't... I don't believe it is from *our world*."

Russell leaned in. "Well then, where does it come from?"

"I don't rightly know. But I think something's happened to Hope's Hill. I think this darkness, whatever it is, has been unleashed upon us like a plague."

"Unleashed? You think someone released this on purpose?"

"Maybe not someone. More like *something*."

*

The heart was secured in Dr. Craven's little black satchel, which was just large enough to contain the mighty muscle. He left it cracked open, thinking it best to give it air. The notion was based in no scientific or medical principle, because the heart defied all known principles. He was running on instinct here—instinct and excitement.

The train car moved forward, dark bloats of steam drifting past the window as Craven looked out upon the hulking presence of Black Mountain. It seemed somehow ominous today in a way it had never struck him before. Perhaps he was just frowning upon this piddle town for the last time, moving on to bigger, brighter places, the throbbing meat in his satchel his ticket to a better life.

His telegraph exchange with Dr. Julius Mumme, a renowned professor at the University of Pennsylvania, had been discouraging at first. A man of science was always a man of skepticism. But Craven convinced the professor to meet with him, using his own mentor's name for credibility. As long as Craven paid his own way in his trip east, Mumme agreed to at least give Craven a few minutes of his time, no matter how precious the professor believed it to be.

Craven settled into his seat.

It would be a long few weeks of travel, but he expected all would go smoothly.

CHAPTER XI

GLENN TESTED THE NIGHT AIR.

Thurston's black magic was moving—moving *fast*. Something had taken it. Was someone in possession, or was it that it had taken possession of them? Where it was going, Glenn could not say. The scent was rapidly slipping away and he could not determine its course. His nostrils flared.

"Something wrong, boss?" Web asked.

The big man had his arm in a sling made from one of his shirts, but the bleeding had stopped. Web was older and didn't heal as quickly as the others, but in a couple of days the axe wound would seal up completely. Rapid healing was one of the benefits of lycanthropy. A normal man would have had to amputate that arm.

"It's on a journey now," Glenn said.

Hiram spat. "Shit."

Dillon moved forward, picking at his bullet wound. He was twitchy, still excited by the day's events, of being a Koyote in general. Glenn almost envied the boy's exuberance and capacity for joy. It would not last. Time had a way of taking away a man's capacity for happiness, every year of his life passing by faster and meaner until he was straddling his grave, grumbling about how he'd never gotten a break, never warmed in his moment in the sun. Glenn knew no true joy, only the momentary ecstasy of violence and the lust he felt for anarchic destruction. He would feel no happiness until he found his place in Hell, a palace he'd built for himself to enjoy his eternal retirement from this world.

"What now?" Dillon asked.

Glenn gathered the reins. The redhead girl's pigtails had made for excellent new bridle handles. "We stay the course. If'n we lose the trail, then we head on to the last place we know Jasper was 'fore he died."

"Where's that?"

Glenn nodded toward the valley of rock. "Black Mountain. The scent has been bringing us to it thus far. Must be where the magic first returned. If'n we find out where it came from, we can find out where it's going."

Hiram spat again. "Yeah, last time we saw Jasper he was headed up that mountain with some of the other boys, but ain't none of them come back. I say it's time we search that bloody mountain again. Turn over every goddamn village that's done sprouted up 'round it. If we have to burn every one of these towns to the ground, then that's what we'll do."

"Where to first?" Dillon asked. "I'm ready to pull foot."

They turned to their leader. Glenn ran a hand over his muttonchops, scratching away fleas. The breath from his nostrils smoked in the cold. He gazed into the heavens and when he spotted Mars he watched it closely, absorbing its arcane energy, seeking guidance from its oxidized iron. He made the men wait until the red planet emanated a rich but invisible force from its ruddy surface, a conductivity only the strongest of wolfen could utilize. When Glenn's eyes fell back to earth, they were the same rusty color of the red planet.

He clacked the severed pigtails and the reins snapped the mustang into stride. He rode on without saying a word and the rest of the pack followed, tufts of dust rising from black hooves and leather shimmering in the light of the moon as the bringers of death thundered onward toward the hills.

*

They reached the cave just before midnight. Glenn had followed the internal compass bestowed upon him by Mars, but as the Koyotes rode deeper into the craggy, frigid core of Black Mountain, he had only to turn his nose to the wind to find the women.

First he smelled the flames, and then saw their glow. An orange orb pulsed upon the black rock, illuminating the shadowy figures of the cave dwellers. They were thin and tall, limbs gangly upon their lithe bodies, the full breasts and thick buttocks out of proportion with their slender frames. At their feet were a litter of wolf pups, some roughhousing while others snoozed before the warmth of the fire. One of the women was eating a live black snake, unbothered by the serpent biting her back. A young girl, hairless in her pre-pubescence, waited for the snake-handler to toss her scraps of scaly skin and then slurped them down and cowered back to her nesting hole of tangled thorn.

Web and Hiram knew these women, but Thad and Dillon had only heard of them and had not yet sampled their sacred pleasures. Glenn sensed the men's hunger and put up one hand to calm them.

"These are not prey."

The men rode slowly beneath the cover of withered branches until they reached the clearing the women had settled in, a barren spot where trees had been torn away, aptly known as a deadening. It suited these lovely, unholy creatures. Glenn rode point, guiding the rest of the pack into the haunt of the firelight, and when the first of the Daughters of Maenads spotted them she spun sharply, alive with the impulse to fight until she recognized Glenn. In her arms was a wolf pup suckling at her naked breast, its paws pressed against her, tail curled. Some of the other Maenads wore loincloths stitched of fawn skins, but most of them were nude, revealing the thin trail of peach hair that climbed up their spines, running from their tailbones to the napes of their necks. The one nursing the pup stepped forward, her eyes reflecting the moonlight in golden ovals, her smile plump and purple.

"Amarok," she said, calling to Glenn.

One of the other Maenads slithered behind her, a young vixen with black hair that fell down to her knees, covering her like a tangle of dead vines.

"The seventh?" the girl asked.

Glenn smiled at her. "They very same."

More pale bodies emerged from the cave, other Maenads awoken by the mere presence of the Koyotes. The men dismounted and stretched, wide grins on their dirty faces, weary from the road but aroused by these nubile females.

"What are they?" Dillon whispered to his pack leader.

Glenn never took his eyes off the woman before him. "They are acolytes. The Daughters of Maenads, worshippers like little sisters to our kind."

The Maenad woman gently placed the wolf pup on the ground beside its dreaming brethren and stepped into Glenn and ran her hands up under his cotton shirt, twisting her fingers in his chest fur.

"I am Thyian," she said. "And I am yours."

Glenn leaned in. "All of you are."

He stuck out his tongue and licked her from her lips to her forehead, leaving a trail of spittle. Thyian ran one finger through the spit and then stuck it in her mouth. She ran her hands up through Glenn's muttonchops and guided his head down to her breast where he suckled at her milking gland. Thyian leaned back and let out a banshee shriek that spooked the forest critters back into their holes. Other Maenads inched closer, hips cocked and swaying, and the Koyotes let them fall in and wrapped their arms around them. The men's dusty clothes came off and the little pups howled in celebration. Thad was the most eager, tearing away a Maenad's loincloth and pushing his way into her body before she was even ready to accept him. Still she moaned with pleasure. Hiram bent a Maenad over a rock to sodomize her, and she purred and clawed the granite with silvery dagger-nails. Another Maenad produced a live bat from a tangle of netting and bit into it, ripping away a leathery wing, and then took Web down to the ground and straddled the big man like a steer. A trio of the women undid Dillon's slacks and fell to their knees before him, licking their lips.

Thyian reached for Glenn's groin but he snatched her wrist.

"First things first."

"But the orgy is ritual, my illustrious one."

"The orgy can commence without me. I'm not here for pleasures of the flesh."

Thyian did not go for his crotch again, but she ran her leg up and down Glenn's, unable to control her desire. He was the head Koyote, the one hell-bound for the fiery, black throne of the next circle. Glenn had earned her adoration, but he chose to reward her for it anyway. Thyian sighed with ecstasy as he took her by the throat and squeezed.

"I will fuck you to the edge of dying," he said. "But first you must give me what I seek."

"Yes, grand Amarok. How may I please you?"

Glenn brought his lips to her ear and her neck fur rose up.

"Take me to Jessamine the Deathless."

*

Wet stalactites hung from the ceiling of the cave like fangs, dripping moisture that electrified the skin. Thyian walked ahead of him, guiding with his hand in hers, and he found himself admiring the way her trim waist curved into plump buttocks. Her could even see her breasts from the back, the Maenad's udders swollen with milk. The whore-beasts were a gift from Hell itself, but their deadening was not where the red planet had been guiding him, merely an oasis.

Glenn grew colder as the cave floor turned to bone. Beneath his feet lay a galaxy of slick skulls that gleamed in the light of Thyian's torch. Bison skulls, moose skulls, fox skulls. Most of all there were the skulls of humans, young and old, including the tiny, cracked heads of those born dead. Glenn inhaled, gathering more information by scent. These were not just Indians buried in the caves for some primitive ceremony. There were whites and blacks, Maenads and wolfen. As the tunnel progressed, the walls too went from granite to compacted skeletons, comprised of the remains of every creature native to this land, some dating back to B.C., others as fresh as that week. The shattered ribs of fallen warriors jutted from the walls like white atlatls. Mummified children stared at him with eyes shrunken to green peas, their mouths offering a rictus grin where lips had rotted away. The flame Thyian carried shrank to a small, blue pyramid and then soared back into a huge fire of purple, as radiant as a dozen moons. Every hair on Glenn's body stood on end. Thyian's ridgeback fur spiked along her spine. He could smell her sex moistening, her nipples seeping, her eyes watering. He was salivating like a dog, his chest hair soaked. The cave thrummed with a song-like moan, effeminate but inhuman, ghostly in the echo chamber.

Thyian turned to him. "She waits."

Glenn stepped forward alone. Here the skeletal floors forged a curved pit in the bottom of the entryway, swirling with brackish swamp water. Glenn stripped nude and waded in, first to his knees, then up to his waist, wanting to prove himself. He dipped one hand into the sludge and drank. It was rancid, diseased, but he swallowed it back. To disrespect the witch's hospitality was to fall from grace. He was up to his chest in the waters now and it was bubbling even as it grew colder. His teeth chattered as he sunk to his neck, and then he let go, dropping into the obsidian chasm, letting the blackness flood his eyes and fill his nostrils and pour down his throat, drowning himself in dedication to the sorceress' witchery. He suffered until the pain threatened to burst his lungs and then paddled back to the surface just before his strength could give out. His inhalation boomed and black birds fluttered from branches.

Glenn opened his eyes. He blinked away the blackish blood.

He had followed the underground tunnel and emerged out of the cave and into a dead forest. The remains of lifeless trees twisted out of the earth in broken spines, their suckering roots running through the yellowed grass like bloodless veins. The tops of the gnarled sycamore were enveloped in poltergeist veils of cobwebs. Rainclouds sulked above them in bulbous swarms, cradling the ravens Glenn had stirred from nests of human hair. Grayness draped across this land. It had soaked into everything, draining all color except for the swamp green of a single house rotting before the tree line. It was a stout, square building of dried mud brick, compacted with dirt, clay, and straw. It looked like a small fort or adobe house, only decaying, oozing. The same musical moaning Glenn had heard in the cave emanated from within.

He went toward it.

A rawhide sheet served as the front door and a pentagram had been carved into the porch. He stepped inside. The light in here was like that of Thyian's torch, an ethereal, metallic glow, green instead of lavender, but the source of it came not from fire, but from the cold flesh of Jessamine the Deathless. She stood before him statuesque, clad in a dress stitched together from the tanned flesh of children who'd gone lost in the caves. Their faces gazed without eyes like grotesque masquerade ball disguises. Jessamine's eyes were sunken in her attenuated face, the high cheekbones jutting out, her teeth worn down to half their normal size. When she spoke, her vocals crackled like the thrum of a beehive.

"The Seventh," she said.

Glenn nodded. "I've come in the name of The First."

The witch outstretched her arms. "Jasper is risen."

"Resurrection?"

"Not quiet yet."

The sorceress came forward, and when she got close enough Glenn could see the scar of the noose around her neck where she'd been hung but had failed to die. In accordance with the law of the time, she'd been set free. It was one of many assassinations she'd survived over the years, including stabbings with bayonets, beatings with clubs, and a single bullet in the back of the head. She'd vanished into the mountains so mobs, angry at what she'd done to local children, had been unable to hunt her down for lynching. They'd still been unable to keep safe any young ones who dared trespass upon her hollowed ground.

"Jasper is dead," she told him. "But the magic? Immortal. His heart is too wicked to die like a man's dies."

Glenn leaned into her. "Where?"

Jessamine the Deathless moved like vapor through the one room shack, drifting past a table of brimstone and a chair of rattlesnake hide that faced out the only window. She liked to watch, liked to wait.

"It travels in another's hands," she said.

"Whose?"

"A man of medicine, it is believed... or a scientist of some fashion. It is difficult to say just now. When the planets are not aligned, the message becomes muddied, Seventh One."

"Where he's taking it?"

"That... cannot be known." She ran her hand upon the table, her fingers withered like wet paper. "But you are not the only one to seek it."

Glenn's jaw tightened.

"There is another," she said. "And he too is wolfen. He too... a Koyote."

CHAPTER XII

BYRNE FELT SICK TO HIS stomach. The mining town of On-yx Banks had been in destitution for many years, but now it was decimated by more than economic strife and illness.

Human bodies lay bloody in the streets, gunned down like bison, some butchered like lambs. Outside the chapel, a nun was face down in the dirt, her skull crushed. Small, broken children were scattered about her in a confetti of gore that had gone black under the sun. The smelting house was on fire and a dead man was hanging out the window, impaled on shattered glass. Beside a cart filled with ore, another man lay with his hacked limbs stacked upon his chest like logs. An old woman was on her side upon the walkway, spine showing where her killer had peeled sheets of skin from her back. There was a fist-sized hole in the back of her skull. Inside, it was hollowed out.

Byrne kept on. He followed a wagon trail to a shredded revival tent where churchgoers and their steeds had been brutally slaughtered. Some of the bodies had been reduced to mere stains in the grass. He dismounted and stepped inside the tent, a cloud of flies buzzing about the rows of the dead. The carnage was worse here. Bodies bore claw and bite marks and had been partially eaten. Black fur was sprinkled across everything.

Wolfen, he thought. *A company of wolfen.*

He sniffed the putrid air, detecting the pheromones of Glenn Amarok and Web Tipton among others. Byrne's old company was indeed seeking Jasper's magic, and they were already ahead of him. Did they know to go to Hope's Hill? Did they know of the purified graveyard where Jasper Thurston had been buried all these years?

He climbed back into the saddle and Bo strode forward, the horse spooked by the presence of murdered mules and ponies. Byrne clacked the reins and Bo galloped, hooves pounding down the vegetation as they sped up. The sinking sun bled the sky into early evening. Byrne fled the horror of Onyx Banks, rambling across countryside withered by the touch of autumn, the once colorful foliage gone coffin-brown as November wound to its end. As the first stars sparkled in the gloaming, he pressed through lurching highland where the timber cleared and hulking shadows grazed. A society of buffalo roamed the knoll, their shaggy winter coats tucking them in the soft embrace of early dark, their horns and ears glowing with ethereal foxfire. He would shoot one for dinner but sojourn here only long enough to eat and rest his horse, having decided they would ride through night.

When dawn broke Byrne spotted a camp of canvas teepees, their wood spokes reaching for a purpling sky. One of their smoke flaps came open, a face peeking out from within. The Indians were too far away for him to guess their tribe, so he tucked his coat back to expose the iron at his hip, just in case he needed it. His horse grew tense and they slowed to a trot. Byrne's ears perked up for the sound of a bow wobbling, an arrow ripping air. But none came. He gave the camp a wide berth as he passed by.

Though they treaded softly, he heard them before he saw them. He could tell they were Indian by the way they rode their horses. They were adorned in bison hide, a single feather in each of their headbands. One was an older male, weathered with hair gray as his teeth. The other was a teenage squaw with deep eyes and a choker of beads around her neck.

Byrne picked up their scent.

He knew then they were a tribe of intermarried Shoshone and Bannocks, likely pushed away by whites from land more plentiful with water. The Snake War had ended with a treaty of peace, giving Byrne hope these two would allow a half-white to pass without any call for violence. When they came within six feet of each other, Byrne and the riders stopped but stayed atop their horses. The man said something in his native tongue and the young woman translated to English to their best of her ability.

"Father," she said to Byrne, "he ask you have tobacco."

Byrne reached for his wedge pack slowly, so not to put them on guard, and retrieved two Henry Clay cigars and offered them to the riders. When the man spoke again, his daughter translated.

"Thanks be to you, traveler. Good smoke is to be shared."

"Happy to oblige."

Byrne struck a match and lit their cigars, then one of his own. The man spoke to his daughter but didn't take his eyes off Byrne.

"You have whiskers," the girl said, looking at his muttonchops. "Father say you are skin walker. Move through night like antelope."

Byrne exhaled smoke. "I'm just a man."

"We believe you are of the Coyote people."

Byrne tensed. Did this tribe know the wicked pack of wolfen, know he'd once been a solider of the Koyotes? Or did they just mean wolfen in general when they referenced Coyote people? The Indians were always the more mystic race, their minds open to the supernatural and therefore better capable of understanding it, even utilizing it.

The old man's face was like a dynamited mine in the dull glow of the rising sun. His gaze was milky with cataracts, his words coming out like mixing gravel.

"Brother Coyote was part of The Great Mystery," the woman said, translating. "The creation. These were peaceful shapeshifters who taught our people to grind flour, make fire. Find herbs to heal our sick. But some coyotes are tricksters of the bad magic. If one of this breed crosses our path, we go home for three days before we go out again. The missionaries told our shamans of Satan. We believe he ride bad Coyotes like steeds."

Byrne shifted in the saddle. The old man flicked ash from his cigar. The young girl blew smoke. There was a beat, filled only by the distant call of morning birds.

"Before you pass, Father want know which kind of coyote you be."

Byrne looked out upon the horizon. "It's true that I am wolfen, but I do not suffer a call to evil in my heart, nor do I run with any pack that does."

The daughter shared a glance with the old man.

"Father say you peaceful man," she told Byrne, "but still your spirit howls."

The old man raised his arm, showing three fingers, and the warriors who'd been hiding out of sight slinked out from behind their coverings and placed their arrows back into their quivers. They walked back to the Indian camp, at ease, but perhaps a little disappointed judging by the scalping tomahawks some of the men carried.

This time the squaw spoke for herself.

"Run on, Brother Coyote. You will be known forever by the tracks you leave."

*

It was high noon when Luther Byrne came home.

Hope's Hill looked different, but at their core small towns tend to stay the same. The hearts of such places are stones that never roll, for they are pinioned by tradition and prejudice and the overrated lineage of old blood. Just to walk upon this dirt again made Byrne's posture go rigid. He watered Bo and hitched him at the post beside the old chapel, passing by the flower garden he himself had helped to dig into existence all those years ago. He'd hated the orphanage then. He'd been ripped from his mother and it left him a bitter, angry child, a boy the nuns had to keep a closer eye on. But could he be blamed for his rage, considering how he'd ended up here?

He'd missed his sweet mother terribly, but had no use for his birth mother, the actual woman who gave birth to him. She was a slobbering drunk who brought home any man at the saloon who'd buy her a bottle of vodka or sneak her some moonshine from a private still. But it was not one of these late night Romeos who had left her with child, but a Navajo Indian who'd been banished from his own tribe for reasons he would not name. Byrne's mother was ashamed to have been impregnated by a man who wasn't white, blaming the affair on the hallucinogenic effects of illegal liquor. She proved incapable of taking care of her son, being a poverty-stricken alcoholic with no family to fall back on. And so she'd taken baby Luther and placed him in the pen with their dog, a Russian wolfhound bitch that raised Byrne as one of her own. From her the

83

young boy learned to sniff what little food they had before he ate it, to walk on all fours, lick himself for personal hygiene, and bark, howl and yipe to express himself. The wolfhound was a caring mother, giving him more guidance than the one who'd spawned him ever would. And though he cursed his birth mother to this day he had come to appreciate that she'd at least had the good sense to place him in the care of someone who would love him, human or not.

By the time young Luther was four years old, his birth mother had drunk enough high-proof spirits to go totally blind. Unable to find her way home after a night in the woods, she stumbled through the streets in a sick delirium, screaming and flailing until she was taken away by lawmen who placed her in a wagon full of other head-sick patients bound for the asylum. She told them of her son, and when the lawmen discovered the feral boy he was taken from the dog pen, howling for his mother, the wolfhound howling back.

Byrne never saw her again.

In time he would learn to speak, walk upright, and eat with utensils instead of his hands, but to this day he still smelled his food before eating it and licked at his wounds until they stopped bleeding.

Bleeding.

That's how he'd served the nun who taught him to be human. Sister Mable and her own version of holy water—the blood and tears of children. For the nuns, suffering was the key to divinity. Byrne had learned there was some truth to that, but it did little to ease his resentment toward the church, to the Christian faith in general. He knew there was a world beyond this one, but had no fondness for the snakes and rats of Christ.

Now, all this time later, he came upon the front steps of the chapel with his jaw and fists clenched. He rolled his shoulders and shook himself loose. Going in with a rough attitude wouldn't help his reason for being here. The door was open, like always. He stepped inside. Out of the sun, his body cooled within the old chapel's walls. He smelled black mold hidden within them, smelled termites and dust in the rafters. An old woman sat in a pew with her head bowed toward the wooden statue of the crucified god-man. Unlike the one in the secret sepulcher below, this one had no special pipes to distill Sister Mable's holy brew. A beam of sunlight fell through the open window and illuminated Christ's slack, dead head, highlighting the dust in the air. Byrne approached the altar where the reverend's podium cradled a massive copy of the Old Testament lay open to Isaiah. He glanced at the page.

See, the day of the Lord is coming—a cruel day, with wrath and fierce anger... I will put an end to the arrogance of the haughty... their infants will be dashed to pieces before their eyes; their houses will be looted and their wives violated.

Byrne thought of all he'd seen at Onyx Banks. He took the remainder of his last cigar from his breast pocket but as he reached for his matchbox a door came open and he heard a familiar voice.

"I've waited for you to come."

It was as if she hadn't aged.

She said, "I sprinkled a special elixir so you'd be able to enter without being singed. A more sinister wolfen would have been singed anyway. Gives me hope for you yet."

Byrne stared into Sister Mable's heart-shaped face, so pale and lovely and arctic. A flood of conflicting emotions ached within him with no way out other than tears, so he swallowed them back and lit his cigar.

"Smoking in God's house?" she said. "I raised you better than that."

"I was raised by a dog."

"You know what I mean."

The old woman who'd been praying looked up at him for the first time, gathered her pocket Bible, and left the building. He was alone with the nun now.

"What made you so sure I'd be back anyways?" he asked.

She stepped around the pews. Even up close, he marveled at how she looked younger than he did now.

"You made a promise," Sister Mable said. "You're a troubled man, Luther, but one of honor."

"Wasn't always."

"Things change."

Byrne shrugged. "Yeah, well. I doubt things have changed in this here church, or up in our lady's orphanage."

"Luther, please. There's no need to bring up the past. Now, I've made up a bed for you and there's a general store at the end of the street. I will send one of the sisters to get some things for you—"

"No need. And there ain't no time for me to rest, good as a bed sounds. Just tell me what'n the hell happened to that grave."

"Do not use such language in the—"

"Where the hell's Jasper's goddamned heart?"

She gasped and crossed herself. "I believed I'd taught you long ago to be human, but you remain an animal. I do not know where Jasper Thurston's heart is, but it isn't where we buried it. Someone robbed the grave, and before you ask again I'll tell you I don't know whom."

"No Koyote still in Satan's palm could set one paw on that holy turf. Wasn't that the point of putting all those dead kids in the ground?"

Her face soured. "We had to purify the land to keep those monsters out."

"Reckon it didn't work, sis. They must've found him and dug him up."

"If they'd found Jasper Thurston things would be far worse than they are right now. You know this to be true."

He did. Of that there was no question. If Glenn and the boys held Jasper's heart, they held its magic, and they would do all they could to unlock its power in full. He had to get busy. Each passing day brought the Koyotes closer to a darkness that could cripple the world, perhaps even destroy it.

"If'n the Koyotes ain't the ones who done swiped it, who is?" he asked. "What kind of degenerate would go digging holes in a graveyard in the middle of nowhere?"

*

"Come on now, Cassius," Vern said, "this here's pure gold, pure as the Virgin Mary. You know it's worth more than a dollar and two bits."

Cassius Sneck crossed his arms and looked down at the capsule. "Dang it, Vern. This is a general store, not a bank. You got my offer. If'n it don't suit you, well, you know where the door is."

Vern shook his head. "Can't take it to no bank, you know that. With my debt they'd only give me the money to take it away again. Just a bundle of low-down dirty thieves is what they are, no better than the bandits who up and rob them. In fact, I'd say a bandit is the higher class of human being of the two. At least he doesn't put his arm around your shoulders like you're his kin before robbing you down to your skivvies."

The door came open and a tall man walked in. Vern and Cassius fell hushed at the sight of this stranger, with his heavy build, dusty clothes, shaggy hair and even shaggier whiskers. His skin was the color of dead leaves. The stranger browsed the wares and Cassius kept one eye on him as Vern continued to haggle.

"I'll take three dollars for her. Heck, you might still make up to five dollars profit on her; maybe even ten."

"Hogwash. This egg of yours could very well be fool's gold."

"No, sir, it ain't! I wouldn't try to swindle you, old friend. I'm on the up and up. This here is *solid gold*. Here, take a gander."

Vern opened the capsule.

"Tarnation!" the shopkeeper said, fanning in front of his face. "Your egg smells rotten. What you been keeping in there, a month old salmon?"

Being a mortician, Vern Pipkin was not as sensitive to odors as most folks. He thought he'd cleaned the inside of the capsule well enough, but…

"It's just a little odorous 'cause of its age. See, it's an antique I'm selling you here, a genuine article if ever you done saw—"

Hands grabbed at Vern's collar. He was spun around. The stranger had pounced upon him with the speed of a mountain lion and looked twice as mean. His knuckles going white as he clutched the golden egg, Vern began to shake.

"Please, friend," he said, "What's the meaning of this?"

In one swoop the stranger ripped the capsule from Vern's grasp. He opened it all the way, found it empty, and glowered at the undertaker.

"Where'n the hell'd you get this?"

Vern swallowed dry. "Why, it's a family heirloom. Belonged to my dearly departed nana."

"Horseshit." The man pushed him. "Where'd you get this? I ain't gonna ask you again; least, not nicely."

"No need for this manhandling, friend. Are we not white men?"

"No. I'm a half-breed and you're a goddamned ghoul is what you are."

Vern's face pinched. "What's that now?"

"You've been nibbling graves."

Though he tried to speak, all the air had left Vern's lungs. There was a loud click and when he turned around he saw Cassius had come up holding the shotgun he kept underneath the counter for just such rough customers.

87

THE THIRTEENTH KOYOTE

"Now you listen good, mister," the shopkeeper said. "I don't want no trouble in my establishment. Now why don't—"

The stranger snatched the shotgun from Cassius with one hand, never even taking his eyes off of Vern.

"Buried things are supposed to stay buried," the stranger said. "You dug up something you'd have been best off leaving deep in the ground." He looked to Cassius. "There's gonna be trouble in this town alright. Mean trouble."

The stranger tossed the capsule over his shoulder and it clattered when it hit the floor. Vern flinched, hoping it hadn't been scratched or dented.

"Where is it?" the stranger asked. "Where's the heart?"

Both men's eyes fell on Vern. He detected a bizarre redness in the stranger's irises.

"Mister... er... what's your name, sir?"

"Luther Byrne. You'd do smartly to remember it."

"Mr. Byrne, I do declare, of such a heart I am ignorant."

"You're lower than a cow paddy but you're no simpleton. And there's no time to waste on this here foolin' around. Tell me the truth and I'll let you live."

Cassius spoke up. "Mr. Byrne, please don't do this in my establishment."

Vern huffed. "Don't you mean don't do this *at all*, Cassius?"

"Ah, hell, Vern, 'course I do."

The one called Byrne took a deep breath. Vern could tell this burly man was holding back a violence that came to him by primal instinct, but he may not hold it in much longer. It may come out involuntarily, an automatic reflex to being lied to. Vern wet his lips. He had to make a decision here.

"Listen good, Vern," Byrne said, "you done cursed this here town. Cursed just about all mankind if'n that heart fell into bad hands. Now, I can forgive you not knowing how important that heart was, but I surely cannot forgive you lying to my face 'bout where you done stashed it. I know you had it at one point. I can smell it on you like shit on a hog farm."

Vern looked away as Byrne's eyes grew redder still, rubies catching sun. This was no normal man. He was as queer as the heart he was enquiring about. Maybe the heart really was dangerous.

"It beats," Vern said. "Beats though there's nary a body to beat for."

Byrne remained silent, waiting for more.

"The doc said he wanted to study it. I gave it to him in the name of science."

"What doc?"

"Dr. Uriah Craven."

Cassius said, "He's the town doctor, mister."

"I follow that," Byrne said. "Where can I find him?"

Vern began to tell him, but Cassius cut him off.

"He's gone," the shopkeeper said.

"Gone?"

"He come in yesterday to stock up on travel supplies. Had a ticket to the teapot, he did. Said he was heading east. I can't recall where to, exactly, but his journey was far enough to call for a loco-motive."

Byrne closed his eyes and released a long breath. Vern turned his head away.

"Sweet gallnippers, mister. Your breath could knock a buzzard off a dung-wagon."

Vern instantly regretted it as the big man pulled him closer, his fists drawing Vern's collar tight around his neck.

"You're to tell me all there is to know about this Craven," Byrne said. "And you'll be helping me figure out where he's headed."

"I'm afraid I have no more to tell."

Cassius leaned in. "Come now, Vern. Can't you see this here man means serious business? Hang up your fiddle, you darned fool, 'for he tans your hide."

Vern would have gut-punched the shopkeeper's round belly if Byrne hadn't frozen him still. He tried to wet his lips again but his mouth was desert dry. And so he told him everything, from the robbing of the grave to the trade off with Craven and how the doc-tor seemed to think he'd come across the find of the century. When Vern was finished, Byrne's grip on him loosened a little.

"Now, I done been straight with you, Mr. Byrne. I done told you it all and there ain't no more."

"Take me to his office."

"But... but he's gone."

"Take me anyway."

He let Vern go, giving him the urge to run. But judging by how quickly Byrne had pounced upon him, he knew he wouldn't even make it out the door. He pressed his coat back into place, straightening the ruffled collar.

"I cannot help you anymore than I have," he said. "Craven's headed out of town. He's like a nigger in a woodpile now; *vanished*. Who knows where he might be."

Byrne released Vern, cracked the shotgun and expunged the bullets before throwing it to the other side of the store. Vern winced as he was took by the arm again, Byrne's grip like a foothold trap. He started them to the door and Cassius remained behind his counter, a dumb look on his face. He would be of no help. Vern reached for the golden capsule on the floor and picked it up on their way out. No way in hell he'd leave it for Cassius for free.

They walked down the street in relative silence, Vern only giving directions. The doctor's office was not far from the general store. What did this ruffian think he'd find there that would help his pursuit any? And who was this Byrne anyway? He hadn't announced himself as a lawman or any other authority. What gave him the right to shove Vern around like he was no better than an Injun? He was a respected member of his community who provided an essential service. So he'd nibbled at a grave in the middle of nowhere—what was the harm? It worried him that Cassius Sneck knew about it now, but Vern would later claim he'd only told Byrne what he wanted to hear, that there'd been no truth to the forced confession of grave-robbing. Still, Cassius was a jabberer and everyone in town bought goods from his shop. Gossip would spread like smallpox.

When they reached the office, Vern took his eyes away from the windows and looked at Byrne.

"If'n you intended to break into the good doctor's office, I will take no part."

Byrne took hold of the doorknob and tried to push, clearly not familiar with the fairly new invention. Vern smirked in superiority and turned the knob for him, then realized he'd gone back on the words he'd just spoken. Byrne shoved him inside and drew back the curtains to allow light. The office was cool and sterile, much like the man who owned it. Byrne rummaged through the office first, then went to the back of the building to search Craven's living quarters, taking Vern along. They opened drawers and lifted the hood of his roll top desk. Byrne seemed to search not just with his eyes, but also with his nose, sniffing every nook. Vern had to look away. The man was simply beastly. When Byrne came to the bookshelf, he snorted at a particular volume and withdrew it. Opening it, he sniffed the pages.

"Gracious, sir," Vern said. "What in blazes are you doing?"

Byrne sniffed once more and placed the open book upon the desk. He pointed at it.

"This," he said. "This is the last page he touched. His scent is all over it."

"How could you possibly—"

Byrne tapped at the header of the page.

The University of Pennsylvania.

CHAPTER XIII

THEY WERE WAITING FOR HIM when he came out of the office.

Russell kept his Colt holstered, but placed his hand upon it. The iron was cool to the touch, the sun having slunk behind the gathering clouds. They groaned, heavy with the cold rain of late autumn. When the big man stepped into the street with the undertaker, Deputy Jake Dover raised his rifle but didn't point it directly at them. The young lawman had been the one to alert the marshal of the break-in, a nervous shopkeeper having come to the station to tell him of a man named Byrne and where he was headed.

The stranger paused, clutching Vern so he couldn't run away. He was a dark and ragged rider, caked the in the grime of a long journey. Russell and his men were skilled at monitoring who came and went in their town. It irked him they hadn't known of this stranger until he'd already committed the crime of trespassing on the doctor's property. Byrne wore iron at his hip, a Colt bigger than Russell's. Deputy Dover spotted it too.

Dover raised his rifle a little higher. "Let's see you just drop that belt and cannon. Nice and slow."

Byrne stood still as granite. The wind picked up and blew his tangled hair about his shoulders. His whiskers fluttered. Russell suddenly thought of what Sister Mable had told him and all he'd heard about the Koyotes. This tall drink of water certainly matched their description. Best not to take chances. He turned the lip of his coat to flash his badge.

"Best do as my deputy says. You don't want to catch a tartar."

Byrne squinted but said nothing.

"That is to say, you wouldn't want to go into something when you're outmatched."

Byrne's face was a death mask. "And what makes you think I'm outmatched?"

Silence fell between the men. A light drizzle came then, promising full rain on its tail. Beyond the buildings the tree line seemed to sway drunkenly, awoken by the witch's wind, and their bare branches cackled against the backdrop of undulating gray. A chill ran through the marshal.

"Stranger, you're close to forcing me to do something I'd rather not. You best drop that iron in your belt."

Byrne shook his head. "Can't come it."

"I'm taking you to my jail one way or another. Wouldn't it suit you finer to not be lying in a cell with a bullet in you?"

Deputy Dover aimed the rifle directly at Byrne. Russell could swear he saw fangs when the man sneered but Byrne closed his mouth too quickly to be sure. Vern Pipkin put up his hands.

"Please, Jake," he said to the deputy, "be careful where you point that!"

Byrne said, "That's good advice, gentlemen."

Russell itched to draw his Colt but didn't want to start a shootout unless it was absolutely necessary. There were townsfolk in the street behind them, watching, too entertained to get to safety. Their rubbernecking might just cost them their lives.

"You threatening men of the law, Byrne?" Russell said.

"You warned me; now I'm warning you. I'll let the undertaker go and be on my way, but I ain't going to no calaboose."

"And why's that?"

"Ain't got time."

"Suddenly you're in a hurry to leave Hope's Hill?"

"Never wanted to come here to begin with."

"Well then, why did you? What's your business in my town?"

"It's *your* town now, is it?"

Vern said, "He's looking for ol' Doc Craven, but Doc's gone on to the old states! This man says Doc took his heart or some such." Byrne shushed him but being between him and the peace officers panicked Vern. He pointed to his temple. "He ain't right in his upper story!"

To Russell's surprise, Byrne shoved his hostage away, giving him up, but he did it with enough force that Vern stumbled and fell face first into the ground. He coughed as his wind left him. Startled by the movement, Deputy Dover nearly fired, his finger twitching upon the trigger. Vern ran, cradling something gold and shiny, a child with a straw doll. There was a silent standoff then, the lawmen waiting for Byrne to make his move and Byrne doing the same.

The rumble of wagon wheels drew Russell's attention and he watched the approaching stagecoach out of the corner of his eye. As it drew closer, Dover turned his head, unsure now who to aim at. These could be friends of Byrne come to shoot his way out of trouble. But as the stagecoach came upon them the lawmen recognized the black-clad man who sat atop it. Russell was amazed the old preacher could see well enough to steer the horses. The wagon came to a stop, Sister Mable leaping out of it in a hurry, two nuns following behind her.

"Jesus," Russell muttered.

Byrne laughed. "Exactly."

Sister Mable drew closer. "Marshal, wait!"

When she raised her hands Russell saw she was not wearing her usual gloves. In each palm was a scar the size of a silver dollar.

"Stay back," Russell said. "All of you get on back in that buggy."

"Please, you must listen to me. This man can help us save Hope's Hill."

Russell looked the outlaw up and down. The last thing he would have taken him for was some sort of savior. Hell, he didn't look worth the worn out boots he stood in. The rain was picking up, so Russell couldn't tell if it was raindrops or tears on the nun's face, but he had an inkling considering the worry in her eyes.

"What're you telling me, Sister?"

"This is Luther Byrne. I know him well because I raised him, right here in this town. If it were not for his bravery, Hope's Hill would be nothing but rubble, and without him it may come to that right soon." A flash of lightning made the pale nun all the more ghostly. "Don't mind *this* rain, Marshal. There's a worse storm coming, worse than any you can imagine. All the signs of deviltry we've seen thus far—the sour land and livestock? It's only the beginning. The true storm will come on a legion of wolfen—the Koyotes. They're returning to finish what their leader started."

Russell still wasn't buying into this supernatural nonsense, even if so many other people in Hope's Hill were convinced of it. But he had to calm his people and a big part of that would involve placating the church. The last thing he needed was for them to start spreading some holy panic through their flock, Reverend Blackwell flapping about on his stage, orating about Armageddon zeroing in on their little town. Town leader Murphy Hyers would want to know why Russell hadn't acted, why he hadn't done it as a show of good faith. And what if Sister Mable had something more than a hunch when it came to the Koyotes? He knew the outlaws from his fugitive list and the brutality of their crimes. What if they really were on their way to Hope's Hill and Mable and Byrne could give him more information? Something fishy was afoot, be it supernatural or not.

He looked to Byrne but spoke to the nun. "So what of him then?"

"Luther's here to help us," she said.

Sister Genevieve stepped forward. "It has been foretold—"

She shut her mouth when Mable glared at her. Russell took note of it.

He turned to Byrne again. "Alright, mister. What's your relation to the Koyotes?"

"I don't owe you my life story."

"Best give me something, or I'll take you in yet, no matter how many nuns you've got backing you."

Sister Mable got close to Russell so to whisper.

"Marshal…. this man is the thirteenth Koyote."

*

"How'd you know where I was going?" Byrne asked. "And that I was in trouble with the law?"

Sister Mable huffed. "You're always in trouble with the law."

"But how'd you—"

"Reverend Blackwell may be half blind but he sees more than most. He has a special vision, a true gift from God."

THE THIRTEENTH KOYOTE

The preacher sat at the back of the marshal's office, head tucked, either asleep or in prayer, maybe having another one of his epiphanies. Byrne couldn't be sure which. The nuns took to the other chairs the deputy had dragged in, but Byrne chose to stand even as the marshal sat. Vern Pipkin was in the corner, wringing his hands and sweating with all the guilt of a man with his hobbies.

They went over all Byrne knew, all Mable knew, and Russell took it in, his eyes tired as if hearing their story made his head too tight. They told him of Byrne's desertion of his former gang, how he'd revolted against the Koyotes and the ruthless Jasper Thurston. They left out many of the more fantastical details of that night, but made the point clear—Byrne was not with the company any longer.

"We need Doctor Craven brought back to Hope's Hill," Sister Mable said. "We need Thurston's heart so we can put it back into the grave where it belongs."

Russell leaned in. "You must realize how batty this sounds."

Byrne said, "Even if you don't believe in the heart's sorcery, I can assure you the Koyotes do. They'll be coming here right quick."

"How would they even know where it is?"

"They know."

"How can you be sure if you left the company?"

"You're a man of no faith, Marshal. You wouldn't believe how I know."

"Tell me anyway."

Byrne rolled his shoulders. "There are things in this world can't be explained by the logic of mortal men. There's darkness and light, gay heavens and a thousand levels of a black hell. All the art of the world can't capture them. Even your Bible fails, I reckon."

"What're you telling me here?"

"That there are worlds *behind* this one, other stars in other universes. What say you if I say this universe you live in is a conscious thing, or that the sun that makes life possible can be yanked from the sky into some queer dimension and cast your planet in a darkness colder than a witch's tit that'll cripple and kill all mankind? What if I say this still-beating heart your doctor snatched holds all the power a Koyote needs to bring that black hell upon us all? I know what you'd say. Like your undertaker, you'd say I wasn't right in my upper story, that I was madder than a rat in a shithouse."

Russell glowered. "Watch your cussin' around the sisters."

"I may not see all Blackwell sees but I know the lusts of wolfen

96

gone mean. Amarok savors—"

"*Amarok?*" Russell said. "You talking about the outlaw? Glenn the Dreadful?"

"The very same."

"He's one of the most wanted men on my fugitives list."

"And mayhaps all the world."

Russell leaned in. "You're telling me he's—"

"He savors all that is evil and if'n you fail to heed this warning he'll unfold the blackest of magic upon Hope's Hill. Your streets will run red with the flesh of men, women, and children you could've saved."

"You talk big for a man with little sense."

"And you listen like your ears are packed with cattle droppings."

The marshal stood. "I ought to arrest you, seeing as you were part of this gang. Amarok runs with Hiram Zeindler, a filthy child-killer. Not to mention Thaddeus Bowman and Web Tipton, and the kid, Dillon Boody—all murderous rakes, some even wanted for cannibalism! Yes, I researched these scoundrels. Unfortunately when I checked my bulletins I found nothing I can throw you in a cell for. Still, who knows how many crimes you've committed. Must be a bounty on your head somewhere."

"I ain't rode with these men in over a decade. You've got nothing on me."

"We'll see about that."

Sister Mable stepped between them. "Gentlemen, please. Your squabbling wastes time and benefits our enemies. Marshal, I too can assure you these marauders will come, just as Jasper Thurston did many moons ago. How much of this curse must you see, how many of us must tell you of this great evil before you accept it as the God's truth? I beg you—do not gamble with the lives of Hope's Hill. Do not let them suffer once more at the hands of Koyotes."

Russell sucked his teeth, considering, and then turned to his deputies.

"Battlecreek Station is the largest in the region," he said. "If Craven's headed east, his train will have to make a stop there. Get a telegraph out to the sheriff. Tell him to stop that train when it rolls in and find the good doctor. I want Craven escorted home. I want to see this beating heart."

*

THE THIRTEENTH KOYOTE

Craven bent over, his hand across his gurgling gut.

Why did I have to fall ill while en route? Of all the times…

It wasn't like him to get travel sickness from riding by train. But this wasn't mere nausea. He was truly sick. Perhaps he'd eaten something spoiled or had caught a simple virus. He was a doctor, after all. He came in contact with the sickly every single day.

His bowels rotated as if in a butter churn. He held a fist to his mouth to cover his belches, already embarrassed for he'd gone to the hooper toilet four times to void himself over the drop chute. It had been coming from both ends and, worse yet, both stool and regurgitation came out *black*. Thank goodness they'd be reaching Battlecreek Station soon. Some fresh air, cold water… a dose of medicine…

The train bounced and he clutched the satchel, fearing for the heart inside. It was just a slight bump but he was growing increasingly concerned for the heart's safety. As important as it had seemed to him upon leaving Hope's Hill, now that he was journeying across the territories with it he felt terribly uneasy. He'd examined it thoroughly, turning it over and under it his hands, prodding it. The heart was precious to him now. He was even having second thoughts about sharing its uniqueness with Professor Mumme when he reached the university. Craven had come to feel jealous somehow. He'd begun to wonder if he was in possession of the heart or if it was the heart that was in possession of him. He tried to laugh away the notion but it kept coming back to him like a Navajo's boomerang.

When the train at last wheeled into Battlecreek, Craven rose from his seat and the other riders, seeing how pale and sweaty he was, let him pass before stepping into the aisle with their bags. He was only outside for a minute before the lawmen came upon him.

*

They were on the other side of the mountain now, the Koyotes riding down the shallow slope and into the sprawling woodland. The gravel was beset by browning chaparral, the walls of the mountain mired by creeper stems that clung to its rock like deer ticks. They came across the ruins of an overturned stagecoach and in the crushed bramble lay two decaying oxen still in their yoke. Wolves and buzzards had picked their bones and now the insects had made their hives inside the gutted carrion. Above the reek of death, Glenn smelled the object of his desires. It was a ripe and pungent odor, the black fragrance of doom and madness.

"It's fast approaching," he said.

Hiram scratched his neck. "You mean it's coming back?"

"I reckon it's riding by air line road."

"A train?"

"Too fast to be by horse. Whoever holds the heart is either riding the rails or has gathered the magic to move like a tireless thoroughbred."

Glenn thought of what Jessamine the Deathless had said, that there was another Koyote out there. How could this be? But if it were so, it could be he who held the heart, he who could become a wolfen warlock and forge his throne. Glenn had not told Hiram or the rest of the company what the witch had said. Some things he kept secret until the time was right, if that time ever came at all.

"Shit," Hiram said, "if the heart's coming back this way, maybe whoever holds it wants us to have it."

"Even a village idiot wouldn't be so daft."

"What I mean is, mayhaps they're on our side, like the Daughters of the Maenads."

Glenn snorted. "I have felt the black sorcery of Jasper Thurston. Though his heart is too much for anything other than a Koyote to handle, its possessor will never accept that fact. Even as it eats their body their soul will cling to it. No one would give up that kind of power willing, even if they knew not what it was."

Behind the leaders riding point, the rest of the company was silent, listening to them, awaiting instruction. Glenn brought Belial to a halt and the horse turned to face his followers.

"Brothers," he said. "Tonight we ride. We go east instead of west, for the heart of Jasper is coming home, back into the arms of we, the blackest wolfen. But we must snatch it while it travels, for if we let it pass we may lose its scent forever. So tonight we ride like a hundred Indians are at our backs. We move like cannonballs and break through whatever gets in our way. We trample woodland creatures and children in their villages and even if our horses' hooves grow bloody we do not break stride."

The men looked to each other, nodding in their silent pact.

Glenn clicked his tongue.

THE THIRTEENTH KOYOTE

The Koyotes roared through the mountainside in a flurry of leather and smoke.

*

Uriah Craven stared at the backs of his hands.

The veins stood out like black roots, enlarged and pulsing as hideously as the heart that beat inside his satchel like a funeral drum. Blood had pooled beneath his fingernails and the little hairs on his wrists had fallen away. He kept clearing his throat and swallowed something tarry each time. Beside him, the deputy from Battlecreek scowled beneath a handlebar moustache.

"What on God's green earth is happenin' to you?"

When Craven tried to speak he felt his lower teeth loosening. Clearly spooked by the doctor's degeneration, Deputy McGath rose from his seat and stood in the aisle. The train was smaller than the one Craven had ridden in, and less comfortable. And now, on top of being sick with an illness even he couldn't diagnose, he was soured by jangled nerves. He'd never been accosted by lawmen before. It had been most humiliating. Apparently the new marshal who'd landed in Hope's Hill had ordered Craven's swift return. Why was this happening? McGrath and his sheriff had been tightlipped about the meaning of this, telling him Marshal Russell would have to talk to him about it himself. Had the new head lawman of Hope's Hill found out he'd been buying body parts? Had Vern Pipkin been caught nibbling graves and run at the mouth, giving up the names of his clientele in exchange for a lighter jail sentence? It would be just like that sniveling rat of a resurrectionist to do such a thing. He'd send his own mother to the gallows if it meant saving a single hair on his pimply ass.

Hair.

Craven looked again at his bald wrist. He rolled up the sleeve of his shirt and arm hair came up with it, blowing away like a cat shedding its winter fur. Black varicose veins made shapes like shattered windows across his graying skin. He looked away, choking back a sob. How cruel was God? If Craven were to die a horrible, cancerous death, could it have not waited just a little longer so he could reveal his great discovery to the medical community, thereby securing his name in the history books? Even a death as confounding as this one would be less painful if he knew he'd made his mark on the world of science. A legacy would be his only solace as he lay in the grave.

He couldn't think that way. He would overcome this, whatever it was. Some new form of leprosy, some alien pox. Perhaps it would not be the dead man's heart but Craven himself who would become the medical anomaly to go down in history books. *Craven's Syndrome*, they might call this cachexia. He groaned and rested his head upon the window.

Night had fallen in full but a waxing moon threw the land in a pale dream. A goldmine of stars poked holes in the sky and Craven recalled how he'd slept under them during the war, lying back in his bedroll and smoking his pipe as his fellow soldiers played cards and told tales of women. He'd been so much happier then—young and spry. Gazing upon the prairie, Craven saw the huge shadow of Black Mountain swallow up the stars and just before the moonlight vanished behind the summit it fell upon the riders heading for the train. Their horses rumbled across the earth, great plumes of dust bursting about the steeds like geysers. And though Craven knew not who they were, somehow he knew what they were coming for.

Other passengers spotted the riders then. Women gasped. Men shouted. Deputy McGrath had already drawn his iron and when the door to the car opened two expressmen came down the aisle. Employed to guard the passengers and cargo, they'd jumped at the sight of the riders and readied their weapons. The expressmen exchanged a few words with McGrath as the outlaws came alongside the train, the horses bolting at full speed. One of the outlaws was already reaching for the rails. The older expressman shoved a passenger out of his seat, crouched into it and raised his revolver through the window and fired three shots but the riders showed no sign of harm in the muzzle's flash. The rookie expressman, an ill prepared tinhorn, was pouring powder into the barrel of his outdated rifle. His hands were shaking and the gunpowder fell about his arms like black snow. When the older expressman aimed out the window again he suddenly screamed and an arterial spray turned his face the color of strawberries. He cried out in his agony and fell back into the seat, the stump at his shoulder gushing where his arm had once been.

Craven gasped as a monster's claw crashed through the window where the expressman had been firing. It tore through the glass and when it hit the sill it tore through the train itself, shredding away the frame like it was paper until the hole was large enough for the burly man to pass through. All about the railcar people were screaming and trampling over one another in an effort to escape, as if there was somewhere to go. Craven just stayed in his seat, watching as this outlaw came at the man he'd just mutilated.

McGrath tried to rescue the fallen expressman. He fired upon the attacker and managed to put at least one bullet in him, but the beastly man did not lay off his assault. He ripped into the expressman with hairy hands, sending red tufts of flesh and bone chips into the air. The rookie got his rifle together just as the back door of the railcar swung open and another outlaw stepped in. He was slender and rat-faced with dirty-blonde whiskers. He had a small cigar in his mouth and a Wesson rifle up at his shoulder. He blasted, taking down whoever stood in his way. The railcar became a hurricane of panic, gore-slick bodies writhing as if in some great blood orgy. The slender man forged a path for the next outlaw, a pale rider with long black hair and yellowed dog teeth. The mere sight of this one made Craven cry out. Clearly this was the leader. This was the man who'd come to take his world away. Craven clutched the satchel so tightly the tip of the heart oozed through the top and he scrambled to get it closed again.

But it was too late. The leader glared at Craven with eyes like red gemstones.

As the outlaws tore through the passengers, McGrath and the rookie expressman ducked and fired but even when their bullets landed true they caused little damage. The slender man caught a ball to the shoulder, but he merely winced as he resumed his attack. McGrath fired at the leader and the outlaw moved like lightning, drew a dagger from his coat, and used it to deflect the bullet. It ricocheted off the blade with a spark and landed in the side of an old woman's neck. She fell on top of a screaming little boy and crushed him into the seats, twisting and breaking his leg beneath her. Craven sat in shock as the leader jumped—*flew*—over the others and landed upon the deputy. The outlaw's face was almost snout-like now, the nose black and wet, jaw wide. McGrath fired repeatedly into the beastman's chest and the beastman grabbed hold of the pistol and crushed it like wadding clay, then shoved the hot mass of iron into McGrath's stomach and dug it into his insides. McGrath's gut opened and hissed. He fell slack in his attacker's arms, his steaming entrails disgorged. The wad of iron burned the innards black and they boiled and fizzed as they dribbled to the floor.

The leader threw the body over his head and McGrath's corpse smacked down the rookie expressman and his pouch of gunpowder burst in his breast pocket, caking his face and chest. The slender man chuckled at this, took his cigar from his lips, and flicked it at the rookie. The gunpowder caught and the young man was instantly awash in flame. The smoke of his burning flesh began to fill the railcar as he screamed and flailed against the dead body pining him to the floor.

Craven closed his eyes as the leader's shadow fell over him.

"You have something that belongs to me."

CHAPTER XIV

WHILE HE WAS LAID BY the whore, Byrne thought of the saloon girl, the one he'd danced away a night with back in the mill town of Steelbranch. The whore's name was Veva, a giving lover worth every bit of coin, dark-haired with heavy rouge and lipstick that made her look more mature than her eighteen years.

When Byrne climaxed he cried out, "Sorrow!"

He collapsed on top of Veva and once he'd rolled off she looked at him with her head propped in her hand.

"Sorrow?" she asked. "Is that always what you say when you get a poke?"

"Ain't what you're thinking."

"I'm guessing it's a name then."

He reached for his discarded coat and retrieved a tobacco pouch, saying nothing.

"It's all right," Veva said. "My name's whatever you want it to be."

Byrne rolled a cigarette, lit it. It'd been too long since he'd enjoyed a woman's charm, so before retiring he'd dipped into The Green Lily for a poke and a whiskey. The marshal had said Craven was on his way back but it would be a few hours before the train arrived at the depot. Sister Mable had offered Byrne a room at the orphanage, but just the thought of going into that building again made him queasy. He'd be more comfortable at Abercrombie's boarding house. He looked forward to catching some sleep in a real bed.

Veva snuggled against him in post-coital serenity and, even if she were just faking, this sweetness still caused him to catch his breath. She was young and tender, a doll baby who smelled of aromatic herbs and fledgling sweat. Her body was freshly ripened and he sensed no stains upon her heart. Though he wished her no harm, his primal instincts assured him she would be delicious. But he hadn't eaten human flesh in years, having sworn off it when he'd decided to be a better man. Not a good man, perhaps, but a better one.

"Best be getting back downstairs," Veva said. "Can't keep customers waiting too long. Ain't but one other whore here."

She sat up and Byrne gave her an extra dollar. "When you sleep tonight, dream of me."

"I never dream."

Byrne envied her for it. His own dreams were always tarnished by memories he couldn't suppress when unconscious. The people he'd murdered haunted him when he so much as closed his eyes. His troubled mind would not allow him dreams of fancy, only nightmares as brutal as his life had been, only the terrors of all he'd seen and, worse yet, all he'd done.

He rose from the bed and slid into his slacks. Once dressed, he bent over Veva and planted a kiss upon her forehead.

"If not a dream, then put me in a prayer."

*

Walking up the stairs to his room, Byrne removed his hat and rubbed the bridge of his nose. Exhaustion had kicked him like an ornery mule. All he needed was a nap to recharge, and then he'd be ready to take that black heart. Though it would not poison him the way it did mortal men, the sheer power of Jasper's heart was overwhelming. He would have to gather his strength to fight all it offered, to not break under temptation. Demonic force lay within that heart. Byrne had craved that power once, had wanted the very thing Glenn Amarok was now after.

THE THIRTEENTH KOYOTE

The next plane.
A new circle of black fire to call his own.

Jasper had nearly become a prince of Hell. Now it was Glenn who sought that laden crown. Byrne thought of all the wild adventures he'd had with Glenn, from their first robbery down to their last ride. They'd been like brothers. All the Koyotes were. Byrne being the sole dissenter, what did that make him?

As he reached the upper landing, another door came open and a young woman exited her room. Seeing him there startled her and she put her hands to her chest.

"Pardon me, sir," she said. "You gave me quite a fright."

"Can't say I blame you, ma'am. I've been long in the saddle. Reckon I could use a bath."

She offered a shy smile. "I was just going downstairs for a glass of milk."

"Can't sleep?"

"I'm afraid sleep has not come easy as of late, things being as they are here in Hope's Hill."

Byrne nodded. "Name's Luther. Reckon I'll be your neighbor for a spell."

"Grace Cowlin. I'm the schoolmarm."

"A true pleasure." He almost shook her hand but remembered where it had been back at the whorehouse. "Well, I won't keep you. Hope you catch a few winks 'fore sunup."

"Goodnight, Mr. Luther."

"Just Luther. And G'night."

She walked past and once her back was turned he looked her up and down, liking what he saw. In another life he might have courted such a woman, taking her to county fairs and on holidays to California beaches and marrying her in the chapel on some sunny day in June. He'd never had something like. Doubted he ever would. It was simply beyond his capabilities to make it so.

Grace went downstairs and vanished in the dark. Byrne found his room and only took off his boots before plopping upon the mattress. He was snoring in less than a minute, and though he got in four hours of sleep it felt as if he'd just lain down when the knock came at his door. Rolling out of bed made his body ache, reminding him of his age, wolfen or not. *Many men die in their forties*, he thought, not for the first time. Before going to the door he drew his iron, just in case.

"Who's there?"

"It's Marshal Russell. Best get yourself together."

Byrne opened the door. "Craven's back, is he?"

Russell shook his head.

"He wasn't on the train?"

"No, he was. But the train never came."

Once outside, Byrne gathered Bo from the stable and joined the marshal and his deputies who all sat their horses. Byrne never thought he'd be riding with men of the law. If he'd told his younger self he'd be doing so he'd have laughed like hell. He climbed into the saddle and patted Bo's neck.

"Reckon you can help us track them," Russell said.

Byrne felt a sudden chill. "Shit. You're telling me the Koyotes…"

Russell nodded.

They rode through the streets in a steady gallop, dawn breaking the meridian with its steel light as morning birds that hadn't fled south serenaded the new day. Faces appeared in windows like jack-o-lantern turnips as they rode through town, their heavy coats fluttering in the cold, their horses snorting plumes, and as they entered the firth of the hillside the sun rose in a pale plate of fire, turning the sky white as winter. Flurries fell soft and slow and then built up, snowflakes dancing in every direction as the riders drew closer upon Black Mountain. They rambled on, following the railroad toward Battlecreek, knowing they'd find the train before they got there.

By noon they spotted smoke, and when they found its source they found the train, far from any station. There was a gathering of lawmen and villagers at the scene, shoveling dirt onto the dying embers and piling corpses in deadcarts. The derailed locomotive lay on its side with the railcars laid out behind it like some great mechanical worm. The cowcatcher was dented on one side and the smokestack was bent into the rock, exhaust steam still trickling out of its spout. The caboose and several passenger cars were still simmering though the flames had mostly died down, and the smoke of combustion swirled about the wreckage. Charred bodies were trapped in the overturned railcars, others scattered in the dirt in pools of blood gone dry and dark.

Byrne rode past a man whose skull had been pulverized. Bloody horseshoe prints covered his back and the ground around him. A woman's severed head stared up at him with a petrified final expression. The crisp body of a man in an expressman uniform was twist-ed in the earth, one arm missing, his chest torn to ribbons. An in-fant was torn completely in half and smoked like a turkey, its bits looking like coal among the fresh dusting of snow.

Deputy Hustley turned to the side and vomited, splattering the side of his horse. "Oh, sweet Jesus."

"This ain't His work," Deputy Dover said.

Russell approached the constable in charge and they spoke, then he returned to his men.

"There were some survivors," Russell said. "Few, but some. They say five men rode up on the train, three of them climbed aboard and got right to killing. Say these men were more animal than man. *Werewolves*, a woman said."

Byrne sniffed the wind. "You starting to believe yet, Marshal?"

"All I know is them boys laid down a mighty evil here."

"Yeah, well. They ain't through by a long shot."

"I follow that and it troubles me plaguily. Reckon you know them better than anyone, Byrne. I am wary to trust a man who could ever ride with such villainy but the church has vouched for your redemption and I do fear for Hope's Hill."

"Koyotes done got what they wanted here."

"Got it from *our* local doctor," Russell said, his face stern. "If they backtrack and figure where their leader must've died them boys are bound to come to Hope's Hill, for revenge if nothing else. May-be Amarok will have other plans now that he's got the heart, but I can't imagine they won't end up in my town come soon."

Byrne gripped the pommel of his saddle and sniffed the wind again, catching no sign of Jasper's heart or the outlanders who now possessed it.

Russell came closer. "Hear me, Byrne. If you're offering help, I could use you. As a former Koyote, you'd be best at predicting what they'll do next."

The sky swelled gray, snow blowing about like dandelion and catching in the brims of their hats. Byrne had the urge to clack Bo's reins and haul ass back east, maybe to Dodge City, Kansas; a mighty fine city for gunslingers to get hired by businesses for protection. It'd be a decent life, and sure easier than what he'd fallen into here. Or maybe he could hang up his gun belt for good and just take up jobs as a wolfer or logger, nab himself a piece of land before he got too old to earn one. But running from Jasper's evil would only buy so much time. Whatever Glenn unleashed from the world beyond would spread its malevolence across the land like a disease. And then the darkness would come. Come and never leave.

Byrne looked at the lawmen. Their chances of defeating the Koyotes were slim, but if they were going to die, they might as well die fighting back.

"We'll be needing more men."

*

The turkey was slung upside down on a clothesline that stretched from two poles some fifty yards apart. Oscar Shies clutched his Whitworth rifle. It was old but trusty, maybe even lucky. It'd done him better than any other, helping him take down five wolves that had been attacking one of his steers, saving its life. No easy feat. Though an expert with firearms, Shies preferred ones like this; guns with no frills or decoration, no nickel-plated pistols or pearl handles. Function outweighed fashion when it came to a man's iron and anyone who thought otherwise was a mere dandy, what Shies referred to as a "two-gun Percy" when he'd been a posseman for federal deputies.

A crisp wind fluttered the dead turkey's feathers as it hung on the line. All the patrons of the Bodden County Fair stood around the scene, some munching on haystack cookies while others sipped from flasks, all having laid down their bets. The man who'd gone before Shies had fired four shots but missed the turkey entirely, not even coming close to the head. The object of the competition was to decapitate the carcass with a round while galloping at full speed. Some fairs kept the bird alive to make it more sporting, but Shies would have none of that. He was an animal lover enough to pet an armadillo to sleep. It had pained him to even take out those wolves. But once this bird was beheaded it would go to a feast and that was noble enough a cause of death.

The ringmaster raised the flag in his hand, called out for them to ready, and waved the flag down. Shies' horse was gray as spent coal yet just as fast as it had been when it was five years younger. Its hooves quaked the ground like steel hammers as he raised the rifle, closed one eye, and took off the turkey's head with the first shot. The crowd erupted in cheers. Once he'd dismounted, some young boys came up to him. They were white children but showed him total respect, idolizing him for his bully shot, the boys smiling like it was Christmas when he shook their hands.

He tied his horse with the others and went to the jakes for a piss, undeterred that it was not a stall for colored folk, then exited and went to the circus tent to collect his silver dollar prize money.

Shies passed by the freak show where a woman with two heads sat on a pedestal, her dual spines warped from scoliosis. Only one of the heads was alive. The other was much smaller, more of a child's head, and it lay limp and withered in death. The living woman's face was permanently pressed against her dead twin's rotting skull.

In a cage was a mongoloid boy completely covered in thick hair. He was eating a strip of raw buffalo. His eyes were white with blindness. When Shies approached the circle of spectators, a tiny man with a cleft lip stopped him.

"Ye wish to enter, mister?"

Shies nodded.

"Be a penny."

"I ain't paying you or nobody else for exploiting these poor souls."

The man scowled but looked away, intimidated by the much larger Shies. He adjusted his bowtie and cleared his throat.

"Well, mister," he said, "then you can't come see the freaks."

Shies stepped past him and the tiny man did not try to stop him. Shies maneuvered through the crowd with little kindness, knocking the men away with his shoulders. Some grumbled before they turned around and saw him—then their mouths stayed shut. When he approached the boy's cage, a man nearly as tall as Shies came over and put his hand over the lock.

"You best just get on," he said with a southern accent.

"And you best let this child go. The woman too."

The man smirked with rotted teeth. "Can't come it, mister. These two belong to me and my partner, ya see? We bought 'em and we own 'em."

Shies clenched his fists. He knew too well what it was like for a human being to be owned. He was a Freedman now, but had been a slave since birth under a plantation owner named John Shies. At age seventeen, he was sold to a Choctaw Indian, one of the many men from the Five Civilized Tribes who owned African slaves. This man's name was Talako but in his adulthood he went by the more 'civilized' name of Wallace Eagle Stone. Shies was with Stone for four years before Stone freed him by manumission. What Stone did not know was that by this time his fourteen-year-old daughter had secretly fallen in love with Shies and even more secretly left with him. She ditched the name Sarah and went back to the one her mother had given her, Nizhoni. As an interracial couple, Shies and his wife knew what it was like to be gawked at and ridiculed, much like these sideshow freaks were now.

"I'm taking these two away from the likes of you," Shies said.

"Over my dead body."

"You can have it your way."

The man sneered and drew back his coat to show the pistol at his side.

"I ain't a-scared a no nigger," he said. "You feel squirrely just make for that iron on your belt."

"You damned fool. Do you not see this crowd full of women and children? You'd fire a pistol here?"

"I don't give a damn 'bout them noways."

Some of the crowd was already backing away while the ones more prone to rubbernecking stepped closer. Shies wore a Colt pistol and would not fear using it even on a white man, if not for his family. He wasn't a posseman anymore. He'd hung up that hat and had put on the one of a cowboy for the sake of his children. It would be reckless of him to instigate a slinging of guns with anyone, but his draw was fast and sure. He had no doubt he could drop this carnie if it came to a gunfight. And he was not about to abandon these prisoners. But he would not pull his iron in such close proximity to innocent people.

"Outside," Shies said. "Unless you're too yellow."

The man pulled his pistol and Shies grabbed his wrist and pointed his aim upward and away. The shot tore through the top of the canvas tent and the crowd scattered like fire ants. With his other hand Shies slugged the carnie under his jaw and the man bit his tongue as a result, blood frothing between his teeth. Shies twisted the carnie's forearm and his pistol dropped to the dirt. He looked to the front of the tent, making sure the carnie's partner wasn't sneaking up on him, but the little man had fled with the rest of the crowd. Shies kicked the pistol away and dragged the carnie out of the tent and flipped him on his side so he would not choke to death on his own blood. He grabbed at the man's jailer ring of keys and went back under the tent and unlocked the boy's cage. The child cowered away. Shies took his time talking to the child in low, calming tones until he allowed Shies to pick him up and carry him, the boy's face pressed close into Shies' chest as if to shield himself against the cruelty he'd known all his life.

The two-headed girl gazed up at him, her mouth wet with drool, eyes misted over with tears. She made guttural noises, unable to speak. Shies saw that her tongue had been ripped out. He took her hand and was relieved to see she could walk. As he guided them out of the tent a woman approached.

"Where you going with them?" she asked.

"To a nunnery on yonder in Hope's Hill. The sisters will do them right, get them medical attention, a warm bed and food."

The woman's face pinched. "You can't think these creatures could have a normal life, do you? They're no better than animals."

Shies raised his chin. "Funny. I was thinking the same thing about you."

CHAPTER XV

THE HEART PULSED IN HIS hands.

Glenn sat shirtless upon the edge of the passage, looking out across the mountainside and the snowy valley below where black birds hopped between the bare branches of the trees in a haunted ballet. The river seemed to pulse in rhythm with Jasper's heart, its waters choppy where it dipped into the rocks. Glenn breathed deep of the cold, clean air.

Jasper's heart bled blackly and the drops absorbed into Glenn's hands, his body electrified by the majesty of it. A sorcery unlike any he had ever felt made his arms shake and he struggled not to drop it.

It had been a long night after a long day and the men lay sleeping, but Glenn was too riled up to join them in their slumber. At last the awesome power he'd been seeking was his. Now he just had to understand it. He was not the warlock Jasper Thurston had been; at least, not yet. He would learn, for Jasper would teach. The magic *itself* would teach. The ooze coming from the heart was no longer blood; it was *ichor*, the watery discharge of the wounds of the gods. As it sluiced through his pores and entered his veins, Glenn's eyes went dark, then entirely black and sunken in his skull. He was struck blind, but felt no fear from it. It was as if he were drifting off to sleep but he knew it was not so.

A complexity of unnatural colors rose from out of this darkness in psychedelic rays and trailing behind them were bulbous creatures foreign to the world. They seemed almost aquatic, their bodies ethereal like jellyfish, appendages slick and boneless, slithering like electric eels through the tapestry of this midnight dimension. And as they passed by the air around Glenn warped like heat waves on a desert floor. His body moistened. The hair on his spine rose.

A roiling array of carcasses drifted past every corner of his vision. Though many were too mutilated to appear human, Glenn knew they were. On every cold, dead face was a red pentagram of light, the same kind young werewolves saw on the foreheads or palms of their next victims. But these victims had already been taken—taken by Glenn himself. Perhaps a hundred corpses. Male and female, young and old. They were dismembered and decapitated, half devoured by his very fangs. The sight of them gave him no remorse, only a stirring in his stomach for more. He could almost taste flesh upon his tongue. The grayed remains of broken women drifted past and Glenn's loins rolled with savory memories of defilement.

He trenched through the piling corpses. Skeletal forms forged a pathway, the brittle bones cracking beneath his feet as he ran towards the meridian where a crimson monolith surged and thundered against the blackness. It was towering brimstone the color of Mars. Its rectangular shape went blurry as it vibrated with the same currents that shook Jasper's heart in his hands.

A door.

But he knew he could not enter from here. He was not at the summit. Jasper was giving him a mere taste of what awaited, and these visions were not a key, but a compass. He clambered up the stairwell of blackened remains, the bodies intertwined and made turbid by their collective rot. Steps made of the flensed skulls of children, the eyeholes stuffed with human waste, teeth knocked out to make necklaces. Mounds of putrid carrion beset these stairs, a lifetime of murder hoisting up a precipice of cadavers. This was his ossuary, his playground.

When Glenn reached the monolith he lifted the heart before it, then brought the heart to his mouth and sunk his fangs into the pulmonary artery. Ichor hit the back of his throat and slid down into his very soul. Black magic entered him sublingually and now he could hear his old pack leader's voice echo through his mind.

"Sacrifice," Jasper said.

The gallery of corpses withered and fell to ashes that scattered in the wind and transmogrified into a gray sandstorm. Each grain shimmered like quicksilver until there was a blinding flash and when Glenn could see again he was surrounded by a different sort of people. They were alive, or at least they had been during the time he'd traveled back to. Glenn recognized them despite the decades that had passed. He doubted these were faces that could ever leave his mind, no matter how old and senile he may grow to be.

Something soft and warm wrapped around his free hand and when he looked up he saw the face of his mother. She was a dark beauty, just as he remembered.

Mother was young. Mother was still alive.

Seeing how she towered over him, Glenn realized he was a boy, maybe eleven or twelve.

And he was *home*.

The entire clan stood within that rocky clearing, the one claimed by the prophets. They were just beyond the caves at the edge of their village, a farming community of houses made of mud and straw. The faces of the villagers were orange suns in the glow of the bonfire. These people were ravaged by poverty. Their mules were on the brink of starvation, their dogs mangy and flea-ridden. Clay bowls were stacked against the boulders to collect dew, for they'd gone months without rain. Their crops were withered by the sun and their cemetery had doubled its occupancy even before the prophets had come.

*

The prophets arrived during the worst weeks of the drought. They were young but completely bald, albino brothers with chalky skin and pink eyes. They were adorned in white robes and wore jeweled bracelets and beaded necklaces like Apaches. They told the villagers they were the sons of Viracocha, the first Incan god who created all the others, as well as the sky and the earth and all the creatures upon it. They told the impoverished, illiterate villagers of a great fortune of gold and silver the gods had placed within these hills. But only through worship could they hope to obtain them.

115

THE THIRTEENTH KOYOTE

The prophets, Timat and Thorn, held rituals in the clearing before the caves, feeding the villagers peyote and smoking herbs. The villagers in turn offered what little food they had to the prophets. The albinos told them they must show their devotion to the gods and held orgies where some of the women gave themselves to the prophets with their husbands' consent, and when Timat grew bored of womanly wiles he was offered up a teenage boy willing to be sodomized to end the drought.

But after weeks of debauchery, the people grew impatient. No rain had come, no riches delivered. They'd pledged themselves to the gods and wanted their just reward. Timat and Thorn claimed they would climb to the mountain's summit to speak with Viracocha, and they vanished for several days, causing the villagers to worry they'd chased the prophets away with their doubt. Many turned on those who had lacked faith, threatening them to behave if and when the prophets came back. So when Timat and Thorn returned, the villagers were doubly obedient, particularly when they were introduced to their new goddess.

She exited the cave in a plume of smoke.

"I am Lady Quilla!"

The woman stood upon the stone platform just above the clearing, her silken robe adorned with jewels and beads that shimmered beneath the summer sun. But no matter how lovely was her finery, it paled in comparison to her own natural beauty. Raven hair hung low, covering her lithe body like serpents, and her eyes were black and piercing, a sharp midnight against her brown skin. She almost looked Mexican or perhaps a white and Apache half-breed. To Glenn, she was the most beautiful woman he had ever seen, even more beautiful than his mother.

Timat and Thorn introduced her as the third power, the goddess of the moon. They confessed that she was even more holy than they were and should be worshipped as such. The orgies continued, growing in number, some of the men of the village joining in, many bringing their children into the mix at Lady Quilla's insistence. And the rituals became more bizarre with the feasting upon raw meat gathered from dead bats and field mice. At first Lady Quilla gave short speeches upon the mount, but in the weeks that followed she began giving full sermons, telling of vengeful deities who would continue the drought until the villagers' very bones were charred if they did not prove their devotion. Soon the albino brothers were an afterthought. Lady Quilla reigned supreme and those who did not adore her feared her enough to obey her whims.

Then the sacrifices began.

It started with a pair of dissenters who'd grown tired of the sexual abuse.

"We only want to leave," one woman said. "That is all."

Her sister nodded. "Please… give us passage."

Glenn would never forget the pitch-black fury in Lady Quilla's eyes when she said, "Execute them."

The goddess's servants snatched up the sisters. Glenn watched from behind his mother as the angry mob took the sisters apart, hacking at them with pitchforks and axes. A small boy pummeled one of their skulls with the mandible of a dead donkey. Timat and Thorn, desperate for some sort of significance, gutted the women with spearheads and held the innards to the night sky in a blood-slick offering.

Glenn's mother tucked him behind her, hiding him, and when they returned to their shack she and Glenn's father put him to bed but he lay awake listening to them whispering in the shadows, plotting.

The next night a man was crucified. He hung there for over an hour before Lady Quilla ordered him burned alive. His screams tore through the village so intensely Glenn could hear them from inside his family's shack. His father held him close and prayed. But Glenn knew he was praying to the wrong god.

"Let us leave now," his mother said early the next morning. "While they are still sleeping."

A blood ritual had followed the crucifixion where the dead man's wife was sexually penetrated with a pickaxe. The blood from the widened hole between her legs had been collected in the clay bowls that had once gathered dew and was mixed with the blood of chickens slaughtered in animal sacrifice.

"I must drink of blood," Lady Quilla claimed, "so I may stay young forever!"

The revelers cheered and celebrated the ritual with copious amounts of peyote. They smoked cannabis and the albino brothers concocted bluestone liquor that they mixed with the blood. Timat and Thorn drank first, then the bowls were passed around, refilled at the dead woman's wound, and passed around again. They danced and sang and had sex until the rising of the sun. Now they slept deep.

Glenn's parents had been part of the few who had not participated, but there was mounting pressure for everyone in the village to partake in the beating, burning and butchering of those selected for human sacrifice. They'd claimed young Glenn was sickly and they had to nurse him instead of joining in the revelry.

That night they'd fashioned bedrolls using blankets and pelts and gathered essentials in a gunnysack. While they'd packed, young Glenn had paced and bit at his cuticles. The thought of leaving home filled him with existential horror, as did the sudden notion that his parents may well be fools, no wiser than jugglers. How could they abandon their homeland and become godless vagabonds? He cursed them, even loathed them.

Just after dawn they waited, listening to the silence, then snuck between tiny houses, ducking low amongst tall fescue that had yellowed in the dry heat. Glenn's father led them to a skinny trail that would enable them to bypass Lady Quilla's ritual cave at a great distance, steering clear of the house the villagers had made for her using soil and paddy straw, having no rice husks. Glenn held his mother's sweaty hand. Her eyes twitched with paranoia, looking behind them over and over again, scanning the hillside like a hare hiding from a red fox. Her fear made Glenn huff and pout. She was being *ridiculous*. Why did his parents not understand a faith so pure and true? They'd witnessed the resurrection of the goddess just as he had, that blessed moment of enlightenment as she'd risen from out the wisps of smoke like some poltergeist comprised of magic and dreams. How could they have grown ignorant of Lady Quilla's majesty and blind to her undying beauty?

They scrambled across to the edge of the village where the river frothed in the light of another scorching day, and when they reached the bank their neighbors intercepted them. Four men from the village, armed with axes and scythes. Thorn was among this group, a leather bullwhip in his hands. His bald head was raw with sunburn. He growled at the family with rotting teeth.

"We were just going to forage food," Glenn's father said.

His voice was trembling, betraying the words.

"You dare dissent against the goddess?" Thorn said.

"No, we don't, we—"

The bullwhip cracked like a thunderclap. Glenn watched as his father's shirt was torn open and the flesh split in a rich, red gash.

Mother screamed. Father yelled at her and Glenn to run and Mother hesitated only for a moment before taking Glenn by the hand to duck into the cover of the thicket, leaving her husband to fight a battle he could never win. It seemed he was making a sacrifice of his own.

As the villagers sliced at his father, Glenn turned to see Thorn and a man with a bloody scythe chasing them and knew what he must do. He grabbed his mother's leg, tripping her, and when she landed in the dirt he snatched up a rock and struck her skull with all his strength. He would never forget the look of shock upon her face as it filled with blood. A man lunged at Mother, tossed his scythe aside, and produced a rope. Thorn, having seen Glenn's betrayal, placed a hand upon the boy's shoulder.

"You have done well, my son."

Glenn smiled, proud. "Praise Quilla."

"Praise Quilla."

His parents were taken alive, their hands tied behind their back and their feet tied just loosely enough for them to shuffle. When they returned to the village they were brought to the clearing where Timat joined Thorn and fitted Glenn's parents with a yoke that locked their heads in place. They were restrained side by side like a pair of oxen, the yoke's wood and iron weighing them down and bending their backs. Father was bruised about his face and neck. There was a gash where an axe had sunk into his shoulder.

When Lady Quilla stepped forward, she gazed upon the heavens with a smile the color of blood. A gathering of gray clouds sulked upon the horizon. The villagers had come out of their houses now and they looked to the coming storm, sweet delight on their faces. They cheered and praised her. When she was told of Glenn's betrayal of his parents, his ultimate act of devotion to the goddess, he was hoisted up on Thorn's shoulders and the villagers gathered around, touching Glenn's feet and the rags of his clothing.

Silent lightning made pink veins across the sky, an undulating, slate-colored firmament celebrating the young boy by baptizing him with the first rain the villagers had seen in one hundred days. The villagers dragged out their clay bowls, barrels, wheelbarrows and oxcarts to gather the rainwater and they danced, cheering and kissing in the downpour, praising Lady Quilla and hailing Glenn. Thorn placed him on the ground again and held him in his arms, whispering.

119

"I am so proud of you, my son."

He kissed Glenn's lips and walked him to his parents who stood sobbing in their yoke—two tortured blasphemers. That look of shock had not yet left Glenn's mother's face. It never would.

Thorn handed him the whip.

The thunder howled and the rain fell in earnest, soaking the delighted villagers as Glenn whipped his parents to death.

*

This childhood memory crashed against the confines of Glenn's mind to shock his very soul. He opened his eyes, no longer blind as he sat upon the craggy passage. He found Mars in the cosmos though it was nearly invisible tonight, and then turned his attention to the moon. Once he'd been a slave to it, transforming at its will. Now he was the keeper of his own magic. Jasper had taught him how to control the wolf within, to be one with the lunar spirit. Now his old pack leader had given him further instruction, and it was a familiar benediction, one as old as all humanity.

Sacrifice.

His lifetime of wickedness had come full circle.

Glenn licked his chops, recalling that first taste of blood in a shack where victims died slowly. It was blood he himself had spilt, the same blood that flowed in his veins, the blood of his own kin. He'd drunk of his mother and fed upon his father's flesh.

He stood and walked through the dusting of snow to the campsite where his brethren lay about the fire like hibernating bears. On a length of chain, Uriah Craven was curled naked before the flames, still shivering. Black lines in his skin made him look like a statue of carrara marble about to crack into tiny pieces. Dillon stirred and looked up at his leader, and judging by the way the young Koyote's eyes went wide Glenn knew the change in him was not hidden. The beast within was surging just below the skin, and it was hungry. It had been starved too long.

"You alright, boss?"

Glenn grinned. "Never a better day."

CHAPTER XVI

"OSCAR'S DONE GONE."

Russell looked at his deputy. "What does that mean?"

"He's on a cattle drive. Gone to transport a herd to a ranch just south of Battlecreek."

"Dang, Jake, it's a marvel we didn't pass him somewhere along the plains."

Russell crossed his arms. Oscar Shies had been the first man he'd thought of when it came to deputizing a small army to go up against the Koyotes, especially after Dover had told him Shies had once been a posseman for federal deputies. Shies was a man of grit and courage, and yet also decency, a rare combination. He'd proven this by taking no guff from the bigots in The Rusty Nail and offering to help Russell escort Sister Mable to that graveyard.

"Reckon he'll be back after two days," Deputy Dover said.

"May be two days too late. Who else we got? You know these townsfolk better than me."

Dover rubbed his chin. "Hell, if'n you'd ask me that but a few weeks ago I'd have thrown up the name Barley Reinhold."

"If that's a bit of humor I ain't laughing."

"Sorry. Course we can't use him. Even if we wanted to, who in hell knows where he done gone."

"I'd sooner deputize that sniveling undertaker than trust in a man who kidnaps schoolteachers whenever crops go bad."

Dover sucked his big teeth, too big for such a short and wiry man. Russell thought they made the young deputy look like a hybrid of man and burro. But he was a hard worker and hadn't griped when Russell tasked him with getting Thurston's grave refilled. Dover had paid a couple of teenage cowboys a dollar each to go up the mountain with him, but they'd been unable to locate the graveyard. It bothered Russell to leave it unattended, but there were bigger problems right now. They needed a team.

"We can pull in Cillian O'Conner," Dover said.

"The boy from that weird farm?"

"The very same. He's hardly a boy now. Think he's past twenty."

"Might be fragile after all he done seen, all that's become of his poor family."

Dover rubbed his chin. "There's Cassius Sneck up in the general store. He's a bit heavy in the belly for riding but I seen him handle a rifle something powerful at the shootin' fair. Oh, and there's Big Chuck Brazzo. A former soldier. He was with the Brownsville Tigers, he was. Fought in the Cortine Troubles; the first war, you know, the *big one*. Come all the way up from Rio Grande Valley. Too bad Doc Craven's gone. He too was a solider once upon time and—"

Russell stopped him. "Tell me more about this Brazzo."

"Not much to tell. He lives down in the valley low. There's a village of four or five shacks down 'round there."

Byrne, who stood in the corner of the office, blew smoke from his cigarette and raised the brim of his hat, joining the conversation.

"I know just whereabouts," he said.

"You know Brazzo?" Russell asked.

"That be one of Big Chuck's names. Went by MacDougall a while back. Called himself Bennett, last I knew. He's a solider to the manner born. Must be over fifty if he's managed to stay alive but I can't see age taking the bite out of that rabid dog."

"He's an ornery sort is he?"

"To put it politely. But he's more strange than anything else."

"You think he'd be of use to us?"

Byrne stubbed out the butt of his cigarette on the heel of his boot. "I'd bet every last coin I had that he could take down a moose with bare hands."

*

The snow had given way to an arctic mist that lingered all afternoon. The manes of their horses stuck wetly to their necks as Russell, Dover, and Byrne trotted into the valley basin, crushing soaked leaves beneath them as they followed the trail to a row of pale adobe houses resembling small, Spanish forts. The path gave way to the clearing where a reddish-brown child was playing with a stick. When he saw the men approaching he ran away to one of the houses and tucked himself behind a door of hung rawhide. On the frame was a rusted horseshoe nailed there for luck. The riders eased their horses on, Russell eyeing every corner a rifleman may hide. His spine went rigid when he saw a teepee of buffalo skins, a thin river of smoke rising from the flap at the central point.

"Didn't say there'd be Indians," Russell said.

"Word was Brazzo befriended the Kiowa," Dover said. "But hell, I didn't know he lived among them as such. I ain't been in these parts in years. Most folks don't come out here."

"Settle yourselves," Byrne told the lawmen. "These people know me."

Russell smirked. "And that's a good thing?"

As they came upon the houses, an old Indian man passed by, dragging a cart stacked with rice husks. He disappeared behind a crumbling wall. Chickens scuttled freely and an old dog sniffed behind them.

A white man emerged from the adobe the boy had run into. He was an ox of a man with a grayed head and squinty eyes. His teeth were bared as if he were hissing. Clad in just a one-piece for sleeping, he wore no shoes despite the ice forming on the ground. He looked at the men and then stared at Byrne.

"You got balls big as an Appaloosa's if'n you're comin' back here without my goddamned money."

Byrne smiled. "Easy now, Chuck. These men have a proposition."

"You owe me five dollars, Luther."

"And you'll get it. But there're bigger things to worry."

Brazzo laughed. "I left my worries back in Texas. Don't need none of yourn."

Russell frowned at Byrne. He just knew letting him tag along would muddy their efforts. What kind of friendships could a Koyote leave behind? It was a wonder Brazzo hadn't come out shooting.

"Mr. Brazzo, my name's Henry Russell. I'm a U.S. marshal."

"Yeah, I recognize yourn badge. You could almost pass for a Texas Ranger if'n ya didn't talk so good."

Russell let the jab at his homeland slide. "I've come to oversee the development of Hope's Hill."

"Then ya best get back to it. This land is out of yourn jurisdiction. We ain't part of that town noways and don't want to be neither."

"Sir, if you know Luther Byrne then I reckon you're familiar with his prior outfit."

Brazzo's eyes hardened to flint. "That I do."

"Well, them boys are coming our way with a vengeance and are just as mean as rattlesnakes. I'm looking to deputize a few men to make a stand against these outlanders if'n they come to my town, and I've heard tell you're a man of grit."

"Shit." Brazzo cackled. "Another militia calling on Big Chuck Brazzo? Can't you see I'm old as Moses? I've hung up my belt and cannons, mister. I collect weapons more than I use 'em. Mayhaps you ought find yourself another solider."

"I could see to it you make a fair salary long as you're under the town's employ. If there's something else that might make you reconsider, I am open to negotiations."

Brazzo chuckled an old man's wheezy laugh. He scratched at his day's worth of stubble. "You must be mighty desperate. You really think them Koyotes be heading yourn way?"

"It's near certain," Byrne said.

Russell shot Byrne a look that told him to hush.

"Lordy," Brazzo said. "Those sons of bitches come for ya'll they may well cross ourn path, and they don't leave nothin' but the bones in their wake. Why'd you have to cross 'em so?"

Russell leaned on the pommel. "Mr. Brazzo, them boys came looking for a dead man's heart. Seems they found it and can trace it back to Hope's Hill. That heart belonged to their former leader."

Brazzo spat. "That's what I think of Jasper Thurston."

"So you knew him too?"

"A man that wretched seldom goes unnoticed."

Russell nodded. "There's history to the Koyotes' vendetta, and maybe there's something more than that. They believe in some satanic power, and though it goes against all logic I've seen things that would make your blood run cold."

Brazzo put his hands on his hips and turned away, staring off to the tree line. The mist coiled about in a gathering veil.

"They ride with the devil," he said. "I've seen men slaughtered in battle. Watched them squirm against the thrust of my bayonet as they lay screaming in the dirt. But even those Mexicans died with more peace than any victim of a Koyote. Those I killed I did so in the name of country. The Koyotes have no country other than the very pit of Hell, and they do aim to impress Old Scratch."

Silence fell. Byrne broke it.

"Will you help us fight them, Chuck?"

"Reckon there's no choice." The old man spat again. "Letting them do the devil's work would be nearly as bad as serving the devil myself. Though I claim no allegiance to men of my own race I will not stand by while wolfen tear this land apart. But a group of men, no matter how strong or deadly in their aim, is no match for the powers of Hell. We don't want to catch a tartar. To fight devils we have to harness power of ourn own."

"I see," Russell said. "Well, we do have a chapel where—"

"Blessings are fine and good but magic they ain't."

"*Magic?*"

"Ya heard me. Now, I don't mean fortune telling and such. I mean a connection to the spirit world. Something to purify us."

There was a shadow in the adobe the child had run into. The rawhide door flapped open revealing a Kiowa woman who stood there listening and eyeing the outsiders. She wore her hair long but shaved on the sides and back. She looked strong to Russell, as strong as any man.

"Kasa," Brazzo said, addressing her. He said something to the woman in her native tongue and she slinked back into the shadows. He turned back to the men. "Come out them saddles and follow me."

The men dismounted. Brazzo guided them toward the teepee and peeled back the flap. Russell stepped inside first and glanced at a very young Kiowa nursing a half-breed baby at her breast. Her eyes were raw with suspicion. On the other side of the teepee an Indian man was shifting the embers of the fire. His flesh was dry and cracked, and yet he was not an old man. Hair ran down to his tailbone and was he was decorated with dangling feathers, armbands tied tight at his biceps. He was shirtless but for a stitching of animal pelts slung across his shoulders like an entertainer's cape, but wore the slacks of white men and a pair of Civil War-style boots. He did not look up until all four men had entered the tent.

Brazzo greeted him with a nod. "Mornin' Setimika."

Setimika nodded back. "You bring guests."

"These are new, er, friends," he said, pointing to the lawmen. He aimed a thumb at Byrne. "You 'member this sumbitch, I trust?"

Setimika squinted in the firelight. His eyes flashed when he recognized the former Koyote.

"The one who runs at night," he said.

Byrne tipped his hat. "Good to see you again, Charging Bear. Been many moons."

Setimika looked to the young mother and she rose and carried her baby out of the teepee without a word.

"Sit," he told the men.

They sat upon the shaved logs and Dover fiddled with the pocket of his vest, retrieving his tobacco pouch with jittery hands. Some whites will never feel comfortable around the red man, Russell thought.

"They're back," Setimika said.

Byrne removed his hat. "Back and headed our way."

"This I know."

Russell blinked. "How'd you know?"

"The stink of a predator precedes him. Especially wolfen."

"What are these *wolfen?*" Russell asked. "They're men, but not, they're...*what?*"

He noticed Byrne stir but the man said nothing, letting the Kiowa do the talking.

"The Cheyenne calls them *shoemowetochawcawe*—high-backed wolves. The Navajo calls them *skin walkers*. They know well the Coyote People. This pack you speak of are not the first of their kind. The spirits haunt both earth and stars and place strange creatures among us."

"Can you help me understand them?"

Brazzo said, "That's what I brought ya for."

Setimika continued.

"There is a story of a shepherd who lived in Window Rock. He was on hunt one night and caught sight of a coyote running behind clumps of mesquite. He came 'round the bush with rifle at the ready, and a woman called to him to not shoot for if he did he would kill a member of his own clan. When the shepherd came closer he saw it was a coyote who spoke, and it pulled back its fur and skin to show a woman's face, one of the shepherd's cousins. He had long suspected his kinswoman of being a shapeshifter. My people know there are many were-animals. The shepherd's cousin was a *skin walker*, for she used the skins of many animals and hid them in her home. When she wanted to celebrate the dark spirits, join with her fellow witches, or move about at night as a huntress of great speed and force, she only need put on the right skin."

Russell watched the Kiowa as he spoke into the flames. Sparks fluttered from the kindling and danced before their eyes like tangerine fireflies.

"Is that what these men do?" Russell asked. "You think they wear magic skins?"

Setimika shook his head. "The Koyotes are a different breed. They no longer need to put on the skins for they've taken the magic into *their own* skin."

Setimika closed his eyes. A low rumble came from his chest, like a cat purring. When he opened his eyes again they were yellow. Russell flinched. Dover scooted back and Brazzo put his hand on the deputy's shoulder.

"Easy," Brazzo said. "Not all beasts are hunters of men."

Setimika nodded.

"You're..." Dover stammered, "you're a..."

"Of the grizzly breed," Setimika said. "The ones who run at night."

Russell looked to Byrne. The man's whiskers stood on end, grayed and burly, and when he smiled Russell saw his canines had grown higher than the rest of his teeth. His eyes were rubies, burning.

"Now do you believe?" Byrne asked him.

He did.

CHAPTER XVII

IT WAS IN THE EARLY morn when another stranger came to Hope's Hill.

Grace Cowlin spotted a rider silhouetted against the violet fire of the morning sky. As they trotted into town, the schoolmarm watched, wary of newcomers after all the goings on. She only wanted to return to her normal routine, to teach the children who were on their way to the schoolhouse for their daily lessons. She'd had more than enough excitement of late, and enough terror to fill a lifetime. She was not interested in living in unprecedented times.

When Grace reached the steps of the schoolhouse, the stranger came into the heart of town. Deputy Norton Hustley had stepped out onto the porch of the station, hands on his hips as he observed the newcomer. He said nothing and never left his post, which Grace found rather odd, but when the rider came into view she realized why the deputy had not considered them a threat.

It was a girl. Not a woman, but a girl.

She wore clothes like a man and rode a pony as confidently as one. Worn boots in the stirrups and a long coat a size too big for her. A rifle in the saddle scabbard and a bedroll to the back. She wore a broad-rimmed hat that had been stitched back together and from out of it fell red hair that was choppy and uneven, just long enough to cover her neck.

Grace came down the steps.

"Girl?" she called out. "Girl, are you lost?"

The redhead brought the pony to a stop. Grace came upon her slowly so not to spook her, but when the girl looked up from under her hat it was Grace who gasped. Amongst the freckles a pink scar ran across one side of her face from chin to forehead and dug into her eyelid where a milky eye rested. The scar wasn't old enough to have fully healed.

"Are you all right child?" Grace asked.

The girl climbed down from her pony. Out of the saddle, she was taller than Grace and musclier, a farm girl raised on manual labor and hard living. But her face was soft with youth despite the deforming wound. There was hardship behind those eyes, but no meanness.

"Might you have a watering hole, ma'am?" she asked.

Grace showed her to the back of the school and the girl tied her pony to a juniper tree and watered it from the school's well, then drank from the gourd. As some of the water rolled down her chin it cleansed it of grime.

"My name is Grace Cowlin. I'm the schoolmarm."

"How do you do, ma'am. My name's Delia Van Vracken. What town is this? I didn't see a sign."

"Why, you're in Hope's Hill."

It pained Grace to think the girl a nomad. One her age needed a home and stability to grow up proper. Where was the girl's family? She wanted to ask but thought it to be bad manners to do so, feeling it would come off as an insult to the girl's parents. She kept her questions neutral.

"Where do you hail from?"

"Back east," Delia said. "A farmland called Cottonwood, not far off from Steelbranch."

"Steelbranch is quite a ways from here. It must be three hundred miles as the crow flies."

The girl certainly looked as if she'd been traveling a long time. Her clothes were filthy. Her bedroll looked well used. When she turned to one side, Grace noticed a gash at her collar.

"You're bleeding!"

Delia reached for the wound and drew back her fingers to examine the blood.

"Wasn't nothing serious," she said. "I fell asleep in the saddle and my pony led us through a thicket. She was short enough to clear a tree branch but I wasn't. Nearly fell out of the saddle when it cut me, startled as I was."

Grace looked closer. "It could use a stitching."

"Oh, I reckon I'll be all right. Don't have the money for no doctor. They charge almost two dollars a call these days."

Grace smiled. "It's no trouble. I can give you a clean stitching."

"You can?"

"Yes. My father was a doctor. He taught me."

Delia blushed. "Forgive me, ma'am. I didn't mean any disrespect with what I said about doctors charging too much."

"No offense taken."

The girl smiled then, looking so much like a child. Grace hated to pry, but had to ask.

"Delia, what has brought you so far from home?"

The redhead looked off into the horizon where the rising sun broke through the dead trees. There was a hardness to her gaze that was beyond her years, a lean, unspoken anger that would not be buried anytime soon.

"Looking for some people," Delia said.

*

She kicked out of her boots and lay back upon the mattress, refreshed from the bathhouse and more comfortable than she'd been in weeks. It was so good to be indoors again. The nights Delia spent on the open range had been mean, December rolling in like a curse. The first snow chased her into a cave that stank of guano and she'd had to cover her pony in buckskins.

It was mighty kind of the schoolmarm to invite her back to her room after giving her enough money to bathe and get a hot meal from the landlady, a kindly woman named Joyce Abercrombie. And her stitches had indeed been gentle and deft, and when Delia got a look at the wound in a mirror she realized just how necessary they were. The generosity of Hope's Hill was enough to tempt her to stay a while, but she had a mission and needed to press on.

But she'd long lost the trail of the men who'd killed her family.

She was saddle-sore and her skin had dried and cracked in the cold. Her neck was stiff from falling asleep in the saddle. It'd been a trying journey across the plains. Her pony was too old to move more than forty miles a day (twenty as they'd rode the mountain trails) and it needed new shoes. If Delia pushed either of them any further they were bound to collapse. She'd be too weak to get her revenge if she didn't care for herself.

Delia decided that, if the schoolmarm would allow it, she would stay a couple of days to get back her strength. Proper rest and sustenance the likes of which she hadn't had since home.

Home.

The mere idea of it, what the word meant, went through her like a soldering iron. The outlaws had destroyed it just as they had destroyed her parents, burning down the house Papa had built with his own two hands and using the flames to light a smaller fire upon which they cooked her infant brother alive. They'd made her watch and pushed her down into the dirt as she writhed and hollered. The leader they'd called Glenn had cut her pigtails off with a knife as if for some kind of trophy, threatening to do the same to other parts of her.

"I could chop off those little titties of yours," Glenn said. "Make them into jerky. Now that you've eaten human flesh, you know how delicious it can be."

"I know no such thing," she said. "I am not an animal like you."

"Oh, but you are."

Delia batted away her tears. "I only did it so I could live."

"Exactly. Mere animal instinct. We're all animals, little girl, be us man or beast. The only ones above that distinction are the gods, but of what worth have they proved today?" She flinched when he reached for her neck. He snatched away her crucifix necklace and held it up. "What has Yaweh given you to deserve such worship? What sort of lackadaisy demiurge is he? All I see here is suffering and death, your kinsfolk dead and boiling in our bellies. What good is a God too powerless or indifferent or downright sadistic to allow such things? Does this not give you pause, or are you too simple a farm girl to question such things?"

"It surprises me not that a man as evil as you knows no God."

Glenn laughed at this. "Evil? Like any man, I do what I need to do in order to make this life to my satisfaction. How then, am I evil? Because I do not obey arbitrary rules laid forth by lesser men who came before me?"

"You killed my family. You killed a *baby boy*."

Glenn leaned in, seemingly excited by the debate. "And what if that was the best thing for him?"

"Bastard!"

"What if it was not killing him that was the sin, but *creating* him in the first place?" Glenn's eyes flashed, his smile devilish and sharp. "Procreation is an act of cruelty. When your parents fucked it was for their enjoyment, and when they brought you and your brethren into this world that too was for their own benefit. They were keeping your Papa's semen as a pet. Procreation is always to the benefit of the creators—never the created. There's nothing consensual about it. Parents get a child they have total control over, to mold and manipulate to their liking and image. All the child gets is a ticket into a world of danger, pain, and turpitude. If the child has a soul, as your archaic religion insists, then surely that soul existed in the peace and harmony of some heaven before coming into this world only to experience loss, old age, and death. If that soul then returns to the heaven from which it came, of what use was being alive at all?"

Delia didn't reply. Her chest heaved with sobs, making it impossible.

"See," Glenn said, "you humans are a true paradox. You're the only species aware of its own mortality. Your understanding of your own frailness—the foresight that you will die—disables your ability to function like normal animals and ensures you lives of tragedy. Your very consciousness cripples you. So you toil in self-deception, thinking there is such a thing as morality, that human life matters. I know this for I was once one of you.

"A wolfen has no such delusions. He reclaims the beast within and abandons the trivialities that plague his humanity. Yes, we killed your baby brother, but what is one moment of pain against a lifetime of them? Human procreation is the true moral evil, for human suffering and death cannot exist without it."

He grabbed her chin and though Delia fought against him it was no use.

"Now," he said, "on the other hand, if I was to put a wolfen child in you, it would be no such evil. A wolfen from birth is stronger than those who become wolfen later in life, for it does not have to unlearn what men have taught them. A birth wolfen is never hindered by man's sense of right and wrong, for he knows there is only one right—the right of his own need. Because he pursues it without regret, he suffers less. And while wolves and men both die, for wolfen that need not be so. We are shapeshifters, always transformative. There is the chance for something better, a new form. And if a wolfen can become immortal than he is the master of his own soul, and then, once again, of what use is your God?"

Delia grit her teeth and managed to shake her head free from Glenn's hand.

"God'll give me the strength to go on," she said, "so that I may live to kill you for all you done."

Glenn's face soured, but only for a moment, then he smiled wider than he had all day. "Well now. You may have just changed everything."

He stood and dusted off the dirt and dried gore from his knees. Delia sat there in the grass, waiting for the deathblow that did not come.

"Come for us," Glenn said.

"I will at that."

"I do not doubt it. You are a study, farm girl. I see something in you. Something cold and mean. I've put a poison in you and it'll amuse me to see it germinate. Yeah, I'll be seeing you again, I reckon, and I do say I look forward to it."

"Not as much as I. I'll kill you or be dragged to hell trying. That's a promise and that's the God's truth."

Glenn gave her one last flash of fangs and then turned and walked off. After their feast, the youngest of the outlanders came upon Delia undoing his pants. Glenn pulled him back.

"There's no time for such merriment," Glenn said. "Leave this one be."

Dillon gave Glenn an odd look. "But boss, this one's ripe for the plucking. Teens are always the sweetest—"

"You question me again and it'll be you roasting on that fire. You hear me, boy?"

As the men saddled up, Dillon gave Delia a sneer and spat on her.

"Shit," he said. "After that whip to the face, who'd wanna fuck you anyway?"

The men rode off into the dying of the light, coattails flapping like the leather wings of vampire bats, leaving Delia bloody and weeping in the devastation. But they'd left Delia's repeating rifle, the one her mother had tried in vain to fight the outlanders with. Delia gathered what few belongings she could salvage from the ruins, finding her parents' hope chest, which had survived the fire, and gearing up in her father's hand-me-down clothes. She saddled up her pony and set out with a saddlebag full of bullets and a heart swollen with fury, a girl of seventeen hunting down a gang of murderous cannibals.

Now in the boarding house, Delia slept all afternoon until the schoolmarm came home. Grace offered her clothes that would fit better but Delia declined. She just didn't want to give up what few keepsakes she had.

"You look to have improved," Grace said.

"I'm mighty grateful for your hospitality, ma'am."

"Oh, now, think nothing of it."

Grace removed granny apples from her bag and offered one. For days Delia had eaten only what she could hunt—gamey rabbit meat and wild turkey, a slab cut from a deer that'd been taken down by wolves some time before. She ate fistfuls of snow to stay hydrated and refilled her canteen with it when it was warm enough to melt. There'd been no huckleberries or other fruits upon the range, the winter having killed them off for the season. The west needed its own Johnny Appleseed, she thought.

The schoolmarm agreed to let her stay on, telling her she was welcome as long as she wished to stay. Later that evening, Delia excused herself and wandered the streets of Hope's Hill alone, remembering things she wished to forget but holding tight to the one memory she would never let go of. She aimed to keep her promise to that beastman who'd wronged her so.

She entered the stationhouse without knocking. A deputy rose from his seat.

"Can I help you, girl?" he asked.

"I'm hoping so, sir."

CHAPTER XVIII

THE TEEPEE GREW WARM WITH the rising fire. Byrne removed his coat. Setimika shook his gourd rattles through the smoke, the seeds clicking like cicadas as he performed the *sing*. While the lawmen squirmed some, Byrne felt no white man's unease. Like Brazzo, he'd been part of the shaman's rituals before and had experienced their efficacy firsthand. If they were going to take on the Koyotes, they would need all the blessings the spirit world could offer. If a man was to do something more than human, he must have power beyond human, and as he'd learned from the Kiowa peoples, all power moves in a circle.

The fire rose and fell with Setimika's movements, in tune with the wizardry the Indian exuded. His voice was high and beautiful, strangely feminine coming from the muscular man. His yellow eyes glimmered before the flames like harvest moons, teeth silvery as atlatl heads. Brazzo, having long converted to the Kiowa's way of life, turned small crystals in one hand and with the other thudded the earth with a jawbone club, the powwow growing in intensity until it reached its crescendo, a great thunderclap giving way to rain. Setimika ushered the men outside.

"Nature has something to say to you."

As they stood there in the downpour, Russell looked to Byrne as if he was about to ask some complex question, but then did not speak, letting his eyes speak for him. Brazzo came over, smiled at Russell, and placed his hands on the lawman's shoulders.

"Keep mind and heart open, Marshal. A man can't fight what he does not understand."

Russell cleared his throat, still shaking off the ritual's *ju ju*. "So. This was some sort of séance. We're being baptized by rain?"

"That's a facile conclusion. But you'll get yourn learnin' yet." Brazzo went to Byrne. "Luther, how many men have you killed since I last saw you?"

Byrne rolled his shoulders. "None worth mentioning."

"And none of consequence, I hope?"

Byrne looked away, rain dribbling from the brim of his hat as it hid his eyes.

"Right," Brazzo said. "You may've left them Koyotes but yer still mean as the devil's nutsack."

"I ain't like I used to be. How 'bout you, Chuck? Still scalping every Mexican you come across?"

"My sins are mine and yourn are yourn. But I've made peace with what I've done, given my honorable motivations. Can you say the same?"

Byrne looked away.

The rain vanished as quickly as it had come, but the clouds remained, the sky alive with rolling heather. Setimika moved beneath it like a phantom in a dream. He offered choker necklaces of blue and black beads and each man took his, even the racially nervous Deputy Dover.

"Do not wear them now," Setimika said. "Wear them when they are most needed."

Russell said, "How will we know when that is?"

"When the time comes, there will be no doubt."

They bade farewell to the Kiowa and rode back to town, Brazzo joining them atop a Quarter horse the color of brimstone, the stirrup fender decorated with insignias burned into the leather and the saddle horn curled about with a vaquero's rope. He'd put on a deerskin coat and a rifle was slung upon his back and he wore parade chaps, pistols on each hip like he was part of some wild west traveling show. A pipe hung between his teeth, something other than tobacco burning in it.

Russell whispered to Byrne. "This old boy all right in the head?"

"Are any of us?"

*

When they got back to the stationhouse a redheaded girl was there with Deputy Hustley. As soon as she saw Byrne her eyes went tight and her fists balled. She strode up to him with chest out, as confident as any man.

"What are you?" she demanded.

Byrne furrowed his brow and removed his hat.

The girl sneered. "I see your whiskers, all tough as roofing nails. And I can smell you from here. It's a wet dog smell, but one I've smelt on certain men before."

"And I smell them on you too," he said. "But you're not one of them and neither am I so you best let this go."

Russell stepped up to the redhead. "What's your name, girl?"

"Delia. Of the Van Vracken family. Or what used to be the Van Vrackens. A gang of savages killed my parents and wee baby brother."

"Indians?"

"No, men white as you but as foul as this one." She pointed at Byrne. "They have his look, his feel, his stink. He was not there, and he may not be of their company, but I'd bet my soul he's of their breed."

"You'd win that bet," Byrne said.

Delia scowled.

Russell asked, "What's your business here?"

"I come looking for the men I speak of—men like wolves."

Russell shared a look with Byrne and the deputies.

"Where'd all this happen?" he asked the girl.

"Cottonwood."

"What makes you think them boys come here?"

"I don't. I'm just lookin' town to town. Came to your station 'cause you're the law. Thought you might know something is all."

"Have you spoken to the law in Cottonwood 'bout your family?"

Before she could answer, Byrne stepped forward and said, "The men you're looking for aren't here, but they're coming."

Russell scowled. "Dang it, Byrne…"

"She's a right to know, if they did to her kin what she says, and

137

I've no reason to think her lying about it."

"They're coming here?" Delia asked. "How do you know this?"

"I just know. I'm of the same breed, 'member?"

"Do not tease me now."

"I would not lie to an orphan."

"You *do* tease!"

"They're called the Koyotes. Their leader is a demonic rapscallion named Glenn Amarok. Ain't that right, kid?"

Delia nodded, eyes going wide.

"They'll be here," he told her.

Instead of the fear he expected, Byrne detected excitement in the girl's eyes, even the milky one.

*

Russell took his supper at the café across from the post office. He was worn from the day's weirdness and still a little shook by his interactions with the supernatural.

Men who are wolves. Men who are grizzlies.

He'd seen it all with his own eyes and still didn't want to believe it. But there it was, clear and cold and real. It gave him a fear the likes of which he'd not felt since being a marshal in Indian Territory, where lawmen were more likely to die than any other place in the country. He ate heartily of boiled mutton and stewed liver, weary but not wanting to admit he might have only so many good meals left in him. It was more than the fear of these Koyotes that had been growing inside him. He was getting old. Past forty now, his hair almost completely gray and thinning at the crown, his body softening where once there'd been hard muscle. The beer he'd once enjoyed now made his stomach roll and when he did not get a good's night sleep it hurt him hard come morning. Worst of all, he was without family. His parents were long dead, as was his younger sister, all gone to one disease or another. He had a few cousins down south he'd long ago lost touch with, but that hardly counted for kin anymore. And as for starting a family of his own, after Caldonia, he doubted he'd ever have what most men took for granted.

It was strange to think of those days with his wife, the happiest days of his life seeming like some funny dream now that she'd been in the ground a score. *Twenty years this Christmas.* Hell of a long time for a man to ride alone. The memories had driven him out of Lonely Bell, Texas. Caldonia's absence tore something in him. It was not just love he felt he'd lost, but the ability to love. Where once he'd been the romantic sort, courting his beloved with his own attempts at poetry, now he could think of nothing so sophomoric. He was not embarrassed to have been so syrupy then. He'd been young. Youth can enjoy such fancy. But even if he wanted to be that way with someone new he felt he would find himself incapable. The part of him that picked wild flowers and strummed a two-string guitar was gone. The amorous *Henry* had been buried in Caldonia's grave too, leaving only the pale, gray ghost of *Russell* behind. There was no love now, only law. No fairness in this life, but hopefully justice more often than not.

He thought of the fiery, little redhead who'd come to the station. Would there be justice for her kin? Delia Van Vracken was full of vim and vigor. There was no question about that. Russell knew the rage that blazed within her heart and it pained him to think of such a young girl going to that kind of rot inside. Even if she penned her vengeance in gun smoke, Delia would never scrape the decay free from her soul. No amount of revenge can bring back the dead, nor can it resurrect the happiness you once had with those loved ones now gone. After a tragedy like this, every good memory becomes a mental pang, a hindrance to your ability to get through another day. Like Russell, Delia would forever be a delinquent heart, eternally longing for the strength to reflect without the fear of never coming back to joy.

After supper, Russell walked back to the stationhouse, wondering what would come next, what his next move should be. How could he prepare for what could not be fully comprehended? He'd gathered a posse and given time he'd recruit more. That crazy solider Brazzo even insisted on sleeping in the jail with the door to his cell open, so he could be "at the ready" if the Koyotes rode into town by night. Russell had only a few strong possemen, but he could not warrant a request for assistance of other governing bodies. It was unethical to call in lawmen from other areas to safeguard a small town based on a hunch.

But the Koyotes would return here. Russell's every instinct as a marshal told him so. All the stories he'd been hearing only added kindling to the flames. If he sat and waited, he may be inviting death to Hope's Hill, raw and gore-caked and merciless; but if he took his posse out to hunt the Koyotes down they'd be leaving the town unguarded, and then that death could be all-encompassing, a great annihilation that would reduce this land to skeletons and ash.

It was a mild night for December and the day's rainfall had melted the snow. He was passing by the Abercrombie house when he spotted Grace Cowlin sitting on the front porch in a rocking chair, knitting. She was lit by a combination of the lantern's orange glow and the abundant blue moonlight, making her look like some ethereal phantom bride. The schoolmarm was young and soft—a creature of fledgling earnestness and yet also a lady well educated. Even under the unpleasant circumstances he'd shared her company, Russell had sensed in her a goodly femininity, the sort of silent jubilation that comes before the usual life labors of a woman, such as motherhood, hardship, or the fear of becoming a spinster or widow. Grace was still fairly new to this world and therefore saw it with unsullied eyes, a virgin to the true horrors of the untamed west.

"Evening, ma'am," Russell said, removing his hat.

Grace stood. "Good evening, Marshal."

"Do not fret," he said with a smile. "I don't come in name of the law this time. Just out for a stroll."

"I'd welcome you either way. 'Tis a nice night for a stroll though, if a bit airish."

"So why are you out here alone? Where's Norton?"

"I released your deputy of guard duty."

"Feeling safe enough to be above-board?"

"Yes. More importantly I cannot allow myself to live in fear. It only allows men like those who kidnapped me to keep me prisoner in another way."

Russell nodded. "Reckon you're right at that."

There was a beat of uncomfortable silence, nether knowing what to say but Russell not wanting to wish her goodbye. Just being in the woman's company made him feel younger somehow, less beaten-down, less afraid of the unknown.

"So," he finally said. "You have a visitor."

Grace blinked. "Oh, yes, that's right. A girl from Cottonwood."

"A girl who just might get herself into something she ought not mess with."

"Why do you say that?"

"She came to the station asking about some bad men, ones she's been looking for since they did her ill service. I'd be much obliged if you could assist me in keeping her out of trouble by encouraging her not to seek her own retribution. Let me and my men handle them boys instead."

From the look on her face, Russell knew Delia had not told Grace all that had happened to her family. He chose not to divulge it now either. Such pain was private.

"I will," Grace said, asking no follow up questions. "Delia has known hardship. That is plain to see. I hope to shelter her in more ways than one."

"You are a goodly woman, Ms. Cowlin. I thank you."

He was about to say goodnight when she asked, "Do you know the other stranger who's come to town? The man staying in this house? Luther Byrne?"

"I do."

"I hate to make assumptions, but he is an intense-seeming fellow."

"Has he upset you?"

"Not as such. I'd have asked Deputy Hustley to stay if he had. I was just curious if there was any relation to his and Delia's arrivals here."

Russell didn't want to lie to her, but also didn't want rumors to trickle through town. Fear led to panic all too easily. He did not suspect the schoolmarm of being a gossip, but figured it best to not test this theory.

"Luther Byrne was raised here and came back for his own reasons. Delia was passing through until you were so kind as to take her in."

He left it at that.

"All right," Grace said, her smile making something flutter within him. "Well, it is getting colder now that it's full dark. I do believe I'll retire to my room."

"Of course, ma'am."

"And I will do my best to keep Delia out of trouble, though it seems if trouble is what she was looking for, she may have come to the right place." She paused. "I'm glad you're here in Hope's Hill, Marshal. Goodnight."

"Much obliged. Goodnight, Ms. Cowlin."

He waited until she went inside and closed the door behind her, and then he walked on, his head down, looking at the pebbled street beneath his boots.

Grace had been right. It was getting colder. And it would get

THE THIRTEENTH KOYOTE

colder still.

CHAPTER XIX

HIRAM WAITED IN THE BACK room of the saloon, crouched upon the mud floor like some dominating ape. The blonde hair on his arms stuck wetly, weighed down by the grime of travel and spilt whisky. Glenn and Dillon were in the main hall, raising a ruckus as they cheered the dancing of the saloon girls. The young ladies were doing everything they could to escape the fate of the saloonkeeper and bartender, as well as the three good Samaritans who'd tried to intervene. Hiram had sat back, watching as Thad drew his pistol and shot the men in quick succession after they'd dared to tell the Koyotes to travel on out, that their bullying would not be tolerated here in Blue Valley. Their attempts at heroism had cost them their very brains, each punctured by a round to the skull. Thad had slapped his knees and praised his own rapid shots, but while the other Koyotes—and even the chained Dr. Craven—celebrated him for it, Hiram had remained silent in his chair, bored by the drunken revelry.

"I know what would cheer ye," Web told him.

An older member of the Koyotes, Web understood the pecking order and the importance of staying in the good graces of someone who outranked him in the pack. He was always sucking up to Hiram and jumped at any chance to please him. This wouldn't be the first time Web had brought him something special without being asked. Web took Thad with him out into the night to search the mill town for what Hiram liked to call his *delights*. And so Hiram waited until he heard the men's voices again, along with the sweet little cries of fear that came from their hostage.

Hiram cracked the door to watch.

Web pushed the boy up against the bar. He was towheaded and wore overalls, a skinny boy, maybe five-foot-three in height. His cheeks were pink from crying and he blubbered when he begged to be released. Hiram wondered where his men had snatched him from, but decided it didn't really matter. Somewhere a mother and father likely lay dead, but if either were alive they would soon wish they weren't, so not to live with what was to be done with their son.

"Please, mister…"

Web boxed the boy's ears, making him keel over. Thad laughed, drunk and all the meaner for it. Glenn and Dillon paid them no mind, still flinging quarters at the dancing girls, hard enough to hurt.

"Sock him again, Webster!"

Web kicked at the boy, swiping his legs out from under him so he fell onto his back. The saloon girls cried out but Glenn cursed them and warned they'd be raped if they dared intervene. Cawing like a crow, Dr. Craven stared, eyes bloodshot and weeping yellow pus. Thad took a running start and kicked the boy in the ribs, both men cackling like jackals as the boy tried to regain his air.

"Please… I cannot breathe…"

Hiram felt all the blood in his body redirect itself. His hands were clammy now, mouth salivating. *Just a little more…*

"Aw," Thad mocked the child, "ain't he all beer and skittles?"

Web said, "How old are ye, boy?"

"Twelve, sir…"

Web smiled, fangs blackened by decay. "Old 'nuff to die."

Hiram opened the door and strode forth with his chest out. He put on a look of outrage and approached the pack, his arms flailing.

"What in tarnation!" he exclaimed. "Get off that boy, you villains!"

Web and Thad stopped smiling. They retreated from the child slowly, saying, "Yes, sir," in unison.

"What in blazes is wrong with you, stomping on a child when both of you be grown men? Have you no decency?"

"We were just having a wee bit of sport," Thad said.

"Yeah," said Web. "Besides, what's he even worth?"

Hiram hissed. "A human life always has merit in this world! Fools! Scoundrels! I'll have your hides for this."

The men looked to the floor in faux shame. Hiram went to the boy and helped him up, wrapping one arm about his scrawny shoulders. He dusted him off.

"What's your name, son?"

The boy sniffled. "Willard, sir."

"You're going to be okay, Willard. These men will not harm you any further."

He walked the boy away from the men and took him to the backroom where he'd put aside a cup and pitcher of water. He gave the boy a drink and spoke to him in a calm and even tone, the voice of a loving uncle.

"It's all right now, son. I'm here to help you."

"I thank you much, mister. Those men… they're just horrible… they… they…"

Willard began to bawl and Hiram pulled him close, embracing him, feeling him. The child smelled of grass in spring and when Hiram put his hand into the boy's blonde hair it was fine and silken like baby flesh.

"You can tell me," Hiram said.

"My papa," the boy said, "they done shot him."

"Good heavens. How badly? If he still alive?"

"I think so. I mean… he was when they done dragged me away. He couldn't get off the ground though. They gut-shot him."

Hiram squinted. "Son, rest assured I'll see these men hanged. But first, we'll find your father and get him to the town doctor. Everything will be all right."

He reached out and the boy took his hand. A quiver coursed through Hiram's every muscle fiber. His heart rate accelerated. He wiped away a tear from the boy's cheek and then sucked on his finger, relishing the salt of misery. The boy froze when Hiram kissed him.

"I'm lying you know," Hiram said. "Nothing's going to be all right. Not now or ever again. Not for you, my sweet delight."

The boy shuddered in Hiram's embrace. Once again, his breath left him.

"They say a gut-shot is the most painful way to die," Hiram said.

"But I can think of many ways worse. Can't you?"

The boy didn't answer. Hiram undid his coat and reached for the hunting knife in its sheath. The blade was long as his forearm and gleamed like a supernova in the backroom's shadows.

"Well, Willard, when it comes to pain, I'm about to expand your imagination."

*

When he was finished, Hiram came out to the bar and got himself a beer. He'd worked up a sweat and one powerful thirst. Most of the pack was drinking on their stools but Web sat on the floor with his arm around the mad doctor, pouring beer over Craven's head. The saloon girls had stopped dancing and now sat in the corner holding each other and shuddering while the men got drunker. Hiram was surprised Dillon hadn't fucked one of them yet. He was surging with young hormones and always went for the girls first and foremost. Maybe the whisky had mellowed him for the evening.

Hiram snatched a rag and did what he could to clear the blood from his chin and between his fingers. Web pulled up a stool beside him.

"Hellfire," Web said. "We could hear that boy all the way out here. Reckon that one screamed worser than all the others put together. What all'd ye do to him anyway?"

"That's between me and him."

"He dead?"

"No. He'll live, but it will not be a good life."

That was part of the allure. Sometimes Hiram slaughtered his delights but with Willard he chose the grimmer fate of letting him survive. The boy would forever limp—maybe even crawl. Children would shriek at the sight of his face. He'd live with the shame of what Hiram had done to his most private of parts and would never be able to enjoy a woman in the biblical sense. Inflicting trauma was the sweetest torture of all, because it was an agony without end. The thrill of causing psychological damage was why Hiram always had Web abduct the children instead of doing it his own self. It gave him the opportunity to rescue the child and fill him with relief and hope only to take them away again. The shock and horror he saw in the eyes of his delights when they realized they had been tricked was even more satisfying than the screams of pain that followed.

"I heard tell of one like ye," Web said. "Name of Marcus the Sod. Got his jollies by adding torture to his sexing."

"You mean the *Marquis de Sade*. But he only *wrote* of such things. Fiction is fine, but I aspire to the genuine article. See, the man I admire is Gilles de Rais. He was the Marshal of France. Rode alongside Joan of Arc in her battles and fell in love with her. So when she was burned at the stake, well, it just drove Gilles plumb crazy. He became a beast of such cruelty no man has yet topped his crimes against society. His God had betrayed Joan of Arc, and so Gilles sought revenge upon The Lord himself."

"Shit. Gone whole hog then?"

"That he did. Gilles left his wife and vowed to never bed a woman again. He done filled his castle with sycophants and wastrels, holding wild orgies and lavish feasts and building labs for alchemy."

"What's that?"

"It was believed to be a way of turning metals to gold. Gilles brought in sorcerers and the like as an affront to Yahweh and as a means to align himself with the Prince of Darkness. To get the alchemy to work, he swore to Satan he'd do the most heinous crimes in his name."

Web chuckled. "Like what?"

"Started out by taking a peasant boy into his castle. He gouged out the kid's eyes and cut his throat from ear to ear and pulled his heart from his breast."

"Tarnation!" Web slapped his knee. "He weren't just having a sport."

"No. He was evoking black magic. Same as the Daughters of Maenads, same as Jasper done did."

Glenn turned their way. He hushed Dillon and Thad and told Hiram to go on.

Always the storyteller, Hiram was enjoying the attention. "Gilles caught the boy's blood in inkwells and used it for alchemical brews and writing evocations. But Ol' Scratch never showed and no metals done turned to gold. But by then Gilles had something more valuable than either of those things. He found great *delight* in slaying that child, more than he ever got from his wealth or orgies or any of his other hedonistic gluttonies."

"Seems he found his inner wolf," Glenn said.

"Some say he *was* a werewolf. Before he was brought to trial,

Gilles tortured, sodomized, and killed a thousand boys. And most times he did it, he did what I done here, having one of his servants capture the kid so he could pretend to rescue him before slitting his throat and violating him. He'd masturbate on them while they were being decapitated, then he'd impale their heads on poles and dress 'em up in whore's rouge and have all the staff in the castle come to judge this beauty contest, having them vote on which dead head was the prettiest."

Dillon winced. "Damn. That's sick even for my blood."

"Gilles de Rais was a genius, a true master of the dark."

Glenn asked, "So what happened at his trial?"

"He was found guilty. Back then they were big on burning people at the stake, so he almost went out like his true love, Joan of Arc. But because of his high position in France he was strangled before being put on the fire, as a mercy. And the tribunal looked the other way when the rich de Rais family had him removed from the burning stake before he got so much as singed. The ecclesiastical were far more interested in Gilles' fortune than seeking justice for a bunch of peasant children, little guttersnipes nobody would miss."

Hiram poured himself another drink. Though he'd spoken of his idol, his eyes were like slate, cold and without feeling. The bliss he'd felt while performing on the boy in the backroom was like any other bliss this world had to offer—short, temporary, a brief reprieve from the inanity of being alive.

The rest of the pack returned to their drinks and Dillon approached the saloon girls after all, perhaps excited by the story, maybe even inspired. But it was Glenn who'd gotten the most out of it.

"Those who think of Gilles as wolfen," Glenn said, "do they also believe he achieved a throne in Hell?"

Hiram sipped, placed his cup on the bar. "Boss, I can't imagine Hell would not have him."

From the corner came the laughter of the deteriorating doctor.

"Lies," Craven said.

Hiram turned. "What'd you say, pissant?"

"Gilles de Rais…. he was no child killer. He was a victim… a victim of Church conspiracy. He had ties to Joan of Arc, who they executed… he was considered guilty by association. The man was framed by clergy."

Hiram flushed. "Shut your hole, worm!"

When Craven snickered, a trickle of black drool appeared at the corner of his mouth.

"He's just as crazy as an Injun," Glenn said to Hiram. "Mortals can't handle carrying Jasper's heart. Turns 'em into whatever creature we see before us now. What Jasper raised out of Hell is quite a study, I do say. Making sense of it all will be a feat."

Glenn poured another as Web and Thad followed Dillon's lead and made for the young women. The pack leader told his second-in-command of his vision, the other dimension he'd glimpsed with its towering ossuary and crimson monolith.

"Sacrifice," Glenn said. "An offering to the dark gods, much like the ones Gilles did. I heard it told over and again in that phantom realm. *Sacrifice, sacrifice, sacrifice.* I believe therein lies passage to my own circle below."

"Okay, boss. I was letting the boy live, but if'n you need to kill him—"

"A single child is too weak an offering, 'specially after all we've done before. Our legacy is written in blood, Hiram. If I'm to gather all the wizardry in Jasper's heart, my pack must bring about a slaughter beyond any this territory has suffered before. We must be more than butchers; we must be *decimators*. We must exfluncticate all that is good and pure and innocent, so much so that the devil himself may beg for us to stop."

Hiram looked into his leader's eyes.

"Right, boss. Let's put Gilles de Rais to shame."

*

The local law tried to seize the Koyotes as they left the saloon. The shootout lasted only thirty seconds. When it was over, there were three dead peace officers full of bullets, all lying about their wounded horses like discarded meat rags. Hiram used his Wesson to shoot the steeds, scattering their brains across the dirt to steam in the winter night. Glenn walked his horse to the bodies and it stopped and pissed, dousing the dead sheriff who lay broken beneath a horse of his own. There were faces in the windows of the buildings, the town watching the outlaws as they strode through the streets. Doors were locked and bolted, prayers being muttered behind them, but no snipers fired from rooftops and no assassins sprung from the alleys.

"Shall we burn it down?" Hiram asked.

THE THIRTEENTH KOYOTE

"When we leave Blue Valley it shall be only rubble."

"This is just a simple mill town. Even if they gather arms these hicks and niggers will be easy prey. *Too* easy."

"This is just the beginning, Hiram. Something to wet our chops. The sacrifices must be legion."

Glenn reached into his coat and stroked Jasper's heart. The muscle was thudding, the magic enticed, waiting for release.

Dillon had bound and gagged the saloon girls after they'd been gang raped and locked them in the backroom with Willard. Thad wanted to set the saloon on fire with the prisoners inside but Dillon protested, so Thad let it be. Glenn climbed into the saddle upon Belial, the other men following suit, and they drew their rifles and Colts and clacked the reins and their horses burst into the clay streets, neighing in the choke of darkness with misting muzzles as their masters went to war.

The five wolfen ripped through the mill town like tornadoes, all black and raging, and though they drew fire from those villagers who were armed, they caught few bullets and would heal quickly. Houses were broken into and people were dragged shrieking into the streets to be gunned down and trampled by horses. The outlaws made torches from broken furniture and set wagons and homes on fire. In the chapel, frightened villagers gathered to beg for divine intervention. The men rode inside, this chapel not possessing any white magic, and Glenn cracked his whip, opening backs and crippling legs, the other Koyotes blasting people to bits, Dillon swinging a sickle-shaped sword to decapitate the preacher. The chapel was set ablaze and the fire traveled across the courthouse and surrounding buildings, driving more victims into the streets to be shot in the back as they tried to run away. Children had ropes tied to their hands, the rope's ends looped around the saddle horns, and the riders kicked their steeds in the ribs and they bolted forward, the children dragged and shredded across the earth as fathers screamed and mothers fainted.

Many villagers fled into the woods, leaving their homes to be raided and burned. But though this riot left many dead, still Glenn wanted more. Jasper's heart was pulsing against his body, titillated by the carnage, and he aimed to release more of its sorcery. He tilted his head back and howled, and the pack followed their leader, adding to his moon song and barking in revelry, sensing the call for murder.

An old woman was hauled naked into the street where Thad raped her with the barrel of his rifle and then fired it, blowing her apart from the inside. A man told them they would burn in hell just before Dillon cleaved his head in two. The dying words only made the Koyotes cheer. Pets and pack animals were killed. A family was marched to the blacksmith's forge and had their heads hammered against anvils while the father took a hot poker down his throat. A little girl was eaten alive.

The Koyotes gathered skin and bones, trophies to decorate themselves and their horses, and just before dawn they returned to the saloon and gathered Dr. Craven and the saloon girls, tying them at the wrists and having them walk behind the horses with ropes around their neck, pulling them along on leashes. The boy, Willard, was carried outside, too broken to walk.

Glenn put a wedge of tobacco between his cheek and gums and stared down at the red craters where the child's eyes had been before Hiram Zeindler had come into his life. He spat out tobacco juice, filling one of the sockets, and the boy stirred, still alive. Glenn looked to Hiram.

"This one's yours. You decide his fate."

Hiram was expressionless. "Already have."

They trotted out of Blue Valley.

CHAPTER XX

THE BOY SHE'D TRIED TO raise right sat across from Sister Mable now as a hard, damaged man. They were in the underground church, Byrne looking up at the towering Christ that had been flushed with his own childhood blood. Mable knew it would pain Byrne to see it, to be in the sacred sepulcher at all, but she had to show him if he were ever to believe her, or ever understand why she'd had to do what she'd done.

"I never meant to hurt you," she said, "nor any of the children."

Byrne kept his eyes on the statue. "*Suffer the little children to come unto Me. Such is the kingdom of God.*"

"You misconstrue in your interpretation of the book of Matthew."

"You taught me Galatians too—*have you suffered so many things in vain?*"

"None of it was in vain. Again, you miscons—"

"And what have you misconstrued, Sister? Or have you followed God's word closely enough to speak for Him?"

Sister Mable flushed. "I would never blaspheme in such a way."

"And what about other ways?"

"Please, Luther, I did not ask you here to bring up the past. I

152

asked you here to save the future."

Byrne smirked. "Do I look like a savior to you? Even if my blood flows in His veins…"

"You must hear me in this hour of darkness. There is far too much riding on us. We've been saddled with an unfathomable task."

"*We?*"

"You, me, the local law, the other sisters and Reverend Blackwell. We're in this together, and if we're not united it only benefits the Koyotes."

Byrne stood and, fearing he was about to walk out, Sister Mable rose and took his arm. She expected him to pull away but he did not. He seemed to be waiting, wanting something.

"I apologize," she said. "I am sorry for the pain I've caused you, the suffering you endured at the hands of the church. But it was your blood that kept the evil at bay. Innocent blood, Luther—that is what is required. And what blood is more innocent than that of children? So yes, we drained you and countless others, but we always nursed you back to health."

"Only the body. The scars left on the mind are another thing entirely." He shifted, pulling free of her now. "What exactly did my blood keep at bay?"

She stepped up to the altar with a sigh, hardly knowing where to begin. She said a silent prayer in the hope God would give her the words to explain something she barely understood herself.

"You know this evil," she said, "even if you cannot put a name to it. The church has long tried to contain it, we nuns especially. We are the brides of Christ but we are also mothers. We lay with no men and bear no babies for we are already the mothers of lost children. Women of the cloth are better capable of keeping this evil force imprisoned and resisting its temptations."

"You mean like those nuns on the night Jasper came to Hope's Hill?"

Mable grimaced. "Some sisters are stronger than others."

"Is that why you built this place? The chapel wasn't enough?"

"Yes. We learned that on that fateful night. A simple chapel can only fend off evil so much. We'd tried to keep the most powerful force of darkness at bay but we needed someplace more sacred and secluded."

Byrne rolled his eyes. "You telling me you caught the devil?"

"Not the devil, but the energy *behind* him. Lucifer draws upon a cosmic darkness that lies within the universe itself. It is the blackest magic, and though it cannot be contained in its entirety we can capture it in parts to diminish its usage by those who would rather see a portal opened."

She watched Byrne, looking for some glimmer of recognition in his eyes. They were deep and black, no longer the soft brown they'd been so long ago, before he'd turned full wolfen, never to return.

"This force infects all wolfen," she said, "drawing them like moths to a flame. Surely you must sense the darkness that has lived within your very core."

"Hell, course I do!"

"You've fought against it since leaving the Koyotes. You've tried to push it out of your soul. I've tried to push it away from our world."

"Yeah. I know it. But what lives within me no longer controls me."

"Because you're stronger than the Koyotes."

"I *am* a Koyote." Byrne drew back his hair, revealing the number tattooed on his neck. "This number is a brand that binds forever. I've merely wandered from my pack. A lone wolf is still a wolf. I came back here to keep them from destroying this town 'cause it's the only home I've ever known, sad as that is to say."

"Luther, please. If you still choose to resent me, even *hate* me after all of this is through, I will not judge or blame you for it. But I beg you—do not let this animosity keep us from working toward a common good. I have something I must show you, something that has been seen only by myself and the other sisters. I only show it to you now so that you may grasp what is really at stake. It's more than this town and the people in it. And it's more than Jasper's heart."

She moved to him and was surprised when he let her take his hand, just as he had let her take it when he'd first arrived at the orphanage. In some ways she could still see that feral child inside. Behind the leathery skin and muttonchops, a youth had been destroyed, a soul tarnished. That he'd ever broke free from a life of wickedness was evidence enough of miracles.

Walking him to the altar, they stepped up to the statue of Christ and Sister Mable dragged the footstool from out behind it.

"Step up," she told Byrne.

When he did, she directed him to the ridges of Christ's abdomen, where the locks and tumblers were so slight they weren't visible until you were at eye level with them. She took the crucifix that hung upon her neck and handed it to Byrne. He did not have to be instructed on what to do next. He stuck the cross into the body of Christ and turned, releasing each lock from its chamber, and the crucifix key began to glow, an ethereal light sparkling upon its brass like St. Elmo's fire. When each lock was opened, Byrne put his hand upon Christ's midsection and pulled open a small door.

Behind a veil of stained glass lay the rectangular artifact. Though it resembled a perfectly smooth and symmetrical stone, it gleamed like a jewel and the body of it was swirling with murk. This red fog encapsulated it, and yet also bent the rectangle in denial of all physics. The stained glass chamber was awash in blood. It roiled about the object within, a churning envelopment forged by the life force of the orphans.

Sister Mable kept her distance, ever terrified by the prime evil that was the Menhir. Though it was but a segment of the great monolith beyond their dimension, it was powerful enough to have passed through into their world, and powerful enough to tear it in two if put into the wrong hands.

"Do you feel it?" she asked.

Byrne looked upon the Menhir with glazed eyes. His hands were shaking, fangs sprouting from swelling gums. Sister Mable hoped she'd judged him correctly. If he weren't strong enough his wolfen core would be compromised, and though he was no sorcerer he was right to say he was still a Koyote. If anything could transform him back into the beast he'd once been...

"Luther?"

"Yes," he said. "I feel it."

"Now you see. This is what we must keep awash in holy blood. This is why Jasper Thurston came to Hope's Hill to begin with. That night, it was in the bottom of the fountain of blood. He nearly achieved enough power to take possession of it. Jasper knew this piece of the monolith was here. As an unmitigated servant of darkness, he felt it calling to him. But as long as we kept it awash in the blood of lambs... that is to say, our orphans... he could not find it. That's what filled him with enough anger to want to destroy the world completely. He wanted the power to split dimensions, to literally open the gates of Hell."

Byrne came down the stepladder, away from the Menhir. He was sweating and trembling. Sister Mable held him by the shoulders for fear he might faint.

"Luther, are you all right?"

"Get me away from it."

They started toward to the stairwell, Byrne bent low enough that Mable's arm could go around his shoulder.

"Never bring me near this thing again," he said. "If you do, I might hurt you, even kill you. I don't know if I'll be able to stop myself. The pull... it's just too strong."

They went up the staircase and into the main hall of the chapel. The other nuns were waiting for them, their faces hard, serious. Behind them stood Reverend Blackwell, his cataract eyes like white marble, unblinking, ghostly. In his arms he cradled the massive Bible.

"Jasper's heart beats on," the reverend said. "It is an amulet of black magic, but also a guide to an even blacker magic, truly the blackest of the black. He still wants the Menhir."

Byrne said, "You always have these visions?"

"Not always. There are times I do welcome them. That's when they don't come at all. But there is no mistaking this vision. It is the clearest one I've ever experienced."

Sister Mable was too afraid to hold back tears any longer.

"The Koyotes will come, Luther," she said, "and Hell will follow with them."

*

Murphy Hyers wanted to lead this town, but apparently he was not willing to lead it into battle. Though he said he would not ride with them because of his importance in the community as its presumptive mayor, Russell knew a yellow belly when he saw one. He lost some respect for Hyers that morning, but there was still a job to do here. Russell's duty did not end just because of a change in personal politics.

As it was he had Byrne, his two deputies, and that crackpot Brazzo. Local barman Zeke Ottoman wanted to stay put and protect his saloon if there really was trouble coming. But he said he'd have his firearms at the ready. Cassius Sneck expressed the same concerns for his general store. Russell debated getting Cillian O'Conner from the orphanage. He'd seen his parents taken by the sort of darkness Russell's regulators were in pursuit of. But Russell worried the boy would vent his anger at anyone who looked at him cockeyed. He wanted a lawful posse, not a gang of trigger-happy malcontents. Most of all, if Cillian were killed it would leave the rest of the O'Conner children in even more dire straits. He decided to pass, at least for now. He had another man in mind.

Oscar Shies lived on a small ranch with a small house and a barn just big enough for the horses and one bovine bossy grazing in the pasture. Having come alone, Russell tied Fury to the hitching post and came upon the porch, the old wood bowing beneath his feet. When he knocked upon the door a young boy opened it, his head just above Russell's knees. He had Shies' intense eyes even at this young age.

"Yes, sir?"

"Hello, son. I'm Marshal Henry Russell. This is the Shies residence, correct?"

A woman's voice called from within. "Tohasan? Who is at the door?"

"Mama. There's a sheriff here for Pa."

"I'm a marshal, ma'am," Russell called into the house. "Not exactly a sheriff. I've come looking for Oscar. I have need to speak with him."

"Tohasan, come back inside."

The boy obeyed and the woman appeared in the doorway. She was a beautiful Indian girl, adult but younger than Shies by a decade if not a score. Her hair was black and so long it fell about her hips, her belly swollen with child. Her pregnancy was so far along it was noticeable even beneath the housedress she wore. It was attire more common to white women, none of the usual dress of her people. Russell removed his hat and held it in both hands.

"What is your need with my husband?" she asked.

"I'm the man Oscar guided up the mountain a few days back."

"This I know."

"Well, ma'am, I'm in need of your husband's help again."

Her eyes tightened. "I did not want Oscar to take you to that graveyard. Such places are best left alone. But he is my husband, so I abide. Tell me you are not taking him to another land of restless spirits."

Russell was never one to lie to a woman. Many white men didn't show women of color the same respect as women of their own race, but Russell's mother had taught him from an early age that ladies were always to be treated as such, without exception.

"Ma'am, all I can say is I'm in need of the help of a few good men, and I've seen goodness in your husband. I only come to ask his assistance in protecting Hope's Hill. I will not, nor would I ever, force such a duty upon him. It's strictly voluntary."

The young woman watched, sizing him as well as his words.

"My name is Nizhoni," she said. "It is cold. Please, come inside."

"Much obliged."

The house was not much more than a country shack, the interior proving even smaller than the outside projected. There was little furniture, all of it chipped and dented, and an old, heavy box stove in the corner provided the room with heat. The little boy sat on the floor playing with a cup and ball. Nizhoni closed the door, retrieved the teakettle from a cooking plate, and poured Russell coffee in a clay cup.

"Oscar went to town," she said. "He came back from his cattle drive yesterday and we are in need of supplies. I am unable to get them while he is away."

"What about the horses in the barn? Could you have not ridden one to the general store in your condition?"

Nizhoni shook her head. "I do not go to town even when not with child. Whites do not want an Indian woman in their shops and are even less kind when she brings her half-breed son. My husband and I wonder which part the whites hate most, Negro or Apache."

"It bothers me greatly to hear you've had bad experiences in Hope's Hill. I plan to change things now that I'm here. You should not fear coming into your own town because of blind prejudice."

"You are a peacemaker then?"

"I like to think so, yes."

She smiled and sat down to ease her burden. "I am Choctaw, but there is a tribe of Kiowa in this valley. They bring me things while Oscar is away. They say Setimika perform a sing on you and your men, to bless you with rain and give you more lightning in the hand."

Russell nodded.

Nizhoni said, "They say you're up against a mighty evil, that there lay wolves the size of men beyond the trees. Is this what you want my husband for? To stand by you as you fight off wolf men and bad spirits?"

The marshal knew not what to say, so he said nothing.

"You need good men, but my children need their father."

She rubbed her swollen belly.

From the moment Nizhoni had opened the door Russell felt he should go. He should have lied to a woman this one time and told her he was just dropping by to say hello. Putting an expecting father in the path of death riders was not something he could live with.

"You're absolutely right, ma'am. Your children do need their father, and they need him more than I." He put the cup down on the table. "I thank you for your hospitality and sure hope to see you in town soon."

He went to the door and she followed behind him, and when the cold wind of winter greeted him he put on his hat and hunched up his shoulders. Nizhoni gave him a small bow, cradling the baby inside her.

"I was raised to distrust the white man," she said. "But where there is kindness there is true strength. A man's strongest hand is not the one that crushes. It is the one that lifts."

Russell smiled. "Good day, Mrs. Shies."

"Good day, Mr. Russell. And good fortune."

CHAPTER XXI

THE RUSTY NAIL WAS QUIET tonight.

Byrne sat at a corner table, twirling his empty glass with one finger. He hadn't meant to get this drunk but something about being back home made him crave numbness and oblivion. Over at the bar, Zeke Ottoman was playing solitaire. Two drunkards were having a political debate and a strawberry blonde saloon girl sat upon a stool, one leg draped over the other, long and lovely in the stockings. Byrne wanted to dance with her but didn't want to get too close to such a woman after being in contact with the Menhir. It was as if he were coming down from a high. The cooling period was necessary if he were not going to rip the men apart and rape the lady right there on the floor. The darkness on the edge of the world still called to him, just as it had when he'd been younger and wilder. He'd done things like that back then, things that kept him up nights.

Sin truly is a good man's brother.

Back when he'd first turned wolfen, Byrne had raped many women and girls, killed innocent people, and even eaten them in his werewolf state. Taming the beast had been the hardest thing he'd ever faced, taking an enormous amount of intestinal fortitude. He tried to tell himself he'd had no control when he'd transformed beneath a full moon, but knew his actions stemmed from his own desires, things he still had the urge to do despite knowing they were wrong. The wolf inside him was under his command now, but the temptation to let it loose remained. He could whip that doggie but never take the bite out of it.

"Shallst I replenish ye?"

Byrne had not noticed the bartender come up with the bottle. Byrne nodded and Zeke filled his glass with whisky.

"I know ye," the barman said. "Know yourn kind. T'was here when ye and them boys come into town. Burned my saloon to cinders, yes they did. Had to rebuild her from the dirt on up."

Byrne squinted. "And still you serve me?"

"Aye. T'wasn't ye who done it, but the others in yourn company. And we all know how you turned on 'em and did what was right for ourn town." He put the bottle on the table. "Yourn money ain't no good here, friend, long as you help me keep this saloon from the fate of my last one."

Byrne was not used to praise or adulation. He felt it was undeserved, despite what he'd done for Hope's Hill some fifteen years ago, and he tried to duck away from it. He kept his hat low whenever he moved through town, not wanting to be recognized by the older residents.

"I thank you," he said, rising to his feet. "But I think I've had enough."

As he walked to the Abercrombie house old ghosts returned to him, clawing their way to the forefront of his mind. These memories had been circling his brain since coming back. Now, in his drunken state, they were even sharper.

He hadn't known Jasper would lead them to Hope's Hill. Had Byrne known that, he might have stayed back with Glenn and the others.

*

Jasper had gathered Byrne and three other Koyotes, not wanting the entire company to leave their base unguarded. They'd taken over a whorehouse in Pope's Rock and made their nest there, the harlots partying with them every night as they came back with more riches. The town was poor and welcomed these strangers and their generous spending. Merchants had set up their carts outside the brothel, trying at all hours to sell the Koyotes various wares. There was food and drink, new clothes and hats and saddles, young women and war beds—all the pleasures the riders could handle and then a little more. Jasper wanted to keep this sense of royalty as long as they could, knowing it was only a matter of time before the lawmen of other towns they'd pillaged would band together to find them. When they did, the Koyotes would have to be ready.

"Should only take a couple of days," Jasper said.

Byrne was still unsure what the point was. "What're we hunting, boss?"

Jasper put his nose to the wind. His muttonchops were long and hung low like a beard, the whispers thick as porcupine quills, and as he tested the air his eyes went red and shiny.

"There's something special out there, kid. Something worth more than gold."

"What is it?"

"Don't rightly know. But whatever it is, I hear it calling like a battle cry, pulling me like the very magnet of Mars. All that makes me wolfen, all that makes me the first Koyote—it begins and ends in this."

Byrne scratched his chops. "So where we going?"

"Everywhere. This thing's either in or 'round Black Mountain. Probably buried in it somewheres. Mayhaps a bat cave or some In-jun burial site. Ye, Corbin, Leroy and Okie all come with me to search. Glenn takes command of the rest of the pack 'til we return."

They spent fifteen days riding through the rough and craggy terrain of the mountain, led by Jasper's upturned nose, a hound sniffing out a meal. All the while Byrne and the other men sensed nothing. They were not inexperienced when it came to black magic—how the moon and stars granted them powers beyond mortal men, how the red planet could bless or curse them with a turning of its axis. But they felt no lure the way Jasper did. Whatever this magic was, it had chosen him alone.

The force that drew Jasper Thurston led him and his followers in a new direction each morning. They'd rise from their bedrolls and go southeast when the previous day they'd headed northwest. They crossed over streams they'd already been to and crushed their way through familiar brush, Jasper taking them up to the summit and back down into the basin only to do it all over again.

"I think he's gone mad," Okie said one night while the others slept.

They were in the bedrolls beside the dying fire, the embers just bright enough that Byrne could make out Okie's yellow face. They spoke in whispers.

"Don't talk that talk," Byrne said.

"Wish I'd stayed behind with Glenn. Sometimes I think he'd be the better pack leader."

"Said *hush it* with that. Quit your yammerin'."

"Aw, shit, Luther. Why're we out here ridin' in circles while our brethren get on in their fandangos, getting their peckers sucked and eating fresh meat each night? They're drowning in beer while I'm down to rationing my last bit of corn liquor. They've got a bath-house, an outhouse, shelter from the rain *and* whores to poke. Best place we ever squatted."

"We'll be back with 'em soon enough."

"Yeah, well, *shit* to *later*, I'm talkin' about *now*. We're gettin' sun burnt and saddle-sore on this here goose chase."

Byrne huffed. "Patience is a virtue you just ain't got. Jasper's shown us pearls."

"Has he? I've seen that little satchel he done carries, a mighty grist of marbles and shiny rocks and teeth. He says they're jewels, for heaven's sake, like he's a pirate of Panama."

"He don't mean they be diamonds and rubies. He means jewels of another kind."

"Yeah, I heard all that hogwash. Calls it his *ju ju* bag. Well I ain't seen no voodoo magic. Maybe he's a four-flusher instead of some warlock."

"Damn it, Okie. Jasper's teaching us how to control our trans-formations instead of letting the moon do it for us."

Okie snorted. "So for that we owe him a debt of blind alle-giance?"

"I reckon. And if you don't feel the magic, just think of things this way—he's making us rich, one heist after another."

"Hell, I robbed them banks too. He didn't do it all for me. I don't owe nothin' to any man. Remember it was *me* who done found that herd of horses we stole from them vaqueros down in Oatman. A whole fifty-six head of paint horses and mustangs, not to mention all them wild burros we found along the way. Sold them horses for a mighty profit, did we not?"

"Yeah, I recollect. That's how you got in this gang in the first place."

"Well, I didn't join up with this company to follow a cuckoo bird to nowheres. Hell, he don't even know what it is he's lookin' for. I'm ridin' back to Pope 'fore sunup. If'n you've got a lick of sense you'll do the same."

Byrne rolled over, away from Okie and the fire that had now gone out completely. He was tired of this trip too, but what exhausted him most was the feeling Okie might be right about the pack leader. Since detecting this invisible force, Jasper had been focused on nothing else. He barely ate, only nibbling on jerky he shared with his horse, not wanting to stop for breaks. His lips were always moving, mumbling to himself. Maybe he really was cracking up. Then again, he'd never seemed all that sound to begin with.

Byrne slept, but not well.

Okie was gone when he awoke, but his horse was still at the campsite.

As the steel light of morning cracked the skyline, Byrne spotted Jasper walking through the thicket beneath a mantilla of shadow-black foliage. He was in his undergarments, the front of which was speckled with still-wet blood. He was muttering to himself again and when he emerged from the bushes Byrne could see his rictus grin and dilated eyes.

Leroy was the first to speak up. "Ya okay, boss?"

Jasper didn't answer. Still grinning, he went to Okie's horse and started removing its saddle.

"Boss," Byrne asked. "Where's Okie?"

"Went on back."

"Without his horse?"

Jasper tossed the saddle and parts into the dirt and smacked the horse on the ass.

"Go on, git!"

The mustang only trotted forward so Jasper reached for the rifle by his bedroll and brought it close to the horse's ear and fired into the air, spooking it. The horse ran off kicking dust.

Jasper spat. "Now his horse be gone too."

Byrne looked to his fellow Koyotes. Corbin had begun gathering his things in silence. Leroy sat still in the dirt, head down so not to meet anyone's gaze. He was a black man and his skin had gone ashy from dryness. Cold moved through the pack then. Something had snapped here. A brotherhood had been tested and failed.

*

That night they raided the first town.

Jasper's nose led them to a village where unforgiving mountain rock gave way to verdant lowland. It was too small to have local law, so the Koyotes were only resisted by men ill-equipped for combat. When one of the villagers was brave enough to walk up to the mounted Koyotes with hands raised, pleading for peace, Corbin drew both pistols and shot him seven times before his body could even fall to the ground. Byrne looked the other way.

"Where is it?" Jasper screamed into the night, questioning the village as a whole.

The townspeople scattered like rodents, diving behind stone fences and climbing through windows. Leroy rode along a row of straw shacks, spitting whisky into a handheld torch to throw the flames. Again Byrne looked the other way.

"The pull of it is strong," Jasper said, more to himself than anyone else. "I feel it in my blood and bones. We're close, damn it. It speaks to me! It wants victims! It needs *sacrifice*! Boys, let's appease it and gather ourn sorcery!"

Corbin and Leroy dismounted and chased a woman who was running from a shack Leroy had just set afire, two teenage children with her. Corbin shot her legs out from under her and when she fell her kids stopped too, crying for their mother. The boy was the eldest and tried to play hero to his little sister, standing in front of her as a human shield. Leroy took his head off with one swing of his tomahawk and when his sister screamed Corbin grabbed her hair, shoved the barrel of his pistol down her throat, and fired. The mother screeched and writhed in the dirt. Still Byrne looked the other way for his eyes had gone red with the madness of his breed.

"Make it worse!" Jasper shouted. "The greater their pain, the louder the call!"

Corbin dragged the woman by one busted leg and tossed her on top of her dead children, pushing her face into her daughter's expelled brains. He climbed atop her, tore apart the bottom of her dress, and sodomized her. When a man came charging at Corbin with a pitchfork, Leroy swung his torch and caught the man square in the face with flame.

Jasper strode up to Byrne. "Busy yourself, Luther. You ain't here to sit back and watch."

Byrne dismounted and took his Winchester from the scabbard. The smell of blood and burning flesh stirred the darkness within him. He felt his canines stretching, his whiskers going thick. He was suddenly hungry. *Starved.* Behind him, Jasper was turning his horse in circles, sniffing for a new lead. A group of villagers appeared between two houses. One man ran away and Byrne shot him in the back. A bolder man charged from an alleyway with a double-barrel shotgun. The blast peppered Byrne but he did not break his stride. His muscles were swelling, coarse hair bursting from under his clothes. He smoked with gunpowder but bled little and felt only a slight pain, like the sting of bees. When the villager brought back the second hammer, Byrne shot him in the heart and the shotgun's blast went wild, taking down a woman who'd been ducking for cover. Part of a rib blew out of her back. She collapsed, gagging on the blood rising in her throat, and Byrne grabbed her around the neck and sank his fangs into her shoulder, ripping the meat away, swallowing it without even chewing. He dug one hand into the gunshot wound and twisted the protruding rib until it snapped free, then began stabbing her with her own bone. He pulled the flesh away and bit into the muscle. His claws tore the woman's bloomers to ribbons and he entered her, forcing himself upon her while eating her alive.

He was not yet in total control of the beast. In this moment, he did not wish to be.

The Koyotes slaughtered nearly forty people that night, many of which were women and children. All the while, Jasper insisted each atrocity only strengthened his inner compass. Before leaving the village they set the little chapel on fire and sat their horses, watching God's house burn as they smoked cigars and passed around a bottle of wine, one of many they'd pilfered. Their clothes hung upon their bodies damp with gore and flies swirled about them in excited black clouds. After more than two weeks of starved drudgery upon the mountain, this revelry was the pack's salvation.

They watched the chapel implode, the flaming roof caving in, walls bowing and breaking into splinters. The cross atop the building inverted and then fell to the ground with a crack. It shattered into burning pieces.

Byrne flicked the butt of his cigar into the blaze.

Torching the church was his idea. It always was.

*

They rode all the night through.

Jasper did not want to lose the lead he'd sensed, so they journeyed across the low valley, onward through grassy slopes and tangled briar, on and off trails that stretched across this desperate land. Sometimes they dozed in their saddles. Jasper was the only one who remained sharp, his nose always testing the wind.

Between sleep and consciousness Byrne was haunted by memories of all they'd done the night before. Now that his werewolf state had passed, he lamented his actions, particularly the slaughter of children before their parents' eyes.

He was a monster. They all were.

In his youth, Byrne had not been so bothered by his behavior when his werewolf side took over. But as he grew to be a man, what was left of his humanity had begun to eat at him. His actions when he'd allowed himself to be swallowed by the beast within were a chain of guilt around his heart. And the more control he grew to have over his wolfen state, the harder it became for him to excuse his own atrocities.

It wasn't until the afternoon that Byrne began to recognize the terrain. He'd been little more than a kid when he'd last rode through this woodland where white willows whispered on the wind and a babbling brook sang like rapture in the belly of the forest. He'd fished these waters many a summer whenever the sisters took the orphans on their little trips to picnic and play as if they were like any other children, as if they could be happy on more than these rare days.

Jasper was leading them north. They would reach Hope's Hill just before sundown.

When they stopped to water the horses, Byrne washed his face in the creek and sat upon a fallen log. He stared into the rippling waters like a bear seeking salmon. He wasn't fishing for food, but rather answers.

Hope's Hill had been bad enough to leave, but good enough to be seen with rose-tinted glasses now that he'd been gone all these years. Nostalgia has a way of smoothing the rough edges of memory. There had been good times among the suffering; he felt that was certain. Warm spring days rolling in the dirt with his moth-

167

er, her licking his head and belly to wash him. Other kids he'd befriended at the orphanage, ones who were adults now and likely still lived in town. It would be their homes and business burned to the ground, their sons and daughters buggered and butchered before their very eyes. And though he still despised the church for the sadism of Christianity, for draining his blood and warping his childhood, even some of the nuns held a warmer place in Byrne's heart than they had when he'd run away. It wasn't until he'd gone out on his own that he realized he'd known love, however dysfunctional. Town after town he'd sought revenge against the cruelties of the orphanage, demolishing churches as payback. But could he stand to see the only place he'd ever called home transformed into a gallery of corpses, all of Hope's Hill rendered to ashes and broken bones?

"What troubles ye?"

Byrne turned to see Jasper standing behind him. The pack leader's whiskers were still speckled with bits of human skin. His towering frame cast a long shadow cold enough to make Byrne's flesh prickle.

"I'm all right, boss."

"Yourn face betrays ye. I see it clear as shit and quicksilver. The look of loss besmirches."

Byrne stared back into the brook, bubbles brewing around the jutting rock, a school of tadpoles rioting just below. He wondered if such insignificance simplified a life, if it quieted a savage soul. Jasper squatted down beside him.

"Stay the course, son. I heard the talk ye had with Okie. I know yourn dedication to the pack."

Byrne dared to say it. "And what of your dedication to the pack, boss?"

Jasper paused. "Sometimes a wolf has to chew off a leg to free himself of a trap."

A breeze rustled the treetops, swallows rising from the birch to serenade the morning sun. Jasper turned his face to the sky.

"Every breeze takes us closer to the magic," he said. "I promise ye it'll all be worth it. Once we unlock the sorcery, earthly riches will seem like yesterday's manure compared to what'll be bestowed upon the Koyotes. That power will not just be mine, but ourn. And with it we can snatch the very sun that shines above ye now. Then all the world's swallows will sing for us and us alone."

They traveled on. With every upturn of Jasper's snout Byrne

hoped he'd lead them away from Hope's Hill, but the prairie was growing more recognizable at every turn. He stirred in his saddle, sweating and chewing his cheek. When Jasper started singing an American variant of "Where, Oh Where has my Little Dog Gone?", Corbin joined in, grinning like a hyena, and Leroy hummed for he did not know the drinking song's words. Byrne filled his mouth with a wad of tobacco just to stay out of it.

"*Oh where, oh where can he be?*" Jasper howled.

Distant thunder groaned in reply and in less than an hour the rains came but Jasper would not let them take shelter beneath a canopy of trees.

"We must follow the scent! This rain could wash it away! Leave us lost!"

So they rode on still, their clothes sticking to the bodies and mud sucking at the hooves of their horses. The cascara trees seemed to sigh about them, relishing in the downpour with leaves brought back from the edge of dying. Clouds frothed like a tide, fermenting into a gray so thick it mirrored dusk, and Byrne hunched up his shoulders as the air grew colder.

It was late afternoon when the strangers rode upon Hope's Hill.

Thunder and darkness followed behind them like a curse. The rain gave up but the clouds remained, sulking overhead, a warning of things to come. As they entered town, Jasper perked up like a child with a new hoop and stick.

"This is it, boys. The source of the power lies herein, in this very hamlet."

Byrne squirmed in his saddle. The town had grown some, featuring more residential houses as well as state buildings including a small courthouse and even smaller jail with a gallows pole out front. There was a bank and land office he did not remember and a feed store built inside a refurbished barn. Streets had been platted but remained messed by wheel tracks.

"Where do we start, boss?" Corbin asked.

Before Jasper could answer a man stepped out of the jailhouse. He wore a two-piece suit and Derby hat, his handlebar moustache perfected with wax.

Leroy chortled. "Who's this spring daisy?"

The man crossed the sidewalks and raised a hand at the riders. "Greetings, friends. Haven't seen ya'll 'round these parts before."

Jasper rode up, splattering mud onto the man's fancy slacks. His face went sour.

"Heavens, sir! Do mind your horse! This suit cost me—"

Jasper swung his boot, knocking the man over. He fell into the filth of the street, a wave of mud covering him, hat disappearing into a puddle. His coat opened, revealing a badge.

"Who the hell are ye?" Jasper demanded. "Don't tell me ye're supposed to be some kinda constable, a dandy like you."

The man struggled to get to his feet, slipping and grumbling.

"You lousy bugger!" he said. "I'll have your hide for this."

Jasper drew iron, a long-barreled, six shot revolver with conical balls that could go through a tree. The lawman didn't even have a gun on him. All he could do was put up his hands when he saw the pistol pointed at him. The Koyotes laughed but Byrne looked away, embarrassed for the man for he recognized his face. The last time Byrne had seen him the lawman was just a young fellow, the son of a shepherd and part of a large, Catholic family. Guarding a town was about to prove more of a challenge than guarding a simple flock.

"What's yourn name, honey?" Jasper asked.

The man's jaw tightened. "Shipman McCain."

"An Irishman, ey?"

"An *American* Irishman."

"You Irish be a trouser stain on ourn great states, no less a nuisance than Injuns and other such niggers."

Byrne thought this an odd comment, seeing as some of his brother Koyotes were Irishmen and people of various color. They'd had three Mexicans and even two Delawares, but they'd all died in a shootout with bank guards that cost the Koyotes eight men total. Byrne himself was half Navajo, though people didn't often guess it. None of his fellow wolfen had ever brought it up, including Jasper. And Leroy was of African descent, a slave who'd escaped to Canada West in 1841, returning to the states after life in the northern country proved too hindered by discrimination. Even though British colonies had abolished slavery seven years prior, racism was overt in Canada and town charters excluded blacks from working honest jobs. Wolfen, however, were not of one race, but one species. Still, Jasper Thurston was an ornery sort, a provoker not prone to kinder epithets.

"Well, 'least the Injuns were already here when the white man arrived," Jasper said. "You immigrants be intruding on the master race's land."

McCain stood, hands still up. "Hope's Hill be a peaceful place, sir. A good, Christian town. We don't take kindly to bullying and won't stand for it. It would be smart of you to recognize me as an officer of the law and show me the proper respect."

The Koyotes looked to one another before breaking out in laughter. Byrne was the only one who remained stoic as Jasper shot McCain in the belly. The lawman crumpled inward but remained standing, shaking like a newborn pup.

Jasper said, "That's what we think of the bloody law, honey."

McCain sank to one knee, blood trickling from the corner of his mouth. His spectacles fell from his face. Corbin drew his iron to finish the job but Jasper raised his hand.

"Nah," he said. "Let him think 'bout it. Let him savor it."

"Right, boss."

They trotted on as McCain cried for his mother through a throat filling with blood. Doors were bolting now, the townspeople having heard the shot, some of them having seen the killing. Byrne lowered the brim of his hat, ashamed in a way he'd never been before. There would be more faces he recognized, more familiar eyes staring up at him as their lights within went out. Could he merely idle in this slaughter? He balked at his own twisted morality. What made these people's lives more worth saving than all the others the Koyotes had murdered? Theirs was a reign of terror, a legacy of brutality, and Byrne had ridden with them since his teen years, taking whatever he wanted, feeding his darkest dreams with hedonistic, selfish cruelty. He'd robbed, raped, killed, and cannibalized. But as he'd matured he'd started taming the beast little by little, using Jasper's teachings against their very purpose. Instead of managing his lycanthropy to weaponize it, he was doing so to regain what was left of his humanity. He wanted to be master of his own fate, to go full werewolf only at his own discretion instead of cycling along with the pack or falling slave to the moon and planets. He regretted what had happened in the last town, the way he'd lost control. Perhaps coming home was the next step to deliverance. But could he emancipate himself from the pack? Did he really even want to?

They took their horses to a hitching post, Leroy and Byrne staying guard while Jasper and Corbin headed to the saloon. Though the breeze was cold Byrne had to wipe his face of sweat.

Leroy's smile missed several teeth. "Ya look tired, brother."

THE THIRTEENTH KOYOTE

Byrne wanted to plead with Leroy, to profess the Koyotes were going too far, growing too evil. Acts of savagery were part of being wolfen, but there was a difference between robbing banks and trying to outdo the devil himself. But while Leroy was not the worst of the pack by any means, he reveled in the freedom the gang offered, no matter how violent was the path to maintain it. With Okie, Jasper had given a message to potential dissenters. The Koyotes were a lifetime pledge. Once you were in, there was no peaceful way out.

"What if he does find it?" Leroy said. "Ya think this thing'll really give Jasper the power he says it will?"

"Reckon so."

"What all ya think he plans to do with it?"

Byrne watched the saloon, waiting.

"Evolve," he said.

The building exploded in gunfire. Glass burst from the windows, freeing the sounds of screams and cracking wood. Jasper and Corbin leapt from doorway, still firing behind them, and when they turned back Corbin lit the rag wick of the bottle he held and tossed it through the window. He fashioned these crude bombs from lamp oil and gunpowder. When they worked, they spread flames in a hurry, and this one worked. There was a loud clang followed by more screams and men came out of the saloon shooting back at the Koyotes. Byrne recognized Zeke Ottoman, older now but just as ugly, the peacemaker he kept under the bar popping off in his hands. Pistols blazed in the fists of cowboys armed to fend off aggressive wildlife during cattle drives.

Leroy joined the battle, drawing his iron and cocking the hammer in quick successions with his free hand. A cowboy took a round in the arm but hardly even flinched. He returned fire, taking off the top of Leroy's ear. A saloon girl joined the vigilantes, drew a hidden Derringer from between the breast cups of her corset, and shot Corbin in the face. The Koyote dropped in instant death. Jasper roared, fangs long like a saber-tooth, and when he ran out of bullets he sprinted toward the horses for his saddle scabbard, spotting Byrne.

"Why are ye just standing there dumb?" Jasper said. "Get yourn ass in this!"

Byrne snapped out of his daze, wondering whose side he was on here. His pistol cleared leather just as the cowboys left the porch but he did not fire, his hesitation costing him a ball in his thigh. The round burrowed down to the bone and Byrne stumbled, and Zeke's rifle went off again, just missing Byrne's skull and hitting Leroy's horse instead. Still tied to the hitching post, it writhed against another steed and all the horses screamed and bucked. Gun smoke made the gray light even grayer and Byrne fired through the fog, dropping one of the cowboys. The man's blood gushed against the saloon girl's face and she shrieked but continued to put a new round in her Derringer, snarling as if she too were wolfen. A lock of blonde hair fell loose and covered one of her eyes, and perhaps this was what failed her aim for the bullet went wild, giving Leroy the opportunity to rise up from behind a rain barrel and shoot her in the shoulder. She flew backward and fell over the windowsill, falling back toward the saloon's flames and glass shards.

With his horse in a fit, Jasper struggled to get the rifle from the scabbard, so he drew his hunting knife from the sheath at his hip and in one swing sent it tumbling through the air where it landed dead center in a cowboy's chest. The saloon had blossomed into an inferno and Zeke abandoned it, choosing his life over his property. He disappeared down a dark alley and though Byrne could have easily shot him in the back he did not fire. A rush of flame wafted from the window like the breath of a dragon and Leroy ran from it, his clothes catching fire. As he dropped and rolled Byrne ripped his bedroll from his frazzled horse and threw it over his brother Koyote, patting out the flames. Through the smoke he spotted the shadow of the saloon girl, taking the same alley Zeke had. He was surprised to realize he was glad to see her alive.

When the surviving Koyotes regrouped, Jasper grabbed Byrne by the throat and lifted him straight off the ground. His protruding eyes surged with colors matching the flames, the sclera gone yellow and bloodshot.

"Ye have gone weak!"

He tossed Byrne like he was flicking a coin and Byrne landed hard onto the ground.

"Fetch my knife!" Jasper said. "Make yourself useful!"

Byrne spat away the mud on his lips and went to the dead cowboy. The knife was so deep in his chest Byrne had to put his foot on the man for leverage to pull the knife out with both hands. He brought the blade to his pack leader and Jasper's nostrils flared, his chin high.

"Now fetch me Corbin you bloody idiot."

Byrne looked at the corpse. "You want his body?"

Leroy said, "We can sell him to resurrectionists down in Onyx Banks."

Jasper clapped Leroy on the back of his head and stepped in close, their noses almost touching.

"You'd chop yourn brother wolfen up for parts, would ye?" Jasper snarled. "Seems I done brought the wrong men on my quest."

"Sorry, boss, I didn't mean... I mean, uh... I'll try and do better."

Jasper nodded his head toward the body and Byrne and Leroy went to it and dragged it to the hitching post. The horses had mellowed. Leroy's mustang was not seriously injured. Jasper patted his steed on the neck and got sugar cubes from his saddlebag and gave each horse a treat. The men propped up Corbin in a sitting position, leaning him against a post.

Byrne said, "You want I should put him over the back of his horse? We can lead it on back to Pope's Rock so the whole pack can give him a proper burial."

"Nah," Jasper said. "We ain't leavin' this here town yet, and Corbin ain't goin' in the ground noways."

Jasper squatted beside Corbin's corpse and raised the dead man's chin. Corbin's right eye was gone. The ball had entered through the socket but had not exited, lost somewhere in the scrambled brain matter. Jasper reached into the gris-gris bag slung upon his necklace and withdrew a small fistful of talismans—a rainbow-colored marble, two pebbles of brimstone, a dead locust, a pewter dog figurine, a child's mummified toe. He shook them in his hand like a rattler and hummed deep in the back of his throat. His eyes closed and his mouth opened, fangs gleaming though there was no sun, and as he chanted thunder groaned in the heavens like the great hooves of a thousand galloping horses.

Byrne watched with bated breath. Leroy's eyes glazed.

Jasper's chant was like that of an Indian shaman, and yet there was menace to it, more invocation than prayer. As flames swallowed the saloon, shouts of panic echoed through the village. The Koyotes ignored them. Jasper's hand became a fist and a strange light that was not light at all beamed out from between his fingers. It was a black radiance, unfathomable, unlike anything Byrne had ever seen, sunrays born of gun smoke and charcoal. And unlike natural light it was bitterly cold, making the men's breath mist. When Jasper leaned into the phosphorescence it illuminated his skull beneath the flesh, large and animalistic. He breathed deep of its vapors and then leaned in to Corbin, put his mouth over his, and forced the blackness into the dead man's lungs. The body instantly convulsed. Leroy stepped back, mumbling as if he were about to piss himself. Jasper took the child's big toe and shoved it into the hole where Corbin's eye had been, the nail facing out like some putrid cornea.

When Jasper uttered something in a foreign tongue, Corbin's good eye snapped open. He let out a cry as he was ripped from death's womb. Jasper helped him to stand and blood trickled blackly from Corbin's ears.

"Welcome back," Jasper said.

Corbin croaked like a toad when he tried to speak.

Leroy gagged. "Jesus! What in blazes ya do to him, boss?"

"Ye speak of resurrectionists. Well, I am one. Not no body-sellin' ghoul like them scallywags back in Onyx Banks. Instead of sellin' off the dead, I've mastered bringing 'em back. Resurrectionist. Necromancer."

Byrne stepped closer to the re-animated man. "Corbin? That really you?"

Corbin looked at Byrne but there was no recognition there. Jasper patted Corbin's shoulder.

"Ye won't find the dead to be much good for conversation."

"He conscious?" Byrne asked.

"His brains might as well be a bowl of custard with that bullet in his head."

"Hell, Jasper. Why even bring him back then?"

"I shoulda known ye'd be washy on it." Jasper shook his head. "Sometimes I think you're just a dog going gimp. We need men here, Luther. That McCain bastard said this be a peaceful town but it looks to me these folks don't shy away from vigilante justice. Corbin here may not be right enough in the head to fire a gun but he can still fight. When the dead come back, I can tell ye this—they ain't in no good mood."

Byrne rubbed the back of his neck, the tattooed number tingling.

"How do we know he'll be on our side?" Byrne asked. "I mean, if'n his mind's up the spout how'll he even know where to direct this rage?"

"Don't be simple. He'll fall in line 'cause I'm his ruler, the one who done brought him back from the other side. He'll kill who I bloody tell him to kill and eat who I bloody tell him to eat. Those impulses are set deep in a Koyote's heart, be they live or dead. All I gots to do is play puppet master."

*

They approached the chapel like the pack of wolves they were, Jasper riding point, the other two men flanking him atop their horses. Corbin's corpse was on foot, moving with legs stiff, not bending his knees. His head kept jerking and snot bubbled in one nostril. Both the chapel and its adjacent orphanage looked exactly as Byrne remembered them. His stomach soured and, though he knew he should not, part of him itched to burn the church down.

Jasper sniffed the air, trying to regain the scent he'd been following. His face pinched in frustration. "Something's clouding the scent. Or someone." He looked up at the chapel's doors. They were bolted shut. "I thought God's house was always open." Jasper chuckled. "Guess the good Lord done tattled on us, warned these Bible-beaters we were comin'. Even God's a snitchin', filthy rat."

Byrne adjusted his coat, suddenly uncomfortable. He knew butchery would soon begin if he did not intervene. He could smell the bloodlust wafting from his fellow Koyotes. Jasper's craving for all that was evil was a palpable thing. As night fell the transformations would begin, and because he was on the same cycle as his brethren Byrne too would change even if it were against his will. Who would he rape and murder his former friends and neighbors then? Whose children would be devoured?

A thought came to him. What if they found what Jasper was looking for? Was it crazy to think he could convince Jasper to just head back after they'd obtained it? Would it spare lives in Hope's Hill? If they tore this town apart looking for it, there would be mass death, but if he could track down this magic bean a mass killing would be unnecessary and time-consuming, would it not?

"I'll bet it's right here," he said, gazing up at the chapel.

Jasper turned. "You're an expert now, are ye?"

"Reckon it makes sense, don't you? If something with magical powers is here, would the church not take possession of it? Wouldn't they be the most capable of trying to keep you from it, clouding the scent and such?"

Jasper looked upon the shuttered doors. "They turn to Christ for protection, using the cross on vampires n' such, or so I've heard tell. Maybe there is power to it yet."

Jasper dismounted and drew his hunting knife, flipping it in his hand, the cowboy's blood having dried upon the blade. The other Koyotes swung out of the saddle and Byrne felt cold sweat at his neck. Hopefully the chapel was empty, but if a few Christians were tossed to these lions in order to save the rest of the town, it was a small toll. And didn't these holier than thou types always preach the importance of sacrifice? Let them bloody well prove it.

The pack leader ordered the door broken down. Leroy went to work with his tomahawk, splitting the dunnage. Byrne fired three rounds until the lock fell away. Corbin in his undead state clawed and chewed at the wood in dumb obedience. When the doors swung open the Koyotes stepped inside. With night coming the chapel was lost in shadow. The pews empty, the lectern unmanned. They looked up at the plain, white, Christless cross and Jasper sniffed.

"Yeah," he said. "Yeah."

He walked toward the pulpit and hopped onto the platform, sniffing deep and growling. In the shadows he looked like a prehistoric beast, roaming nebulous and raw through the house of the holy.

"Smell that?"

"Yep," Leroy said.

Byrne did too. There was no mistaking the savory stench of blood.

Jasper fell silent, ears perked. Over the low rumble of thunder, Byrne heard the voices coming from the backroom. He expected fear in them but instead he heard delight. They were female voices, moaning like whores paid to do so. Leroy snickered and adjusted his crotch. Beside him, an idiot Corbin giggled spit bubbles. When Jasper spotted the door leading to the backroom the Koyotes followed him to it, weapons at the ready in case this was a trap. Byrne bit his lip. Smelling blood in this place again made his inner child shrivel in terror and that enraged the man he'd become. Part of him wanted to lay down wrath here, to avenge that lost little boy. When the Koyotes opened the door they stepped back. Even Jasper's jaw dropped.

Three nuns were writhing on the floor in a deluge of blood. One had her gown up around her waist and was driving a crucifix in and out of her sex. A teen choirboy lay beneath an elderly nun who was riding him, her saggy tits flapping in his face like loose saddle bags. Another sister wore only her wimple headdress and was slathering herself in the gore that gushed from a fountain meant for holy water.

On the wall was another cross, one much cruder than the one in the chapel hall. It was manufactured from pieces of freight boxes and pages from the Bible were pinned to it with barbed wire.

Byrne's breath stopped in his chest.

Hung upon this cross was Sister Mable, railroad spikes driven through her palms. Her gown was slick with blood and her wimple had been removed so another tangle of barbed wire could sit upon her skull. She managed to look up and her eyes locked with Byrne's, recognizing him instantly despite how he'd aged, and though Byrne had never seen her without her headdress there was no mistaking that lovely face, not even when it was twisted in agony.

"Luth…" she muttered, unable to finish.

Jasper stepped forward, blood pooling around his boots.

"It's here," he said.

But Byrne knew that. The power was so intense any wolfen could detect it. In this force's presence, Byrne shuddered in unmitigated horror. It chilled him to his marrow. This was a writhing mass, without form or color, an energy so nefarious and depraved it brought tears to his eyes and stopped his breath.

The nun who'd been masturbating tossed aside her cross. Her gown was split, one pale leg sliding in and out of view as she came toward them. She wore the smile of madness. When she reached Jasper she pulled off her wimple and her long, brunette hair tumbled about her. She slung her arms around his neck and kissed him like a new bride.

"You are wolfen," she said, more statement than question.

Jasper nodded.

"It told me you'd come," she said, speaking quickly, excitedly. "I was pouring the children's blood in the fountain but I spilled it by accident and it knocked the Menhir free from the amulet. The ecstasy of it was like rapture. I've never felt such divinity before, not in twenty years of service to Christ."

Jasper ran the back of his hand across the nun's cheek.

"Where's the leader of this flock? Where be yourn preacherman?"

"Reverend Blackwell is away." She smiled and bit her bottom lip, a girl alone with a boy for the first time. "He is on an exorcism in Steelbranch. I think that's what made it possible for the Menhir to release its power and show us how erroneous was our blind allegiance to the Lord." She looked up at Sister Mable. "This one tried to stop me. She bolted up the church and tried to drown out the call of the Menhir with holy blood. But I knew someone would answer that call, a great sorcerer like you."

"Ye done good," he said. "There'll be reward for ye yet."

"All I ask is for you take me with you."

The gore-slick, naked nun chimed in from her pool on the floor. "We've tasted so much pleasure but still desire so much more. Teach us! Show us!"

"Take us with you," the brunette nun pleaded.

"First things first. Take me to this Menhir, as ye call it."

She took his hand, giddy as a schoolgirl, and guided him to the fountain of blood. Byrne followed, glancing at Sister Mable, wondering how he could get her down and if he really wanted to, as torn as any man who'd grown up with an abusive mother figure. When they reached the fountain Jasper reached into it but drew his hand back, hissing as he was burned.

The nun blinked. "I knew I was not strong enough to take it, though Lord knows I desired to. I thought a wolfen wizard as yourself would be able—"

Jasper plunged his knife into the nun's stomach and twisted it in her intestines. She vomited blood and collapsed, voiding her bladder and bowels. Byrne looked away, limbs shaking. He could feel the hair sprouting from his back. The choirboy and the old nun stopped having sex and got to their feet, him slipping in the blood. Jasper's eyes went red as he looked upon his men.

"It needs more. With every evil act we grow more worthy of its power. Human sacrifice is what will make this Menhir mine!"

Leroy lunged at the old nun and sunk his tomahawk into her shoulder. The brittle bone split as he withdrew the weapon and swung it again, and as she fell the blade chopped her head in half horizontally, the top separating from the bottom. The top half slid across the floor, the nun's eyes wide and staring, the broken nose dribbling with bloody snot. The choirboy screamed and tried to run but Corbin knocked him down and started hammering his head into the floor with both hands, the blows sluggish but hard. The nude nun slunk backward into the corner and covered her eyes, her whole body convulsing in fear. Jasper approached her, grinning, and when she peered through her fingers her reflection looked back at her from his bloody blade. Byrne took one step forward, but Jasper was too fast. He grabbed the nun by the hair, swung back with the knife, and decapitated her with three quick blows to the neck. As her stump gushed, slathering her breasts in gore, he tossed her head into the air and when it fell back toward him he punted it and the head burst through a window and out into the night.

Sister Mable groaned and Jasper smiled up at her, spinning his blood-slick blade.

"You're a pretty one, ey? Little for teets but a face to make up for it. And yourn cunt is virgin. Be a damn pleasure for a poke."

Byrne's stomach turned. "I say we let her hang there. Having her die a slow death is more wicked, especially when it's in the style of her Christ."

"Mayhaps. But I can think of other things we can do to her while she hangs up there, things that'd even make them kikes who killed Jesus weep."

Corbin shot up from his victim, his mouth and eyes wide. He let out a long groan like a dying hound. Jasper put his hand on Corbin's shoulder and the dead man guided his master to the room's only window. Lightning lashed a firmament black and swollen with rain. Corbin punched through the glass, splitting his knuckles, and pointed at the larger building across from the chapel. Byrne's hackles raised when Jasper tested the air.

"You're right, Corbin," Jasper said. "I smell 'em too."

Corbin winked with his toe eye, a proud rictus grin on his face.

Jasper turned to his men. "Children. Lots of 'em. Up yonder in that there building."

Leroy shrugged. "So we torch that bloody orphanage with them little ones still in it. What could be a better human sacrifice than that?"

"Sometimes you're smarter than I give ye credit for, Leroy."

Hair curled out of Byrne's forehead. The skin of his nose grew coarse and black, his face elongating. It was not the moon or Mars that turned him now, nor was it the cycle of his fellow Koyotes. *He* was controlling this transformation, the beast within awakened by his own rage. When Jasper turned away from the window he saw Byrne was changing form.

"Luther!" he said. He slapped his knee. "Ye gots it, brother! You're masterin' yourn lycanthropy!"

Byrne snarled. "Don't make me stop you."

"Stop me from what?"

"That orphanage. I can't let you kill them children. I won't stand for it."

Jasper and Leroy shared a glance.

Leroy pointed at Byrne. "Brother, what in bloody hell's wrong with you."

Jasper moved in. "I was hopin' I was wrong 'bout you, Luther. The way ye led us here, I hoped ye were back on track. Now I see my previous inclination was correct. Ye done gone soft on me, on all us Koyotes."

"Don't—"

"What bloody right have ye? Growin' a conscience like this after all ye done. All the people you murdered... those dead are yourn! And what if we do kill these orphans? Why does it peel your skin so? You've killed children yourn own self."

"That's right," Byrne said. "I own that and carry it all the days of my life. But I'm under my own power now. Ain't no longer a slave to my cycle. I won't let you burn those children, Jasper. I can't come it."

Jasper stepped in, hair climbing up his neck like writhing worms.

"You don't give the orders here, boy. I do! Remember who made ye wolfen in the first place. Ye drank of my blood willingly and took yourn number upon thy neck."

"Don't claim otherwise."

"Then show me due gratitude."

"I owe you no debt."

"You owe me yourn very life! You'd been dead a hundred times over had I not made ye one of us. You were shot even today! And already that bullet has popped from your leg and it be healing over. I gave ye power beyond your dreams—*pearls*, you said. It's time for you to return that favor. This Menhir *must* be mine. I'll see a million children suffer and scream if'n that's what it takes. And if I first have to kill ye dead I'll hesitate not, brotherhood be damned. This is yourn last bloody chance, Luther. Are ye a Koyote or are ye not?"

Byrne returned Jasper's red stare, the two men nearing full transformation. Leroy had drawn his iron but held it down at his hip. Byrne had no illusions about whose side he would take. The aroma of blood further stirred the Koyotes, the inner beasts pushing their way out, and thunder cracked, announcing a duel, and Byrne lunged at his mentor.

*

The werewolves roared.

Leroy had raised his pistol but Jasper barked him away, wanting the dissenter for himself. Byrne struggled beneath his massive opponent as Jasper got the upper hand, clawing him with nails like ram horns. Shreds of hair and clothing and flesh spun. The puddle of holy blood singed their skin and as they rolled away from it Byrne snapped at Jasper and caught his snout in his jaws. He shook his head back and forth, lacerating Jasper's face until he retreated. Byrne rose to his feet, hands on the ground like paws. His fur dripped crimson, some of it Jasper's, some of it his own, and some of it having belonged to the children the nuns had drained, just as they'd drained him.

Before Jasper could attack, Byrne ran at him, battering Jasper into a wall. It shattered in splinters and the Koyotes rolled out into the night, rain hammering down upon them as they twisted in the mud. A shard of wood had pierced Byrne's forearm and he yelped as Jasper pushed it in further and then swung Byrne by it, hurling him into the chapel's cemetery. Among the tombstones and iron crucifixes these creatures tore each other in a tornadic war, flashes of lightning revealing their freakish forms to those villagers who could see the graveyard from their homes. Byrne dove into Jasper's waist and lifted him in the air, then swung him down with all his weight pressed upon Jasper's torso. With the shard of wood still sticking through his arm, Byrne used it to stab at Jasper's body until it broke free, each Koyote taking a piece of it with them and slamming into graves and howling to heavens blacked out by the storm. A witch's wind whistled in the trees, branches clacking like rattlesnake tails, and thunder groaned within the belly of a diabolical cosmos.

Snarling, the werewolves ripped an ocean of gore. Like demons they fought, brothers mutilating one another in civil war, and when Jasper managed to pin Byrne down upon a fresh grave he thought for sure he was at the point of dying. Nothing warm flashed through his mind. There were no memories of a sunnier time that had once made life worth the going. There was no joy for him to relive. Instead his soul shuddered with sad recollections of all the pain he'd caused others, all the horror and butchery and death he'd brought upon his fellow man. Though his body was covered in wounds he suffered most from this regret, the painful reflections like some final contrition before his soul was lost forever.

Byrne growled.

Letting Jasper live would mean his evil would go on. Hundreds would be slaughtered still. Perhaps thousands. If the Menhir was as powerful as Jasper believed it to be, what foul villainy would he lay upon this world? The misery would be catastrophic, and it would all start with the murder of the orphans, children who'd suffered the same way young Byrne had, and that was suffering enough.

He shot his hands into Jasper's mouth and before Jasper could snap his jaws Byrne pried them apart, stretching Jasper's head until the jaw cracked. His tongue hung loosely and he yowled in pain. As Jasper fell backward, Byrne reached for the iron crucifix that marked the grave, pulled it free from the earth, and plunged it deep into Jasper's heart.

The first Koyote gargled one last howl.

Then he died.

Byrne rose to his feet, standing upright as he slowly started to transform back into a human. But he'd only taken one step when Leroy shouted over the rain. Byrne looked up. Leroy was standing at the cemetery gates. He'd taken Sister Mable down from her cross and held her against him like a human shield, his pistol at her temple.

"Just get on out," Leroy said.

"Say again?"

"Just leave, Luther. Ya killed Jasper fair and square. I always followed my leader but after seeing what he done did to Okie, I doubt he valued anybody but his own self. But you always been a brother, so you just take your leave now. I'll tell the boys you two done killed each other. You get on with your life and I get on with mine."

"And what kind of life might that be, Leroy?"

The big man's eyes flashed. "That thing Jasper were after. It'll be mine now. I get that power and I'll be the new leader of the Koyotes."

"I won't let you torch those orphans as sacrifice."

"Then I'll kill this nun of yours."

Byrne glowered.

"Yeah," Leroy said. "I saw the way you looked at her. Like a sad little puppy. I heard her try and speak your name. You done told me how you grew up, remember? I could tell this was the place. I could sense it even if Jasper was too focused on his own game to pick up on it. I know this nun means something to you."

"I'd kill that bitch ten times over to save those orphans."

"Let's test that theory."

"Stop this, Leroy." Byrne sloshed through the mud, nearly human again, or as close to it as a wolfen can get. "Let's end this, brother—you and me together. No more rape and murder. No more sadistic wickedness. We can rise above it all."

Leroy shook his head. "You've gone plumb crazy if'n you think I'm gonna give up everything—the money and women and whisky, all the *power* in my wolfen blood. Reckon you're one mighty fool to be giving it up yourself."

"Ain't giving nothin' up noways. I'll be wolfen 'til my last breath but I don't want to be a Koyote no more, not if we're going to let loose this kind of evil. I know you felt it in there just as I did. Whatever that Menhir is, it carries with it all of Hell!"

"Then all Hell shall be mine. People wouldn't treat me like a human being because I was a Negro. With the power of that rock, they'll have to treat me like a king—that, or die."

Byrne inched his hand closer to his Colt. Leroy snarled.

"You're not the shootist I am," he said. "Your pistol won't clear leather 'fore I put a bullet in ya."

Byrne was hoping for Sister Mable to jam her elbow into Leroy's balls or bite his ear, anything to give him a moment to take Leroy down. But the nun was dazed and broken. Even if Leroy didn't kill her, she still might die.

Corbin crashed through the hole in the chapel.

Leroy flinched and Byrne drew iron and fired. The round went into Leroy's throat, crushed the Adam's apple and thyroid cartilage, and exited through the back of Leroy's neck, severing it from his spine. He collapsed, bringing Mable to the ground with him. Byrne ran at them, smoking gun still in hand, and Sister Mable crawled away from Leroy as he shuddered in the mud, paralyzed and bleeding to death. She reached for his pistol but her pierced hands were useless. Corbin wandered past her, directionless without his master, and Byrne came upon them and put Leroy out of his misery with a headshot. He then stepped to Corbin and shot the abomination in back of the head. Corbin fell dead for the second and last time.

Byrne stared down at Sister Mable but did not help her up when she reached for him. There was an ethereal glow about her, a pale blue that played tricks on his eyes.

"Luther…"

"Don't cry to me, lady."

He looked back at the body of Jasper Thurston and spat. In dying, he had returned to his humanoid form but his heart, having been impaled upon the cross while he was still a werewolf, remained in werewolf size, pitch black and so huge it broke through Jasper's ribs and out of his chest.

"Burn 'em all," Byrne told the nun. "And what won't burn bury deep in blessed earth."

"The Menhir…"

"What the hell is it?"

Sister Mable clutched her chest. "The sisters fell under its spell… the darkness… they could not help themselves. Forgive them."

"I don't give a damn. God's the one who's supposed to forgive, ain't He?"

"I thought it would be safe inside the amulet, but all it took was one mistake… Sister Angela dropping the blood… the chapel is not enough to contain it. We need something stronger, somewhere better to hide it from the likes of wicked, bloody men."

"Now look, I don't know what that Menhir is and frankly I don't want to. Jasper can't hunt it no more and I don't want nothing to do with it. You're the one with the power of Christ behind you. Let the church figure out how to cage Satan's dinner bell."

He took a cigar from his pocket and lit it. He started his way out of the graveyard but blood loss made him woozy and he had to lean against a tombstone. A bit of tobacco smoke rose out of a wound in his chest that had pierced his lung. Mable cried for help from the villagers across the street, but after all they'd seen no one left their houses. She balanced herself against the wall of the chapel in order to walk.

"What if others come for it?" she asked. "Will you help us then?"

"Ain't nobody gonna come now."

"But if they do? Promise you'll help me fight."

Byrne shrugged. "Only thing I promise is to keep the world

185

from ending, and only 'cause I ain't through with it yet."

Mable sighed and moved across the chapel.

"I'll get the doctor," she said. "Bring him back to help you."

"Save it. You go to him and get yourself fixed up. I just want to smoke my cigar in peace."

"You could bleed to death."

"I won't."

The nun looked away. "Of course. You are wolfen now. How, Luther? How could you have gone so far astray? How could—"

"Don't speak. Just leave."

"And what of you, Luther?"

Smoke poured from his nostrils. "By the time you come back, I'll be gone. Gone for good."

CHAPTER XXII

NEEDING THE REST, OSCAR SHIES sipped another gin sling. His shoulders ached from pulling a steer out of a mud bank at the river where it had sunk up to its quarter. A pair of cowboys had lassoed a rope around the poor creature's neck in an effort to drag it out, but this had only served to choke the steer. Shies got down from his horse, undressed fully, and waded into the muck and pulled the bight from under the steer's dewlap, tossing the rope aside. The stunned cowboys watched then as the giant man took the steer by the horns and started pulling it toward the embankment. Shies' muscles popped and gleamed like gunmetal beneath the sun, his teeth grit and his eyes shut tight. The steer moved little at first, but with the rope freed from its neck it could breathe again, and as Shies helped the animal it began to help itself. It came loose from the sucking mud and climbed out, Shies guiding it so it would not fall. When it was over, he called the cowboys damned fools and climbed atop his horse, riding naked and muddy until he reached part of the river that ran clear. He bathed himself in the waters and redressed before heading back to town for a drink.

Zeke Ottoman wiped down the bar. The Rusty Nail was empty this early in the afternoon, but Zeke had hired a fiddler on and when night fell the saloon would be lively again. Shies finished his drink and was about to head home but when he put on his hat he saw the marshal's face reflected back at him from the mirror behind the bar. He turned and they shook hands.

"Good to see you, Oscar," Russell said.

"Likewise, Marshal."

"Buy you one?"

"Well, I was just about to be on my way, but I never turn down a free drink."

Russell gave Zeke the order and the two men stood at the bar.

"Heard you came calling for me," Shies said.

"I did at that."

"Thought about coming down to the station to talk to you about it."

Russell shook his head. "No need."

"I disagree. The wife don't take kindly to the notion of me being a posseman again, but with the baby coming we'll be needed the money. If you're willing to pay a decent wage, I might be interested, if you're still looking to hire a man on, that is."

"I promised your wife I'd leave it be."

"And I promised her I'd take care of our family. I took her away from her tribe and brought her all the way out here to start our own. I can't have my children's bellies go empty and have my Nizhoni dressing in rags. I won't stand for it. She is a goodly wife and will abide my choices."

"She's with child and the risks of riding posse are high."

"I've stared down risk without flinching all my life," Shies said. "If I could read better I would've surely made deputy back home. Might have even made sheriff, of a black town at least."

"You don't understand what we're up against, friend."

Shies faced Russell head on. The marshal looked back at him with tired eyes. He seemed more worn than the last time Oscar had seen him, older and grayer.

"You look like someone's done shot your dog, Henry. I've heard tell of bad things going down in this territory. Heard of a mining town where they've had to bury nearly fifty people who'd been slaughtered at their own tent revival. Heard of a train wreck whose survivors spoke of monsters, men described as wolves or demons. My wife told me about your visit with Charging Bear and how he performed a *sing* for you and your posse. I lived among the Choctaw a good chunk of my life. I know a thing or two about the spirit world, including its darker corners. If something is coming down from it, you'll need all the help you can get."

The marshal looked at the floor and Shies put his hand on his shoulder.

"You're right to think I have a duty to protect myself for the sake of my family," Shies said. "But if something wicked is on the crest of our town, how does it protect them if I don't try and stop it?"

*

As Vern Pipkin took his horse to the town line, the rolling cart dragged behind. Yonder the dirt road forked, a thinner trail on either side of the main path, both leading upward to the unrelenting crags and briar of Black Mountain. It was a frigid day and the sky sulked gray. Vern pulled his coat tighter and hunched his shoulders. In the cart were his excavation tools—shovels and pickaxes and lanterns—and his buck-hunting rifle was resting in the scabbard at the right side of the saddle. After his encounter with that giant ruffian in the general store, he doubted he'd go without some sort of weapon from now on.

He'd lain low after being taken to the marshal's station. Though there'd been no suitable evidence to arrest him, rumors of Vern being a marauder of graveyards had trickled through the town like so much dog piss. It was a risk to go back out grave-robbing again, but there were many bills to pay yet and with Dr. Craven gone he had to meet the demands of other resurrectionists who'd hired him, those serving as middlemen between Vern and clientele of the medical variety.

His pony neighed and Vern patted its mane.

"Easy now, darlin'. You've been up this way before. You can do it."

The road wound through a prairie white with snow, branches of shrubbery like skeletons burnt at the stake. When he came upon the O'Conner's dead farm Vern swallowed hard. The land was black as a starless sky, the vegetation lost to ashen ruin. The remains of the house lay singed in the gray dirt, broken and twisted beneath the collapsed roof. Though the windmill still stood the blades were hole punched and blackened by the fire, looking like great moth wings as they spun gently in the December wind.

Vern's brain panged when he thought of what had happened. He'd told no one, not even Uriah Craven, that as he'd rode down from the mountain with the hideous heart the wheel of his cart had hit a rock and Vern had fumbled with the golden capsule in his lap. It fell to the ground and when it cracked open the heart rolled out of the casing and tumbled down the path to the O'Conner's farm and went lost in their cornfield.

"Sweet merciful Christ!" Vern had hissed.

It was not quite dawn yet but the first blue light had cracked the horizon by the time he found the heart among the rows. Had it not left a trail of blackish blood for him to follow it might have been lost forever to the plentiful autumn corn. It lay there in a pool of its own wet tar, the liquid stretching out in all directions. He'd watched with mouth agape as the cornstalks were watered by it, their husks turning black upon impact. The fluid ran on toward the barn beyond and the horses bucked and whinnied as they tried to dance around the streams. Vern scooped the heart back into the gold canister, careful not to touch it with his fingers while he scooped, and ran to his pony and trotted away just as the first rooster began to crow. He carried on then, back to his parlor with the pink haze of daybreak as his guide.

That night at the town meeting, when he'd learned how the O'Conners and their farm had been plagued as if by some gypsy curse, his air had caught in the back of his throat. Had it been that horrible, horrible heart that had caused the poor family's devastation? He could not get rid of the blasted thing fast enough. Though he'd pushed Dr. Craven for more money, he would have settled for less just to make a little coin and get the blasted thing out of his life.

He rode past the O'Conner farm now, trying not to look at it but somehow drawn to the utter ruination. The hair on his arms stood and his mouth went dry as Texas. When at last he passed the wretched place he led his pony up the slope through snow gone black by wagon wheels. He traveled on, the cart rickety and threatening to break free, but still they climbed, up into the icy crags where the corpses of red oaks bent over like mourning mothers. As the gloaming gave way to full dark, a third quarter moon offered little light and when he reached the clearing he looked back and forth, his brow furrowed.

"Shit. I could've sworn that little cemetery was right up here."

The darkness didn't help his sense of direction. He'd felt certain this was where he'd stumbled upon that hidden graveyard but here there was only wilderness. Perhaps it was to the east rather than the west? He trotted his pony and circled back to the trail and when he reached the next clearing he saw the first row of little crosses marking the graves.

His smile didn't last long.

Gathered in the cemetery was a group of men, watching as Vern approached. They were hard-looking riders with long coats blackened by travel and the threat of their shadows tempted Vern to turn back. But that would raise suspicion as to why he was out here this late with a cart full of excavation gear.

But, well, why were these men out here then?

Vern moved on, aiming to bypass the cemetery as if he'd just wandered off the trail by accident. He did not look at the men, hoping it might keep them from being triggered. It was a dull hope indeed. One of the men came out of the trees and stepped before Vern, making the pony stop. He was dark enough to be an Indian or African, but the moonlight made it hard to tell, as did the thick muttonchops that hid much of his face.

"What ye doing up here?" the burly man asked.

Vern had no saliva to wet his lips. "T'was just turning around, friend. Seems I moseyed off the path."

The other men were drawing closer. Though his rifle was beside him, Vern dared not touch it, having no doubt these men were armed.

"Ye ain't lost," the dark man said.

A skinnier man came up to Vern, his coat back and the moonlight reflecting off the silver-plated revolvers at his hips. He had a face like a possum but Vern doubted he would play dead in the face of trouble, no matter how great.

"What's your name?" the skinny man asked.

"Vern Pipkin, friend," he said, forcing a smile. "And you are?"

"Name's Hiram. Hiram Zeindler. And I'm anything but your friend."

Vern's bowels went cold. Another man came out of the darkness of the graveyard, his long, black hair like a woman's but his body like that of a lumberjack. He sniffed at Vern.

"It was you," he said. "I can still smell you on his corpse."

"Pardon?"

"The heart. You dug up Jasper Thurston's grave here."

Vern could not keep the quiver out of his voice. "Goodness, sir. What has been implied here?"

Hiram reached up for him so quickly Vern didn't realize it was happening until he fell off his pony. Pebbles ground into him as Hiram dragged him screaming into the graveyard, the other men walking alongside. They came into the circle and when Vern was dropped he sat up and saw two other men with the same whiskers. At their feet were young women wearing only their bloomers. They were covered in bruises and cuts, rope leashes around their necks like lassoed cattle.

A frog croak rose from the brush behind them, and when a pale face poked out of the shadows Vern gasped, recognizing Dr. Craven. The look of death was upon the doctor. Craven's skin was like alabaster in the light of the moon, except for the putrid rot that had blackened his hands, which were now without fingers. The rot continued across his flesh in black varicose veins. His lips had decomposed and fell away some time before, his teeth in a fixed chatterbox rictus. He wore only an unbuttoned blouse and, much like his lips, his genitals had oozed away from decay, leaving a gaping hole of brackish sinew where his manhood had once swung.

Vern screamed and the doctor cackled—undead, insane.

"Lordy!" Vern said. "Uriah, what has happened to you?"

Hiram pulled Vern up by his collar. "The same thing that's gonna happen to you. Unless you want to tell us what brought you here in the first damned place."

"I don't know what—"

A blow to the stomach stole Vern's wind and he would have dropped to his knees if Hiram were not holding him. The one with the long hair stepped up and grabbed Vern's face with his hand. His eyes glowed in the darkness, red like an albino alligator's.

"How'd you take the heart without it poisoning you?" he asked. "You some kind of white magic master?"

"No, sir."

"No mere mortal can carry it in their hands."

"I never touched it!"

"So you admit you stole it from the grave?"

"No… er… I mean… Oh, all right. I took it, but I didn't think I was *stealing* so to speak, and I sure wasn't after some dead man's heart. It was the capsule I wanted."

The man let go of Vern's face. "Capsule?"

"Yes, sir. It was made of gold, it was. Had all sorts of mystic engravings on it, a mighty pretty piece indeed. Well worth the taking. That man in the grave certainly didn't need it."

"Where is this capsule?"

Vern looked up and away. "I sold it."

"Horseshit."

"I tell you no lies, sir."

"You'd fib to your mother on her deathbed, Pipkin. The stench of liar upon you is outweighed only by the miasma of your cowardice. Now I'll ask you once last time. Where is the capsule?"

Vern whimpered. If he were socked in the gut again he might just mess himself. From the looks of these men, they would not stop at just another body blow. There would be many.

"Wait," he said. "That's right... I remember now. I was *going to* sell it, but the man down at the general store wouldn't offer a fair price. Yes, yes—I have it at my parlor. I'm the undertaker in Hope's Hill, you see? I must have gotten mixed up about what I did with the capsule, sir. I just made a mistake."

"I'll say you did."

The man nodded to the others and suddenly they were upon Vern with ropes. He squirmed and kicked, fearing he was about to hang at the end of a noose, but there was more than one rope and the loops were being tied at his wrists and ankles. He was dragged through a pile of fresh droppings left by one of the horses, and when the feces filled his eyes he could not see what was happening until it was too late. He heard the men talking, horse hooves shuffling. He felt each of the ropes go tighter around his wrists and ankles, and then he was rising off the ground, his limbs stretching out.

"No!" he cried. "Please, Lord!"

When he managed to blink away the turds he saw four of the men were on their horses, each holding one of the ropes tied around the horns of their saddles. Each horse was facing a different direction—north, south, east, west.

"Oh, sweet merciful God!"

The only man not upon his horse was the leader with the crimson stare. He stood off to the side with a bullwhip in his hands, his hulking frame a soulless shadow, a ghost of utter darkness, inside and out.

"God can't help you," the man said. "Never has."

Vern began to sob.

The leader yelled with a crack of the whip. "He-yah!"

The horses ran in each direction at full gallop, and as his arms popped from his shoulders and his legs broke free from his hips Vern did lose control of his bladder after all. His limbless torso spun in the night as he fell back to earth. Blood shot out of him in arterial geysers, and just before he lost consciousness the leader stepped up to him and kicked him over, face up. The leader took something large and meaty from out his coat and held it over Vern's face, and when the tarry, black liquid dribbled into his mouth Vern realized what the object was.

*

They used the undertaker's pony cart to carry Jasper's corpse out of the cemetery.

Propped up beside the corpse was the undertaker himself, pale from losing nearly every pint of blood but still alive, or at least undead. Dr. Craven stumbled along on his rope. On the other leashes were the saloon girls who'd been used to satisfy the Koyotes' needs along the trails, keeping them from stopping at bordellos or raping villagers. There was no time for such things. Those pleasures were trivial compared to what lied in wait.

The Koyotes and their captives moved down the mountainside, a cavalcade of monstrosities and white slaves journeying like venomous pilgrims across the jagged rock, their horses clinging like goats to crags they struggled to see as storm clouds drowned the moon. And at the head of this hellish procession was Glenn Amarok. He rode atop Belial as a nobleman of the darkest sorcery, the zombie heart of his mentor in his coat and pulsing hot against his breast, telling him all he need know.

Hiram strode up next to him.

"Still surprised we could set foot on that holy ground," he said.

Glenn pushed tobacco under his bottom lip. "T'was the heart's magic. Without it, we may never have passed into the graveyard."

"Why Jasper's body, boss? Is it magic too?"

"This is the Koyote's greatest adventure yet. We owe the boss one last ride."

But this was not Glenn's true motivation to bring Jasper's carcass along. He felt if the heart was this powerful then perhaps the body would prove useful yet.

As may that golden capsule.

CHAPTER XXIII

WOLVES SURROUNDED DELIA.

She'd been running with her baby brother cradled against her bosom, but with each step the ground grew softer, pulling at her heels like quicksand. When the wolf pack closed in, she screamed and dropped baby Leonard, sacrificing him so that she might escape.

She awoke in a cold sweat and gulped back a cry. Even her subconscious mind wouldn't let her forget, wouldn't let her forgive herself. She hadn't given up her brother for slaying when the Koyotes had come, but she hadn't been able to save him either, and it was his death that stung her most. She was the big sister. Leonard was a helpless infant. She'd failed him more than she had the rest of her late family.

Delia wrote her big brothers letters to tell them the tragic news but wasn't sure the address was valid anymore, her brothers working at a logging camp one year and a pig farm the next, cowboy vagabonds to their core. She was essentially without kin now, on her own save for the kindness of Grace Cowlin who slept beside her. Delia was on the floor in her bedroll, having refused Grace's generous offer to take her bed. The woman was a good Christian and

Delia liked to think God brought the schoolmarm into her life as a reward for keeping the faith. Heaven knows He'd tested it.

Feeling restless, she removed the nightdress she'd borrowed and put on her clothes. She went downstairs for a glass of water, gripping the banister in the dark, and when she came into the parlor she spotted Luther Byrne smoking a cigarette on the front porch. She came out to join him. The big man nodded a hello.

"Got another?" she asked.

He took a pouch from his pocket and handed her a paper. Delia had learned to roll cigarettes for her father and older brothers and had the perfect thin fingers for it. Byrne lit her up and she inhaled deep, waiting for the relief a good smoke brought.

"Was hoping you could tell me more," she said.

"Yeah? 'Bout what?"

"Them Koyotes. Figure the more I know, the better off I'll be."

"You aim to see them hang?"

"No, sir. I aim to kill them myself."

Byrne shook his head. "Then you really do know nothin' about them."

"So educate me. You're of their kind—a wolfen. I know they ain't human. I've seen their fangs and red eyes. Men who eat a baby boy can't hardly be human noways."

"They did that?" Byrne said, his eyes downcast. "I am mighty sorry, kid."

She stepped into him. "What are they?"

"Wolfen are only part human. We got wolves inside us, see? A beast within that makes us transform, makes us hunger for human flesh and do terrible things I won't share with a young lady."

"You can't shock me, mister. Not after all I done seen."

He sighed and rubber the back of his neck. With his shaggy hair pushed back, Delia could see the number thirteen tattooed on his neck.

"When you first become a werewolf," he said, "you have no control. You change with the phases of the moon and stars. The planet Mars pulls at your soul. You kill, you rape, you devour—whether you're a wicked man or not. If you join a pack, you tend to transform at the same time, a sort of group cycling. The power of that makes you more aware of what's happening, but it takes time to master your own lycanthropy, to transform at your own will and no longer be a slave to it. Once you hit that phase you're always part wolf, part man, only letting the full werewolf out when you wish to."

Delia flicked ash into the cold winter air. "The one called Glenn said some are born wolfen, but what about the others? How does one become a werewolf?"

"There are a few ways. You can be initiated into a pack by drinking the blood of another lycanthrope. If you're bitten by a wolfen in their full wolf state you have a fair chance of being infected and becoming one or at least gaining some of their abilities, like the advanced hearing of a dog or a more powerful nose. But it's something you have to want. The spirit of the wolfen lies in the hearts of mortals. Some are merely human but still have a beast within that makes them more susceptible to the curse. If you're driven by anger and lust and a desire for violence, you're asking to be wolfen whether you know it or not."

Delia considered this. "And what of you, Mr. Byrne?"

He blew smoke and looked away. "I was a boy then. Just a little younger than you, I reckon. Ran away from this place, ran from all the pain and let my heart swell with meanness. I saw a chance to join a pack and I took it. I knew nothin' about wolfen then, but I sure learned quick. But by then it was too late to turn back."

"But you have now, right?"

"To the best of my ability."

"You're not a Koyote. Just a wolfen who has it under control. That means you can utilize it for good instead of evil."

"You just don't understand."

"Do you not believe in redemption?"

Byrne shook his head. "Some things can't be forgiven."

"God forgives those who come to Him on their knees and let Him in. If there is true repentance in your heart there can be redemption for your soul yet, especially if you offer up an act of contrition. The arms of Christ are open to all God's children."

Byrne stubbed out the cigarette butt. His shoulders had dropped, lowering along with his gaze. He seemed suddenly very tired, drained.

"Sometimes you're just damned, kid," he said. "If God didn't give up on people, there'd be no need for a Hell."

Delia decided not to press the issue of faith. Father had taught her religion was not felt by insistence, but rather by patience.

"There's rumors going 'round town," she said. "Rumors about

the Koyotes."

"Yeah?"

"Some folks say the marshal's building a posse in case they come back. But you're expecting them for sure, ain't ya?"

"Let's just say them folks would be better off shuttin' their yappers and get to packing their bags. Get out while the getting's good."

Something turned over in Delia's chest. There was fire in there, hot as any scorching desert, burning like the Battle of Atlanta. Byrne gave her a hard look.

"You ought leave town," he said, "before you end up like your poor family."

"Nah," she said, her eyes just as hard as his. "I ain't going nowheres. If the marshal wants a posse, I hereby volunteer."

Byrne's sardonic laughter made her scowl. "No lawman in his right mind would deputize a little girl."

"I ain't little. I am nearing eighteen and raised farm strong. Plus, I'm a sharpshooter to the manner born. I'll bet I can drop a horsefly from fifty yards. Won me some ribbons for my shooting, I did. Beat grown men in contests at the county fair year after year since I was but fourteen. Heck, I can wield *any* weapon—even forge them given a straight-peen and anvil. I'd make as good a posseman as any. And after what them Koyotes done to my kin I probably have more a right to hunt them than any of you."

Byrne had no reply to this. Delia flicked her cigarette butt into the night, watching the tiny red light sail in the blackness, reminding her of Glenn Amarok's baneful eye. She would stare into those eyes again even if it meant she'd not live to see another day.

"I'll be a part of this posse even if they don't allow me to, Mr. Byrne. This I vow."

The big man looked at her, as if sizing her up. "Of that I do not doubt. Just remember what I done told ya."

"What's that?"

"Those with fury in their hearts are the ones who turn wolfen the quickest."

Byrne wished her goodnight. He went up to his room but Delia remained on the porch, gazing up at the cosmos, thinking of the power they held over these millions of minuscule earth creatures. It made human life seem so insignificant, particularly her own. It often made it hard to see the glory of God's love, hard to view His gift of life as a gift at all. Mankind had been cast out of paradise. Now there was only a world of horror and pain to live in. She thought of Glenn's harsh words about procreation and human suffering, his macabre antinatalism and bleak godlessness. The words haunted her always, especially when they began to ring true. It made her realize he'd taken even more from her.

Part of her had died along with her family, something snatched from her soul by the claws of Koyotes. It was a part of her more special than she'd realized, the sort of human nature one took for granted until it was suddenly stolen. Love was so easily replaced by pain, regret, and sorrow. It could harm as much as it healed, ruin the very things it had created. She now understood that much of what we learn about love is taught to us by those who've never loved us at all.

She went back inside, going from one darkness to another. In the distance there were the cries of normal coyotes, hunting in the blackness of the rocky terrain, eager for blood.

*

Glenn had loved his father.

His birth father had been a decent man, but it was his second father he'd loved, the prophet Thorn who raised him after the raid on the village. A large group of cavalrymen had ridden into the cult's community and, having caught the villagers in an orgy among flayed and vivisected human bodies, they'd fallen upon them with all the hammers of the law. Glenn had watched in horror as the cavalrymen seized Lady Quilla. The goddess screamed, professing her greatness and warning the soldiers of the retribution of the mighty and dreadful Incan god Viracocha, he who would lay his vengeance down upon their heads if they dared put her in chains.

But the cavalrymen had no fear and no wrath came down from the heavens, no lightning from Viracocha's fingertips, no avenging angels with wings afire. And Lady Quilla herself was shockingly powerless, which more than frightened Glenn. He was disturbed. Why was the goddess unable to defeat mere mortals?

He was even more rattled when he saw Timat, one of the very prophets who'd brought Lady Quilla to them, swing an ax at the attackers only to be shot dead. There was no invincibility, no resurrection. One bullet stole his life away, same as it would any man. It put a sick, hollow feeling in the pit of young Glenn's stomach. As the villagers fought in vain to rescue their goddess, Thorn took Glenn behind a straw shack and led him through a tangle of brush, wiping tears away after seeing his brother killed.

"Why does she not stop them?" Glenn asked.

But Thorn did not answer. He rushed them through the woods, leaving behind the only place Glenn had ever lived, abandoning villagers who had loved and praised him, worshipping him as the golden child. After Glenn sacrificed his parents, Thorn took him in, becoming his new and more powerful father, adding to Glenn's perceived royalty among the village. He was leaving more than a home here; he was leaving a life of luxury and privilege, denied his role of prince.

"Goddess Quilla," he whimpered as they fled. "Please…"

They were the only ones who managed to escape.

The raid killed several of the villagers and the rest were rounded up and brought to the nearest jail. Thorn took Glenn across the range until they reached a small farm and stole a horse from the barn. They traveled north, living off the money Thorn kept in a leather pouch, riches given to him by his worshippers. For days they rode, Glenn riding bareback and holding onto Thorn from behind. They journeyed through a changing landscape, the edges of great cliffs giving way to sandy trails alongside streams of freshwater where they stripped and bathed.

"Where are we going, Father?"

"Home. My old home… and our new one."

Six days later they arrived at a plantation. Upon acres of cotton, African slaves toiled under a merciless sun, the rags of their clothing sticking wetly to their malnourished bodies. Thorn dismounted and guided Glenn off the horse and they walked up to the manor house, a two-story mansion with huge white pillars surrounded by a ring of maple trees bright with summer. On the front porch an old black woman was sweeping. When she saw Thorn she stood up straight and put her hand up to shade her eyes.

"Young Master Pete? That you?"

"Yes, Emmy. I've returned."

"Lordy, lordy. I'll go on 'n fetch master Sherwood. Your pappy'll be so glad to see you." She smiled at the boy. "And you've brought a guest."

"This is Glenn. He'll be staying with us from now on."

THE THIRTEENTH KOYOTE

This was where Thorn had come from. Not the heavens, not some parallel world beyond, but a white's man castle. Glenn learned his father's birth name was Peter Sherwood and he came from relative wealth. And when he gave his own father the bad news about Timat, Glenn discovered the other prophet's name was Jonathan and he was actually a cousin, not a brother. Thorn told his father they'd been riding a steep mountain range when a black bear came out of the woods, spooking Jonathan's horse, and the horse bucked him over the edge of a cliff. Thorn said a search party had proved useless for Jonathan had fallen down the mountain wall and into a river to be lost forever. He told his father Glenn was a young orphan who'd been under his employ and he'd decided to adopt him. The lies, the different names, and the sprawling manor itself made Glenn's mind roll.

"I don't understand," he confessed in private.

Thorn patted him on the head like a dog and rustled his black hair.

"Be patient, my son. All will be revealed when the time is right. You must not lose hope. Lady Quilla is depending on us."

Glenn took this to mean they would return to the village and hunt down the cavalrymen and kill every single one of them, rescuing the goddess and their brethren. But as the days rolled on, it became obvious he'd seen the village for the last time.

One day a lawman came to the manor and Thorn hid Glenn in the root cellar and warned him not to make a sound. He sat huddled in damp darkness among spider webs and Mason jars, listening but only making out some of what was said. The lawman mentioned Jonathan—Timat—and how he'd been involved in some sort of scam, that he'd been shot while trying to evade authorities. This was when Glenn first heard the term *cult* and first heard the name Guadalupe Sánchez. This only brought up more questions, but when he dared asked any, Thorn hushed him.

"This is a test, my son. You have to have faith."

After the visit from the lawman, Thorn and his father had argued, his father calling him a bold-faced liar and a shit. But they stayed on the plantation, Glenn eating better than he ever had before, defecating in a clean, indoor Victorian bathroom and sleeping on a mattress stuffed with feathers. He learned to ride a horse and train the gentler ones. He was taught to wrangle the slaves by cracking a whip, using fear to motivate them when they drooped with exhaustion. His new father was teaching him to how to lead both man and beast using mental manipulation and brutish intimidation.

But it was Glenn who decided to make sweat boxes out of old chicken coops to box the blacks inside of when they got uppity or tried to escape. He kept them locked in these vivariums, curled into a ball so to fit, cooking in the summer heat without food or water, often for days.

As Glenn grew older he lost his virginity by having his way with one of the slave girls. When her brother tried to stop him, Glenn whipped and beat him to the point of crippling him forever. He took to raping the women regularly, impregnating two slaves with babies who would be raised up to become slaves themselves.

For almost two years he had a good life at his grandfather's plantation.

Then the U.S. Marshals came.

Thorn was brought to the jailhouse and Glenn was taken from the plantation by force as his grandfather threatened the lawmen with litigation that would take their badges. At the constable's station, Glenn was handed a gazette. It was of a former year and his old village was front page news, the story covering the shocking case of a crazed cult led by a female charlatan named Guadalupe Sánchez, a Mexican prostitute who'd been rented out to men by her brother since the age of seven. After her brother was stabbed to death in a saloon fight with an Indian, she'd come up through Arizona Territory, selling her body on the streets and robbing her customers at knifepoint.

"They hired her," the constable said. "Pete and Jonathan were two rich cousins out seeing the country. Guess they'd grown tired of their hometown and wanted to experience new things 'n sow their oats. They had no need for money and dabbled in crime just for the thrill of it, robbing stagecoaches and general stores in their travels. When they came upon your village they watched you all from afar and decided to pull their biggest scam yet. Them boys saw an opportunity to brainwash simple mountain folk with cactus wine and penny magic tricks— flashes of gunpowder and such. Cheap illusions."

He waited for a response Glenn did not give. Then he went on.

"They turned the villagers into sex slaves and took them for every ounce of coin they had, promising them a treasure. When the people grew restless, they brought in the whore and dressed her up as an Egyptian goddess or some such. Seems the bitch got more crazy each day."

Glenn sneered when the constable called Lady Quilla the bad name. He looked down at the paper again. A doctor was quoted in the article, saying Guadalupe Sánchez had developed intense religious delusions and had been placed in an asylum while awaiting trial.

"The villagers were pressed to testify against Sánchez, but they all refused to do so. They still believed her to be their goddess. It wasn't until one of these men saw his brother hanged for murder that he came to his senses and started telling the truth. I've suspected for a long time now that Pete Sherwood was involved in all this but his daddy has enough connections and money to buy off Lady Justice herself. But we've got us a new governor now. One who comes down hard on killers. And the public just won't let this thing go. Frankly, neither will I."

Glenn kept his eyes on the floor as the constable went on, lecturing as much as questioning. Glenn gave him simple, one-word answers when he gave answers at all.

"Son, I know you was just a kid. You ain't in no trouble here. But the man in that cell is not your father. In fact, he probably had your daddy killed, along with your mama. The things this cult did, I don't even like to think about, less they keep me up all night."

Glenn glowered. "What happened to her?"

"Sánchez? She was hanged along with the other killers."

Glenn looked away in an effort to hide his tears.

"I know you done been through a lot, son, but I need you to help me. I need you to testify against Pete Sherwood."

It was that day Glenn first developed his loathing for men of the law.

He thought about it now as he led the Koyotes toward Hope's Hill.

CHAPTER XXIV

"THEY'RE COMING."

Russell stood. "You're certain?"

"Certain as death," Byrne said. "I sense 'em. Even smell 'em. They're coming by way of Black Mountain."

"How long do we have?"

"If they don't stop I reckon they'll be here by nightfall."

"Son of a bitch." Russell leaned over his desk, his hands in fists upon the wood. "So we got only but a few hours? I thought you could sense them from farther away than that. Ain't that what led you here to begin with?"

"They're more powerful now that they've got Jasper's heart. I reckon it's cloaked them, made them harder for other wolfen to detect."

Big Chuck Brazzo came out of the cell he'd made a room of, cracking his knuckles and grinning like a jester. "So it's wartime, is it?"

"Reckon so," said Byrne.

"Heh-heh. 'Bout time. I was getting bloody bored."

Russell looked at him. "Thought you said you were happy to have hung up your pistols."

"Yeah, well… guess this old dog still enjoys a foxhunt."

Deputies Jake Dover and Norton Hustley joined the men. Dover already with his hand resting upon the butt of the gun at his hip, as if the Koyotes were already at their door. Brazzo noticed and chuckled.

"Gonna take more than pea-shooters to take down this gang of bastards, kid. But don't worry, I've got something special I've been saving."

Russell said, "What's this I hear?"

"Got me a mean piece of weaponry stashed at home. Didn't want to bring it into town 'less we knew for sure these rascals were on the way. It'd only scare the turds out of every one of yourn citizens. But if'n you've got a tow cart we can go fetch it."

"A cart? You need a whole cart for it?"

Brazzo only laughed. Russell told Hustley to fetch the tow cart from out back, take Brazzo to his village, and come on back in a jiffy. As the two men went out he turned to his other deputy.

"Jake, you go out to Oscar Shies' place and get him on back here, fast as you can."

"Yes, sir."

As Dover went out the door, Russell rubbed his chin, thinking.

"We set up an ambush," he said. "At the edge of town, just down the mountain trail."

"Might could work," Byrne said, "unless they be expecting us."

"Don't suppose you can sense that too."

"Not until they're close enough for it to be too late. I don't know all what powers Jasper's heart has given Glenn the Dreadful. Second sight may be one of them, I don't know. We can set up an ambush but we should protect the town too, in case the Koyotes have separated. Maybe post an assassin on a rooftop."

"No, I think we'll need all the men for the ambush."

Byrne sat on the desk and took out his tobacco pouch to roll a smoke. "Yeah, well, I was thinking of using somebody else as an armed lookout. Someone outside of this here posse."

Russell raised his chin. "Who might that be?"

Byrne didn't answer. He took up his coat and headed toward the door.

"Luther?"

"I've got to go warn Sister Mable and the rest of the church."

"The church? What in blazes—"

"Trust me on this one. I'll go by the chapel right quick. Then I've got just one more stop." Smoke gathered beneath the brim of his hat. "I'll be coming back with a sniper."

*

As Byrne trotted through town he diverted from the main streets so not to see anyone he might know. Behind the rows of buildings he followed a trail that made a circle through the valley wide and let Bo relieve his bladder. They moved on again, closer to the woodland on the edge of town, and over the smell of horse urine Byrne detected another scent. He tested the air and when he picked up on their musk he came down from the saddle and stepped toward the thicket.

One of the wolves poked its head out from a bunker of snow.

"I remember you," Byrne said. "You're a long way from Battlecreek. Didn't you like it there?"

The bulky pack leader took a cautious step. Behind him were the five pups hopping about their mother. The other adult wolves looked on curiously, sixteen of them in all.

"The pack's growing," Byrne said, smiling. "Hope you haven't been snatching sheep from no farmers. Why'd you come this way? You following me?"

The pack leader trotted over to Byrne now and nuzzled against his leg. Byrne petted him and scratched him behind the ear. The wolf made a friendly grumble.

"You probably smelled my horse piddling," Byrne said. "Thought you could gang up on him for dinner. But Bo's my friend too, so you'll have to find yourselves different prey. Here…"

He reached into his coat pocket for the strips of jerky and tallow he carried to keep his urges at bay when he was around tender humans. As he fed the pack leader, the other wolves came forward and gathered around the lupicinus. He fed the puppies and mother first, then offered pieces to the others by hand, emptying the gunnysack.

"You'll find some wild mules up that hill yonder," he said. "Plenty of hares too. But I don't recommend staying in Hope's Hill. There's a mighty evil coming."

*

THE THIRTEENTH KOYOTE

Reverend Blackwell was in the garden when Byrne arrived, raking fallen leaves now that the snow had melted. As Byrne's horse approached the preacher turned and waved.

Byrne tipped his hat. "You see good for a man supposed to be blind."

The preached chuckled. "Tales of my blindness have been greatly exaggerated. I've lost sight in one eye but God replaced it with a more important vision."

Byrne climbed off his horse, his boots rising dust.

"And what do you see right now, preacher?"

Blackwell's face was cracked, white leather. His pale eyes swam behind cataracts, the lids withered around them.

"I see a storm coming," he said.

He pointed skyward and Byrne turned around to see heavy clouds the color of slate. They sulked above Black Mountain like a plume of volcanic ash, churning slowly. It was an ominous change of weather, something more threatening than a rain shower or even a snowstorm. A gentle wind fluttered from the same direction, cold as an icebox.

"Where's Mable?" Byrne asked.

"Down below, feeding Christ."

Byrne put his hands on his hips. "Old man, if I had more time I might finally ask why you let that bleeding go on so long."

"And I'd tell you it was not my decision."

Byrne stepped past the preacher and Blackwell took a few steps toward the mountain in the distance, gazing upon it like a child would a shooting star. When Byrne entered the chapel, Sister Genevieve turned around in the front pew. She held her rosary in both hands clutched to her bosom, tears streaking a face soft with youth. Seeing her, Byrne had to stifle a pinch of hunger for human flesh. He felt the floorboards vibrating beneath his boots. From the door behind the pulpit came an unnatural, reddish light.

"I couldn't bear it," the nun said.

"What's happening here?"

"The Menhir. It's getting... *bigger.*"

Byrne grit his teeth. New hair curled up from the back of his hand.

"I could not bear it," the nun said again. "I could not be in its presence any longer. I'm not as strong as Sisters Mable and Evalena. The Menhir fills my mind with sin and wickedness until I cannot feel God's love."

Byrne began to vibrate just as the floors did. Saliva filled his mouth as his fangs began to inch out. He stepped backward, away from the doorway that led into the underground church where the blood of children struggled to contain the blackest magic. He had to leave. He had to leave *now*.

"Tell Sister Mable," he said, "tell her they're coming."

Sister Genevieve gave him a sad smile. "We already know."

He ran out of the chapel before the Menhir could force him to transform, force him to rip the young nun to fleshy ribbons and violate her virgin insides. He went to his horse, petting Bo to calm himself as the wolf within slowly retreated.

Blackwell came up behind him.

"The sisters had a choice, Luther. Bleed the children or let the devil take them."

Byrne turned to face him. "Bull."

"Not long shall you live to think so, if you don't heed my warning. The Menhir, terrible though it may be, is only one small piece of a mightier evil."

"What in the hell is it?"

"A proper choice of words—*hell*. The monolith has been with us since the dawn of man. Like Stonehenge, it is one of many blocks. Most believe they were here before we were, perhaps as old as God Himself. It is said that Cain slew Abel not with a stone, but a fragment of a monolith, what we call Menhirs. He did so to assure the future of civilization by building cities and fathering a long line of descendants, all of which were influenced by Menhirs. There are lost pages to the Bible that tell of apostles—twenty of them, not twelve—battling through a plague of beastmen to get the monoliths. They succeeded, but lost eight men, and could not destroy the powerful rocks. They could only break them into pieces and scatter them across the world, the many Menhirs put into the hands of the holiest of men and women to be hidden in Christian lands. Separating them lessened the power they had collectively, a power that could end the universe as we know it."

Byrne stroked his chin as he watched the clouds roll like a black ocean.

"So it's some sort of devil stone," he said. "Satan's rock."

"Not just the devil—*many* devils; the collective power of all the sons and daughters of Cain, the servants of Lucifer. The evil is legion." Blackwell took his crucifix in his unsteady hands. "The Crusades and holy wars—all were fought with the Menhirs in mind, whether those battling knew it or not. Even Joan of Arc had a piece of it. She had it sewn into her bosom for she was the most pure soul in all of France. No one else could contain the Menhir's influence. This is why many of her men became so violent and merciless. They could not stay sane in the Menhir's presence, not even with its power muted by Joan's divinity. This is why she was burned at the stake."

"What happened to the Menhir inside of her?"

"It was taken by priests and now lies within the skull of a bishop buried deep within the Catacombs of Paris, an ossuary which holds the remains of six million people. It's been there since 1789, hidden under the bones of ten thousand clergymen."

Byrne shook his head at the ground. "I've heard some crazy stories in my day. And I've seen enough queerness to understand there's more out there than the known world. But this… this… I mean, how in blazes did this Menhir end up in Hope's Hill?"

The thunder groaned and the two men looked skyward.

"It was brought to this country in 1620," Blackwell said, "carried across angry seas by Pilgrims seeking the religious freedom required to contain it. The Menhir poisoned over a hundred souls on that voyage. It was larger then, so it was broken into several pieces and brought to different locations across the land. This particular Menhir came west via the Oregon Trail in the '40s. It was—"

"Damn it, preacherman! I ain't got time for a history lesson! Just tell me why's this object of evil kept in this little town? Hope's Hill is a totally insignificant place."

"Precisely why it was chosen!" Blackwell's face went pink, veins rising at his temples. "Don't you see? If the Menhirs were kept in massive, beautiful palaces such as the Cologne Cathedral, Notre Dame, or the York Minster, it'd be the same as handing out maps to every wicked man alive. These holy shrines to God are the first places they would think to look. But keeping them in small, *insignificant* chapels in underdeveloped country… well, who would think to search there? Even if word got out that they were kept in such places, there are far too many in the world to choose from. It makes detection nearly impossible."

"Not impossible enough, I reckon."

Blackwell took a deep breath. "My son, centuries of study and prayer have blessed us with the best methods of containment we can muster. But evil always finds a way."

The breeze grew colder, biting at Byrne's neck tattoo. The preacher reached into the pocket of his coat and retrieved a large bottle. Byrne was disappointed to see it wasn't whisky. He sure could use some. A bolt of lightning made cracks of pink across clouds that had grown bigger and blacker. The thunder was triumphant, almost musical.

"The Bible says there shall be seven trumpets heard on Judgment Day," Blackwell said. "Each of which brings nightmarish consequence."

Blackwell started walking.

"Where you going?" Byrne asked.

"Everywhere God allows."

Byrne shouted after him but the preacher kept on up the street. "The Menhir, Blackwell! Who brought it here? Was it you?"

"I did not." The preacher didn't turn around as he spoke. "I've dedicated my life to The Lord, but still even I am not holy enough to resist The Menhir."

"Then who?"

The old preacher spoke no more. He walked far up the street, dragging the rake behind him as he sprinkled the soil with the bottle of red liquid. Byrne didn't have to guess what it was. He climbed atop his horse and tapped his heels. As he rode through town he watched the undulating clouds, phantasmagorical tombstones twisting like humongous worms in a dilating sky. Lightning illuminated the storm's underbelly, and as that white light flickered he saw the blackest of the clouds shatter into pieces, swirl through the air and then regroup, only to band back together again.

That ain't no cloud.

It was an enormous flock of ravens, surging as one amorphous blob, tornadic with menace as they danced, as if they were of a single consciousness. Their caws were applauded by thunderclaps and Bo neighed between Byrne's knees, sweat appearing on the horse's taut neck. The air filled with electricity then, causing Byrne's muttonchops to stand on end, and when he sniffed the wind there came a foul, familiar stench.

It was not just the Koyotes he smelled.

It was death.

*

Grace Cowlin had lit a lantern against the dimness in the room and turned it all the way up as the clouds blotted out all sunlight in a false dusk. Delia watched from the window as hundreds of black birds swarmed across the face of the mountain. She thought of a line from one of her favorite poems.

To the fowl whose fiery eyes now burned into my bosom's core... prophet! Thing of evil—prophet still, if bird or devil!

Something within her tightened, this unkindness of ravens making her hug herself. She moved away from the window.

"Delia?" Grace asked.

Before she could answer there was a knock at the door. Somehow Delia knew to take her repeater rifle in her hands.

Though Grace Cowlin pleaded with her not to go, Delia saddled up her pony and joined Luther Byrne on his way back to the station. She spotted Deputy Dover trotting through the streets, issuing a call of curfew, telling the residents to pass the word and get inside their homes. Delia was suddenly breathless, her pulse quickening. The deputy was telling people the coming storm was the cause for curfew, but she knew it wasn't so.

When they reached the stationhouse, the marshal was there with a black cowboy who looked tougher than a crocodile. Russell took one look at Delia and the rifle in her hands and turned to Byrne with wide eyes.

"Are you bloody mad?" the marshal said.

"Says she's an eagle eye with this here repeater."

"An eagle eye? Seems one of them's been... compromised." He seemed embarrassed to reference the whip mark on her face that scarred her eye. "Besides, she's a child!"

Delia stepped up. "I see all right from this milked-over eye, and my other one's clear as day. And I'm no child, Marshal. I'm a woman—a *proud* woman of the Van Vracken family. I come here seeking justice and I'm gonna see it followed through."

"What does Grace Cowlin think of you coming here?"

"She didn't like it but she also didn't take me to raise. She's my friend and a goodly woman but she is not my keeper. I'm my own woman."

Byrne smiled at the marshal. "How 'bout that, Henry?"

Russell looked away. "Can't come it."

"What's that?" Delia said.

"I can't deputize no young girl—er, lady. This here is men's work. Lawmen's work."

Delia came almost toe-to-toe with the lawman. Her eyes drew to flint.

"Who here is your best shootist?" she asked.

"Ms. Van Vracken, please."

"I'll wager you, Marshal. Put me up against your best shootist and, with all due respect, I'll make him look a tinhorn. If I can't out-shoot your man, I'll leave here without another peep. But if'n I win you make me a posseman and let me see my vengeance through."

Russell looked to Oscar Shies and the big man approached Delia, grinning.

"I respect your gumption," Shies said. "But while I'm not one to brag I'm something of a shootist myself. And I must agree with the good marshal when it comes to you tagging along, girl. I'm a father and can't imagine putting a young'n like yourself in harm's way. So I'll take your wager. Three targets. Whoever does the best job wins and when it's done you get on to somewheres safe."

"Only if'n I lose."

"Sorry, lil' miss, but you will."

They went out back of the stationhouse, Delia with her repeater and Shies with his Whitworth. Russell tossed bottles in the air for Shies first. Shies took out two but his rifle misfired on the third. Before it could hit the ground Delia turned and shot, blasting it to bits.

"Figured I'd help ya," she said. When Russell came up with three more bottles, she said, "Throw 'em all at once."

Byrne chuckled. "Lordy, she is cocky."

Russell threw them in the air without warning but Delia's shots rang true, blowing the bottles out of the sky in quick succession.

"Some nice shooting," Oscar said. "Let's try this. Get on that pony of yours and I'll sling up some cans n' such on this here line. You keep stride and hit as many as you can."

He lined up ten in all, the cans and bits of rubbish swinging from the clothesline stretched across the buildings. Delia put Bessy into a full gallop and as the pony flashed past the stationhouse she released the reins entirely, shooting and feeding fresh rounds into the chamber, the bolt growing warmer in her hands. She ripped the rimfire cartridges from the magazine just as quickly, and before she'd passed the station she'd taken out six cans, missing none, and she grabbed the reins with one hand just long enough to turn Bessy around and then came circling back through her own gun smoke, obliterating the remaining targets without missing a single shot.

"Hot damn!" Byrne shouted, slapping his knee. "Now that's some bully shootin' if I ever done seen some."

She rode up to the men and dismounted, her stare now flint making sparks, red hair fluttering in the rising wind like the very flames of hell. Shies stared clapping, not mockingly but genuinely impressed. He turned to Russell and put his hand on the marshal's shoulder.

"Maybe we oughta reconsider."

Byrne said, "We keep her safe as we can. She'll be our sharp-shooter in the sky. Put her right up on the roof of the station here. If we can't keep the bastards from riding into town she'll be here as a reinforcement sniper."

Russell looked at Delia, rubbing his chin, speechless.

"I'm gonna shoot these buggers anyway," Delia said. "Might as well work together."

The sound of iron tire wheels made them turn their heads. Three riders were approaching with pack animals hauling carts. One was Deputy Norton Hustley. The other two Delia did not know, one an Indian and the other a wild-looking white man. But what really drew her eye was their freight.

Clearly these men were ready for war.

*

"What in blazes?" Shies said.

Two donkeys and a reindeer hauled the three tow carts. One of beds held a long, bronze tube. The other held a carriage and wheels. In the third cart was the ammunition—all of it large, round explosive shells.

Russell said, "Lordy, Big Chuck. You brought us a goddamn cannon?"

Brazzo got off his horse. He was adorned in war paint that covered his entire face in a red skull mask.

"Ain't no cannon, Marshal. This here's a mountain howitzer. Just look at this fine, smoothbore twelve-pounder, eh?" He slapped the giant tube. "Ain't she a beauty?"

"Where in hell you'd get such a war weapon?"

"Why, in war, of course!" Brazzo laughed. "We used these mean buggers all the time in the big conflict with the Mexicans, but I stole this one here from a couple of dumb Confederates down in Mississippi. Them Graybacks were so slobbering drunk on 'shine they didn't even notice when my buddies and I looted every bit of weaponry they had."

Shies felt compelled to shake Brazzo's hand. He'd seen him around the Kiowa village but did not know him well, but any man who stole from the Confederacy was a friend to Oscar Shies.

He looked at the Indian who'd come along with them. "Howdy, Charging Bear."

Setimika nodded. "Greetings to you, Oscar Shies." The Kiowa looked to the other men. "Your necklaces, my friends. Now would be good time to put them on."

Setimika dismounted, bringing more of the beaded chokers from his saddlebag. Byrne drew his own from his pocket, as did Russell and Dover. Brazzo was already wearing his. Setimika gave one to Shies and one to the girl too. The Kiowa's was bigger with a third row of beads and what appeared to be the small bones of birds.

"You've come to join us in our fight," Shies said.

The Kiowa's face was grave. "Me have little choice." He raised his face to the rumbling heavens. "There be a terrible storm coming, clouds swollen with the bad blood. Koyotes dragging darkness now. We must fight with all our courage, for they will not rest until they bring endless night."

The posse went into the station, gathering around a table covered in weapons and supplies. There were pistols, rifles, and hatchets. Kiowa blowguns and blades. There were ball rounds and magazines and wadcutters, cleaning jags and blackened pouches of gunpowder. Setimika had an atlatl, a Henry rifle, and a war club furnished from an elk's jaw, the teeth still intact. Big Chuck Brazzo had his rifle, the two pistols on his belt, and a tomahawk he'd sharpened until he could shave with it. Byrne and Shies had their rifles and, along with Marshal Russell, wore Colt revolvers at their hips. The deputies carried their state issued firearms. Along with her repeater rifle, Delia was given one of these, a Smith and Wesson pistol that opened from the top to expose all six cylinders, giving its shootist extra swiftness when it came to reloading.

"Look at these," Brazzo said. He held up three sticks of dynamite.

Russell shook his head. "No. We don't want to blow up the whole town."

"Not the whole town, Marshal, but maybe a small part of it."

"Best put those away."

Brazzo shrugged and put the dynamite sticks into a sack.

Looking at the arsenal laid out before them, Shies swallowed hard. Judging by the weaponry, this wasn't going to be a mere scrape. This was war the likes of which he hadn't seen in many a year. But he'd seen fair action during his days as a posseman. Even when he was owned by Wallace Eagle Stone, his wife's father, Shies had served as Stone's bodyguard and risked his life more than once in gunfights protecting the Choctaw Indians from more savage tribes as well as whites displeased with the notion of a red man having modest wealth. In the years before he was freed, Shies was rewarded for his bravery, being allowed to eat at the house table. He'd been honored at the time but now he figured such a seat was not worth taking that bullet in his left leg and risking being put in a noose by white bastards inspired by the Ku Klux Klan's uprising. What *had* made it worth it was being sat across from Nizhoni whenever it was suppertime. That's where their love began.

He thought of her now, all swollen in the family way, a woman he thought stronger than he could ever be. He thought of his son Tohasan and the haunted look the boy had given him after seeing tears of anger well in his mother's eyes when Shies aimed to leave.

"Why must you do this?" she'd demanded.

"We've been over this, darlin'."

"I wish to talk of it again. You told me your gunman days were behind you, that your toughness was to be spent on breaking horses with badder tempers than your own."

Shies took up his lucky Whitworth. "When evil never dies there's always the chance of one last fight."

"And what of me? I am to stay here, swole up with child with only Tohasan to help me with the horses and bossy? Left to stare out the window in fear of you not coming back? What of *that* evil? The evil of a woman left heartsick by the abandon of her husband?"

Shies took his wife by the shoulders and dragged her to him, locking eyes with Nizhoni for a silent stare. He kissed her brow but she moved away.

"There's no recourse," he said. "If'n I stay here this town may well burn."

"Then let it burn. I'd just as soon dance before the flames of a place that treats us as unwanted, its townspeople who call me red nigger."

"I tell you they ain't all like that, but even if they were I can't sit idle while the Koyotes rip 'em all to hell. It ain't right. There are women and children in Hope's Hill."

"There are women and children in this very house."

"All the more reason for me to fight. I will not let my son think his father a yellowbellied coward."

"Yes. You'd rather he look at you and see a fool."

His wife turned away from him then, her long hair braided at the back, covering her like a second spine. She was so petite, so fragile. Her words came out in whispers in effort to drown out the tremor in her voice.

"Tell the marshal he is a scoundrel for lying to a woman carrying child. Father was right. There is no heart in white men."

Shies shook his head. "I still hope you can unlearn the old man's teachings and see the error in your own prejudice, my darlin'. But that's a fight for another day. As for right now there's a mighty evil comin' down the mountainside, and I aim to see it stopped in its tracks."

He took his hat from the nail upon which it hung and opened the front door. Outside, Deputy Dover sat his horse, watching a mean storm rolling beyond that very mountain. Shies put his hand on his son's shoulder and told him to watch after his mother, that he was the man of the house until his father returned. The boy nodded emphatically and Shies kissed his forehead. But when Shies went to his wife she turned away from his kiss.

"Promise me," she said. "Promise me you will come back alive."

He took her in his arms and this time she did not resist his affection.

"I swear on my sweet mother's grave," he said. "Nothing bad's gonna happen. Least not to me."

Thinking of those words now, he could only hope they were true. The great mound of weapons seemed to say otherwise.

CHAPTER XXV

"SHE WAS RIGHT," GLENN SAID.

Hiram looked to his leader. "Who's that now?"

"Jessamine the Deathless. She spoke of another wolfen out here. Not just a wolfen, but a Koyote. One of Jasper's clan. One of us."

"Hell." Hiram furrowed his brow. "That just can't be right, boss."

"I tell you it is. I can sense his presence down below."

They were walking the horses so not to risk a fall, the trail too thin and craggy on the edge of the mountainside. Hiram didn't know why Glenn wouldn't let them take the easy path into Hope's Hill, the one the grave robber had taken up. Behind them, the rest of the pack was singing "Poor Old Slave", a southern Negro song only Web knew all the words too. For such a goon of a man, he had a high, pretty voice. It reminded Hiram of his time as a choirboy, something he'd rather forget, but he let the men enjoy themselves, figuring they'd earned it on the long, exhausting quest. Towed behind them were their slaves, including the babbling torso of the undertaker in the little cart.

"How's that possible?" Hiram asked his boss. "How could there be another one of us?"

"Reckon your guess is as good as mine."

"Maybe one of the boys put a Koyote baby in some whore."

"That ain't what Jessamine meant. She didn't mean a new litter of puppies, she meant a Koyote just like you or I."

"But we five are the only Koyotes left, boss."

The pack leader spat tobacco over the cliff's edge. "Maybe not."

"You think one of our boys didn't up and die during Jasper's last stand?"

"Thems the only ones I didn't see die with my own eyes. I watched my men drop when we was fighting Injuns, stealing horses, robbing banks or whatnot. But Jasper, Leroy, Corbin and Luther— we didn't actually see them die now did we?"

"No. We were back at that old whorehouse."

"Right. Now we know Jasper done died 'cause I hold his heart and we've seen his grave. We got his bones. The others, though..."

"Come on, boss, They'd of come back to the base if'n they were alive."

"Jessamine only spoke of one. I believe there was just a single survivor of Jasper's last stand."

Hiram pursed his lips, watching his footfalls carefully as the trail tightened further. He thought of his old friends, as if he could analyze them down and figure out which among them had lived.

"Maybe they were locked up," he said. "Maybe this survivor didn't get killed but got himself caught and thrown in the hoosegow. Or maybe he got wounded and had to lay up and hide somewhere for a spell."

Glenn squinted. "And maybe he done changed his mind."

"About what?"

"About being one of us. About riding with the Koyotes."

Hiram grunted. "I can't believe that about none of our fallen brothers."

"The dead have a way of building themselves up in the memories of those they've left behind. We put our dead brothers on pedestals, some of which they don't deserve. Corbin was a mighty good soldier for this pack. He'd have killed his own grandmother if it pleased Jasper. He'd never give up the brotherhood of the Koyotes. But Leroy and Luther, well, I don't know. From what I recall, those two were sometimes weakened by their own consciences."

Hiram sniffed. "I don't recollect. Not that way."

"Hell, they were mean sons of bitches and weren't yellow noways, but they'd come to start feeling guilty for some of the things they'd done and what their brothers were still doing. I think that's especially true of Luther Byrne."

Hiram looked to the west, the sky shrouded by storm clouds. There had been a time when he'd thought Byrne was destined to rise up the ranks before he would. If he had survived the battle and come back to base, he'd surely have become Glenn's right hand instead.

"Thought you two was thick as thieves," Hiram said.

"We *were* thieves." Glenn chuckled. "But you're right at that. I introduced him to Jasper my own self and once he'd drunk of Jasper's blood I taught Luther everything there is to know about being wolfen. Us being the same age, we grew from boys into men side by side, into Koyotes worthy of the brand. We were the young bloods back then. Seems so long ago now, and yet like yesterday at the same time."

Hiram shifted, not used to Glenn showing any sentimentality.

"But see," Glenn went on, "I moved up the chain faster than he and became Jasper's right hand man. After that, things changed between me and Luther Byrne. It wasn't bad blood but just... different, I don't know. But I know this—whichever Koyote is out there, he's not a lone wolf, at least not anymore."

"What're you sayin'?"

Thunder grumbled above, the rocky crag crackled below.

"I'm sayin' this—Jasper's heart has been telling me things, see? Talks to me like his ghost though I can't always make out his words. But he's telling me if'n we take the trail directly into Hope's Hill we'll be walking into a trap, one this Koyote has helped set up for us. That's why we're going this less traveled trail instead of taking the quick route into town."

"Shit. An ambush? How they even know we're coming?"

"A fellow Koyote can sense Jasper's heart, just as we did."

"Damn it, if it is Luther or Leroy or whoever else why in hell they'd want to sabotage us, unless..."

He looked to Glenn as the thought hit him, mean and hard and heavy.

"Unless," Glenn said, "our brother's turned on us."

"Why would they do a thing like that?"

"The *power*. The force behind the blackest of black magic. Ol' Jasper was on to something, see? There's something worth hunting for down in Hope's Hill. That's why he took them boys searching to begin with. What Jasper felt then I feel now. You know I've always been more aware of the presence of the magic than others in our pack. Other than Jasper there's only one man who was ever as keen to its call as I, and that man is Luther Byrne."

They took the long way down the mountain—wolfmen, ghouls, and white slaves marching in a macabre parade, an unkindness of ravens circling above them in black decadence and gray thunderclouds following wherever the men traveled. They stopped on occasion so Glenn could test the air, and when the men complained of hunger they unchained one of the saloon girls and cut steaks from her thighs and buttocks and ate them raw, Hiram chewing on the girl's severed ears and savoring the flavor while the flesh was still warm. The excoriation further weakened the girl and left her in trauma, but still the Koyotes made her march instead of putting her in the tow cart with the undertaker.

At one point, Hiram rode alongside the cart so to speak with him.

"You like your work?" he asked.

Vern looked at him with bloodshot eyes. His gums were still black from the magic gore Glenn poured into his mouth to keep him alive. He was not quiet a zombie for he had not died and returned, but instead was kept at the threshold of death's door.

"You like it?" Hiram asked. "Burying people and holding funerals all the time? Death gives your life meaning? Or maybe you just like gussying up corpses. Putting rouge on them and such—kind of like a girl with her dolly. Is that what you like?"

Vern spoke in croaks. "I do, sir. I enjoy my vocation most greatly."

"Now why's that?"

"The dead make better company than the living."

Hiram laughed. "What about your family? What do your folks think of you being an undertaker and a grave robber?"

"It doesn't matter. Ma and Pa are in hell where they belong."

Hiram laughed even harder. "Well, I reckon you'll be seeing them soon enough now won't ya?"

Vern closed his eyes. "I reckon you're right."

It was late afternoon when they came to the base of Black Mountain and rode through a somber basin, the horses trotting in a smooth gait, excited to be on flat land again. Here the ground was still damp from melted snow and the slush spattered onto their hooves but did not slow them. They were coming upon Hope's Hill from the back end of town, and as they drew closer Hiram spotted a small homestead and a stable of horses. A dark-skinned child was dragging a sack of grain from out of the barn and, when he saw these riders with their human train of the bound and the mutilated, the boy turned and ran, calling for his mother, as if she could save him, as if she could save herself.

CHAPTER XXVI

THEY'D BEEN WAITING TOO LONG, far longer than it should have taken for the Koyotes to come down Black Mountain and enter Hope's Hill. The men kept turning to Byrne, asking him if he was sure they were coming. Back at the station he *had* been sure. Now he wondered if he'd been mistaken.

Brazzo stood on a bluff behind the howitzer, chewing a cigar. Now that it was assembled, Byrne could see just how powerful the weapon looked, a small cannon that packed the same bite. The rest of the men were scattered around the woodland that flanked the road leading into town. Beside Byrne was Marshal Russell, his rifle at the ready, sweat at his brow despite the flurries of snow that flew on the December breeze.

"Something's wrong," Russell said.

Byrne nodded. "Yeah."

"Them boys should've been here by now."

"Yeah."

Russell glared at him. "That all you got to say?"

"What ya want me to say?"

"You're the one supposed to have a sixth sense. You said they'd been coming this way soon. Where are they now?"

"Don't rightly know. I've sort of lost the scent."

"Either you have or you haven't."

"Make it have then."

"So this is just a goddamned goose chase now, is it?"

"No, I sense them all right. They're coming but somehow they've led me off course. The Koyotes can sense me just as I sense them. Mayhaps Jasper's heart has made Glenn better than me at this sort of tracking. Maybe it's even cloaking them."

Byrne sat down upon a fallen log, his rifle resting in his lap. He made a church with his fingers and watched the skies.

"Them thunderclouds," he said. "That ain't no natural weather. That's *them*."

Russell gave him a quizzical look. "The Koyotes?"

"Their darkness is getting stronger—taking physical form. I'd say we could use them clouds to track the Koyotes but they're so big they cover up nearly the whole blasted sky."

"And them birds?"

Byrne leaned forward to better see the swarm. *There must be near a hundred of them ravens now.* Their meaning eluded him, but there was no denying the reason for their presence.

"Birds of death," he said. "Maybe they're celebrating the Koyotes' warpath or maybe they're serving as a warning to us of the Koyotes' approach. Either way they're linked to them."

Russell huffed and began to pace. "I don't like this at all. There's too many of us here if you ain't sure they're even coming this way. I'm a darned old fool for leaving Hope's Hill guarded by nothing more than a tinhorn girl, be her a fine marksman or not."

The marshal looked across the range in the direction of town. He rested the rifle over one shoulder, snow collecting in the brim of his hat. Byrne thought he looked like some sheriff of legend then, a frontier man from some *Beadle's Dime Novels* paperback, determined to civilize a wooly land whether by politics or pistol.

"I'm taking some of the posse back to town," Russell said. "Reckon you best come with. See if you sense them there."

Byrne got to his feet and they made their way through a thicket gone pale. The flurries intensified, promising accumulation, and the intense silence of falling snow gave the woodland an ominous presence, one that had not been there when the men first arrived. Russell gathered Norton Hustley but left Deputy Dover so there'd be a lawman present. Shies stayed behind for they needed a sharpshooter, and Brazzo stuck by his howitzer, not wanting to miss an opportunity to use it.

Setimika chose to return to town.

"The spirits," he said, "they are awakened."

Byrne felt he understood what the Kiowa meant.

The four men rode off, leaving the others to sit back and wait.

*

Delia's breath stopped in her chest.

Five horses, coming on slow.

It was hard to tell from this distance, but it looked as if some of them carried more than one rider. The gray mustang at the head of the formation trotted along with the others seeming to await its every footfall. Delia scooted to the other end of the station's rooftop for a closer look. She forced herself to breathe and steadied her repeater.

There were two riders upon that horse. The one riding bareback behind the saddle was a large man with hair black as coal smoke. She could not yet make out his face for the person in the saddle in front of him, a woman pale as death and slathered in blood, was tied to the man by a length of rope, her head down, filthy hair hiding her face. The man held another length of rope in one hand, a leash for his human-pet who staggered in the lead, his spindly body a black tapestry of veins, mouth bubbling with froth. Delia looked to the other riders, all travel-tough rakes. A second woman was tied to one of the other riders, her limbs bruised purple and yellow. It was hard to tell if she were alive or dead. But what mortified Delia most was the quadruple amputee slung about one rider like a breastplate of flesh. The amputee was still alive, his head bobbing as he spoke back to the man who wore him, a man Delia recognized.

It was the one called Web, the octoroon she'd hit with the hatchet on that fateful day. But while the sight of him made her seethe it was the skinnier man who made her cheeks flush pink with rage. He was the one who'd carried her baby brother by the ankle and called out for a feast.

And there was Glenn the Dreadful, looking rabid-mean with the naked, gore-slicked woman as his shield and a slobbering derelict stumbling at the end of a leash. With his other hand Glenn held the bridle he'd made from Delia's hair. She thought of the promise she'd made to him, a vow of retribution underlined by death.

She put the butt of the rifle tight against her shoulder and her every breath sounded loud as dynamite blasts in her skull. Squinting against the snowfall, she steadied her aim, but whenever she tried to lock in on Glenn his horse would bounce the slumped woman and Delia feared she might kill her instead. The poor girl deserved an attempt at rescue instead of just dismissing her life as a causality of war. But that was if she were still alive. Given the sadistic cruelty of the Koyotes, Delia figured she very well was.

The men passed by Sneck's General Store. Delia recognized the one called Thad. He had no human shield and neither did the young one, Dillon, the bastard who'd wanted to rape her. She drew her aim on him and waited, but for what she did not know.

Shoot him, she told herself.

Delia had no doubt her shot would land true, sending this killer's brains out of his ears. But she hesitated. Though Dillon was more monster than man, she had never shot another human being, let alone killed them. It was different than pulling the trigger on a rusty can. Even when she'd shot living things it was for a purpose, the turkeys and possums making for a good supper. The rifle's only purpose here was vengeance. Was it not foolish to go into it in a rage? If she shot Dillon, the other Koyotes would surely spot her before she could take them all out. They'd return fire and siege the stationhouse, find her on the roof, and rape and murder her, or maybe burn the building with her in it. It would be a tragedy of vanity if she were to believe she could take these men out alone.

And so she waited, watching as the sons of bitches came into town, hiding behind their bound victims, iron at the ready. When Delia saw the bullwhip at Glenn's side she shuddered, the horror of her mother's slaying coming back to her in a vivid, unforgiving flashback. Her own injuries seemed to warm at the sight of it.

Her trigger finger had never itched so badly.

If the men took to attacking unarmed people, would she have to shoot at them? Until then she had to stand her post, had to be patient. Hours had passed since the posse left. Surely the marshal would return to check on her, to check on Hope's Hill entirely. It was best to—

Delia gasped at what she saw.

The one called Hiram was carrying a fetus.

The unborn infant was no bigger than a cottontail, a pinkish doll of slime and membranes. The eggshell of its skull had been opened. Hiram dipped his fingers into the underdeveloped brains and brought them to his lips. Delia would have shot him then if her hands had not begun to shake. Here was the same scoundrel who'd taken the first bite of her baby brother, and now he was eating a child who'd not yet even been born. She urged to turn away but did not want to lose sight of the men for even a second, so she saw when Hiram snapped off one of the infant's fingers, sucked the tissue away, and then used the bone to pick his teeth.

Though Delia did not fire, there was a gunshot.

*

A bullet landed into the chest of the saloon girl in front of Glenn, bursting one breast and putting her out of her misery. He turned in the direction of the gunshot, spotting the barrel of a shotgun sticking out from the doorway of the general store. Glenn drew his iron and fired twice, the door proving a less effective shield than a dead body, and the shopkeeper fell but was still alive, scrambling to regain his rifle as Glenn rode up on him and kicked wide the door. He shot the man in the face and was done with him. If this were the protection Hope's Hill had to offer, the Koyotes would take nary a scratch.

"A-yup!" Glenn called, and all the horses sped their trots.

The townspeople who had been in the street were scrambling to get indoors. Glenn eyed the windows of every building as his men fanned out, searching for any other good Samaritans. Clearly the posse was not here. The sorcery had camouflaged the Koyotes, leading astray the one who'd turned on them. It gave Glenn a solid head start in his search for the capsule the undertaker had spoke of, the one that had contained Jasper's heart while it lay trapped in the grave. He assumed this capsule must be the amulet that held the great power he was seeking, the very black magic Jasper had searched for.

He pulled Uriah Craven back with his leash.

"Where's the funeral parlor?" he demanded.

But the doctor could not speak with his lips and tongue decayed. He could only point the direction with his rotted nub of a hand.

"Move."

He clacked the leash and Craven shuffled forward, taking them

227

past The Green Lily brothel where fledgling harlots watched like housecats from windowsills. As they passed by a boarding house Glenn paused and sniffed the air around it. There were two distinct odors here, that of a Koyote and that of a young woman whose scent was familiar but he could not place. The smells were faint, telling him their owners were not inside. Ahead were the livery and a saloon where a row of horses were tied to the hitching posts, their riders inside and half-drunk, laying low. Just beyond these buildings was the funeral parlor.

"Hardly worth making human shields," Hiram said. "Ain't nobody 'round to stop us."

Dillon said, "Gimmie some of that would ya?"

Hiram tore a leg from the fetus and handed it to him.

"Quit foolin'," Glenn said. "This ain't no time to be cavalier. Hiram, drop that nigger baby and draw your iron."

Hiram pursed his lips, muttonchops still wet with gore, and flung the infant's remains to the street. He drew his pistol and held it shoulder high. His saloon girl winced at the sight of it, having been pistol-whipped daily among other tortures. The other men clutched their weapons as well and as they moved past the saloon Glenn fired at one of the hitched horses, dropping it. Dillon laughed and fired upon the other trapped animals, killing two more horses and a mule. Thad curled his lip, revealing green teeth, and shot the final one through the neck, the appaloosa crying out as it fell into the freezing dirt.

"Be sure to reload," Glenn said. He'd wanted to get his men in the mood for violence but didn't want them emptying all their chambers. "We're bound to have some entertainment now."

A pair of cowboys came out of the saloon with revolvers in their hands. Hiram shot one down before the poor fool could even aim. Taking the bullet to the gut, the man fell forward, tumbling off the porch and into a puddle of slush. His friend popped off rounds as he ran across the porch, trying to dodge fire, but Thad wouldn't allow it. He rode forward and as the man fled Thad shot him twice in the back. The cowboy fell against the hitching post, rolled down among the slaughtered animals, and died like one. Turning back, Thad fired at some of the faces watching from the windows of the saloon, laughing in a blood-fever.

No one else came out to confront them.

When they reached the funeral parlor Glenn raised his hand to stop the procession. The pack sat their horses and he tested the air. The snow was getting thicker now, freezing out all odors. He sniffed long and deep, his every breath puffing like gun smoke. If there were other men waiting with firearms, they'd likely be here. He felt certain they'd be guarding the capsule.

The Koyotes waited. There were no gunshots, no hidden assassins.

Realizing where he was, Vern Pipkin squirmed in his confines. "Home sweet home."

"Hush up," Web said.

"Web," Glenn said, "take the undertaker inside. Have him show you where the capsule is."

Web untied Vern and carried him to the ground with a carefulness that confused Glenn, but then he dropped the undertaker accidentally and two teeth flew out of Vern's mouth.

"Aw, shit," Web said.

Glenn trotting over and booted Web in the side of the head.

"Tarnation!" Web cried, holding his skull. "What'd ye do that for, boss?"

"I didn't keep this here grave robber alive just so you could knock his brains out of his skull. I want him alive until we find what I've come looking for! Now be more careful with him or I'll box your ears!"

Web reached down for the hat that had fallen off his head and brushed it clear of snow. He snorted and picked up Vern and slung him over one shoulder. The undertaker babbled something about a woman named Sarah, professing his undying love as if she were standing there with open arms.

"Seems he's dying anyways," Web said, "or at least his brain is."

"All the more reason to get your arse moving."

As the big man started toward the door, the Koyotes turned back at the sound of another man's voice calling to them from someplace unseen.

"Glenn Amarok!" a man said. "You and your boys just drop them weapons and get down from your horses right slow. We've got you surrounded!"

PART TWO

THE RULES OF HELL

CHAPTER XXVII

TUCKED BEHIND AN ASSORTMENT OF crates, Russell yelled out to the riders with his Colt in hand, Deputy Hustley beside him with the barrel of his rifle sticking out between two stacks of freight boxes. Hearing the gunshots as they'd rode into town, the lawmen took their horses around the backs of Main Street's buildings for cover and snuck up on foot to the post office across from the funeral parlor, just two buildings down from the station where Delia sat sniper. Byrne and Setimika had gone off on their own so the posse could surround the Koyotes to the best of their ability, but Russell had no idea where they were now. There had been little time to form a plan.

Russell grimaced. The Koyotes were a horrible sight, adorned in bloody bodies, one of which he recognized as Vern Pipkin, or what was left of him. Beside Russell, Hustley was silent and rigid, his paleness revealing his frazzled nerves. Russell could only hope his deputy's aim would stay steady.

The leader of the pack trotted forward. None of the Koyotes had dismounted. Something told Russell they wouldn't leave their saddles unless they dropped out of them dead. Behind the Koyotes was a cart carrying a pine box coffin.

"I said drop your weapons!"

Glenn scowled. "On whose order?"

"I am U.S. Marshal Henry Russell, representing the town council! Me and my deputies been expecting you boys, and we're damned sure ready. Now you can bet your very lives on that, or you can give yourselves up."

Glenn spat. "And face a hanging."

"I don't run a lynch mob, Amarok. You'll be given fair trials, same as any."

"With a jury made up of the people of Hope's Hill?" Glenn chuckled. "We've been in this town less than an hour and already slain their sons and neighbors and horses. You think they'll give us a fair shake, do you?"

"It was your choice to come in shooting. Now if you turn yourself in peacefully it'll look well in the eyes of a judge."

"*Peacefully*?" This time when Glenn chuckled, the other Koyotes joined him. "Marshal, you know who I am—know my gang. Surely you must be aware that Koyotes never do anything *peacefully*."

The hair on Russell's arms stood up. He peered over the barrel in front of him, searching for any sign of Byrne or Setimika, of some kind of ambush no matter how sloppy. His grip on the Colt grew moist. Though coming slow, the Koyotes were indeed coming.

"This is your last warning, boys!" Russell said. "Lay down your guns!"

Russell gasped as the eyes of each Koyote shone the like garnets. Their smiles bore jagged fangs and their whiskers rose as if triggered by static. Glenn clacked the leash and his naked prisoner began pulling like a dog, foaming at the mouth as if rabid. The Koyotes growled, their horses snorting mist into snow that flew sideways, and the sky echoed the mad caws of ravens, a flapping circle of doom spiraling closer to the earth.

Russell was pulling the hammer back on his Colt when a shot came down from above. At first he wasn't sure if it were a gunshot or crack of thunder, but then he saw the youngest of the Koyotes knocked off of his horse in a spray of red.

It was a shot that unlocked all of hell.

Atop their horses, the Koyotes unloaded upon the lawmen's meager barricade. Slivers of wood exploded about Russell's body, splinters nicking his face. He had to squint to protect his eyes and so his shots flew wild. Hustley popped off his rifle, sinking a round into the neck of Thad's paint horse. It crumbled into itself and Thad became pinned under it, screaming as his leg broke beneath the horse's weight. Web, still on foot, ran to his fallen brother, blasting off his pistol with the limbless undertaker swinging from his shoulders like a grotesque medallion. Russell would have returned fire if he'd not feared killing Vern Pipkin, but as Web knelt to Thad's side his back was turned and Hustley shot the man in his bottom. Web howled like the beast he was and rolled through the snow clutching his butt.

Glenn charged, a fearless predator, and unloaded upon the lawmen as they cowered behind the crates. The wood was being obliterated. Soon they'd have to run. Russell came up from his hiding when Glenn's pistol clicked empty and shot at him, twice hitting the dead girl tied to Glenn, but the third bullet went into the pack leader's arm, causing his pistol to fall from his grip.

Another shot rang out from the distance and hit Hiram in his shoulder. He winced but did not buckle as a mortal man would. Russell watched the Koyotes. Their wounds were dreadful but they seemed to shake off the pain like so much fleas. Another of Delia's shots blew Hiram's hat from his head.

"Assassin!" he shouted, pointing.

Hiram clacked the reins and his horse galloped toward the stationhouse. He'd spotted the girl. Russell grit his teeth. *Where the hell are Byrne and the Kiowa?* He turned to Hustley to tell him they had to make a break for it, but before he could get the words out a round ripped through the deputy's face, obliterating his cheekbone and rising upward to exit the back of his skull. A nugget of brain matter splattered against the post office window. Hustley fell forward, knocking down what remained of the freight box, and Russell shouted the man's name as if he could hear it, as if he ever would again. Glenn was still atop his horse, his rifle drawn from the scabbard and smoking from the kill shot. Russell returned fire and when his pistol ran empty he pulled Hustley's revolver from the dead man's hip. He managed to shoot Glenn in the neck this time. The outlaw slumped forward and his startled mustang trotted away from Russell's gunfire.

Web fired upon him. He was lying behind Thad's fallen horse, using it as a bunker. Bullets rose tufts from the ground surrounding Web, Delia trying to assassinate him, but he'd swung Vern over his back so she only aimed at his legs. The amputee was cackling with laughter, his mind gone. Russell spotted a shadow to his left. Through the gun smoke came Dillon, who had gotten back to his feet and snuck up on him. Russell did not have time to turn and fire before Dillon started shooting, so he tucked and rolled, one bullet nicking him, opening his coat sleeve and the flesh beneath it. He fell onto his back. Dillon raised the barrel of his gun and gave Russell a smile brightly crazed, and as Russell's eyes closed he thought of his late wife, Caldonia, and what she'd once told him.

Henry, you seek justice and meaning in a world that lacks both.

These words had stayed with him always, for his wife had spoken them just a day before her suicide.

Dillon spat blood. "Say your prayers, you shit."

But Russell was godless. He tried to remember Caldonia's face, the soft and lovely features that had won her a beauty contest in her youth, but his memory was hazy and Grace Cowlin's face seemed to merge with that of his dead wife. The schoolteacher might have been good for him, might have been something to live for. As things were now, he found life was not so much to surrender, though he resented it being taken by this dumb animal of a man.

"You'll hang for this," Russell said.

But he wouldn't.

A pole appeared in Dillon's chest, a pointed spearhead at the end of it, dripping with gore that steamed in the cold. Feathers attached to the atlatl ran heavy with blood. Dillon's eyes and mouth went wide and he paled and dropped his firearm as he clutched at the spear with both hands. He fell to his knees, the spearhead having been driven through his back, ribs, and one lung.

Behind him stood Setimika. Dillon turned on his side, trying to draw the atlatl from his body, but it was too long and when he moved it he cried out in agony. He thrashed and kicked at Setimika, so the Kiowa got down on one knee, raised his jawbone club, and hammered Dillon in the face until he lay still.

Setimika's beaded necklace was pulsing with blue light. Russell wondered if his own necklace was too, if they'd made it possible for Setimika to get there just in time to save his life. He turned away when Setimika's blade came out. The Kiowa pulled Dillon's head back by the hair, slicing the flesh at the hairline, and scalped the young man, exposing bright tissue as the cap ripped free.

Russell asked where Byrne was but he'd gone temporarily deaf from the gunfight and couldn't even hear himself. Web had reloaded and was firing at them again, so Russell snatched up his Colt and the men ducked behind two rain barrels at the other end of the porch, Setimika tucking away the scalp and drawing his bow from off his shoulder instead of the Henry rifle crisscrossed over the other. He pulled an arrow from the quiver and shot it in an arc. Web cursed and ducked low behind the horse, but the arrow went through his arm anyway. He yelped like he'd stepped into a bear trap. Another shadow moved up on Russell just as he was reloading his Colt and Setimika launched an arrow straight ahead, piercing through the undead Dr. Craven's neck, tossing him down into the snow. He would never rise again.

More bullets fell from heaven. Web cursed as Delia landed a round in his thigh, and then he got up to make a run for it but found himself limping. He fired upon the men to cover himself, leaving behind Thad who was still stuck under his dead horse. In his pain Thad had sprouted hair all over his body and his clothes clung tightly to his bulging, wolfen form. His face had transformed, snoutlike, his bared teeth a picket fence of fangs. He shoved at the horse's carcass and it began to budge.

Russell peered through the smoke but was unable to find Glenn. He wondered if he'd managed to kill him but doubted it would be that easy. Hiram was long gone.

"We have to get to Delia," he said. "Where is Byrne?"

"At your station," Setimika said. "He lies in wait for wolfen he know will come."

*

Glenn raised his head with some difficulty, but the bullet was already being forced out of his neck, pushed by the very tissue it had punctured. The muscles in his arm had shoved a round out too and it was sealing up quicker than his injuries ever had before. Jasper's heart pumped in his pocket, a black mist coiling around Glenn's torso, healing him, guiding him. The golden capsule awaited, but first he had to see this posse suffer and die. Trotting Belial toward the stationhouse, he undid the ropes and let the dead saloon girl fall away. Her arm shattered when she hit the ground, folding up behind her back in a cruel question mark, as if asking her creator why she'd been forsaken.

Up ahead, Hiram had reached the station and swung out of the saddle. He'd pulled his Wesson from the scabbard but the bullet in his shoulder made him struggle when he tried to place the butt of the rifle to it. He too had discarded his human shield, but his saloon girl had survived the battle. She was curled up in a ball upon the snow, shivering and whimpering, her eyes sunken into sockets purple with bruises and sleeplessness and the kind of madness one never returns from. Rather than showing mercy by shooting her, Glenn swung out of the saddle and used her for a landing pad. The woman groaned as her breath left her and something in her back popped, the sound giving Glenn a ripple of pleasure.

He'd lost his favorite pistol when the marshal shot him, so he refilled the holster with his spare revolver he kept in his saddlebag. A bullet whizzed by him. He sprinted with the mustang's reins in hand, guiding it to the alley and hitching it there. Hiram had left his horse to run wild but it remained in the alleyway, waiting for its master. The cart and coffin had been abandoned.

Hiram pressed his back against the wall of the station to avoid the fire of the rooftop's assassin. Glenn went to him.

Hiram sneered. "Think it's our boy up there? The dissenter to the pack?"

"I reckon."

"Mighty cowardly to hide up on that roof. That ain't the Koyote way, playing it safe."

"He ain't safe."

Glenn shattered a window with the butt of his rifle, knocked away the shards of glass, tossed his rifle inside, and climbed in. The stationhouse was dark, the dim light of the late December noon drawing shadows across the walls. Every corner posed a threat, every doorway as dangerous as the entrance of a bear cave. Outside, Hiram had stepped away from the wall in a fruitless effort to shoot at the sniper.

As Glenn got to his feet, a claw sprung out of the darkness, taking him by the throat. The bullet lodged in his neck popped out and fell to the floor and Glenn grabbed at the wrist of whoever was choking him. All he could see was the blood-glow of the wolfen's eyes.

He sniffed the air. "*You!*"

Glenn's long-lost brother leaned closer.

Luther Byrne had aged, his face worn from many tragedies, his skin the color of canyon rock. His muttonchops hung long, a touch of gray coming in. But there was no mistaking his wolfen kin no matter how far he may have wandered from the pack. In Glenn's pocket, Jasper's heart heated up, enraged by the dissenter's presence.

Glenn said, "Fifteen years, ey, Luther?"

He shook himself free and Byrne drew his Colt, aimed it.

"Best not go for that iron at your hip," Byrne said.

Glenn's canines inched up. "Bold talk for a man who hides during a shootout. Your friends could have used you back there."

"They ain't no friends of mine."

"Oh, that's right. Turns out you've always been one to backstab your friends, ain't ya?" Glenn spat the last bit of blood from his mouth, the neck wound sealed now, developing scar tissue. "Or did you just forget your way back to the pack all them years ago?"

"I've got a good memory."

"Why, Luther? *Why?* Hell, you were a high-ranking member of this company. You're the thirteenth Koyote, dammit. Think of all the men you could have led. There've been many after you, up to almost fifty over the years."

"You're down to five now."

Snow fluttered through the open window on a mean gust.

"We've lost more than a few Koyotes," Glenn said. "After Jasper died, some of the boys didn't take kindly to me taking over. Had us a civil war, you might say."

Byrne smirked. "Some brotherhood."

"That why you left, Luther? Huh?" Glenn tilted his head, a dog awaiting a trigger word. "Our pack not good enough for you?"

"Guess I didn't want to ride with a bunch of buggers and cold-blooded killers no more."

"You're one to talk, you murdering son of a bitch." Glenn guffawed. "Hell, I've seen you burn men, women, and children alive just because you wanted to see a church house go up in flames. I've seen you force a fuck from plenty a woman who tried to kick their way out from under you."

Byrne nodded. "That was before I had control of myself, control of *it*."

"Bull. I think you just turned yellow. You got some kind of abscess that done grown in you, like a horse with something caught between its hide and the saddle. That abscess is your vanity, Luther. You think you're too good to be what you were born to be, that you can redeem yourself. But a Koyote is always a Koyote. Instead of letting that abscess fester you should've cauterized it. Nipped it in the bud before it done ruined you."

"I ain't ruined. It's you who's about to die."

Jasper's heart hissed in Glenn's pocket, whispering to him on slivers of black smoke that sluiced into his pores. He knew the truth now, confirming his suspicions.

"You mean like you killed the last leader of the Koyotes?" he said.

Byrne's face twitched but he said nothing.

"After all Jasper done gave you, you betray and murder him?"

"All that old bastard gave me was a curse."

"Bull to that too! I pray you—why'd you do it?" He bared his fangs, a growl growing in the back of his throat. "It was the sorcery wasn't it—the black *ju ju*? Jasper finally found it but you wanted it for yourself. Only you were too weak to take it into your cowardly soul. The force of it would just leave you curled up in a pool of your own piss. Ain't that right, Luther?"

Byrne cocked the hammer of his Colt. "I didn't want it, but I also couldn't let him take it. I may be a bloody, lowdown, murdering son of a bitch, but that don't mean I want to open the gates of Hell."

Glenn leaned in, smiling in excitement. "It's that powerful is it? Tell me, I must know."

"Doesn't matter now."

"Like hell."

A window exploded.

*

As the werewolf crashed into the stationhouse, Glenn went for Byrne's gun and it went off, hitting Glenn in the stomach but not slowing him down. Byrne tried to shoot him again but Glenn had both hands on the barrel now, unhampered by the heat of the iron. Byrne spun, taking Glenn with him as the Koyote who'd come through the window lunged. It was fully transformed except for one leg, which was still in human form and all broken and twisted, forcing him to run on all fours. From the scent of this wolfen, Byrne knew it was Thaddeus Bowman, Koyote number twenty-two.

Outside the stationhouse a hail of gunfire commenced, additional rifles and pistols popping off as other gunmen came upon the station. Byrne could only hope some of them were on his side. He tried to twist against the two Koyotes but Thad had knocked him to the ground, pinning him as Glenn ripped Byrne's iron away. He aimed it at Byrne's chest but then froze as he looked into his old brother's eyes. Byrne's teeth grew so quickly his gums bled. Fur climbed up his neck and his nostrils turned black.

"Thad," Glenn said. "Get off him."

Thad hesitated, his wolfen form filling him with a bloodlust that was nearly irresistible, but Glenn snapped his jaws and Thad cowered back, resting on his one good haunch. Glenn holstered his pistol and smiled down at Byrne, the smile of a holy man about to put someone on the rack for blasphemy.

"Can't just shoot you," Glenn said. "Wouldn't be proper."

As Byrne got up on his elbows he realized Thad had raked his torso while pouncing. His shirt was shredded, four cuts weeping blood.

"On your feet," Glenn demanded.

Byrne rose, not so much scared of dying but definitely scared of failing. His life was expendable, even to him, but he couldn't let these bastards win, couldn't let them bring black hell from a malevolent dimension behind this universe.

"You're a betrayer," Glenn said. "Need to make an example of you, Luther Byrne, a message for wolfen and mankind alike. The world needs to know what Koyotes do to those who dare cross them."

He reached into his coat and produced a long kris dagger, the blade curved like a slithering snake. Byrne recognized it well. They'd made many human sacrifices in the name of Mars, tearing out the entrails of young virgins after cutting them from their gullet to their sex. It was always Glenn who did the honors. He had a certain knack for offering up sacrifices, as if he aimed to please a god he'd once failed. Byrne had never done these killings himself, but he'd not tried to intervene either. It was all part of being a Koyote.

"You want to make a sacrifice of me?" Byrne asked. "First you got to take me. Think you can do it, ol' boy, or are you too yellowbellied to find out?"

Glenn smirked. "You don't really think you'll win this war, do you?"

"I ain't alone in this here scrap. You might rip me apart but we ain't gonna let you rip the goddamned world in two."

Outside a nightmare raged—rifles blazing, horses braying, people screaming. He heard the battle cry of the Kiowa and the footfalls of the girl running across the roof overhead. He smelled blood and terror-sweat and tears of pain.

Bullets whizzed through the stationhouse's walls. Another window burst. Byrne dove into Glenn to tackle him but a stray bullet struck his side and he fell short. Glenn ran in a crouch to his rifle on the floor. He turned to Thad and clicked his tongue, and Byrne's heart sank as the werewolf ran up the stairs.

*

The idiots stood at their windows. Some of those further away were even on their porches. Russell grimaced. What was the point of upholding the law when the townspeople you'd sworn to protect put themselves in harm's way just for entertainment?

He and Setimika had reached the station but so had the Koyotes. From the alley, the outlaw Hiram Zeindler was keeping Russell and the Kiowa back with his Wesson rifle, tucking behind the corner when they returned fire. Setimika had slung the Henry rifle from his shoulder in favor of the bow and continued the gunfight when Russell scanned the surrounding buildings for signs of Glenn and Web. Delia had shot Web in the leg and ass but after seeing Thad toss his dead horse off himself to escape, Russell didn't doubt Web could be running at full speed. Russell saw no sign of him but when he turned back he noticed the long barrel of a rifle coming out of a broken window in the stationhouse. Setimika was too busy exchanging fire with Hiram to notice.

"Get down!" Russell shouted.

But it was too late.

The rifle cracked and Setimika spun, a ring of gore suspended in the air for an instant before raining down. Setimika collapsed, clutching his chest and spitting up blood. Russell put his hands under the Kiowa's armpits and dragged him behind the cover of a horse-watering basin.

"Marshal," Setimika wheezed. "Leave me be."

"No. I'll get you to a doctor. You'll be—"

Setimika's face began to change. The skull shifted, crackling as it became boxier. His eyes went dark and fur pushed through his skin.

His mouth came open with the grin of a grizzly bear, his tongue huge and gray behind the jaws.

"Even bears cannot survive a heart shot," Setimika said. "The spirits are calling me home for the great comfort. Here." He took the bloody scalp from his side and passed it to Russell with a hand becoming a paw. "The hide of coyotemen make one a skinwalker, only for a short time. Use it, Marshal. Use it here or die beside me." The Kiowa reached to his hip for the jawbone club still tacky from caving in Dillon Boody's face. "We can club a man to death, but a wolfen we must club ten times as hard to get same result."

He handed Russell the jawbone club, then motioned to his glowing blue necklace, urging Russell to take it too. Russell unhooked it from around Setimika's neck.

"Save this world," Setimika said. "Save my loves and children."

The Kiowa's eyes closed.

Then he died.

CHAPTER XXVIII

THE ECHO OF GUNSHOTS DREW them from their post. Oscar gathered the reins of his horse and though Dover was the lawman he looked to the older Shies for advice, as if he were the one in charge.

"They're in trouble," Shies said. "Let's ride."

He turned to Brazzo who was still behind the howitzer.

"You stay here," Shies told him. "Maybe we can ambush these boys yet."

*

His side was still screaming from the stray bullet he'd taken, but as Byrne continued to transform the round began to ooze out, as if it were the head of a squeezing zit. He got to his hands and knees, breathing heavy as he crawled toward his pistol on the floor. Glenn heard him and turned away from the window, his rifle still smoking after shooting Setimika. Byrne had already gut shot him and when Glenn walked he bent at the waist in an effort to thwart the pain. The two Koyotes held their wounds, similarly weakened.

But Glenn was healing quicker than Byrne was.

"Fight me now," Byrne said. "While we're equal."

"You flatter yourself."

Glenn tossed the rifle and came at Byrne with nails like vulture talons, and as he lunged Byrne lunged back, their jaws unhinged with canines turned to tusks, coats ripping at the seams as their backs ballooned with muscle, hair turning coarse as a boar's and eyes bright as bonfires. A slithering veil of evil coiled about Glenn's limbs, a living fog that steamed out of Jasper's throbbing heart as it whistled like a teakettle. The darkness came at Byrne with tentacles of smoke, wanting his soul for itself, and as it blew across his snout he smelled the miasma of rotting flesh and bubbling bone marrow.

The Koyotes collided like locomotives, crashing and thrashing, ribbons of skin tearing free from their bodies, fur filling the air. They roared, mountain lion mean, and bit at each other's ears and gnawed their skulls and tore hunks of flesh away, moving as one and cracking the hardwood floor beneath them in great, thunderous rolls. Glenn flung Byrne across the room and he slammed into a framed picture, knocking it from the wall, but Byrne rebounded off the opposing wall with both legs and shot his body like an arrow, landing claws-first into Glenn. They rolled and roared. Glenn was growing stronger, inculcated by Jasper's sorcery, and he picked Byrne up over his head and body-slammed him down onto the marshal's desk, splitting it in half and sending a broken plank through Byrne's back. Pain seized him, but he moved just in time to dodge when Glenn jumped, and Glenn crashed into the remains of the desk. Byrne grabbed him about the ankles and spun, sending Glenn flying through the station's front door and into the street.

*

A monstrosity came for her.

It had burst from below the roof hatch like a cannonball and flew into the air some fifteen feet above Delia's head. She shrieked. This was not the *half wolf, half man* state she'd seen the Koyotes in before. But for one crooked human leg, this was a *full* werewolf, a colossal creature from the most terrible dream. He roared in the snow and wind and she raised her repeater and fired. The Koyote yelped before hitting the rooftop with a thud. Delia shot him again. Then again.

The monster charged her and as her rifle went off he batted the barrel away like it was no more than a fly and it spun from her grip, flew over the edge of the roof, and disappeared into the alley below.

"No!" she cried.

The Koyote took her by the throat and lifted her in the air, his one hand so large it closed completely around her neck, throttling her. He brought his hideous face so close to hers his spittle hit her lips when he howled and she shut tight her eyes. The beast stank of gore and sulfur and ugliness. He carried her like that, her feet kicking helplessly.

He's taking me to the ledge!

Delia had almost forgotten about the six-shooter the deputy had given her. She grabbed for it just as the Koyote reached the rooftop's end and unloaded it into him, emptying each chamber. His grip loosened and as Delia was dropped she thought she might land on the roof yet but she missed it by mere inches and flung her arms forward to grab the ledge, barely catching herself. She swung two-stories high, then started to pull herself up, but the werewolf, though he lay on his side bleeding, gnashed his jaws at her and she pulled back, loosing her grip, and as she fell she cried out, the Koyote watching her from the ledge, his wounds pouring blood down her screaming throat.

*

A pair of beasts tumbled out of the stationhouse.

Russell watched them slash and bite, the snow below them turning rose red.

He almost couldn't believe what he was seeing.

Byrne?

He heard Delia scream and when he looked up she was falling out of the sky. Russell gasped. The girl hit the porch's overhang roof, but at least she hadn't fallen both stories to the street. She was shaking and hacking up blood. From somewhere on the roof there was an animal mewl of agony, but Russell knew it was partly human.

He turned to where Hiram had been hiding in the alley, but hadn't seen the outlaw or heard him fire in some time now. He wondered if Hiram was out of bullets or if it was a mere ruse to get Russell to come out from behind the watering tank. And he had still seen no sign of Web Tipton. That bastard could be anywhere. Still, he had to get to Delia and help her down from the overhang. As for

Byrne...

The werewolves were in frenzy. They tore and ripped and mangled and mutilated. One had a black coat of hair, the other the color of chimney smoke, their clothes tight on their bodies, seams splitting. Russell took the black one to be Glenn—the one who appeared to be winning. He was straddling Byrne now, raking his chest, and the ravens made a tornado of feathers all about them, knifing through the black smoke enshrouding the beastmen. The snowstorm went pink with lightning and the thunder roared as if it too were a werewolf, the largest and meanest of them all. And as Glenn brought up his hand his claws glowed with a strange light that was not light at all, a dark luminescence that shined like polished onyx.

Russell took aim.

CHAPTER XXIX

NECKERCHIEF IN HIS TEETH, WEB broke off the tail of the arrow in his arm and then pulled at the arrowhead lodged in him, trying to get the damned thing free. Splinters pierced him from the inside and he grunted into the knot. His arm hurt. His legs hurt. Even his butt hurt from where he'd taken a shot to his setter. The pain had almost made him transform but he didn't want to go that route yet. He wasn't as good at controlling his shapeshifting as some of the other Koyotes were and wanted to have his wits about him, dullard though his brothers thought him to be.

He pulled the arrow further, sweating and hollering into the wadded neckerchief, and when it finally popped free it dragged the end of a torn vein with it and blood poured out like an overturned bucket.

"Tarnation!"

He removed the neckerchief from his mouth and tied it tight around the wound, cursing, then took his flask from his pocket and poured some whisky under it, then took a long chug for himself. He leaned back against the standing cabinet.

Web didn't want to get shot anymore and sure as shit didn't want to take any more arrows. He was mighty sick of this adventure.

Maybe Glenn cared about this stupid capsule but it didn't mean a lick to him. Looking at it now, Web wondered what in the hell was so important about it. The damned thing didn't lure you in like Jasper's heart did. It was just a big ol' golden egg.

"More like a stinkin' goose egg if'n ya ask me."

The funeral parlor wasn't much, but at least it had a roof and walls to hold back the cold. Out on the range he'd had only a bedroll—not even a tarp to cover it with when bad weather came. He wasn't as young as he'd used to be. The cold was meaner now, as sadistic as Glenn himself was to keep them traveling this long. The ground was harder to get rest upon. Web was saddle-sore and his horse had worn down its hide. Poor thing needed new shoes and a long rest. Hell, so did he.

Web knew he should get back to the battle, but wouldn't be much good if he didn't stop and lick his wounds first. Wolfen or not, he didn't heal as quickly as the rest of the pack, another kick in the balls caused by old age. Web had always thought turning fifty was something that happened to other people. He'd hoped being wolfen would keep him young forever, that he'd never die. He'd been a damned fool.

Taking another pull on the flask, he tried to get up and his legs twitched and the wounded tissue twisted into charley horses of pain.

"Son of an onion." He shook his head, remembering the face he'd seen up on the rooftop of the stationhouse. "Crippled by a little ginger who done ass-shot me. Tattooed by an Injun's arrow. Here I am bleedin' like a stuck hog and for what? All so Glenn can have this highfalutin', goddamned egg." He dropped the capsule and let it roll against his boot. "Shoulda been me who took over this damn company, not him."

The sound of gunfire was dying down. Web scooched across the floor and got up on his knees to look out the window and his hat fell back, the stampede string catching it at his neck. He'd already reloaded his pistol, just in case anyone had seen him duck into the parlor. Had he not been so low on ammo he might have put a bullet in this babbling undertaker propped up in the corner, but maybe there'd be use for the bastard yet.

"Got any laudanum in here?" he asked.

Vern blinked out of sequence. "Certainly not. That's a bad habit indeed. Addicting. Why, my brother fell into the opium and he told me that—"

"Yeah, well, I need something for the pain. Ain't ye got nothin'?"

"I'm an undertaker, sir, not an apothecary."

Web looked to the bottles of liquid on the counter. He squinted at the labels even though he was almost totally illiterate.

"What's all them say?" he asked.

"Those are embalming solvents. You wouldn't want to ingest those."

Web sighed, glowering. "Fine then. What's the fastest way out of this town?"

"Past the stationhouse, I reckon."

"Dammit. That's the fastest way to the grave, ye dang fool."

"Oh no, no. The graveyard is by the chapel. Unless you mean the one on the mountain, where I was so lucky as to come across you gentlemen."

"Ain't what I mean and ye know it. I need a quick way out of this stinkin' place, but one that'll keep me hidden. There's gotta be a trail or somethin' behind these here buildings."

"And leave your dear friends behind? *Tisk tisk*."

"Don't shake your head at me, Pipkin! I'll put *you* up in that graveyard and bury ye alive 'less you help me!"

Vern's eyes rolled back as another shiver went through him. He slobbered but had no hands with which to wipe his chin. Web had seen men in this state before, possessed by a voodoo zombie curse. It wouldn't last, though. Eventually Vern's brain would turn to black pudding and his blood would freeze in his heart. When Vern's eyes settled he looked at Web, a rictus grin distorting his face into a joker card.

"I can't save ye," Web said, "but I can give ye a quick and easy death, rather than let you suffer this one. Now are—"

"*Mysterious death!*" Vern shouted, "*who in a single hour, life's gold can so refine, and by thy art divine, change mortal weakness to immortal power!*"

Web blinked. "What'n the hell does that mean?"

"It's Louisa May Alcott, sir."

"Who?"

"The great poet. She wrote like an angel plucked from heaven."

Web blinked again. "I don't give a good goddamn 'bout some bloody scripture written by a heartsick whore, you idgit!"

He moved to Vern and lifted the man's chin with the barrel of his pistol. Vern's flesh was a summer cloud fraught with vein clusters like Daddy-Longlegs spiders. The stumps where his limbs had been oozed blackly, bits of spoiled meat dribbling off broken, protruding bones.

Web picked up the golden capsule.

"Giddy up, undertaker. Let's get back to that tow-cart. Us and ol' Jasper's corpse are gettin' the hell outta here."

CHAPTER XXX

MISFIRE.

Russell had a clear shot at Glenn Amarok, but Setimika's Henry rifle failed him, the bullet never coming when he pulled the trigger. He tried again but there were only more misfires, so he threw the rifle down and cursed.

The battle of the werewolves was now one-sided. Glenn was slashing Byrne and slamming his head into the earth like he was trying to split his skull in half. Russell had to do something and do it fast.

He looked to the bloody scalp of Dillon Boody and remembered what Setimika had said about its temporary power. His face soured at the thought but he took off his hat and put it on the ground.

"Jesus…"

He placed the scalp upon his head like a powdered wig and it clung sticky to his hair. He wiped away blood as it dribbled down his forehead.

This is insane, he thought. *This world's gone mad and taken me with it.*

He snatched the jawbone club and started toward the Koyotes, his heart hammering. If the Kiowa magic failed he would surely die, but if he sat back and waited for it to show itself it might be too late to save Byrne. And so Russell ran up behind Glenn, the jawbone held high in both hands, and as he came crashing down upon the back of Glenn's massive head Russell felt something shift within his muscles, as if he'd suddenly de-aged, gaining back the strength of his youth and then some. The club came down, the elk teeth ripping into Glenn's head and knocking him off of Byrne. Glenn tumbled but got up quickly, and when he saw the marshal his face went slack with shock.

Russell could feel the change Glenn was seeing. His body twitched and pulsed and when he looked at his hands brown fur was crawling out of the backs of them like inchworms. His bones grew hot and his belly hungry. He could smell the blood with the greatest clarity.

Glenn wasted no time. He lunged and Russell spun into him, swinging the club at the Koyote's weeping wounds. Glenn yelped and turned but Russell was faster, charged by the sudden force of his newfound wolfishness, and the club crashed across Glenn's teeth and when he fell forward Russell batted at him again and again until the jawbone club split in two.

Had Glenn been in his human form, Russell would have done his best to uphold the law and bring the outlaw in alive. But trying to get a huge werewolf into a cell seemed ludicrous. Would killing Glenn even count as killing a man anymore? He looked at his own hands again, seeing the thick, yellow fingernails and black paw pads. Did *he* count as human anymore? Was this a lawman taking down an outlaw, or just two big dogs fighting in the street? When it came to animals, did the laws of men still hold value?

Glenn mewled in the dirt, holding his head with blood pouring between his fingers. The hair on his back began to recede, sinking into the flesh and revealing just how many wounds the man had. His vertebra shifted. His every breath seemed to hurt him.

As Russell approached, Glenn drew a dagger from his belt and seemed ready to use it, but when he raised his arm his shoulder crackled and the weapon fell from his grasp. Russell growled, wanting to put fear into the Koyote, the same fear of dying Glenn had put into the hearts of so many others. With each step Russell took, Glenn curled a little further into himself, and Russell sneered at his cowardice, so typical of bloody men when the time came for them to pay for their misdeeds. He'd seen so many villains weep and call for their mothers while standing upon the trapdoor of the gallows with a noose around their neck. Repentance came only when they realized their sins had cost them something, the one thing that makes all a man's dreams, loves, and hopes possible.

"Any last words," Russell asked, "before I put you in a tree?"

Glenn was breathing heavily into his chest, his face hidden. He said nothing.

"I'll take that as no comment."

When he reached for Glenn he was met with a cloud of dust, and just before he shut his eyes against it he saw the little bag in Glenn's hand as he blew this black sand into Russell's face. He fell to his knees with eyes burning and Dillon's scalp was pulled from his head. Instantly he began to return to his normal form. He blinked away the grains but a swirling, purple aurora made a halo around his head, the Koyote's witchery disorienting him. It was more than sand he'd blown in his face—it was something wicked, something *powerful*. Russell struggled to even get to his hands and knees, the sorcery trying to paralyze him.

"Some bully effort, Marshal," Glenn said. "But you should've killed me while I was still down. Your foolish nobility will be the end of you."

Russell tried to speak but his mouth felt wired shut.

"This spell won't kill you," Glenn said, "but it'll hurt worse than any dying you can imagine."

Russell's muscles seized. Blood dribbled from one nostril and he lost bladder control. Glenn stood but was too wounded to do more damage to his enemy. He gripped the dagger but ultimately sheathed it at his side.

"I'm just going to rest now," he said. "I'll murder you momentarily. But it won't be no hanging. That's too easy a death for a man with a badge."

Foam sluiced through Russell's clenched teeth. Looking at Glenn, he saw little more than a pale blur, a waning moon in a galaxy without stars.

"I'm getting hungry," Glenn laughed. "Lawmen taste like shit, given that's what they're made of, but I've never met a human heart I didn't enjoy eating."

With the crack of a rifle Glenn flew backward, a jet of blood rising from his chest. He rolled in the dirt and tried to hide behind Russell's body as the sound of hooves rumbled upon the earth. Russell had gone blind, but he heard the muffled voice of Oscar Shies.

*

He could only hope they were still alive.

The marshal was on his side in a puddle of his own piss. Byrne was on his back, half naked and covered in hundreds of cuts. Beneath him the snow had blossomed red. He wasn't moving, didn't even appear to be breathing.

Atop his horse, Shies aimed the Whitworth rifle again and fired upon Glenn Amarok as he crawled on his elbows, leaving a crimson trail behind him. The bullet just missed and Glenn raised his head and clicked his tongue three times. A horse neighed from the alley beside the stationhouse and Shies turned to look, seeing the mustang pull so hard against its ties that it took down the hitching post before charging toward Glenn.

Deputy Dover fired at the crazed horse but it was clear the beast was more than a mere steed. It snorted black mist, eyes burning like hot coals, and its hide was so thick the bullet ricocheted off of it. The posse's horses whinnied and darted out of its path, and before Shies could stop it the mustang ducked its head toward Glenn and he hugged onto its neck, the horse lifting him out of the snow and riding off, Glenn dangling from it like a gore-slick decoration.

Shies kicked his horse in the ribs and it charged after the Koyote, Deputy Dover falling in line next to him as they gave chase. Glenn managed to pull himself into the saddle and when Shies raised the rifle in one hand the snow before him rose in tufts as bullets were fired at him. He turned to see another rider galloping from the alley and into the street, his pistol blazing. He was thin with a pinched face, riding light in the saddle, and his horse caught up with Glenn's quickly, the outlaws heading straight up the trail leading into town. The snow was merciless now, a full blizzard ripping through the territory in a hurricane of ice, and Shies struggled to see his target, firing blind.

Dover yelled. "Holy mother of God!"

Shies looked up. Some sort of massive animal was leaping across the rooftops, sprinting from the stationhouse and onto the top of the bank, the sounds of it landing like the rumble of a stampede. It moved with a speed that defied its size, like a bison with the skills of a squirrel, and as it sailed down from the rooftops and into the street it bellowed out a wolf's howl and ran after Glenn and his sidekick, fast enough to tail the horses at full gallop, the three strong legs making up for the injured one.

Snow whipped at Shies' face and he had to turn his head away. The buildings became blurs gone black against a whitewashed world and as they rode up the slope leading to the surrounding woodland he lost sight of the trail, lost sight of the Koyotes all together.

"There!" Dover shouted, pointing ahead.

Shies saw nothing but Dover kicked his horse, pushing it harder as he pursued the outlaws. Shies followed, his vision not as good as the young deputy's, but as they drew closer he realized the snow was going gray, and then suddenly it was black ice falling from the sky. Dark dust made a sandstorm about their heads.

Dover cried. "Jesus! What'n the hell did he throw at us?"

But Shies couldn't answer. He was too busy vomiting. He lost grip of the reins and tried to hold the pommel, but his limbs had gone numb and tingly and he was powerless to stop himself from falling from his horse, puking until he was only dry heaving but still unable to stop. The black snow receded like a tide going out, and as the whiteness returned Shies saw Dover had also fallen from his horse. The young deputy was shaking on his back. His mouth was open, a luminous darkness rising out in a black rainbow.

CHAPTER XXXI

SLIDING DOWN THE POLE OF the awning, Delia ran to her fallen posse members. Byrne was a red disaster, almost certainly dead. Russell was alive but writhing, his face tight. She got down on one knee.

"Marshal?"

He wheezed when he tried to speak. Delia rubbed his chest to comfort him and felt something hot there, so she opened up the coat to check that something else wasn't inflicting pain. She reached into his breast pocket and pulled out a beaded necklace, the white one the Kiowa shaman had been wearing. It glowed and throbbed in her hand. It was merely an impulse to put it around the Marshal's neck, but one that quickly proved beneficial. A ghostly, blue radiance quivered across Russell's body, and as it coiled about him his shuddering eased until it stopped altogether. His clenched jaw opened, eyes going clear.

"Breathe," she said, patting back his hair.

He took long, labored breaths as his pupils shrank, the bright expression of agony fading, his seized body going slack.

"Oh, Jesus..." he muttered.

Delia smiled. "God is good."

Russell sat up slowly. "Thank heavens, I can see again. I don't know what that stuff was, but it was one powerful poison." He coughed. "We need to get help for Byrne."

"Is he alive?"

"I don't know. Help me get him to the station."

They raised Byrne over Russell's shoulder and went into the stationhouse and laid him upon a long table. Delia had never seen a man naked before, and while Byrne still had some of his raggedy clothes on they no longer covered his nether regions, and she'd blushed and averted her gaze until Russell removed his coat and draped it over Byrne to keep the man warm. He took his wrist and placed an ear to his chest.

"Slow pulse," the marshal said. "But he has one. His heart's still beating."

"I'll fetch the doctor."

He shook his head. "Only doctor in this town was Doc Craven, and he sure can't help us now."

Delia turned and ran for the door.

"I'll be right back," she said. "I know someone who can help."

*

Grace Cowlin stood over the dying man, her hands still shaking from the opera of violence she'd witnessed from the windows of the Abercrombie house. The gunfights had been terrible enough, but the sight of men transforming into blood-crazed monsters had nearly made her faint. She muttered a prayer before getting close to Byrne, having seen him shapeshift, the most unholy act she'd ever witnessed. Clearly the man was in allegiance with the devil, or at least had once been. To think she'd been sleeping right next door to this abomination.

Though the blizzard had blurred her view, she'd also seen Russell transform after putting that disgusting scalp upon his head. When first he'd done that she'd thought he'd gone mad, but when he began to shapeshift she thought it was she who was losing her sanity. She did not doubt the goodness of the marshal's heart, but also could not explain how he'd become a werewolf, unless he too was involved in deviltry, the very sort of witchcraft she'd once been falsely accused of.

Russell looked at her, eyes pleading. "Can you help him? Delia says you know medicine."

"Well, I suppose, but I'm hardly a nurse, Marshal."

"You're as best we got. Please, save him."

She took a deep breath. Byrne's true saving would be up to God, but doing everything she could to keep him alive was her Christian duty. Even if the man were a beast, he had been fighting for good against those other werewolves in an effort to save Hope's Hill, just like Marshal Russell and this incredibly brave young girl. Perhaps Byrne had freed himself from the wickedness of his condition. Grace believed that sometimes it was not what a person was that mattered, but what a person strived to be.

Taking to Byrne's wounds with needle and thread, Grace washed them, sterilized them with bichloride of mercury, and stitched him up, ceasing the blood loss considerably. What concerned her now was the bone sticking out of his calf.

"Help me push it."

Russell put his hands on the crooked leg and they pushed, popping the shin back in place as best they could. Grace nodded to the shattered desk.

"Delia, break off two pieces of wood, about two feet long each." She looked to Russell. "Rip off the sleeves of this coat."

He cut them free and when Delia returned with the planks they placed them on either side of Byrne's leg and tied them tight with the sleeves. Sweat had formed on Grace's brow. Her mouth was dry as a clod of dirt. Outside, the storm clouds had drifted away as if following the Koyotes, and pale winter sunshine shone through the broken windows of the stationhouse, casting them all in a ghostly hue.

"I'll need some medical supplies," she said, "so I can tend to both of you too. And I'd like to do all I can for Mr. Byrne to prevent infection, which I'm afraid is not much at all. In most cases like this, the leg would have to be amputated before it poisoned him, but amputation is a complicated process I'm not comfortable doing. He'd likely die of exsanguination.... but then again, if he gets a bad infection he'll die regardless."

"He should heal better than mortal men," Russell said.

"Because of his... *condition?*"

"Wolfen aren't immortal but I've seen they're regenerative and tough as railroad spikes. We'll have a little more time with that leg. If it's got to come off, we'll take it off. I've helped do amputations during the war, so much so there were piles of limbs in the field hospitals."

"Good heavens."

"What we do is cut the leg with a bonesaw and tie off the arteries with horsehair, then smooth out the bones and fold the remaining flesh over the stump and sew it up, leaving a drain hole. Then we patch it with isinglass. Reckon it's worth a try to keep him from going gangrenous."

Grace went pale and she put her hands to her belly. "Oh my…"

"Hopefully it won't come to that." He turned to Delia. "You get on over to the doctor's house and fetch us what we need—bandages, bonesaw, stitching needles and thread." He told her where Craven had lived. "Whatever else you can get from the apothecary on my order. Make sure to get laudanum for Byrne's pain. You just tell Mr. Greene I sent you."

"Yes, sir."

The girl left and Russell took a deep breath, the deepest of the day.

"Oscar and Jake are still after them," he said. "I have to try and catch up before the snow covers all tracks."

Grace's eyes went wide. "But your wounds—"

"They're minor, all things considered."

"That poison may still be in you."

"If it is there's little I can do about it. I feel a little worn and tired, but I don't feel the heavy effects of that stuff anymore. My men are out there right now, going up against Hell's personal army. I'm the town marshal. I can't let them do this without me."

Grace's heart plummeted into a stomach already filled with butterflies. She'd seen so much horror today and feared if Russell pushed his luck any further he might not return home. Her feelings for him surprised her. Though she'd seen him turn into a wolf man, her schoolgirl crush on Russell remained. It had even intensified upon seeing his great courage and strength, superlative compared to other men she'd known. He'd been making her feel safe since the night he'd rescued her from a kidnapping. If he were to perish, she might never feel safe again in this town.

"Marshal…"

But she knew not what to say. Russell turned to her and took her hand, their eyes locked.

"Call me Henry."

*

"You sure that stuff from your little bag killed them?" Hiram asked.

"Most likely."

"Maybe I oughta go back and pop a few rounds in their heads."

Glenn gestured to his shredded body. "Can you not see my state, Hiram? We must get to shelter, so that I may lick my wounds. We can't risk going back."

"Not even for ol' Web?"

"Ol' Web proved himself useless today, did he not?"

"What about Jasper's body?"

Glenn grumbled. "We'll get it back yet."

The snow had faded to a haze that enveloped the promontory, but above Black Mountain flurries tumbled from the sky on the back of an arctic breeze. The white firmament was growing dim, the gray soot of the gloaming closing upon the earth like the wings of some great archangel, and the packed ice of the knoll crackled beneath hooves. The Koyotes were trotting now, their horses wet and exhausted. Beside Glenn, Thad was in a slow gait and an even slower transformation back to his human form. Though his face was a man's his body was still bulging with hairy muscle and he was on all fours to support his bad leg.

"Why don't you get up?" Hiram said, patting the back of his horse. "Give that leg time to rest and heal."

"Much obliged."

Thad walked behind Glenn's horse and started toward Hiram's, but as they passed by the bluff there was a deafening sound and the earth shook beneath them. The horses bucked as a large, round projectile flew toward the Koyotes, the wet earth and snow bursting all around them just before the gunpowder detonated.

Thad exploded.

Blood and hair and fingers and teeth splattered across Glenn in a red mist and he fell backward off his horse. His mustang had survived the blast but Hiram's horse, being closer to the detonation, had its front legs torn out from under it, its hair singed and the skin burned away like mere kindling, the flesh beneath going black with gunpowder as it sizzled into the sinew. Hiram flew over the horse's neck, rolled, and immediately tucked behind the fallen horse for cover. He tried to pull his rifle from the scabbard but his horse was writhing too much for him to reach it. He moved away just in time as the mangled steed turned in the snow, nearly crushing him before he could scurry away.

Glenn looked in the direction the blast had come from. He listened closely. Someone was laughing in the brush. Glenn clicked his tongue and Belial charged over to him and he pulled himself up and slung his leg over the saddle cantle. He had his gris-gris sack but could hardly use the black dust on an enemy who remained to be seen. Hiram still had his dual pistols and he returned fire, shooting blindly into the bushes, screaming without words. Still there was laughter in the scrubland. Glenn rode up to Hiram and reached down and Hiram took his hand and climbed atop the horse. A gun popped off, the round just missing them, and this time Glenn spotted the red-faced old man crouched in the thicket and the bronze tip of the howitzer sticking out of the shrubs, still smoking. The man had a repeater rifle and was filling the chamber again. Hiram took aim and fired his pistol into the thicket, but still the old man laughed, as if violence itself was a jester dancing for his amusement.

"Like them apples, do ya?" the old man cackled.

He's a madman, Glenn thought, *a bloody madman.*

The assassin was white but wore the war paint and feathers of an Injun. He moved behind the brush again, cloaked by the snow-capped shrubberies. Glenn heard a larger chamber being open, something heavy being dropped inside it.

"Shit!" Hiram said, having heard it too.

Glenn kicked his horse's ribs and Belial went into full gallop, more than happy to get out of there before a projectile could come for his legs too. Though the snow drew thicker and pulled at his hooves the horse was fueled by his master's sorcery and plowed through. Glenn steamed behind his clenched jaw, eyes tinted with fury. They were down to two Koyotes now, just two men and one horse. Thad and Dillon were dead. Web probably was too. And the strange swarm of ravens had abandoned them. They'd lost weapons and supplies, lost the cart with Jasper's corpse. And they hadn't even found the golden capsule. They'd been so damned *close*.

He kicked Belial again but the horse could go no faster.

When the howitzer fired a second time, they were halfway over the bluff and Belial leapt into the air, the men holding tight as they went airborne, and the rocks and ice erupted behind and above them as the horse hit the lower ground in full gallop, the bluff's edge taking the fiery detonation and enabling their escape. Above their heads came a small avalanche of dirt and ice and sludge, the mess spattering over their bodies already slick with the steaming gore of their dead brother. They rode on through the wintery landscape, onward toward the mountain, through the bones of dead birch and pine, struggling to stick to a trail the blizzard had stolen from them. They looked as if they'd been tarred and feathered using human gore and dog fur, these stains the only evidence left that Thaddeus Bowman had existed at all. And when they bypassed the border Glenn spotted the blackened rubble of a farmhouse that had burned to the ground. There was a seasoned barn there in which they could recuperate and plan their next method of attack, for nothing about this was over.

CHAPTER XXXII

PLACING SHIES AND DOVER IN one of the carts, Russell and Brazzo led the pack animals and horses back to the station-house. Brazzo was hesitant to leave the howitzer behind, but getting the poisoned men to safety took precedence. Russell had found them first and was struggling to drape the men over their horses when Brazzo had come along. Now they returned to town a smaller posse than they had been before, and when Brazzo learned of Setimika's fate the man openly wept.

"I dread to bring this news back to the tribe."

Shies and Dover were still breathing but unconscious. Dover's face was covered in the same sort of black soot Glenn had blown into Russell's and his eyes were jaundice yellow, wide open though he remained comatose. By the time they reached the stationhouse and got the men inside, Shies was coming awake but Dover remained unresponsive.

As Grace Cowlin tended to them, Russell took a seat and bent over, putting his head in his hands, wrought with a feeling of failure even though they'd killed a couple of the outlaws and seriously wounded the others. One of his deputies was dead. Another was knocking on the reaper's door. Setimika was gone and Shies was drained as if the Gods had swooped down and pulled his very heart out. And Byrne, if he lived at all, might become an invalid for the loss of his leg. At least the girl was all right. Delia was a little bruised from the fall but the young bounce back easy.

When she'd done all she could for her patients, Grace came to Russell and escorted him to the washroom where she had him undress to his undergarments so she could wipe him of dirt and use the antiseptic on his many cuts and scrapes. The room was small and dim and they took a lantern with them, the burning oil giving the enclosed space the illusion of warmth, an orange glow that seemed to romanticize their closeness as she stitched the arm where the bullet had grazed him. Not for the first time, he admired her beauty and thought her named suited her. Even as she was faced with mutilated bodies and saddled with the difficult task of tending to war wounds with limited medical knowledge, she exhibited grace that bordered on sainthood. Her fingertips on his naked flesh riveted him and he had to bite his bottom lip, this being the first time a woman had touched him in these places since he'd become a widower.

"You're a brave man, Henry." Her eyes were soft with brown shadows. "And I believe you have a heart like a diamond. But I was hoping I could enquire... that I could ask..."

To marry me, he thought, despite knowing it was ludicrous. Maybe she wanted to steal a kiss. Maybe even take him to bed. No. That was silly too. He was so much older, so much more tainted. His heart was no diamond. It was shards of glass no more salvageable than the station's busted windows. Grace Cowlin was still ripe with youth and laid out before her was a world rich with possibility. She deserved a man with those same qualities, not this rusted, old anchor stuck at the bottom of his own miserable sea.

"You can ask me anything," he told her and meant it.

She hesitated, then said, "I saw you turn—into a wolf, I mean. I saw it with my own two eyes. It troubles me most plaguily."

He hung his head, rubbing his chin. He suddenly felt even older than he had a moment ago.

"Troubles me too," he said, "but I don't think it'll happen again."

"Why is that?"

"It was temporary spell, put on me by the Kiowa shaman only to save my life. Reckon it did the job. I apologize for it upsetting you, ma'am. It shames me that you had to witness me in such a ghastly state."

Grace looked down. She closed up the wooden box of medical supplies and placed it upon the washbasin.

"They'll return, won't they?" she asked.

"Without question."

There was a silence between them then, but Russell found it was a comfortable one. He wanted to stay in this private place with her forever, the façade he'd dreamed up going uninterrupted as long as they both shall live.

Instead he began to redress.

"I must inform Norton Hustley's wife that she is now a widow."

*

After breaking the awful news to Mrs. Hustley, Russell brought Deputy Dover to the Abercrombie house, insisting on a room for him to rest in. Dover lived alone and Russell did not want him to go unattended to. Town leader Murphy Hyers and the rest of the council could pay Joyce Abercrombie an extra dollar a day to have her take care of him. She agreed to do so, saying she was always happy to support local lawmen, but she did insist on evicting Luther Byrne.

"I will not have a devil in my house," she said.

Russell figured this was why she wouldn't let him inside either. Her eyes were not as kind as they'd been before, and she was not alone in looking at him funny. Too many of the roomers here had seen him change and those who hadn't had already heard all about it. He reckoned it was only a matter of time before the council came for his badge, maybe even coming with guns and a stake to burn him at.

Russell didn't want to take Shies back to his family just yet, not in the terrible state he was in. He couldn't have beared to face Nizhoni. He was prepared to board Shies with Abercrombie as well but the cowboy had regained his senses and would not hear of it.

"I feel like I'm getting over the flu," Shies said. "That's all. I have to get home to my wife. Word travels fast and I don't want her to think I'm one of the fallen."

Shies left but promised to return, as did Brazzo who went back to his village to bring Setimika's body home to his family and send

266

men to fetch the howitzer. Russell took Byrne to the only place that would have him. It was a small house with only one bedroom and had been provided to him by the council upon his arrival to Hope's Hill, the great U.S. Marshal from Texas here to solve all their troubles. Dealing with a rattled populace of witch-hunting locals and hired thugs would seem like a vacation to him now. At least those evils were ones he could understand.

Murphy Hyers would have to orchestrate gathering the dead, burying the shopkeeper and the cowboys at the saloon, as well as those the Koyotes killed through windows and one man shot through the throat by a stray bullet. Russell would see to it Deputy Hustley was buried with honors. He was a good man lost too soon. But the dead were dead and less of a pressing issue right now. There were monsters in their midst and they would not hide in the mountains long.

He made his way to the chapel.

*

They'd hidden in the underground church at Sister Mable's command. She needed them all there to keep the Menhir secure, for the devout made the most durable shield. Even Sister Genevieve, who had wept with fright, was a protector by her very faith alone, by the sacrifices she'd made by dedicating her life to the word of God. She admitted her temptation, but Sister Mable had faith in her and baptized her with three drops of child blood upon her forehead to keep wicked thoughts away.

All through the gunfight and wolfen war, Reverend Blackwell had stood at the foot of the stairwell, staring up the steps as if waiting for Satan himself to appear, telling the nuns what the visions enabled him to see, which good men were dying and how many Koyotes were sent back to Hell. Sister Evalena had helped Mable keep the tubes of the Christ statue lubricated, repeatedly flushing the Menhir with innocent blood to weaken it, making it harder for the outlaws to detect.

Anxiety had left them all exhausted, and now that the Koyotes had all either fled or perished Mable exited the underground church and went up to her room for a rest. Night was falling and the snowy landscape appeared as blue as the flickers that filled her hands when she called upon the white magic. All of town was still and silent, a false calm. Once in her room, Mable took the wimple off and let her golden hair fall about her shoulders. She slipped out of her robe and got down on her knees before the bed and put her palms together in prayer.

"Our Father, who art in heaven, hallowed by Thy name; Thy kingdom come; Thy will be done; on earth as it is in Heaven. Give us this day our daily bread. And forgive us our trespasses, as we forgive those who trespass against us." She thought of the merciless Koyotes and knew their trespass would go unforgiven in her heart, though she knew it was a sin. "And lead us not into temptation, but deliver us from evil." She thought of Luther Byrne and the path of wickedness he'd chosen, and wondered if God would ever have him. "For Thine is the kingdom, the power and the glory, for ever and ever."

She felt suddenly cold, and so very tired of being on this earth.

"Amen."

Crawling into bed, she thought of all the years she'd spent in service to The Lord. Where once she'd been so passionate, the decades of her life passed by so quickly and brought with them so much suffering and hardship—her father dying terribly of cancer, screaming in his bed and unable to move, and then her mother falling ill with paratyphoid fever and perishing just a few months after her poor husband. Sister Mable had also buried both her brothers due to separate wars. And her only sister, Sarah June, had been traveling to a new settlement with her husband and their five children when they were killed by an army of Navajos, the Indians slaughtering Sarah June's husband and children before her eyes and then taking her back to their camp to be raped and beaten and starved to death.

At times Mable had felt like Job and confessed this sin to Father Blackwell with great shame. But the loss of family was only but a morsel of the feast of pain God had offered up to her. She fell sickly and only barely recovered from a fever that had threatened to kill her. She suffered bone spurs and tendonitis and spent even her best days aching. Her devotion to Him was rewarded with a devastating sense of loneliness, of being a mere witness to the world around her rather than a participant, and she broke down and was put in an asylum, told she was plagued by hysteria, and was kept there for over a year. When she was released she went right back to the church and donned the cloth once more, for it was the only life she knew and she feared change even more than the wrath of God or Lucifer's lies.

Then the Menhir had come into the church's possession.

God made her guardian of a sinister talisman that could never be destroyed, only cloaked and contained. For the last twenty-six years she had not aged, her body always in a perplexing middle state, and though she was over fifty now on a good day she could pass for a girl of nineteen. Not that everlasting beauty did her any good. She'd never known the touch of a man. She was a bride of Christ and by His rule could not marry nor have children of her own. There were only the orphans, and she had to bleed them to keep the power of the Menhir subdued, to keep wicked men like Jasper Thurston from taking possession of it and ripping wormholes through universes, some of them portals to Hades.

She was just about to fall asleep when the knock came at her door.

CHAPTER XXXIII

SHIES JUMPED DOWN FROM HIS horse so quickly he stumbled to his knees. Despite the pain of the fall he bounced right back up, adrenaline raking his heart, making his whole body shake.

No. No no no no no.

He ran to his son.

Tohasan was lying bent over the hen house. His pants were around his ankles, buttocks splattered with blood. Tears blurred Shies' vision as he went to his little boy and took the limp body up in his arms. He screamed into the sky and clutched the child to his chest. Part of Tohasan's face had been torn from the skull. Shies could have sat there in the snow and cried until his dying breath. Insurmountable grief compelled him to do so, but he had to find his wife. Trembling, he placed Tohasan on the ground and ran to the house and flung open the door. The stench hit him first, and then the terrible sight.

The woman he'd loved nearly all his life was on her back upon the floor. She'd been eviscerated, her once round belly torn open and now housing insects instead of their unborn child. She was nude and strips of flesh had been deftly peeled from her body, revealing this had been done not by a bear, but by a man. Nizhoni had been decapitated and her flensed skull was placed upon the supper table like a horrible centerpiece. Eyes that had once emanated such love for him had been scooped out, lips that had kissed him chewed off. Shies' legs went out. He slid against the wall, sobbing and dry heaving and thrashing on the floor, a man broken and on fire, changed forever.

CHAPTER XXXIV

"I JUST THOUGHT THERE MIGHT be something you could do," Russell said.

They stood over Byrne, Sister Mable clutching her rosary, the marshal holding the lantern above the dying man.

"Do?" she asked. "Do what?"

"I don't know."

"All I can do is give him his last rites."

The nun's eyes misted over. Russell put his hand on her shoulder.

"Sister, I've never been a praying man. Until a few days ago I would have told you there was no such thing as gods and magic and werewolves. But I've seen things—even *felt* things—that have turned me upside-down on everything I once held to be stone-solid truth. Now, you told me you buried Jasper Thurston up in that child's cemetery for a reason and I have come to believe you wholeheartedly. I now believe in witchcraft. I believe in evil. But if there's evil magic it stands to reason there must be good magic to balance it out. I've seen this sort of magic in a Kiowa shaman and experienced the power of it firsthand. Something tells me you're no stranger to it either. I'm guessing you know a mighty good deal about it, in fact."

She turned to face him and the enchantment of a beautiful woman standing so close to him struck Russell for the second time that day. He had the urge to hold her, as if this might be his last chance to hold anyone at all.

"There is white magic," she said. "But I do not possess it. It comes at times by the grace of God."

"Then shall we pray on it?"

She nodded and took his hands in hers. He followed her lead by tucking his chin. Her words were flowery like poetry, a gospel of hope and healing that made him breathe slower, soothing as a mother's lullaby. When she was finished they both looked at Byrne. He hadn't moved or changed in any way.

"Patience," Sister Mable said. "That's one of the things He asks of us."

She went to Byrne and placed her hands on either side of his face. She surprised Russell by leaning down and kissing the wounds on Byrne's cheeks. Rosary in hand, she whispered some words in Latin and lifted his head and placed the rosary around his neck, same as the Kiowa necklace.

Russell hoped they would be enough.

They returned to town together, night having fallen in full. December was an ornery thing now, biting and bleak. Russell had found one of his old coats in his trunk and Mable wore several layers over her gown and long, wool stockings beneath.

"What will you do now, Marshal?"

He wished he knew.

"I'm going to meet with Murphy Hyers and try and contact the council. I need more deputies, more possemen. Maybe some cavalrymen. Whatever this thing is the Koyotes want, they didn't get it today, so they'll be back once they're fit to fight."

She looked down. "I fear you're right."

"Maybe we should get that thing out of Hope's Hill altogether."

"Wherever the Menhir goes, they will pursue. At least here it's mostly secure."

"Once I've got a full posse, we'll be watching the chapel close, but if we surround it that'll only lead them Koyotes right to the Menhir. We'll be giving away where it is."

"You're right at this as well, Marshal."

They parted ways at the chapel and Russell backtracked to the home of Murphy Hyers but the windows were dark and no one answered when he knocked. He left the porch. He would have to talk with Hyers in the morning. Right now he needed rest and lots of it, but doubted his eyes would stay closed for long.

*

Delia woke up hungry.

No. Not hungry—*starving*.

Before bed, Joyce Abercrombie had served the whole house a fine meal, obviously trying to keep her roomers after the carnage that had transpired here in town. There'd been a feast the likes of which Delia had never seen outside of Thanksgiving, with roasted duck, cornmeal, pumpkin pie, and potatoes enriched with cream. There was even a small barrel of beer. Delia ate and drank until she'd felt ready to bust. But now, just hours later, she felt as if she'd been fasting a week.

She sat up in bed and her belly growled. She burped an empty burp. Getting up, she put her coat on over her nightdress and started downstairs for whatever leftovers remained.

Her arms were shaking. She attributed it to the cold at first, but when she looked at her hand on the banister she saw her fingernails had grown long, the peach fuzz at her wrist darker. They would not be noticeable to someone else, but knowing her own body Delia gasped at the change and brought her hand up for a closer look, going to the window for moonlight. Both hands were changed this way and the flesh of her palms was coarse with fresh calluses that were much darker than the rest of her skin.

Standing in the light of the moon, she began to shake harder, an uncontrollable convulsion, and her stomach pinched tight again so she went to the piano stool to sit. Away from the window now, she was covered by shadow, and the convulsing settled back into a mild tremor. She just sat there, breathing, trying to deny her suspicions. When the hunger became too great she went to the kitchen and devoured the remains of the dinner, eating only meat.

Soothed now, she returned to bed but could not sleep a wink.

*

It seemed to take forever to get up the knoll. The undertaker's pony was old and moved like molasses. Even when Web tossed his empty bottle at it, bonking the pony on the head, it still didn't pick up its pace. It seemed frightened by the snow on the ground, its every step ginger, like it was crossing a shaky bridge of planks and rope. It would almost be faster just to walk, but he couldn't pull the cart himself and wasn't about to leave Jasper's coffin behind.

They followed the thin trail through the hinterland, Vern guiding them deeper behind the brush so they wouldn't be spotted. The undertaker was beyond pale now. His skin was nearly translucent and because of his torn open shirt Web could see his skeleton and the blackened lungs and swollen intestines beneath. Vern's face was a death mask, so morbid it disturbed even Web.

"You look like dog shit gone white in the sun," he said.

Vern smiled at this, delirious with sickness. Flurries had collected in his hair and eyebrows.

"Are ye cold?" Web asked.

Vern guffawed. "I'm dying!"

Web stopped the pony. He rose slowly, buttock aching from the bullet in it. He climbed onto the cart. Opening Jasper's coffin, he lifted the frail remains and started removing the dead man's blazer. The corpse was so withered he feared he might break an arm off at the shoulder, but Jasper was big-boned and did not shatter easily. Web managed to get the suit coat free and he placed it over Vern, more to not have to look at his rotting guts than anything else.

"We gotta get indoors somewheres," Web said. "We'll catch our death in this weather."

"We should visit the O'Conner farm... or what's left of it."

Web doubted he had the strength to kill a whole family right now. "How many of them are there?"

"Not to worry. They've gone to perdition."

"Dead then? All of 'em?"

"Dead as William Henry Harrison."

Web furrowed his brow. "Reckon I'll take your word on that. I don't know him no ways."

"Why Webster, he was our great nation's president for a whole month."

"I don't give a good god damn! Where's this stinkin' farm? I'm 'bout to freeze my setter off!"

Vern advised him to follow the dwindling trail and they rode alongside a creek heavy with ice. The moonlight made long shadows from the dead tree limbs, spooking Web now and then, making him think they'd been followed, that a posseman was stalking them. But no one appeared. The trail gave way to a larger path and the pony struggled to haul them up, exhausted by the constant travel.

"Come on, you lil' bitch!"

It was a good half an hour before they came upon the O'Conner farm and when Web saw the rubble of the house he took off his hat and smacked Vern with it.

"Ye coulda told me there wasn't no house left!"

"I thought it was implied when I said they were all dead."

"I oughta cut your damned fool head off like the rest of your parts."

Vern scoffed. "Hardly a threat at this point."

"Shit."

Web clacked the reins, his face brightening when the moonlight revealed the silhouette of a barn. He hooted.

"Finally, a little luck!"

They wound through the misery of the dead cornstalks and past the remains of the house, and when they came upon the barn Web stopped the pony. The wind and snow continued unabated and he sighed with relief at this promise of shelter, however flimsy. He approached the barn slowly, wanting to scan it before leading the pony and cart inside. There could be all sorts of critters living in this abandoned place, and not of all them would be friendly. The last thing he needed was a pony crippled by wolves or a bear, or for he himself to catch rabies. That'd be just the perfect grand finale to this turd soup of a day. When he heard something shuffling in a stall he drew his iron and cocked the hammer. A horse snorted in the shadows.

Why would someone leave a horse behind? Hell, even if it were lame it would make for good eating.

He thought he sensed something—wolf or bloodhound or...

Web lowered the pistol and stepped into the dark, not seeing the fist come at him until it was too late. Web's nose crunched sideways and he fell back, and as he tried to catch himself his pistol flew from his grip. Landing in the snow, he got to his knees just as the shadowy figure came at him again, kicking him in the face. When the man came closer, Web saw his eyes were glowing red.

"You yellow belly!" the man said.

Web recognized the voice. Despite the beating, his fear began to dissipate.

"Boss?" Web said, smiling blood. "Boy, ye had me buffaloed! It's me, Web!"

Another boot to the head. Web spun back to the ground.

Glenn growled. "I know who you are, you moron! You're a yellow son of a bitch with the brains of a fruit fly!" He came at him again and Web scurried backward like a crab. "Where in the hell did you disappear to?"

"I was all shot up, boss. Had to take cover."

"We were all of us shot up, but you're the only one who bowed out!"

"I had an arrow in my arm!" He pointed to the tail of the arrow still in his forearm. "And with this bullet in my setter I couldn't hardly walk."

"A few bullets in the arse is hardly enough to take down a true wolfen."

Web moaned. "But, boss, I ain't as young as I used to be. I don't heal up so good."

Another shadow emerged from the barnyard.

"Maybe we ought show him mercy, boss," Hiram said. "Ain't like we got many men left. Our pack has thinned to a trickle."

Glenn's lip curled as he considered this. Web waited, not daring to even get up from the snow. He really was getting old. He hadn't even sensed his brother Koyotes' presence here. When Glenn spotted the pony and cart, his rage began to dissipate, his snarl leaving his face. He walked over to it.

"You brought Jasper back," he said.

Web got up now. "Yes, sir. I surely did. Oh, and I brought ye something else too, something you'll be right happy 'bout, yes indeedy."

He took the golden capsule from his coat pocket and when his boss took it his eyes went wide, amazed.

"Hell," Glenn said, grinning. "I don't believe it."

"Ain't ye proud of me, boss?"

Glenn didn't take his eyes off the capsule. "Best decision you ever made."

"Yeah?"

"Yeah. If you hadn't of done all this, I'd be ripping out your guts right now and feeding them to you."

Web looked away, sniffing back bloody snot. Glenn spotted Vern lying under the dead man's blazer, sprinkled in the cobwebs of the grave.

Glenn chuckled. "Lordy, Web. Now I'm starting to remember why I keep you 'round in the first place."

Web perked up. "Why's that, boss?"

"You make me laugh."

They guided the pony into the barn and secured the cart, Web carrying Vern inside and placing him atop of small mound of rotted hay.

"He some kind of pet now?" Hiram asked.

Web only shrugged. He looked around the barn. "Where's Thad?"

"Dead," Glenn said. "It's a damned shame too. He was a true warrior, a Koyote worthy of the breed. It should've been you."

Web said nothing for there was nothing to be said. He'd known Glenn long enough not to challenge him. At least Hiram had spoken up for him. Glenn might well have kicked him to death otherwise before he could even show him the capsule their pack leader was fawning over. Glenn turned it in his hands, squinting at the engravings.

"What's it say?" Web asked.

Glenn frowned and sighed with frustration. He threw the capsule against the barn wall, making Web wince.

"What'd you do that for, boss?"

"Because it's worthless."

"*What?*"

"If you could read Italian you'd know that and wouldn't have bothered with it. But you can hardly read English as it is."

Web frowned. "I can read some."

"You couldn't read your own name on a wanted poster."

Hiram leaned in. "Glenn, you really telling us this capsule is worthless?"

"It is to us. It was not carved by the hands of hell or even wolfen like us. They're engravings done by those of the Catholic church, old Italian prayers and incantations meant to seal Jasper's heart. The blessed capsule must make it possible for mortal men to pick it up without succumbing to its sorcery. That's all. That's why this undertaker here could steal it and not fall under its spell. The doctor, however… he must have poked and prodded it with bare hands. That's why he went full dark."

Hiram jumped up and threw his hat to the ground. He went to a stall door and kicked it.

"Dammit!" he said. "We went through all of this for nothing? Thad's dead. Dillon's dead. All for nothing? Damn, Glenn, why didn't you figure this out sooner? You're the one with second sight!"

Glenn glared up at him. "You'd do well to watch your tongue with me, Hiram. I don't take guff from no man, least of all my subordinates."

"I thought we were seeking some greater power, thought you felt its presence."

"I did feel it. Still do. There is a talisman in Hope's Hill—this is beyond doubt. I was only mistaken in thinking the capsule was this talisman." He went to Vern, nudging the man to open his eyes. "If anyone's to blame it should be you, grave robber."

Vern grunted. "So kill me."

"What'd you say, pissant?"

"You heard me. Don't you understand? I feel myself decaying. The pain will only grow greater. Far better to just kill me now."

"Why didn't you tell us the capsule was made by Christian hands?"

"How was I to know? I am no theologian, sir, just a scoundrel robber of graves, like you say. I've been no use to you and nor shall I be going forward. Best to rid yourself of my presence right quick."

Web stirred, somewhat surprised at the urge to get between Glenn and Vern. Maybe Hiram was on to something by calling the undertaker his pet. He found he was fond of the weird man's company, at least as a form of amusement. Luckily, Glenn didn't grant Vern's wish.

"I don't do mercy killings," the leader said.

Vern looked away, closing his eyes again. A sudden wintry wind blew through every hole and crack in the barn and Web pulled his coat tighter, hugging himself. He licked at his wounds.

"I'm hurtin'," he said.

Glenn said, "We all are. Even wolfen bodies have their limits. We'll need something more to get at full strength again."

"Anybody got any nose paint?"

Hiram grumbled. "No whiskey. No nothing."

"Aw, shucks."

"What we really need is a plan."

Glenn nodded. "They've got us outnumbered now, outgunned.

If'n we go back to Hope's Hill we're as good as buried."

"Tarnation," Web said. "We're giving up?"

"No, you dolt. We just need to go about this another way."

"What way's that, boss?"

The wind picked up again and the barn shuddered. In the stall, Belial brayed, as if he knew something the men didn't.

"We go back up the mountain now," Glenn told them. "I must speak with her again."

CHAPTER XXXV

HE WAS IN TOTAL DARKNESS.

Byrne blinked against it, seeing no difference when his eyes were opened or closed. His heart fluttered with the fear of having gone blind. His mind struggled to separate the dream he'd just come out of from the nearest reality he knew.

Glenn, he thought.

His old brother had been on top of him, tearing him apart.

Am I dead?

When he moved he felt the bedding beneath him. He tried to get up but pain coiled around his leg and he yelped, gripping the blanket against heavy rivers of agony. He fell back against the bed, his every bone aching, muscles raw, sweat boiling across his flesh.

"Hello?" he called out. "Is anybody there?"

He heard footsteps and wondered if he'd made a big mistake by opening his fool mouth. What if the Koyotes had captured him and were keeping him here to be tortured? They might be waiting for him to come out of his coma just so they could eat him alive and have him writhe between their teeth while squealing like a hog. Hiram would sodomize him just to prove a point and rip out his liver and suck it like a goddamned honeycomb. Glenn would devour his still-beating heart and use his skull as an outhouse.

He managed to sit up when the door came open, the soft glow of the lantern revealing a man in long johns. It was Henry Russell.

"You're awake," the marshal said. "Thank God, you're alive."

"For a moment there I wasn't so sure." He blinked and looked about the room. "Where are we?"

"My house."

"Lordy, I hurt… my leg…"

Russell came to the bedside, a glass bottle in his hand filled with a purple liquid. He sat beside Byrne and poured some of the liquid into a spoon and fed it to him. Byrne's face soured.

"Jesus, Henry. This tastes like a skunk smells. What'n the hell is it?"

"Laudanum. May taste dreadful but it'll kill the pain for a while. We had to set your leg."

Russell drew back the blanket and when he saw his swollen, discolored leg Byrne winced and had to look away.

"Son of a bitch," he said.

"It's bad. I'm hoping with you being wolfen and all you'll heal up better than most. If not, we might have to take that leg off."

"Son of a bitch!" He slammed his fists onto the bed. "What in the hell happened out there? Last I remember, Glenn was killin' me. But then…" The memory began to return, trudging through a mental fog. "There was some other shapeshifter… one I didn't recognize… he… he saved my life."

Russell nodded. "Yeah."

"Was it Setimika? Looked more like a werewolf than werebear, but I might be mistaken."

"No. It was me."

Byrne raised his head and felt the first tickle of the laudanum begin to take hold.

"*You?*" he asked. "You're wolfen?"

"I was for a moment. Setimika scalped one of them boys and gave it to me as a danged hat."

Byrne laughed and even though it hurt to do so he could not stop.

"Easy now," the marshal said. "You need your rest."

"Wish I could have seen you decked out in such finery!"

Now it was Russell who laughed. "Thought I told you to shut up."

"Thank you, Henry. Thank you for saving my life. I owe you."

"You want to thank me, you just get better. We got a lot of them bastards. Made 'em retreat out of town for now but they ain't all licked yet. I need you Byrne. You know Glenn. You understand what it is he wants."

*

Russell left the house at daybreak and went into town dressed in his most respectable suit. He hoped by looking clean and official it would emphasize the fact he was a man, not a monster. It'd been a serious snowstorm. Not many would have been able to see him transform, only those in the buildings closest to the action. But all it took was one person to spread gossip like wildfire—someone like nosey, old Joyce Abercrombie. There were enough people in her house who had witnessed the battle close up. It was a tall tale indeed but the superstitious folk in Hope's Hill might just swallow it. After all, it was true.

He stopped off at the boarding house first. By now the sun was up and there was movement behind the windows. He hoped Grace or Delia would be the one to answer his knock but, of course, Abercrombie herself greeted him, her crone's stare thrown at him like circus knives.

"I've come to check on Jake Dover," he said.

"I believe he is sleeping still."

"I'd like to check on him either way."

The landlady huffed. "Well, I'll have Ms. Cowlin see to him and she can give you a report."

She began to close the door in his face and Russell put his boot in the jamb. He gently pushed the door open again.

"Ma'am, I'm the town marshal and Jake Dover is my deputy. I expect to see him whenever I wish."

Abercrombie crossed herself for dramatic effect, her hooked nose resembling more witchery than he'd ever seen.

"Mr. Russell, I'll not have a creature such as yourself in my building! This is a godly house and shall remain one as long as I'm here to keep it so."

He crossed his arms. "Your insults are uncalled for and your concerns are groundless. I am not a beast, I am a human being."

"I saw you turn into a—"

"You saw mere illusion."

Her jaw dropped. "I beg your pardon! I know what I saw."

"Think rationally, Ms. Abercrombie. If I were truly a werewolf why would I have fought the other ones and chased them out of town?"

The landlady put her hand to her chin and looked at the floor.

"What you saw was a mere trick of theirs," Russell said. "An illusion forged by the devil to frame goodly men. Now, if you don't believe me, you must only go down to the chapel to have Sister Mable and the Reverend Blackwell set you straight again. Unless you'd think them liars too."

Abercrombie paled. "Goodness, sir! I would never doubt the reverend's word. He speaks on behalf of my Lord and Savior."

"Then kindly step aside, for I assure you he will vouch for me."

She moved out of his way.

When Russell reached Dover's room Grace Cowlin was already there, sitting at the deputy's bedside. She turned around when he entered, mouthing two words to Russell so Dover would not hear.

He's dying.

Russell stepped to the bed and when he saw Dover his breath stopped in his chest. The young deputy looked ancient. He was diminished by cachexia. His skin was a ruin of wrinkles, his muscle mass gone, leaving only a jaundiced, skeletal frame. His hair had fallen out and his skull was blemished by liver spots, eyes white with cataracts like an old dog. When he spoke one of his upper teeth fell out.

"Marshal..."

"Easy now, Jake."

"Did... did we do it? Did we get them sons of bi—?" He stopped himself then, seeming to remember there was a woman present. "I pray you. Tell me we got 'em."

Russell nodded. "Yeah. We got 'em, Jake. Couldn't have done it without you."

"I chased 'em... chased 'em hard as a lion. But that big one... he done blew this weird dirt in my face. Oscar Shies got some too, but I took the bulk of it head-on. It done poisoned me."

"I know."

"I ain't gonna make it."

"Come on, now, Jake. You can—"

"I'll soon walk those golden streets of glory. See my mother and all those who done gone on, just like that old "Wayfaring Stranger" song says. Guess I'm a wayfaring stranger now. Don't know why I'm so scared of going to Heaven."

Russell had no words. All he could do was be there. Grace had closed her eyes, head dropped toward her chest.

"I was gonna turn twenty-three come spring," Dover said, chuckling. "That's a good age to get married, start a family. Could you picture that, Marshal? Jake Dover a daddy?"

"You'd make a fine father, Jake. You're a kind man, a brave man worth his salt."

"Heck, I don't even have me a sweetheart, let alone a wife. I thought there'd be time, you know?"

Dover's eyes misted over but he held his tears in. Russell understood the man's need to remain strong even on his deathbed, to show no such weakness. It was important for a man to keep his dignity, especially when it was all he had left.

"I had me a dog though," Dover said. "He was a good ol' boy. That's kind of like a son, I reckon. I mean, I had to take care of him and all. 'Course he got snake-bit and died." He sighed. "Wish that good ol' boy was here now, Marshal."

The golden daylight had inched its way through the window and fell across the disintegrating body of Jake Dover. The young man turned his head, following the sunlight though he could no longer see it and never would again, feeling its warmth touch him and savoring it for as long as he could.

"I named him Bandit," he said, chuckling. "How do you like that? His name was Bandit and here I am a deputy."

He was still smiling when he died.

*

Russell walked into town hall and went directly to the office of Murphy Hyers, finding him behind his desk, the man's large belly pressed against it as he wrote. When he looked over his spectacles at Russell, his face darkened.

"You've one hell of a nerve coming here."

Russell stopped before the desk. "How's that?"

"Are you joshing me, Henry? You know damn well what! You put together a posse without the council's permission and turned my town into a battleground!"

"It was peaceful before Glenn Amarok and his henchmen came. All I did was stop them. Reckon I deserve a little more gratitude for that. Hell, my posse just saved this town!"

Hyers rose from his seat. "*Saved?* I've got sixteen bodies at the funeral parlor! That's including a deputy! And to make matters worse nobody seems to know where that little creep Vern Pipkin's disappeared to, so we've got no undertaker to handle them. Had to ask a favor from allies in Battlecreek to get us one."

"You knew things were going to get bad here. That's why you brought me to Hope's Hill to begin with, to take care of the trouble so you could solidify this settlement and make yourself mayor."

"Yes, well, that's hardly relevant now." Hyers went around his desk and gathered up some of the papers, flustered busywork. "After what happened yesterday, nobody's going to invest in this forsaken town or even want to live in it for that matter. People are packing up and getting out already. They're not just scared of outlaws—they're scared of bloody *monsters*! Ridiculous, superstitious nonsense! These are grown adults and they're telling me this place is overrun with werewolves. First they were hollering about witches and now it's wolf men, for heaven's sake. These hicks don't deserve a township or the railroad I was trying to get through here."

Russell stepped in front of him. "Then why'd you bother in the first place, Hyers? Why'd you tell me you wanted to save this village if you were just going to give up on it at the first sign of trouble?"

"I thought we were just dealing with the threat of a lynch mob forming over the cattle giving sour milk! I thought the matter had been settled after you and your deputies put a stop to that schoolteacher being kidnapped. I didn't think I'd have to deal with gunfights in the streets! Hell, this might as well be Fort Griffin or Canyon Diablo with all these bullets buzzing about!"

"Then give me more men," Russell said, his eyes going hard. "Dover just died. I've no deputies left. You're town leader. Go to the council! Tell them we need more officers of the law. Have U.S. Marshals sent up from—"

"Forget it, Henry. The council's not going to throw a fistful of good lawmen to a one-horse town just to get themselves killed. Gunfights, bad crops, bad livestock—and a whole mess of terrified citizens bound to just keep acting crazier. Our best course of action here is to gather our things and head on out. And do it fast."

Hyers hitched up his suspendered slacks and went to the door, opening it for Russell. The marshal stared at him until he looked away. Russell walked to the doorway and then turned to face Hyers one last time.

"I'm not leaving," he said. "You and the council can tuck your tails and run, but I'm still the marshal of Hope's Hill and I'll protect those who choose to stay."

Hyers shook his head, giving him sad eyes. "Do as you wish, Henry. But soon enough you'll have to face the facts. There ain't no hope left in Hope's Hill. I pray you see that before it all caves in on you."

CHAPTER XXXVI

ON THEIR WAY UP BLACK Mountain the Koyotes crossed paths with a man traveling alone and without a word Hiram shot him in the face and stole his blue roan. The horse was young with a powerful build and Hiram was pleased to be back in a saddle. There were no weapons or ammo in the man's bag but he did have some greenbacks and a jar of moonshine. Web was the only one interested in the liquor, but Glenn ordered him to go easy on it. He wanted him sober enough to fight if they ran into trouble.

The winter sky burned the color of the snow beneath it, a motionless mist hovering across the frosty knolls where white birch trees rose twisted from the earth like skeletons returning from their graves. The men rode slow, the wheels of the cart creaking a funeral dirge as the worn pony dragged it up the crags, trudging through the slush and ice and general misery the mountain provided. And at the summit the ravens that had followed them into battle hovered in a circular flight, cawing, beckoning.

Glenn rubbed at his swollen neck. It hurt worse than the claw marks Byrne had left on him, worse than the arm that had also taken a bullet. His lower back ached and he had a mean headache. Maybe he'd take a sip of that shine after all, but not until they reached their destination.

He thought about the farm they'd left that afternoon. There was a vibe beneath that poisoned land. A darkness had fallen upon the O'Conner's farmhouse, taking lives. He was certain of it. As the men rested, Glenn had gone to the house's remains and sifted through the debris, feeling the vibrations of the earth there, digging his claws through the dirt like a hound, and like a hound he found himself a bone. Then another. And another. His suspicions had been correct. Something bad had happened here—something delectably evil. He gathered three femurs and two radiuses, a humerus and busted scapula. A pocketful of fingers. Buried deep was a cream-colored nugget and when Glenn pulled it up a vertebra was revealed like an unwound serpent. Holding the bones in his hands, there was a strange heat to them that somehow burned cold. He carried the bones back to the barn and placed them inside an empty feed sack and tossed it in the cart bed. There was *ju ju* in these bones. They might prove useful.

Night fell upon the riders in a gathering shroud. The moon became a homing beacon to the Koyotes as they followed it up the mountainside, as if they were climbing to the cosmos.

"Moon's sure got some light tonight," Web said.

The undertaker giggled. "The moon has no light of its own."

"The hell you say. I'm looking at it right now."

"It is merely sunlight reflected."

"Who says?"

"Leonardo da Vinci."

Glenn said, "Web, you best shut that grave robber up."

"Oh?" Vern said. "Am I pinching a nerve?"

"I'm gonna rip your nerves out of your very body if'n you don't stop your jaw flappin'. You may wanna die, but I can see to it you suffer far worse than you already have."

"Impossible."

"Don't test me, Pipkin."

Web turned back to Vern. "Best do what he says."

Vern pursed his lips and titled his head back, gazing at the starry night. The clouds had cleared and the universe was a dazzling tapestry.

Glenn spotted Mars. The red planet's power radiated through him in a gentle wave.

When they reached the plain they dismounted and stepped

through the thicket and into the deadening. There was no fire burning tonight, no legion of Maenads playing wet nurse to wolf pups, ready to welcome the Koyotes in celebration. The cold had chased the exotic creatures into the caves they called home.

"Glad we came here," Web said, his excitement visible. "I could use me a good poke."

"And healing," Glenn said.

He and Hiram started toward the mouth of the main cave and Web took Vern up and draped him over his back with the rope sling. Vern rested his chin on Web's shoulder, facing forward, making him appear to be a man with two heads. The entrance of the cave glowed a yellowish orange, the shadows of the lithe she-creatures rising, sensing their arrival.

The one called Thyian came to Glenn with eyes once again gone bright with desire. She bit her bottom lip and curled her hair in both hands like a schoolgirl. The Daughters of the Maenads gathered around the Koyotes, pilot fish around sharks. They were dressed in animal hides and some wore tiaras made of snakeheads and rotting human toes. Around Thyian's neck hung a necklace of wire run through a series of testicles dislodged from men who'd been lured to the deadening by the Maenads' siren song. She placed her palms on Glenn's chest, gasping at the sight of his wounds.

"Seventh One," she said, "you are injured."

She placed her lips over one wound and started sucking, her saliva a salve to his gored flesh. The Maenads started disrobing the Koyotes. Vern was placed on the floor of the cave and Web pulled down his pants so the black-haired Maenad could suckle the second hole that had been made in his ass. A young blonde with a short tail sticking out of the back of her loincloth took to mending Hiram's shoulder and he closed his eyes against the erotic nature of this nursing.

Carrying a torch, Thyian guided Glenn through the speleothem to a more private area where mother wolves slept beside their pups. She laid him down on her bedding and caressed him, fellated him to full arousal, and then straddled Glenn and slipped him inside. Though it was the nature of Maenads to ride men like they were rodeo bulls, Thyian was gentle, using her body to soothe him and regenerate his flesh. Her tongue darted in and out of the open cuts on his chest and she sucked his chest hairs between her teeth. Glenn milked her nipples and drank heartily. The mother wolves peeked at the lovers with eyes aglow.

Thyian quivered when Glenn climaxed inside of her. He figured he owed her that much. The sperm dribbled down her thigh when she stood—ethereal, shining blackly.

Thyian noticed his puzzled expression.

"Your seed is responding to my fluids," she said. "We could create an incubus."

"*You* can create one. It's your damned seed now."

She hung her head. "Of course, Seventh One. I misspoke."

Rejuvenated, Glenn rose and stretched. His neck was a little sore, but the wound had fully closed. His arm felt tingly as if asleep, but was otherwise fully functioning. Even his headache was gone. Thyian offered to guide him but Glenn remembered the way and, his passions spent, he no longer wanted the Maenad's company.

But a thought came to him.

"There remains one thing you can do to serve me," he told her.

"Anything, my king."

He grabbed her by the throat with one hand, and though fear leapt into her eyes she did not resist him. He began to squeeze, the palm of his hand turning black with rising paw pads, his fingers thickening, nails sprouting. Still the Maenad did not fight him. A tear rolled down her cheek.

"Sacrifice," was all Glenn said.

He dug his nails into her neck and blood bubbled at the corners of her mouth. She cried out but the sound was muted as he crushed her larynx. The trachea popped. As her neck was pulverized her head flopped to one side and a look of calm came over her as he leaned in for one final kiss, lapping at her plump and bloody lips and slurping the gore that now dribbled from every hole in her head.

He dropped Thyian and her body cracked as it hit the floor of the cave. It was not as good as sacrificing an innocent human being, but it served as a reminder to the satanic forces that offered him power. He was as devoted to the evil ones just as much as this dead Maenad had been to him. He would stop at nothing to serve Hell.

Still nude, Glenn maneuvered through the cave until the rock turned to a pavement of bones, the stalactites made of compacted tangles of skeletons tied with hemp and horsehair, the stalagmites forged with compacted skulls packed with clay. He passed through the obsidian pool once more and emerged into the dead forest, dripping sludge with every step. The unkindness of ravens was there, cawing in the sycamore, and looking up he felt as if the area was encapsulated in a gray globe, as if this were a small, drab dimension of its own. Perhaps it was. When he reached the adobe house he stopped upon the porch's pentagram, smiling as it glowed the same red as his eyes, and then drew back the rawhide and stepped into the gloom.

Jessamine the Deathless was the source of all the light in this one room shack. Her face seemed even more attenuated than when he'd last seen her, body looking starved beneath the dress of the tanned and sewn-together faces of lost children.

"I knew you would return," she said.

He despaired. "I came so very close."

"You have the heart of the First Koyote, but not the talisman that very heart sought."

"Maybe so. But I found Jasper's body."

Jessamine looked at him with pale eyes. He ran his hand over his head, slicking his hair. The black slime of the pond dribbled down his forehead and when a drop hit his lips it tasted like vomit. Jessamine put her hands to her chest and inhaled, and when she exhaled a cloud of spider webs left her lungs and drifted up into the ceiling like cigarette smoke. Glenn looked up and saw it was covered in these webs and had trapped a litany of insects and lizards and small frogs on which Jessamine would feast.

"Take me to him," she said.

*

Web pried the lid from the coffin at Glenn's command but could not take his eyes off the ghostly woman who stood between them. Something about her made his scrotum draw tight and the hairs on his wounded ass stand up. At least his setter wasn't stinging anymore. It would make riding on the hard seat of the cart a lot easier.

When Jessamine approached the carcass she placed one hand upon Jasper's sternum and stood there as if waiting for something. Web didn't know what. Frankly, he didn't want to know. He was plumb tired of all this witchery. Tarnation, he just wanted to rob a bank and use the coin on a bath and a hot meal, get drunk on wine and sleep in a real bed for a change!

When he'd found Glenn and Hiram back at the barn, he'd actually been disappointed. It meant he had to ride with the pack again when he'd been entertaining the idea of going off solo. Well, not solo if you counted Vern Pipkin. Web wouldn't leave him behind. As long as the undertaker was still alive he made for good chatter along the trail with all his little facts and tidbits. It would keep Web from getting lonesome and he'd be learning new things too. But now he was back with his gang, back to this strange witchcraft.

The glowing-green woman was sprinkling something over the corpse's skull now, the black grains falling into the hollow sockets where his eyes and nose had once been. Jasper had sported quite a honker when he'd been alive, but now there was just a sliver with two teardrop holes. When the black sand entered them, the skull began to rattle.

"Lordy," Web whispered.

Jessamine climbed into the cart. Glenn joined her. Together they removed Jasper's carcass from the coffin and placed him upon the cart bed. Jessamine hitched up her dress of flesh and straddled the corpse as if she were saddling a mare. Web saw she wore nothing underneath. She leaned over and kissed Jasper on the teeth. Web recoiled at the sight but kept watching through one eye. The witch clacked her fingers up and down Jasper's broken ribcage as if she were strumming a guitar, and when a centipede crawled out she snatched it up and ate it.

"Give it to me," she told Glenn.

He reached inside his coat pocket, revealing the huge, pulsing heart. It had gone from black to a dark crimson, and when Jessamine took it her own seaweed glow entwined with the heart's red light, creating an aurora borealis that swelled in the night. She plunged her arms under the ribs and placed the heart where it had once rested. She began grinding her hips, pushing her labia into the rotted pelvis of the dead man. Her bush was a briar of mildew, glistening wet. Web recoiled further. He'd never seen anything so perverted. Even Hiram buggering kids didn't seem as vulgar as this. The witch was smiling now, her filed-down teeth flashing in the ethereal glow like straight razors. And when she reached a masturbatory climax the corpse suddenly shot up, jaw dropping in a great intake of air, the first breath of a long-delayed resurrection though it had no lungs to enjoy it with. The carcass turned its head, blind without its eyes, and when it raised its arms the bones crackled like a bonfire, dust and powdered flesh falling all about it like so much snow.

Web swallowed the lump in his throat.

Jasper Thurston was back.

CHAPTER XXXVII

THE POPULATION OF HOPE'S HILL had been cut in half in less than twenty-four hours. Even though townspeople would be leaving behind their own houses and businesses, still they fled in droves, too terrified to stay and too weak to stand their ground against an evil they did not fully understand.

Russell watched from the stationhouse as another series of wagons rolled through the pebbled streets. Gentle flurries whipped through the air. Winter wasn't going anywhere. He shook his head. For families to travel this far north during this time of year was borderline suicidal. But his concerns had been voiced and rejected. The place he'd sworn to protect was crippled by fear and abandoned by its leaders.

Russell thought of Hyers and sneered at the man's putrid combination of selfishness and cowardice.

He saw Brazzo coming up the walkway and rose from his seat. When the man came inside his face was grave but his eyes held their grit, the stare of a warrior done wrong.

"My people want retribution," he said. "They want their beloved Setimika to be avenged, so that his spirit may rest peacefully."

"I am sorry for your loss."

"And I'm sorry for yourn. But it's them wolf men who are gonna be truly sorry. I regret I was only able to blast one of them bastards to smithereens. I wish I had them here right now. I'd gut 'em like trout."

"You may get your wish yet. Unfortunately, I don't think we've seen the last of them boys."

"I see that not as a misfortune, but an opportunity. Vengeance will be ourn."

Russell went to the windowsill, watching the parade of deserters go by. Brazzo joined him.

"This was a tiny village when I first came here," Brazzo said. "Now it's a full town, even if it is on the smaller side. It deserved a chance to grow, its people to prosper. Irks me plaguily to see it falling down about ourn heels."

Russell only nodded.

Brazzo asked, "How's Luther?"

"Alive, at least."

"That bad, ey?"

"Shape he's in, it's a marvel he ain't gone too."

"Hellfire. We need him if'n were gonna make waste of them bastards. He's of their kind. He'll have that sixth sense, that *link* to 'em."

"We'll be needing a whole posse, what with my deputies having passed."

"You're darned tootin'. I've got Kiowas ready to fight for their fallen tribe member."

Russell scratched his cheek, considering. "How many?"

"Five men and two women, both strong as oxen."

Russell's eyes went wide. "Why, that's a small army. They fight well? Can they shoot a rifle?"

"Some are familiar with firearms. Mostly they're accustomed to arrows and tomahawks and the like. But I've got me an arsenal."

"So I've learned."

Brazzo clicked a laugh. "And the women are especially gifted."

"How so?"

Brazzo put his hand on Russell's shoulder and leaned in, grinning like a madman.

"They're skinwalkers, Marshal! Werebears to the manner born! Ever seen a grizzly eat a coyote before?"

Brazzo laughed again, his cackle echoing through a stationhouse made lonesome by the absence of Hustley and Dover.

"Can't say as I have," Russell told him.

"Well then, I reckon we're both in for a treat!"

*

Freezing rain tapped upon the rooftop.

Grace watched the wagons roll on, her neighbors leaving Hope's Hill forever. It was a notion that had come to her as well, but she did not want to abandon the students who would remain here. She also did not want to leave Henry Russell without some sort of assistance, especially if they needed to remove that poor man's leg.

She had a bad feeling in her belly when it came to the creatures that had terrorized her town, one that assured her the battle had not yet been won, that this was merely an intermission. The good marshal would soon enough return to war and would need all the help he could get. While she was hardly a soldier, she could serve as medic. She prayed it wouldn't come to that.

She turned from the window and looked at Delia sleeping. What would come of this young girl if she faced those monsters again? She'd been lucky so far, having only taken a fall that had hardly caused any damage, but good luck had a way of taking off when you needed it most. Delia was just barely out of childhood and was already a lonesome nomad. Lone men became rakes and ramblers. Would a lone woman fall to those same trappings? Would Delia's life be wasted in saloons and gambling halls, soused on whisky and getting into scratches with those who tried to cheat her? It pained Grace to think of the girl transforming into a woman who raised pistols instead of children. It was the path to perdition.

At least she won't be a spinster.

Grace scolded herself. She was too young to fear such misery. Though many women married at a younger age than she was now, by no means did this condemn her to a life of barren loneliness, a life as loveless as the one she currently lived. Yes, of course she wanted to be a bride, wanted to be a mother. But now, watching man after man ride out of town, she wondered if she was sabotaging herself by not doing the same.

But there was still time—plenty of time.

Or at least that's what she kept telling herself.

Looking at Delia, she decided she'd like to have a girl, but then reconsidered. Having a boy first would assure her daughter would have a big brother to protect her.

When you're a woman in the west, protection is worth more than gold.

CHAPTER XXXVIII

JASPER COULD NOT SPEAK. HE was blind and deaf and still utterly dead.

And yet he was alive.

Glenn rode beside the cart, alongside the reanimated corpse. It was sitting upright, its fleshless face to the wind. Glenn thought of what Jessamine had told him before they'd left the deadening.

"The heart will be more powerful when returned to its rightful owner."

Glenn had sneered. "The power of that heart is mine."

"As it should be, Seventh One. You needn't be jealous of Jasper's carcass. It will not take your place at the head of the pack. It is merely another tool for finding the talisman you seek."

"I still don't even know what I'm looking for."

"But you'll know when you find it. The body of Jasper Thurston still holds some of the wizardry the man possessed while living. He can identify the talisman, and the talisman will take you to a portal."

"Portal? Is that what it shall be?"

"A gateway to the darkest dimension, where the throne we've long known you were destined to sit upon awaits. In this vortex lies the very throat of Hell. Therein lies enough blackness to tear the sun from the sky."

Glenn had nodded then. "Cast the world in darkness."

"Darkness eternal."

Jessamine reached into a skin flap that made the dress' pocket and pulled out a tow sack made of jute. It was sealed with candle wax, the blob in the shape of an inverted star. She handed it to him and he took it without another word.

The Koyotes rode on, descending through frozen brush, their horses snorting smoke against the cruelty of the rain, the assembly of black birds following despite the downpour. The men were nearly back to full strength, emboldened by the addition of the zombie sorcerer whose arm was outstretched as if pointing the way.

There would be no retreat this time.

The only outcome would be success or death.

*

Byrne walked down the hallway and back. Russell had been aiding him in this physical therapy, encouraging him to use his muscles again, and Grace Cowlin came to see him and changed his dressings. The redheaded girl visited too, going so far as to pick a bouquet of posies to give warmth to the room. The laudanum relieved the pain but with every dose he needed more for it to work. There was no time to worry about addictions. The Koyotes were coming down the mountain. He sensed their presence drawing nearer like a tsunami.

He was grateful to hear Charging Bear's people would join the fight. By now the Koyotes would have found assistance too. Glenn would have sought the Maenads to nurse the pack back to health. He would return with full force, recharged with fresh ferocity. They would have to fight back with the same fury.

"I'm going to see Shies," Russell said.

"We could use him."

"I just hope he'll be up to it—that his missus won't smack him upside the head just for thinking about it."

"Wouldn't be a bad decision on her part."

Russell paused in the doorway. "I reckon not."

*

The man stood pissing at the rear of the little covered wagon, his back turned to them. Hiram licked his lips. He could use a savory liver—some nutrition to energize him before combat. As they trotted forward the man heard them and spun around, his pecker still out and dribbling. His handsome face soured as he put himself back into his pants.

"Howdy," he said, not offering a smile or wave.

As the cart drew closer the man spotted the corpse and albino amputee. He put his hand over his mouth. "Oh, sweet Jesus!"

He went for his wagon and Hiram drew one of his revolvers and fired at the man's feet until he froze.

Glenn said, "You got a peacemaker in that wagon, you'd best just let it be. Unless you want that piss hole you just made to be your final resting place."

"Yes, sir."

The Koyotes sat their horses. The young man looked to the undertaker and blinked.

"Vern? That you?"

Vern looked his way. "Yeah, it's me. That you, Barley Reinhold?"

Reinhold winced. "Lordy, Vern. What all'd they done to ya?"

"I don't believe there's even a word for it."

Hiram was reloading his pistol, but his eyes never left the young man. "What're you doing out on our mountain, Mr. Reinhold?"

Reinhold's eyebrows drew closer together. "*Your* mountain?"

"This land, as far as you can see, will be ours right soon."

"Lordy…" Reinhold paled. "I know you men. Your whiskers give you away. You're the dreaded Koyotes."

Glenn rolled his shoulders. "Web, check the wagon. Make sure this turd is alone."

Web climbed out of the cart.

"I am alone, mister," Reinhold said.

"Didn't ask."

Web pulled back the flap and peered inside. "It's clear, boss."

He reached inside and came back with a Sharps rifle and a small, wooden crate of ammo and a box of gunpowder.

Vern fluttered his eyes as if he'd just come out of a deep sleep. "Where's your family, Barley? I heard you all were run out of town."

Reinhold looked away. "The wife up and left me. Took the little 'uns to her Ma and Pa's out in Californy."

"Well now that is an American tragedy."

"You ought to look in a mirror, Pipkin. There's a might tragedy if I ever done saw one."

Hiram dismounted and joined Web at the wagon. There wasn't much inside but it was clear Reinhold had been living in it for some time. He came back out as Web pillaged the meager possessions.

Hiram got close to Reinhold, close enough to smell the blood pulsing in his veins.

"Run out of town, were ya? What for?"

Reinhold sighed and looked away.

"You steal another man's horse?" Hiram asked. "Or maybe his wife?"

"Certainly not."

Vern laughed from the cart. "Such dignity for a kidnapper."

Reinhold turned red. "You lousy scoundrel!"

"Well, well," Hiram said with a smile. "A kidnapper. That's more fun now, ain't it? What'd you do, snatch a little girl from a schoolyard swing?"

"Certainly not!"

Hiram punched Reinhold in the gut and he instantly dropped to his knees. Hiram bent over, pointing a finger in Reinhold's face.

"You raise your voice to me one more time, son, and I'll cut out your tongue so you may never be a sassafras again."

Reinhold groaned. "Yes, sir. I apologize."

"That's better."

Vern said, "You're more right than you know, Hiram. T'was not a schoolgirl but a schoolmarm. Ol' Barley thought he'd caught himself a witch!"

Hiram grinned. "That right, Barley boy? You were out for a witch burning?"

"Yes, sir," Reinhold said. "Err, I mean... we was just going to question her. Things had gone all to hell once she'd come to town and—"

Glenn interrupted. "Hope's Hill?"

"Yes, sir."

"You know the town well?"

"Born and raised there." Reinhold got back to his feet. "Lived there all my life and still they let some new lawman just run me out. He'd only been in Hope's Hill ten minutes, the lousy bastard. I'd like to kick him in the teeth for what he done to me. Lost my home, my family, my job at the church."

Glenn's eyebrows rose. "The church?"

"Yes, sir—the town chapel. I was a choirboy as a kid and became groundskeeper and stagecoach driver when I was old enough. On my last ride, I swear I saw *proof* of a witch's curse. I still say I was right to kidnap that witch."

Glenn dismounted. Reinhold stepped back and Glenn grabbed him by the lapel of his coat and drew him near.

"What did you see? Tell me everything."

Reinhold obeyed. He told Glenn of the O'Conner farm, how the corn and rye had gone to ruin and Shane O'Conner had gone mad under demonic influence. He told of a black radiance that had swallowed the farmhouse, taking some of the O'Conners into oblivion and making orphans of their children.

Glenn rubbed his chin, his eyes with a touch of red. "I knew there was something about that place."

Hiram looked to the pack leader. Glenn knew something the rest of them didn't, something he wasn't sharing. He did this often—*too* often. Hiram crossed his arms and dug the dirt with the toe of his boot.

"It was like a door opened," Reinhold said. "Like the land there just opened up and brought all Hell with it."

Hiram said, "Like a portal."

Glenn glanced at him but Hiram could not read his expression. The leader was like a smooth slab of stone, blank and just as cold.

"Yes, sir," Reinhold said. "Like a portal to Hell."

A silence fell between the men, filled only by a cold wind coming down from the mountain. Hiram was downwind from Reinhold and the man's odors made his stomach grumble. Glenn took his lariat from the side of the saddle and tossed it to Web who put Reinhold's arms behind his back.

"Wait," Reinhold said. "Of what use am I to you? I'm a pariah now. Nobody'll pay a ransom for me."

"Never said they would."

"Please, just leave me be. Surely I have suffered enough these past few weeks."

Glenn laughed. "You don't know what suffering is, boy. But you will learn. Learn the hard way."

Hiram put his hand on Reinhold's shoulder. "We've no more use for you, except to ring the supper bell."

"You... you want me to cook?"

The men laughed and Hiram said, "Naw, son. You'll be the main stew."

Reinhold trembled, a mouse cornered by a snake. Sweat appeared at his hairline, his eyes flashing.

"Please. I... I can..."

Web finished tying him up and stepped before Reinhold, face to face.

"What's it like, boy?" he asked. "What's it like to look into the eyes of a man who's gonna eat ye? Your brain—everything that makes ye who you are—will be turned into feces in my belly and dropped into the jakes."

Reinhold was shaking now. "I—I can—*help* you!"

Glenn stared. "Go on."

"I know more than just the layout of the town. I know things men like you will want to know. Things about the chapel." He closed his eyes against the sweat rolling down his brow. "There's something there. A *relic*. I've seen it with my own two eyes, I have. The nuns took the blood of my boyhood just to keep it safe."

"Safe from what?"

Reinhold took a deep breath. "From men like you."

*

Seeing the wooden crosses sticking out of the ground, Russell's chest went tight and cold. These graves had not been there before.

Oscar's dead, he thought. *The poison took him after all, just like it did Jake Dover.*

But what of the other two, smaller graves? Had the poison been contagious?

He climbed down from his horse. Twilight was coming on and the crest of snow looked alien in the dying light. To the west, a sunset of blood made a mystery of the sky. As he came closer to the house he spotted the shed around back. The door was open, the shadow of a large figure inside.

"Oscar?"

The shadow turned but did not speak, face hidden in the dark. Russell's hand inched cautiously to the Colt at his hip. Perhaps this man had dug the graves for...

"That you, Oscar? It's Henry Russell."

Shies stepped out of the shed. Russell was relieved to see him, but the relief didn't last long. Shies stood only in his pantaloons, bare-chested and barefoot. A few days worth of gray beard made a nest of his face. It had gone much darker, much harder. His eyes were lifeless and bloodshot.

"Mercy, Shies. What're you doing out in this cold like this? You'll catch frostbite."

Shies remained stoic. "What do you want, Marshal?"

"Figured you'd already know. Them boys are—"

"They killed them."

Russell froze. "What?"

"My family." He nodded to the graves. "They were slaughtered."

Russell understood the three wooden crosses now—wife, son, and unborn child.

"Jesus…" Russell hung his head. "Oh, Jesus…"

"Had to be the Koyotes. They must've come by here on their way into town. Tore my wife and son apart. Ended my baby's life 'fore it had even begun."

"Oh, Oscar… I am deeply sorry." Russell had to look away, unable to face the man. His heart was in his gullet. "Lord have mercy, I… I just don't know what to say."

"I should have been here."

"You couldn't have known."

Shies gazed off into the distance. "Doesn't matter, does it? I was supposed to protect them."

"You *were* protecting them."

"Then I failed. Failed as a husband and father."

Shies started walking and when he turned Russell saw the assortment of scars across the man's back, likely where he'd been whipped by his owners when he was a slave. Though deep and disfiguring, it was not these scars that crippled Shies, but the ones that could not be seen, the scars upon the heart of a shattered man.

Shies went into his house and shut the door. Russell stood there a moment, watching the sky swirl into a velvety pink that reminded him of his dead wife's lips when she would whisper "I love you", long before her own personal darkness had taken her. He and Shies were bonded now in the worst possible way. And though Russell understood the man's pain and had years of experience dealing with it, he'd amassed no means to diminish it, no tools to ease the agony of a sorrow so great.

THE THIRTEENTH KOYOTE

He was climbing back into the saddle when Shies emerged from his house fully dressed, his coat and hat on, his Whitworth rifle braced over one shoulder and a revolver holstered at his side. He lit the cigarette in his mouth and blew smoke from his nostrils. The look on his face was vicious enough to chill even Russell's spine.

"Promise me one thing," Shies said.

"All right."

"We take them not to jail, but to the grave."

CHAPTER XXXIX

THEY GATHERED AT THE SCHOOLHOUSE just before dawn, close enough to the chapel to watch it without being spotted. The men had armed themselves with stationhouse firearms and Brazzo's weapons, which were enough to fill a wheelbarrow. Byrne looked like he'd been tied to a buggy and dragged across jagged rocks, but he was still standing. Delia was concerned for him, and also for Mr. Shies, who had returned to the posse with a pall of gloom cast upon him, hanging heavy as warship anchors. Something had happened to the man, something too dire for her to dare ask about.

Along with the marshal and posse, Grace Cowlin joined them and Brazzo had brought along a Kiowa woman. She had long black hair on the top of her head but the sides and back had been shaved clean, revealing a galaxy of tattoos—a Gila monster, rattlesnake jaws, and a crescent moon surrounded by stars. She was a muscly woman dressed in bear furs and hides and her face was hard. Brazzo introduced her as Kasa. She was Setimika's woman, a mute.

The posse also had backup hidden far behind the tree line where Hope's Hill gave way to the woodland—more Kiowa warriors lying in wait with clubs and atlatls, their quivers heavy with arrows. It gave Delia some comfort to know they had reserves, especially after Byrne told them all about the Menhir, this strange stone from Hell which the bad men were after. She wanted to feel reassured by this stone being in the hands of the holy, but she simply was not heartened as some Christians might be. She could pray God would protect His devoted ones from these demon spawn, but He worked in mysterious ways indeed, His divine plan just as likely to lead His people to death as it was to bring them to safety. And if their death was His will, of what use was praying for the opposite outcome? She'd never thought this way before the battle they'd had with the Koyotes, seeing good men die while evil ones fled still alive. Her doubts troubled her but she had to put them aside for now. There were other worries more pressing, and not just the battle.

She'd noticed her senses were heightened. Better hearing and a much stronger sense of smell. Even ten feet away from others she could detect their body odor, powders, and perfumes—even smell their last meal. The russet hair on her limbs had grown thicker and she made sure to keep herself covered, her shirt buttoned all the way up to hide the fuzz growing from her belly up to her collar bone.

She knew what was happening, despite her desperate prayers. Something wicked had been passed on to her, ever-deepening the morass her world had become. It had to have been the blood. The Koyote had been hemorrhaging when he'd tossed her off the roof of the stationhouse, and as she'd screamed the blood splashed down into her face and filled her throat. She'd been infected, diseased by the very wickedness she'd sworn to exterminate. She could only hope God would save her before it was too late. The thought of being powerless to control herself made her stomach curdle.

To think she might hurt others...

So she tried not to think about it at all. They were at war. No matter what sickness she'd taken on, she would not abandon the posse when there was so much at stake. She was not full wolfen yet. When the battle had been won—*if* it had been won—she would saddle up her pony and leave Hope's Hill for good. She could not allow herself to be a danger to Grace Cowlin and the marshal and all the others she'd come to think of as her only friends. She would just have to learn to live alone and stay far from others. The life of a hermit was the only life for someone so afflicted, unless they were prepared to be a bringer of death.

She looked to the group. Brazzo was cleaning his pistols, a stout cigar in his mouth.

"If we still have daylight," he told the group, "the Kiowa will send up a smoke signal when they see them boys coming. From up on the bluff they should see 'em no matter what path they take into town."

"But the Koyotes could go for any place," Grace said. "What if they attack residents instead of coming right here?"

"They'll come here," Byrne said, scratching a muttonchop.

"But how can you be certain?"

"I sense them. And I know Glenn Amarok, know his hunger. He dreams the same black dream Jasper Thurston did. If he gets his hands on the Menhir there'll be far more horror than anything the Koyotes might do without it. Half of Hope's Hill's folks have up 'n gone. Whoever's left, well… they'd be unfortunate deaths, but not as unfortunate as the end of the world."

Grace put her hands to her chest. "Oh, dear me." She looked to Russell. "Henry?"

He nodded. "Byrne's right. Sometimes you have to prioritize. This ain't just about Hope's Hill now."

The schoolmarm said no more.

Delia took Grace's hand and they smiled at one another, but it was a smile without joy, a minor comfort in a world going to ruin. There was the soft rumble of thunder in the distance, strange for December, clearly a warning of what was to come.

*

Dark clouds followed the Koyotes.

Wind was at their backs, the smell of ice cleansing the air, and the rain had vanished but still the clouds thickened. The Koyotes traveled on, hauling prisoners and corpses. Barley Reinhold squirmed in his binds. Jasper's carrion drizzled ash. Vern hummed a children's lullaby. The ravens drifted overhead like buzzards over a dying man, their caws occasionally drowned out by another lion's roar of thunder.

Glenn patted Belial. The horse was sensing his owner's excitement and it gave him an excitement of his own. Both were feeling lethal. Both had fire in the blood. He breathed deep the crisp air and the savory stink of man filled his nostrils. He raised his hand and the horses stopped. He sniffed again.

"What is it, boss?" Web asked.

Glenn scanned the woodland below but saw no movement.

"Men and women," he said. "Injuns."

Web and Hiram sniffed.

"Yeah," Hiram said. "I smell 'em now."

Web shook his head. "Hell, why I don't?"

"Because you're old," Glenn said. "Your hearing will go next. If you were a horse I'd shoot you."

"They must be on the trail," Hiram said. "Probably set up a camp there."

"Doubt it. I think they're off trail and waiting on us. That's why we can't see them—they're hiding."

"You think the posse in Hope's Hill made friends with Injuns?"

"There was one fighting alongside them last time."

Hiram spat tobacco. "Shit. Why do white men mingle with such filth?"

"Maybe the town embraced them; maybe not. Remember, Luther Byrne is half Indian. I forget what tribe exactly. He never spoke much about it. These ones could be friends of his."

"How many you think there are?"

"It's a mighty odor for this far away so it must be at least five, but I'd say no more than ten."

"An ambush?"

"Nah. They can't ambush us 'cause they don't know which way we'll be coming from. I think they're reserves. The marshal is padding his posse." He trotted Belial to the shoulder of the trail and peered over the cliff. "We go off trail."

"Hell, boss. These mountains ain't all that forgiving."

"I said we go off trail."

Hiram and Web looked to each other with unease. Glenn clicked his tongue and the horses moved off the path and cut through a grove of trees, the cart's wheels struggling as they went downhill through mossy boulders and over exposed roots. They rounded the mountainside onto a thin pathway of black crag barely wide enough to support the cart. They moved slowly, cautiously, clinging to the mountain wall and watching the path for any further thinning, wary of tumbling over the edge and down to jagged rocks more than fifty yards below. The horses grew skittish. The cart creaked in protest. Still they pressed on. And when they rounded the western wall of

Black Mountain, the less-traveled path vanished into ossified briar attenuated by winter's backhand. The smell of the Kiowa and their pack animals grew stronger. Glenn could practically taste them. When they first heard the distant murmurs, he raised his hand in signal and the Koyotes climbed down from their horses.

Hiram drew both pistols. Glenn gripped the Colt at his side and Web took up Reinhold's Sharps rifle. They moved between the rows of dead trees, their footfalls gentle and drowned out by the caws of their fowl familiars and the low, belly-rumbles of thunder. They tip-toed up the bluff that overlooked Hope's Hill and stayed low when the assembly of Kiowa came into view.

Six men and one woman, armed with the weapons of their people and the same damned howitzer that had blasted poor Thad to smithereens. Half of them were sitting on a large stitching of hide stretched upon the snowy slope. The woman and two of the men were standing at the edge of the bluff looking down with telescopes at the main trails that led in and out of town—watching, waiting.

They wouldn't have to wait long.

Glenn motioned to Web and he came jogging over. They crouched behind a fallen log and Web placed the barrel of the Sharps upon it and closed one eye. Glenn nodded upward to Hiram and he went around the clearing where the tribe was gathered and took up a spot behind a boulder. Thunder rolled and some of the tribe members gazed up at the sky, their backs turned, and Glenn raised his Colt and fired, hitting the skull of the man closest to him, the round forcing fragments of bone through his brain. He spun, his face lost behind a gushing exit wound. As his fellow tribesmen drew arrows from their quivers, searching the trees for their attackers, Web fired at the female and her chest blew open, the blood macerating one lung, parts of which burst from her back in gore confetti.

Glenn laughed as the remaining tribe went into a battle cry. From the safety of his boulder Hiram unloaded upon them, both pistols blazing, the flung arrows breaking as they hit the shield of stone. A third Kiowa raised a rifle but was quickly gut-shot. A fourth had his knee blown out as he tried to crouch for cover. When he fell to the ground Web raised his Sharps and put a second bullet through the man's heart.

"Ye damned red nigger!" Web shouted. "That's for that arrow ya'll put in me!"

With every gunshot came a thunderclap. The savory stench of

blood filled the air, raising the hackles of the Koyotes and making their jowls foam. Their eyes went as red as the crimson jets spraying from the arteries of those they murdered and a fog of gun smoke filled the forest and the ravens moved as one great membrane in the sky, surging like flames and confusing the Kiowa with deceptive shadows. Glenn fired and another tribesman fell dead. The last one made an effort to escape and Hiram ran out from his hiding spot and sent three bullets into the Kiowa's back.

Glenn stepped through the thickets and into the deadening. The gut-shot man was singing a ballad for the dying up to the spirits, his hands clutched to his belly in a hopeless attempt to cease his exsanguination. Not wanting the man to find peace in his chant, Glenn shot him through the mouth. Glenn turned. There was a weird sucking sound coming from the woman who'd been shot through the chest. He walked up to her as she struggled to breathe with the one lung she had left, gasping and wheezing, the air drawn loudly through her ribcage.

He holstered his revolver and took the kris dagger from its sheath, crouched, and pushed the tip into a piece of lung that had been blown out of her body. He lifted it to his mouth and chewed. Hiram and Web, seeing their leader eating, slinked out of the thicket and gathered around the dying woman. Web's fangs were so far out they ran down his chin like a viper's. Glenn pushed his finger into the bullet hole in the woman's breast and turned it back and forth, plunging deeper. She screamed blood. He sucked the finger clean and when he looked to his men they were grinning.

"Feast," he said, "but keep her alive as long as possible. Make the bitch feel it. Make her suffer."

*

Vern was no longer sure what was real and what was hallucination. He was on his back, wondering if he were finally lying in a deadcart where he belonged. But when he managed to turn his head he saw Barley Reinhold bound beside him, and sitting above them both was the demonic carcass, dead yet alive. Every time Vern opened his eyes there were more ravens flying overhead. Some had perched on the sides of the cart and they gazed upon him with black, devil eyes.

Suddenly Web appeared. He lifted Vern in his arms.

"How're ye doing, friend?"

Vern groaned. "Is it time to die yet?"

"Come on, now. Don't be that way. I brought ye some vittles."

Vern had no appetite, but even if he had he never would have taken a bite of the human innards Web clutched in his hairy paw.

"I'll pass," he said. "Maybe I can starve to death."

"Consarn it, Vern. Don't be gloomy."

"Gloomy?" He laughed. "My dear man, there's nothing gloomy about death. Why, I've made it my life's work. Death can be such a lovely thing."

"Shit." Web snickered. "That's crazy talk. Ain't nobody looks forward to dyin'."

"Perhaps not, but there's a world of difference between dying and being dead."

Web shook his head. "Vern, ye are a study. Sometimes I don't know what you're jabbering 'bout. How is dead and dyin' any different?"

"Dying means pain and fear. There are no such sufferings once we are dead. The anguish is behind us. That's why they say *rest in peace*." He looked into Web's red eyes, seeing something there, something one could almost mistake for human. "Please, sir. If you call me friend, then treat me as one. Give me rest. Give me peace."

Web chomped down on a string of guts, slurping and belching. Vern knew what Web would say before he could even swallow.

"Can't come it."

Vern sighed. "Have you thought about *your* death?"

"Hell no."

But Vern could tell this was a lie. All men think about their inevitable demise, even wolf men.

"Come now, Webster. Think of it—you laid out in a cheap wood coffin provided by a town council after some sheriff hangs you or a bounty hunter shoots you down. Your wake would be quite a show—a famous outlaw, half man half beast, all dead and powdered in his box."

Web's face soured. "Hush with that, now."

"Heck, I've had outlaws far less famous than the Koyotes laid out in my parlor and they still drew in a small crowd. I made some coin on those wakes, but with a Koyote, well, I could charge darned near a nickel a head!"

"I said shut yer yapper!"

"Oh, alright, alright. I suppose I can drop the price to a penny for the children."

With a roar Web tossed him into the air, Vern cackling with laughter and still laughing when he hit the ground. Glenn strode over. His face was slick with blood from diving face-first into the woman's neck and drinking like some nosferato before tearing her head free from her body.

"Quit fooling around with your toy!" he told Web. "I want you tending to those bodies."

Vern didn't know what that meant, but Web seemed to. He walked away. Glenn picked a globule of fat from between his fangs and squatted next to Vern and took a small gunnysack from his pocket—the one the witch had given him—and untied the string. Vern watched as the Koyote upturned the sack's contents into his other hand—the petrified leg of a bullfrog; yellowed teeth from either man or monkey; some dried holly leaves; a human eye too small to have belonged to an adult; a single buttercup as fresh as a spring morning; and a live tarantula with its legs impaled on sewing needles that pinned it to a metal pentagram pendant. Glenn sifted through these queer artifacts, his gaze locked in concentration.

Vern squirmed when Glenn picked up the pentagram, the tarantula shaking, trying to pull itself free. As a child, Vern's older brother had locked him in the cellar as a goof, and as Vern blindly felt his way through the darkness he'd collided with an entanglement of webs and had been bitten and covered by spiders until his screaming alerted his mother and she came down to rescue him. Since then he'd suffered acute arachnophobia. It was so bad the mere sight of a spider made him leap across a room. But now, with no legs to run and no arms to bat it away, he could only shiver as the tarantula was placed upon his chest. He would have screamed if he'd been able to breathe.

Glenn went to the cart. Vern listened to the man shuffle things around, and when he came back he had the feed sack they'd been hauling along since the barn. One by one Glenn removed human bones from it, mumbling words in a language Vern did not recognize.

Vern shut his eyes, wincing as the first bone was slid into one of his stumps.

With each word Glenn muttered, the pentagram grew warmer. Bones were forced into the holes where Vern once had legs, twisting the torn tendons and exposed nerves. He cried, sweating and shuddering as bones were pushed through the grayed meat where his shoulders had once connected to arms. He was about to pass out when he felt the legs of the tarantula pattering across his chest on its way up his neck. It was free now, free and on a mission. And as a femur was stabbed into his side the massive arachnid wiggled its way over Vern's chin, pushed past his lips, and entered his mouth.

CHAPTER XXXX

THUNDERCLAPS HAD DROWNED OUT every gunshot, so the posse did not know their backup army had been annihilated. Still Byrne sensed something was amiss. The odor of death was wafting down from the mountain, the smell as clear as a wood-burning fire. There was blood and lots of it. He told himself it could be anything—bears, wolves, or bison. Best not to jump to conclusions and frighten the already tense group.

He rubbed down the barrel of the Winchester with a rag, fidgeting more than cleaning. He hated waiting like this, hated being here at all. Everything hurt and he craved more laudanum and a long soak in a tub. He found he had no desire to bed a woman, not even if this was his last chance for a poke, but the image of the lovely, young saloon girl danced across his mind just as she'd danced with him on a night more worth living than this. If he could just have one more dance with Sorrow, feel her tiny hands on his shoulders and breathe in her sweetness. If he could see her blush when he stared at her too long, if he could linger on her every word, if he were just given another moment to hold her as if she were his, as if he knew what love was.

"Something's coming!" Delia said.

She was at the rear window, a pair of binoculars in her hands.

Russell went to her side. "It them?"

"I dunno."

"Let me see."

She handed him the binoculars and he took a look.

"What in the hell?" Russell said.

Byrne moved forward, rifle clutched in both hands. "What is it, Henry?"

"It's a cart. Just a mule pulling a cart. There's something sticking up from the bed of it. A log or something."

Brazzo got off the table he'd been sitting on and drew a pistol. The woman called Kasa got up with him, slinging her quiver over one shoulder and carrying the bow.

"Careful," Russell said. "Don't go out all guns blazing."

"Trouble's brewin'," Brazzo said. "Best we brace for it. Can't just sit here pickin' at the setter of ourn britches."

"We don't want to be seen. It'll give away our position."

"Ourn position is sitting ducks if'n we don't make a stand."

"We don't even know what this is, Brazzo."

"I never saw me an unmanned mule cart that didn't have foul play behind it."

Byrne stepped up. He could feel incipient violence building.

"It's a trap," he said. "Or at least a distraction."

Delia took up her repeater. Byrne noticed a gleam in her eyes that had not been there before. He sniffed. There was a new musk about the girl now. He figured he was imaging things.

Brazzo headed toward the door with Kasa tagging behind him.

"Okay," Russell said. "But if we're going out there we cover each other's backs."

Brazzo grinned and said something to Kasa in her native language, and then they opened the front door. Oscar Shies stood up with his Whitworth, hulking above the others like an Adonis. When Byrne went to join the others, Russell stopped him.

"You and Delia stay here," he said. He pointed to the east and south windows. "You're our snipers."

"I'll sense them better from outside."

"You could barely walk yesterday. Conserve your strength. We're bound to need it later."

Byrne looked away. He never liked taking orders or feeling like he was the weakest member of a team, the runt of the litter. But while his pride insisted he could do things, his body told another story.

He went to the south window with his rifle. Delia went to the east, and when her arms came up with the repeater he saw hairs sprouting from the cuffs of her shirt.

Now he knew for sure.

*

Russell's heart rose in his gullet. Looking at the thing coming toward them, he clutched his iron like a frightened child would their mother's hand.

Brazzo whispered. "That ain't no mule."

The creature pulling the cart walked awkwardly, as if its legs were different lengths. Russell squinted, the gathering storm clouds casting long shadows over the cart and whatever it was that hauled it. There was no driver and no men on horseback. When he scanned the surrounding woods, he saw no one and heard nothing, nothing but the wheezing creature steadily approaching.

The thing's limbs came into view. They were thin and spindly, misshapen, and Russell gasped when he realized there were more than four. The creature moved as if it was walking for the very first time, unsteady in its steps, but still it pressed on.

In the bed of the cart was a totem pole.

"What in blazes..."

The creature's head was drooped, facing the ground, so all Russell could see was the top of its head. The body was alabaster white and streaked with black veins as if it were a living hunk of marble.

And it was humming.

Russell swallowed hard when he recognized the melody.

Ring around the rosy, pocket full of posies...

"Halt!" he said, aiming his Colt.

But the thing kept coming, the cart grinding, and when lightning flashed Russell gazed in horror upon the totem pole it carried.

Decapitated human heads were stacked on top of one another. There were six male heads and one female, all of them Kiowa. They were all impaled on one long atlatl, the tip of the spear planted into the boards of the cart to keep it in place. Jutting out between some of the heads were bloody hands and feet. Penises were hanging out of the mouths of the skulls, except for the head on the top of the stack, which wore a bullet-torn breast like a hat.

Brazzo gasped and the creature doing the hauling looked up.

Russell recognized the undertaker. Flensed femurs and radiuses had replaced his arms and legs. A long humerus served as a fifth appendage and sticking out of his rectum was a full vertebra he dragged along like a limp tail. Skeleton fingers had been pushed through his cheeks, giving him exterior jaws like spider pedipalps, pinching the air before a mouth full of webs.

Russell shivered. "Jesus…"

The first gunshot rang out.

*

Below the earth, Sister Mable crossed herself. The other nuns looked to her, but she had no words of her own to console them. And so she turned again to Scripture, reciting the Good Book from memory, each page filed and catalogued in her devout brain.

The pitcher in her hands was still warm, the blood that fresh. Climbing up the ladder, she held the jar to her bosom, as if its contents could somehow calm the rapid beating of her heart. She could hear her own pulse even over the vacuous moan of the Menhir. Reverend Blackwell watched her climb, his arthritic fingers wrapped around a rosary, his lips trembling in prayer. And the great statue of Christ vibrated as she poured the children's holy blood through the tubular veins, muting the Menhir, but not for long.

*

Brazzo flew backward as the bullet went through his shoulder. It came out the other side in an aureole of wet flesh. He fired the pistol in his good hand but the shot went wild. Russell got low and braced his arm over one knee and started shooting, but in no focused direction for they did not know where the first shot had come from. From the windows of the schoolhouse, Delia and Byrne blasted suppressing gunfire.

Oscar Shies put the butt of his rifle to his shoulder, waiting for the next muzzle flash instead of bombarding the open range, and when he saw it spark from the tree line he returned fire. His ears were deafened by the shots, so he did not hear the horses until they charged down the street behind him. He turned. Seeing two of the

Koyotes, his chest burned like an inferno. His limbs shook from the fury and he struggled to maintain his aim. The oncoming riders were firing off round after round, their pistols filling the air around them with wisps of black smoke, and the sniper continued shooting from his position behind the trees. Shies was hardly sure whom to fire upon first.

Tucked behind a shrub, Kasa fired arrows and rifles popped from the schoolhouse as Delia and Byrne tried to cover the posse. The Koyotes were drawing nearer, the hooves of their horses kicking up filthy snow. An arrow landed in one of the horses but it did not break stride. Its nostrils flared a cardinal glow and its teeth flashed deliriously.

Glenn Amarok held out one hand and when he opened it he blew hard, sending a spray of black ash that gleamed like quicksilver when it caught light. A gale picked up and a black galaxy of birds descended upon the posse. The flock was tornadic, spinning as one terrible mass, their shrieks at a deafening volume. As Shies and Russell fired upon the Koyotes, the unkindness of ravens threw themselves into their bullets to protect their masters, sometimes doubling up to make sure the bullet wouldn't just pass through one of them.

Shies gasped, hardly believing his eyes.

Brazzo was at his feet again, but when he raised his pistol he was engulfed by a flock of ravens that pecked at his face and body. He swatted at them with his good arm but was too outnumbered to fight. Kasa drew her club and hammered at Brazzo's attackers but another shot rang out from the trees and cut open her arm and she fell backward, her arrows scattering from the quiver.

Shies fired at the Koyotes and when the birds came for him he used the old Whitworth as a club, batting at the teeming flock, sending pulverized birds in every direction. When one clawed at his face he gnashed his teeth and caught the bird in his mouth. He bit down hard and the raven burst between his jaws like a spoiled plum and bled and shat and screamed.

Russell had picked up Kasa and was sprinting to the schoolhouse. He called to Shies to run with him. Shies put his head down and charged into the storm of ravens like a battering bull, his huge body plowing through the assault of the shrieking fowl, swinging his trusty rifle and snapping his teeth, taking off the claws and wings of birds foolish enough to get close to his face. Many of the flock retreated to the sky, but others pecked at his shoulders and legs and tore flesh from the back of his neck. They ripped at his scalp and tugged skin free from his brow. Shots rang out and birds dropped and thunder growled above and he could barely see from the blood pouring into his eyes as he tumbled into the schoolhouse, spitting out the severed head of another victim.

CHAPTER XXXXI

THE WALLS SHUDDERED.

Some of it was the wind the storm brought to Hope's Hill. Some was the beating of the ravens' wings and the loud staccato of their beaks as they tattooed the building, trying to get inside.

Grace's cheeks were wet with tears. Shies was freckled with bloody holes. Brazzo had been ripped apart by the swarm and Kasa was clutching her arm. Grace went to nurse her.

Russell was trembling. He'd never been so afraid. Though he'd faced vicious men without a quiver of his lip, never flinching even when he was outnumbered, the Koyotes were villains he did not understand, and therefore could not predict. They were incongruous, the epitome of evil.

Byrne and Delia were still at their posts, but now when they shot from the windows it was mostly in an effort to keep the birds away. If they closed the windows they wouldn't be able to fire upon the Koyotes at all. They had to keep trying.

"Grace, please tend to Oscar's wounds too and—"

Oscar waved his hand. "I'm fine. It's only flesh."

Russell thought if the man could see himself he might think differently, but he chose to let it be. There was no time to argue. No sense in it either.

"Marshal!"

It was Delia. She'd slammed the window shut to reload her weapon and her eyes were wide, lips gone pale. He went to her and she pointed outside. Russell opened the window and looked, and though he'd seen werewolves and wrathful birds and an amputee made into a giant spider, what he saw now made his jaw drop.

*

Glenn led his horse through the garden to the far side of the chapel, so that the building would be between them and the schoolhouse where the marshal's posse cowered. Hiram followed and tied the blue roan. Glenn took the kris dagger from his side and made quick work of expunging the arrow in Belial's chest. The horse was so powerful the head popped out almost on its own.

"Boss, look!"

Hiram pointed to the clearing where Vern was pulling the cart. The corpse of Jasper Thurston had been propped up behind the totem pole of the dead, but now it was standing up in the cart.

It began to walk.

The Koyotes stared with mouths agape as their old pack leader stepped down from the cart and started toward the chapel, his stride as steady as if he were a living man instead of a carcass buried fifteen years now revitalized by the sorcery of a witch's lust. He walked casually, a man out for an evening stroll to settle his supper.

Glenn couldn't help but chuckle.

"What the hell is happening here?" Hiram asked.

"Guess ol' Jasper thinks he's still destined for the throne." Glenn spat. "I got bad news for him."

Up the road came the clip-clop of the old pony Web rode upon. Hiram was the better sniper, but Glenn had wanted him at his side when they rolled in, so he'd left Web to take shots from the shadows of the snowy thicket. Behind Web sat Barley Reinhold, no longer hogtied but his wrists bound behind his back. The pony struggled to support the weight of both men. Reinhold's face was chalk and his eyes were bloodshot from lack of sleep. Web got off the pony, grinning like he'd just won a hand at faro.

"Didn't even get shot," he said proudly.

He grabbed Reinhold by the shirt and pulled him from the pony,

323

letting him fall to the ground with a thud. Reinhold groaned in pain.

"Shut up," Web barked. He looked around the side of the building for the cart and smiled when he saw Vern. "He done good too, ey?" Then he saw Jasper. "Tarnation! Look at the grand, First Koyote! Walking 'round like he's the danged mayor!"

Glenn punched Web's arm to hush him. Jasper stepped up to the front door of the chapel, but when he got there he only stood staring at it, as if he had eyes.

"What's he doing?" Hiram asked.

Glenn didn't know but didn't want to admit it, so he said nothing. Instead he looked to Reinhold and nudged him with his boot.

"Where's this underground church you speak of?"

Reinhold sat up, blowing snow from his lips. "I'll show you. If you'll just untie me, I can—"

Glenn punted him in ribs and Reinhold bent forward with a yelp.

"You tell me where it is," Glenn said, "or I'll add you to that totem pole."

"If I tell you, you'll kill me 'cause you'll think I'm of no more use to you. But that's not the case, sir. You'll need me in there as your guide."

Glenn smirked. "You'll betray your church, the one where you sang hymns as a choirboy, where you grew to have such noble profession as *groundskeeper*?"

Reinhold flushed. "These people turned on me when I needed them. When I was run out of town, they said nothing. Why should I care if this chapel falls?"

Glenn studied the young man. He was sniveling but telling the truth. There was hate in his heart, hate almost black enough to be a Koyote's. His sense of being wronged hung about him in a miserable shroud.

Glenn said, "What is it you really want, Reinhold?"

The young man took no time to answer.

"Revenge."

*

The break from battle gave Byrne a moment to gather his thoughts.

These earthly weapons wouldn't be enough this time. Glenn had returned with a greater sorcery, something powerful enough to create monstrosities like the one pulling that cart of the mutilated. For all the Seventh One had thus far done, he'd been rewarded with the blackest witchcraft.

Byrne looked out his window, seeing what caused Delia to cry out. Walking between the schoolhouse and chapel was a living skeleton, and inside its ribcage pulsed the lurid heart of Jasper Thurston. There was no mistaking it. The First Koyote had been resurrected in this abhorrent new form. But how conscious could he be with his brain gone to the worms? Surely it was his heart's desire that empowered him, but Jasper himself was no longer the seeker— it was the black magic itself.

"God in Heaven," Delia said, watching the corpse move.

Byrne grumbled. "He's of no help to us."

Oscar said, "What are we gonna do now, Luther? You're the wolfen. You know more about these monsters than anybody else."

They all looked to him. He removed his hat and ran his hand through his sweaty hair. He thought about the things he'd seen during his time running with the pack, the carnage and the witchery and the powers of Hell he'd only caught mere glimpses of. And though he may not have harnessed sorcery the way Jasper and Glenn had, he still had supernatural endowments of his own.

"I'm going out there," he said.

Delia tensed. "But the birds…"

"I know."

"You're injured. You're too slow to—"

"I've got me an idea. I have some friends up in them hills yonder. They might could help."

"Friends?" Russell asked. "What are you talking about?"

"I can't promise nothin'. But it's worth a go."

He reloaded his Winchester, and though the others tried to talk him out of going they couldn't argue they had any better ideas.

"I'll come with you," Shies offered, drawing his Bowie knife from out his coat. "Not all of them birds will attack. I spooked a lot away."

"What are you gonna do with that knife? Stab 'em all?"

"I figure I can slash at 'em."

"Hope them birds didn't attack the horses. I can't travel far without one." Byrne turned to Delia. "You cover us, shootist."

The men exited the back entrance and looked to the sky. A few dozen ravens remained, perched on the roof of the chapel like gargoyles. The horses were hidden behind the schoolhouse, tied to the hitching post near the well. They were unharmed. Byrne breathed a little easier seeing Bo waiting for him, the most loyal friend he'd ever known. Oscar had to help him into the saddle. Once the men mounted, they headed away from the chapel, sneaking between buildings so not to be spotted by their enemies. No shots were fired. No birds came swooping. And the Koyotes were too preoccupied to notice. They had other business. Byrne could only hope there'd be enough time.

They headed to the woods.

*

When the marshal joined her at the window, Delia caught the man's scent and her stomach pinched with hunger. She salivated and had to swallow it back before it hung from her lips like a dog at a dinner bell. Even her loins stirred.

"What're they waiting for?" Russell said.

The Koyotes were crouched behind the cart for cover, watching the corpse. It was just standing there like a statue on the front steps of the chapel, an unwelcome visitor if Delia had ever seen one. She thought of the visit the Koyotes had paid to her family and again itched to fire upon the bastards but thought better of it. As long as all was still, it bought Byrne and Shies some time. She had no idea what Byrne had been talking about or what friends he was going to see. She just hoped they didn't live far. And though she did not fire upon her enemies now she kept her repeater raised, just in case she was offered a clear shot. Given the chance, she'd take every Koyote's head.

*

They galloped away from town and entered the rich expanse of the valley. A gentle snow was falling now and the cold gave a calming numbness to the holes the birds had made in his flesh. Shies clutched the reins, tucked low against the wintery air, the hooves of his gray horse like cannon fire as the sound echoed across the desolate plains. Byrne was taking the straightway toward a dense forest. Shies rode alongside him, and though he had questions he asked none for there was no break for them.

When they came upon the tree line Byrne stopped and Shies pulled back his gray. They sat the horses and Byrne turned his face to the sky and took deep breaths through his nose.

He began to howl.

Shies shuddered. This was not the sound of a man imitating a wolf's howl—this was a *wolf howling from the throat of a man*. Shies knew the moon song of wolves. He'd heard them many times out on the range, especially in the bowels of the mountains. The sound Byrne made now was identical, a canine call to the cosmos.

"Holy hell," Shies muttered to himself.

Byrne continued his crying hymn. Shies' horse stirred and he patted its neck. The wolfen man's calls carried through the trees and rebounded off the horizon, the distant Black Mountain creating an echo chamber of the wilderness.

Something howled back.

Instinctively Shies reached for the rifle at his saddle scabbard but Byrne touched his hand and gently pushed it away. There came another howl. Then another. The hidden wolf was not alone. His gray stirred, rowdier this time, and Shies had to pull the reins, the horse as uneasy as he was.

The leader of the pack stepped out of the shade, a wolf more massive than any Shies had ever seen. Its fur rippled in the wind, the noble face raised to it, yellow eyes like citrine touched by rain. As it moved into the deadening, six more wolves came out of the woods. Shies caught something in the corner of his eye and turned—five more wolves slinking from the coppice to his right. They were closing in on them, surrounding them.

"Jesus," Shies said. "Just what we need."

Byrne spoke calmly. "Actually, it is. Don't be afraid."

"Wait… *these* are the friends you spoke of?"

The man nodded. "I am a lupicinus. A wolf-charmer."

More wolves came forward, almost twenty. They were large and silvery and muscular. A few puppies tailed close behind, almost as big as normal-sized adult dogs. Shies tensed when Byrne swung out of the saddle and approached the pack leader, but Shies did not go for his Whitworth this time. Byrne crouched. The head wolf nuzzled him, purring cat-like as he was scratched behind the ears. When the others gathered around, Byrne took a woolsack from his coat and fed them pieces of tallow and hog fat.

"You always carry that?" Shies asked.

THE THIRTEENTH KOYOTE

But Byrne was focused on the pack. He whispered to them as they ate, and Shies could swear he saw the head wolf nod.

CHAPTER XXXXII

THE CORPSE VIBRATED.

Jasper's heart seeped blackness, the tarry ooze slicking his ribs and slithering up his shoulders and neck. The Koyotes watched as the skeleton twisted in place, dancing without moving its feet.

"What's he doin'?" Web asked.

But no one answered.

Glenn watched as the slime sizzled, giving off black mist, and when the heart pulsed it swelled larger until it was so big it stressed the sternum to the point of cracking. The ravens cawed from the rooftop, some perched upon the large cross at the pinnacle, shitting on it.

"That's it," he said. "The chapel's too purified for a Koyote to simply enter. They've strengthened their guard since Jasper's day. The holy site below the earth has been touched by some sort of white magic."

"Shit," Hiram said. "You saying we can't go in? That we'll burst into flames or something?"

"I don't know what will happen. But look at the size of Jasper's heart. Jessamine was right. Putting it back in his body has made it more powerful, perhaps powerful enough to break this white seal."

THE THIRTEENTH KOYOTE

The corpse's bones creaked loudly and when it bent over the vertebra grew at the tail. Jasper squatted on his haunches and pulled his arms back, chest out and growing wide. His shoulders crackled as they doubled in size and his fingers grew to points. When his head came up the skull was enlarged, the face contorting into a snout, a row of fangs protruding.

"Tarnation," Web said. "He's transformin'."

The werewolf skeleton raised its arms and planted both claws into the front door, roaring as it tore at the wood.

*

The earth seemed to quiver all about the sisters.

Mable crossed herself for what must have been the twentieth time that day. She felt the familiar warmth within her, a force that was comforting to have but terrifying to use, so she'd used it only sparingly throughout the decades. It'd been the driving energy that had helped keep her alive when Jasper Thurston had first come to her chapel. Now, fifteen years later, his disciples were knocking at her door. She had to use what little power she had, no matter how unpredictable it was, no matter how little control she had over it. Mable was merely a vessel for this blue incandescence. Whether it was by grace of God she could not say. All she knew for certain was that it was not of this world.

Sister Evalena was tending to the giant Savior, keeping the Menhir as secure as possible by sprinkling the hallowed blood upon its chamber. The stone was humming now, the ballad of Lucifer calling to his minions. Down on her knees, Sister Genevieve continued to draw crosses upon the altar with a piece of chalk, believing there was strength in quantity. Though Mable did not agree with this belief, she did not argue it, wanting the terrified young sister to cling to whatever gave her hope in this dark hour.

Mable could actually *feel* the blackness above. It was coming just as surely as was death.

Reverend Blackwell stepped beside her. "It won't be like last time. I'm here, unlike before. That alone blesses us the church with higher divinity."

She took the old preacher's hand. "You're the only one left who has guarded the Menhir longer than I."

"Three score and seventeen years."

They fell silent then.

Mable's eyes misted over. "What if we cannot keep it secure any longer?"

The earthen walls shuddered with underground thunder. Sister Mable swallowed hard, remembering the earthquake she'd experienced eight years ago while on a trip to northern California. The ground had torn open and inhaled a row of houses, the families inside screaming as they were buried alive in mere seconds. Mable had been riding inside the stagecoach and Barley Reinhold had put the terrified horses into a full gallop in the other direction, the earth shaking beneath the wheels of the wagon and cracking apart behind them, Mable gripping the seat with white knuckles and mumbling prayers.

She offered up a new prayer now, for there would be no running away this time.

*

They took the shorter way back, charging up the street toward the chapel, guns drawn, horses snorting, a company of wolves running alongside them. The flurries had intensified, flakes swirling in all directions as if hinting at the coming chaos. Byrne's heart drummed. The pull of Jasper's heart was as strong as a freight train. And when he and Shies reached the schoolhouse they did not stop. The monstrous skeleton was ripping its way through the barricaded chapel door. They led the horses in a wide arc and rounded the backside of the chapel, going straight for the Koyotes on the other side.

The ravens rose in a black cloud of wings, cawing to alert their masters, and as they came swooping Byrne fired his Colt, killing one. Delia appeared in the schoolhouse window with her repeater and the front door came open, Russell at the ready. Byrne and Shies climbed off of their horses to get closer to the ground, closer to the protection of the wolves, and when the flock of birds flew down the wolves barked and charged, leaping into the air to snatch birds with fangs, slashing open their bellies, tearing them in half in mid air with a swipe of their paw.

Byrne spotted Glenn and ran in a brazen, careless assault, his pistol popping off round after round. The Koyotes ducked behind the cart as the bullets came for them and one tore across Glenn's thigh but he barely flinched. Byrne put his back to the side of the chapel to cover himself as bullets tore the air in front of him. The chapel was trembling like a newborn fawn and the pungent aroma of Jasper's ooze seemed to emanate from it.

Byrne stepped backward toward the window on the side of the chapel and glanced inside. From this angle he could see the front door from the interior. It was being torn apart, holes offering the white daylight of winter as skeleton hands pawed through the wood. Using the butt of his Colt, Byrne shattered the window and pushed away the shards, but when he tried to climb inside a mean heat made him recoil. He felt suddenly nauseous and weak. He had not yet fully recovered from his injuries, but knew this was not the cause of his sudden spell, for as soon as he backed out of the window the sickness receded.

The church house was protected against Koyotes, even the re-formed ones. Mable must have fortified it since he'd last been here, using some sort of holy purification in preparation for these hellish villains. But Jasper was seeing to that. His heart was pushing its sorcery through the doorway, flooding the chapel and crippling its divinity under a pulverizing darkness.

Byrne put his arms through the window, both hands on his pistol, aiming straight at the door as it split down the center.

*

Russell had no choice but to run through the madness. He dodged past a war of wolves and ravens, the vision of a nightmare world come flesh. Beside him, Kasa was slinging and firing arrows, assisting the wolves in the bacchanalia. When she ran ahead, Russell noticed her nose had turned black and wet, her face somewhat elongated. She pulled arrows from the quiver with a speed that defied human ability. Rifle in his hands and iron at his hip, Russell headed toward the chapel where Shies was crouched behind the low fence, his Whitworth cradled upon it as he fired upon the Koyotes. The wolfen were shooting back and their bullets tore through the planks, but Shies knew when to roll to camouflage his position. Smoke and splinters and snow made a dizzying effluvium.

Web fell backward, a spurt of blood rising. He groaned but got to his hands and knees, searching the ground for his gun. The crack of Delia's rifle from the window behind Russell made his skin gooseflesh. The air was heavy with gunpowder and blood—some human, some animal. Snow made his targets harder to spot. He had to get closer. Delia and Shies would have to cover him. He motioned to Shies and the man nodded, and Russell moved between the shrubs that lined the garden, going to the side of the chapel opposite of where Byrne had gone, hoping they could attack the Koyotes from both sides.

Glenn and Hiram were shooting back at the schoolhouse now, Web still looking for his pistol, all of them too preoccupied to spot the marshal drawing near, hidden by the snowfall and branches. He was coming upon them when he saw the pony and the man beside it with his hands tied behind his back. Russell hadn't seen the hostage from inside the schoolhouse. Though the man's head was down, his blonde hair covering his face, Russell could see he was young, probably had a wife and little children.

He snuck his way closer. The pony was far enough from the cart, standing behind the taller horses. He had to be fast and couldn't be gentle about it. Taking a deep breath, Russell ran, faster than he had since his boyhood, and when he reached the spot he dropped his rifle and grabbed the man around the waist and pulled him up. The man landed on his feet but still stumbled, and Russell drew his Bowie knife and cut the binds, freeing his hands. The poor fellow was dirty, hair matted, face darkened by soot and several days growth of beard.

"Come on," Russell said.

The man seemed to come awake. He looked at Russell and blinked out of his fog. Russell took up his rifle and nudged him to run and they sprinted back to the garden, tucking behind the shrubs.

"You alright, mister?"

The young man nodded. His eyes were hard, wrought from the horror he'd seen while in the Koyotes' possession. He seemed vaguely familiar but Russell could not place him. Another man from town he'd yet to memorize. It would have been easier if he weren't so disheveled. He might be unrecognizable to his own mother in the sorry state he was in.

The gunfire of the battle became a deafening staccato, every gun blazing at once, growls and barking and caws, the piercing screams of man and beast. All about them a psychotic war raged, a horror that shook the blood in his heart.

Russell drew his Colt for his hip.

"You ever fire a pistol, mister?"

333

THE THIRTEENTH KOYOTE

The young man nodded again. He reached out and Russell gave him the pistol, handle first. Russell returned his attention to the Koyotes. Hiram had changed his position and was reloading. He was wide open and oblivious to the marshal's presence. It would be easy, a clear headshot. Russell raised his rifle to his shoulder and steadied it, but the gun that went off was not in his hands.

CHAPTER XXXXIII

THERE WAS A BREAK IN the gunfire and Glenn made a dash
to the chapel's front door. Or what was left of it. Jasper had broken
inside and the blackness followed with him, drowning out the con-
secration the nuns had put in place. Glenn doubted he could make
it inside without catching a round, but it hardly mattered. He was
emboldened by the magic he now possessed and motivated to obtain more of it, even if it meant taking a bullet. He felt not only lethal—he felt *invincible*, fueled by a force beckoning him to his destiny, his throne upon a new level of Hell.

A shot rang out from the schoolhouse and the sniper's bullet
struck him but he did not break stride. The pain in his arm was
there, yet insignificant. But when he entered the chapel and walked
among the pews another shot rang out and this one knocked him
back. This shot had come from the window to his left. His chest
was bleeding but the round missed his organs. Glenn raised his iron
and blasted away at the window but saw no one in it. His assailant
had either ducked for cover or ran off. He got to his feet, watching
the window with his pistol honed in on it, and walked among the
pews, feeling the strange pull of an energy he could not identify.
When he reached the end of the row he turned around and walked

backwards so he could watch the window for any sudden movement, the bullwhip bouncing against his hip.

The walls were shaking. A painting of the Last Supper fell from its hook. Glenn grinned, his teeth sharp as arrowheads, and the floor beneath him seemed to breathe then, rising and falling as he backed up to the altar, and when he reached it he saw the doorway and the corpse of Jasper Thurston laid out before it, the skull shattered, but the heart still pounding.

*

Byrne had been unable to stop the black magic. Though he'd dropped Jasper by blasting his head to bits, every shot the corpse took to the heart was merely absorbed by the mass, as if it were eating the bullets. It was too strong to die by the weapons of man.

He'd clipped Glenn good before taking a bullet himself. Glenn's return fire just missed Byrne's head but caught his left shoulder, severing the tendon from the rotator cuff. The arm would be mostly useless for a while, but at least it was not his dominant hand. He still clutched the iron. It was hot and smoking as he put in more rounds. If he showed his face at the window it'd be met with a bullet between the eyes, for Glenn was a defensive gunfighter and inhumanly patient.

Byrne pressed his ear to the quivering wall, hoping he might hear the man's movements, but the roar of gunfire was too overpowering, even for wolfen.

He had to get inside.

*

Web had taken another damned arrow, this one right through the back of his hand as he'd been pawing at the dirt for his weapon. He mewled and tried to pull it from the ground with his other hand, but the earth was frozen and he couldn't get the damn thing to budge. He was pinned.

"Hiram! Help!"

But Hiram was engaged in a shootout with two opponents, the black man and whoever was in the schoolhouse.

Another arrow flew by Web's head and stuck into the side of the cart just inches from his face. He had to move fast or die, so he put his other hand around the pinned one's wrist and began pulling it backward, the meat and bone separating as the arrow shaft slowly tore the hand up its center. He squealed like a sow being branded, ripping his own hand in two to save his life, and pulled free just as another arrow came at him, landing just where he'd been a second before.

He crawled to the other side of the cart and tucked himself behind Vern. The undertaker was chuckling through his own cobwebs. Web would've smacked him if his hand weren't a bloody flipper.

"Hello there," Vern said. He sounded like a hive of wasps.

Web followed Vern's gaze to where his pistol was lying in a small pocket of slush. He took it up with his good hand. He wasn't as good of a shot with this one, but at least he was armed. Now he could fire back at that Kiowa bitch! He got to his knees, iron at the end of his arm, but when he saw the woman coming he knew a mere bullet would not stop her.

Hell, *six* wouldn't.

She'd tossed the bow. From the looks of her she wouldn't need it. She was twice the size of Web now, a woman almost fully transformed into a grizzly bear. Her attire had burst to ribbons, the strap of the quiver having snapped away. Only her breasts and belly were without the thick, brown fur. The eyes were human, but her face was a snout and her ears had rounded and moved higher on her skull. When she roared, enormous yellow teeth glimmered.

Because of the pain, Web's body had gone into overdrive, flooding him with wolfen endorphins and kicking in its healing properties. He was not in full werewolf state, but he was nearly there—eyes like roses, fangs out, muttonchops blowing long in the wind.

He braced himself as the werebear pounced.

*

Reinhold stood over the first man he had ever killed.

Marshal Russell was crumpled on the ground, the bullet having gone straight through the heart, the lawman slain by his own gun. Though he'd killed bison and ducks and deer for slaughter, Reinhold had never even thought of shooting a man before, at least not with any serious consideration. Even now he hadn't considered it much. He'd simply acted. Maybe it was the insanity of all that was going on around him, the gunfight and the butchered Indians and the human tarantula. Maybe it was just his personal vendetta against the lawman for taking away his livelihood and the family he loved. Whatever had pushed him to murder, there was no excusing it away.

I am a man killer, he thought.

He tucked the Colt into his pants, hissing as the hot barrel singed him. He simply wasn't thinking straight. More comfortable with a rifle, he picked up the marshal's and inched alongside the chapel wall. He wasn't sure whose side he was on here. Probably nobody's. But if he were going to make it out of this alive it would be wise to have assisted the winning team. No one had seen him kill Henry Russell in the garden. It didn't play into whatever decision he would make.

A monstrous roar froze him.

That's no wolf.

He peeked around the corner of the building and saw the source of the noise, a massive she-bear hulking above Web as he unloaded his pistol into it. Still the werebear attacked. The bullets may as well have been beestings. But Web was shapeshifting too, and as he did so his strength increased. When the werebear fell into him and swung a paw he was able to catch it in both hands and snap the bone. The beast countered with the other paw, clawing at Web's face, leaving four bloody trails as it opened his flesh. The top of one ear flew off like mud and though Web fought back the werebear was far more powerful. He screamed as it mauled him, blood and sinew making a mist that changed the color of his attacker's fur.

Reinhold made his choice.

He fired.

The werebear yelped as the round shattered her teeth. Several flew out the other side of the beast's face and disappeared into the rage of the snow. The werebear saw him then, but as it rose to its full height Reinhold fired again. Considering how enormous his target, it was embarrassing to have missed. Web still had some fight in him and his nails went to work on the werebear's underbelly. The beast seemed conflicted now, not knowing which man to attack first, which posed the more immediate threat. She grabbed Web's head, lifting him completely off the ground, and began to squeeze, the big man mewling as the pressure to his skull increased. Reinhold aimed again, steadying for accuracy, but when he pulled the trigger there was only the click of an empty chamber.

"Shit!"

Web was going to die. But if Reinhold could find the marshal's ammo he might be able to reload in time to save himself. The only other option was to run but he doubted the werebear would take long to catch up. He kicked the dead man in the shoulder to turn him further on his side, then crouched down and sifted through his coat until he found the box of rounds and reloaded. It wasn't until he was finished that he remembered he had the Colt tucked into his pants and could've used that to rescue Web. But oh well. One less Koyote in the world was no tragedy.

A strange screeching sound made his ears ache. He slinked around the corner again. The werebear was spinning, trying to paw its own back, for the Vern-spider had pounced upon her shoulders, its skeleton legs stuck into her body, one rising and falling, stabbing the werebear in the back of the neck.

Web was moaning in bloody slush, horribly wounded but still alive.

The undertaker had come to his rescue.

*

Shies couldn't get a clear shot.

If he fired he would likely hit Kasa, and even if he did hit the man-spider on her back his bullet would likely go right through the human torso and hit her anyway. With Hiram returning fire, Shies was unable to charge, but if the Kiowa woman were to be saved he'd have to get closer. He'd been crouched low throughout the gunfight and did not know where the rest of the posse was, if they'd gone inside the chapel or not. The snow was falling so heavily now. He could barely see the cemetery's headstones. But he'd seen Glenn go inside the chapel. Shies was torn now, wanting to rescue Kasa but fearing they'd all perish if he didn't go after Glenn, so he took a deep breath, got into a crouching run, and made for the church house, too angry to die.

*

The blue phantasmagoria swirled beneath the earthen sanctum, a perplexing murk that drifted like morning fog, coiling about the towering Christ and sluicing through every fold and crevice of Sister

Mable's body. Though she'd never known a lover, she shivered as if being touched by one. The mist was almost fluid, cradling her in its womb of white magic. This energy was not fully at her command. She was merely a vessel, here to carry it like a genie's lamp.

The others were at her side, a human barricade at the foot of the stairs, alerted by the low growls and canine stink of the descending abomination. His boots appeared first, black leather with spurs made of human teeth and finger bones. With each step, blackness emanated from his soles, the residue of Hell.

Reverend Blackwell quoted from Ephesians.

"Be strong in the Lord and in His mighty power. Put on the full armor of God, so that you can take your stand against the devil's schemes."

The preacher stepped forward. When Mable tried to join him, he gently pushed her back. She hoped he had a plan. He'd been serving God far longer than she. Perhaps he was ready for Glenn the Dreadful in a manner she did not understand. If he'd had a premonition, he'd not shared it with her. Sisters Evalena and Genevieve stood fast, the beads of their rosaries encircling their wrists, crosses clutched in their shaking hands. Genevieve was crying, but despite the young nun's fear Mable knew she would not flee, such was her devotion to the Lord and faithfulness to her Christian duty to her fellow man.

Glenn entered the underground church, the throbbing heart of the blackest sorcerer cradled in his arms like a newborn. The heart's tubes had climbed up his left forearm, the inferior vena cava long and snake-like, the fleshy pipes of the aorta connected to Glenn's pulsing veins like fat leeches. When he separated his hands, the heart clung to him, an unholy abscess. He looked about the underground church, smirking at the candelabras and multitude of crosses, and when he gazed up at the mighty Savior he spat upon the floor.

Blackwell pointed at him. "Creature of evil! I cast thee—"

Glenn moved like a viper and the preacher was grabbed. Mable started and stepped back, the three nuns huddling closer together, as if they could transmogrify into a collective force for good. But God offered no such grace. The Koyote seemed completely impervious to the white magic that drifted about him, and even as his hands fell upon Blackwell's shoulders they were not singed or broken or harmed in any way. He snatched the preacher by one wrist and one ankle and lifted him over his head like he was no more than a straw doll.

Mable screamed. They all did.

Glenn flashed his fangs and bit into Blackwell's belly, then chewed away the fat and sinew, creating a tear through the preacher's midsection. He didn't even have time to cry out in pain. Glenn pulled in opposite directions and Blackwell was torn apart, his upper body ripped from the lower in a bloody explosion of hot and gassing guts.

Tossing the pieces behind him, Glenn came at the sisters. Genevieve closed tight her eyes, shrieking and sobbing, and when Evalena stepped before her as protection Glenn drew his bullwhip from his side and with one swoop it split the air and slithered around Evalena's throat in a leather noose and snapped her neck, killing her instantly.

Sister Mable glanced to the statue of Christ, wondering, not for the first time, where God was. Through the glass chamber she watched the Menhir glow like a crimson star, the blood it swam in bubbling, steaming. So many children. So many souls. She tugged at Genevieve but the young nun would not budge. Fear had crippled her. Mable had no choice but to leave her as Glenn came upon them, half transformed now, his eyes afire and his muttonchops dripping with the gore of the bisected preacher. As she ran toward the statue she heard the whip cracking over and over again, Genevieve's screams making Mable bite her lip and bat away the rising tears.

When she reached the barrel beside the ladder she slid off the lid, removed her wimple, and dunked her head into the blood of the five orphans the nuns had murdered the night before. They'd chosen the children who were the sickliest and would not live long anyway, smothering them while they slept and then bringing them here for exsanguination. The nuns had done their best to drain all ten pints from the children's veins, and though it broke something in each of them, they had to keep the Menhir safe. A few drops would no longer do now that evil so tremendous had come for it.

The Menhir needed protection... but well, so did she.

Mable tore out of her gown and gave herself a whore's bath with the blood, slathering her arms and neck and breasts, covering her torso first to protect her vital organs. When she went to lather her legs the barrel slipped from her grasp and she cried as it spilled across her feet. And so she got down upon the altar and rolled in it

THE THIRTEENTH KOYOTE

as if she were on fire, weeping and screaming in place of Genevieve, who'd gone silent.

CHAPTER XXXXIV

IT WAS A TIGHT FIT, but Byrne managed to squeeze through the window, catching only a few slivers of glass. The sorcery of the Koyotes had split the seal that had previously scalded him, and he was able to enter the building without physical harm. Screams filled the chapel in a horrid chorus, rising from the subterranean pulpit. Stepping over the bone pile of Jasper, he noticed the heart had been expunged and Byrne followed the trail of tar down the steps, trying to transform but struggling to in his weakened state. He grit his teeth. His left shoulder was throbbing and it pinched around the lodged bullet when he tried to raise his arm any higher than his chest. He worried about blood poisoning. Given his injuries, his wolfen side should be taking over, kicking in instinctively to heal and protect him. But he'd asked a lot of his body of late and its superhuman resilience was spent. He'd needed more time to recover, but time was something they were out of.

Byrne reloaded and headed downstairs.

Into the swarming blackness and pinpoints of blue light, into the stench of blood and the screams of the dying and down, down, down into the pulsing tomb at the end of the world.

*

When the black man ran for the chapel, Hiram got his chance.

Firing in quick succession, he dropped the big bastard. Hiram sighed with relief. The man was a good shot and had clipped him several times throughout the exchange. Rising from his position behind the cart, Hiram saw what all the commotion was about.

Hiram had seen a lot of bizarre things in his day, but this beat all.

Web and the grizzly and the creature Glenn had made of Vern Pipkin were rolling, clawing, and biting each other in an orgy of violence. Hiram looked to the open door of the chapel, drawn to the black light, feeling the tug of the Menhir. He raised his rifle, spun, and unloaded upon the werebear until it fell to the ground. In the process he'd blown off one of Vern's bone legs, causing him to fall off the grizzly as it slowly faded back into the form of a woman.

Hiram glanced at Web. He was a mess, but he might survive, being the stubborn old buzzard he was.

There were more important things to attend to.

*

Reinhold ran after all.

The sheer insanity of the shapeshifters and walking skeletons, combined with the fact he was now a bona fide man-killer, snapped his very last nerve. So he fled through the garden and evergreens, past the fallen black man moaning in a mound of red snow, and when he reached the fence near the cemetery he ran in a crouch.

He'd chosen to join the Koyotes only because he felt they might win this war. He hoped shooting the werebear would count for something. Maybe he could even join up with them, become a member of the company. He certainly had no other prospects and now that he'd killed once he was confident he could do it again.

He looked all around. The gunfire had ceased and the snowfall made the fresh silence all the more stunning. He had to get to cover while things were still calm.

Reinhold lurched toward the schoolhouse.

*

Delia didn't want to smack Grace Cowlin, but would if she had to.

It would be the most disrespectful thing she'd ever done, but the schoolmarm, while well-meaning, was impeding her. Delia was here as a posseman. She was here to fight. But when she tried to leave the schoolhouse Grace kept pulling her back, her eyes bright with worry.

"You can't go out there, Delia! They'll kill you!"

They'd seen Oscar Shies take bullets and drop. They'd seen Kasa shot down too. Brazzo lay shredded by demon birds. They didn't know where Russell or Byrne were now, and that just made Delia all the more uneasy.

"I have to help them."

"You won't be helping anyone by dying."

Delia pulled her wrist free from the schoolmarm's grasp. "I can't do anything from here. They're all in the chapel. What if Mr. Byrne and the marshal really need me right now? What if they're in big trouble?"

Grace didn't have time to respond. The front door came open and Delia spun with her rifle, hoping it was one of their friends returning but prepared to fire upon a Koyote. The man who entered was neither. The stranger closed the door behind him and pressed his back to it, breathing hard as he looked at the women. Delia noted the rifle in his hands, the barrel of which was directed at the floor. She did not lower her own, especially when the stranger grinned. There was something she didn't like to that smile, something disingenuous, a sales pitch.

"No," Grace whispered.

Delia glanced at her. The schoolmarm was the color of camellias, her body gone rigid. The stranger stepped forward without a word and Delia raised the barrel at his face.

"You just stay right there, mister."

His ironed-on smile grew bigger and he stared at Grace, ignoring Delia completely.

"I should have known," he said. "Hell, I *did* know!"

Grace fell mute, so Delia did the talking. "Stay back, I say."

"All this witchery," he said to Grace, "all these monsters and shapeshifters. *You* brought them to Hope's Hill! *You're* the head witch. I've known it all along but these ignorant people just wouldn't listen. They had to stop me from doing God's work. Well, nothing's gonna stop me now."

Delia shouted. "*I'll* stop you!"

He was quick, but not quick enough. The stranger spun toward Delia with the rifle at his side and when he fired his bullet landed true, but he also caught a round to the chest for his efforts. Delia's bullet knocked him off his feet whereas the round he'd grazed her arm with only made her wince. She ran to him, kicked his rifle away, stuck her own in his face, and stepped on his chest wound.

"I will end you if that's what it takes, mister."

"You Satan spawn! You're just another witch, no better than—"

She pressed down on his wound and he writhed, causing her to lose her balance, and while she righted herself he went for the rifle in her hands, pushing the barrel away as she fired a second time, the bullet going wild and hitting a desk. He swept her feet out from under her and slammed her to the floor and tore the rifle from her hands as she gasped for air, the wind knocked out of her.

He pushed the barrel of the rifle under her chin. "Die, you little bitch!"

The top of the man's head came apart.

His skullcap flew from his head like a skipping rock and slid across the floor on a stream of blood. Brain matter burst from his ears, his nostrils a fountain of red, and one of his eyes popped from the socket with a wet hiss before he keeled over. Delia didn't have to see this for she had closed her eyes tight, certain the sound of the gunshot was that of the bullet which would take her life. When the man fell off her she batted away the blood in her eyelashes and saw Grace Cowlin standing above her, the dead man's rifle in the schoolmarm's hands. Delia got to her feet, still trembling from her near embrace with death. Grace was even paler now, tears falling in silence. Delia went to her and kissed her cheek, wrapping her arms around her.

"Barley Reinhold," the schoolmarm said. "His name was Barley Reinhold."

Delia looked at the weapon in Grace's hands. "Dear Lord. That's Marshal Russell's rifle."

*

The nun was encased in a sphere of light the color of a summer sky, the blood she was caked in looking purple beneath the radiant shroud. Her nude body was completely slathered in it, making her look like a corpse, but even if Glenn hadn't seen her douse herself in it he'd have known the blood was not hers just by its smell.

Children. He smacked his lips. *They used children.*

A sudden jolt went through him. Jasper's heart was flooding his veins with a special blood of its own. When he looked at the arm it had attached to, it was entirely coal black and glistening like wet bat wings, the muscles rippling and bulging. He stepped over the corpse of the young nun he'd lashed to death, another offering for the great lords of Hell. But Glenn grew nauseous as he approached the nun sitting on the floor with her legs drawn to her chest and her head tucked, her shield of innocent blood serving its purpose. When he tried to get close his stomach roiled, bowels churning, throat filing with bile. He moved away from her and the dizzy spell began to recede.

"Bloody white witch," he said. "You're of little consequence."

He chose to let her alone for now. The suffering he was to unleash upon this earth would be punishment enough for her, for every pointless human life.

Glenn gazed upon the towering edifice before him and took his first step upon the altar. The Menhir was spinning in its chamber now, the blood swishing, waves of young gore bending the black illuminations into a kaleidoscope of unnamed colors, a cosmic lava that climbed the stone and mortar walls and rippled in the earthen ceiling like flickering stalactites. The Menhir beckoned. It longed to be free from this confine of Christ, awakened after centuries of unwanted slumber. Already it was bleeding fresh visions into Glenn's mind. He absorbed them hungrily, the satanic wisdom of the ancient masters blessing him, damning him, flooding him with the blackest enlightenment.

Glenn kicked out of his boots. He lifted his hand. His wolfen claws were now tough as a blacksmith's anvil and just as hot, causing smoke to billow up from Christ's leg as they sunk into it. He reached up with his other hand and dug in, and then pulled up his legs, the black pads of his soles attaching to the statue, his dewclaws like pickaxes.

He began to climb.

The Menhir released a long, bellowing wail, howling for him with a desire beyond what he'd known in a woman, even a Maenad. Its howl was that of a legion of wolfen, millions of years of lycanthropes and other earthly demons all singing at once, a ballad accumulated over the course of all evil. The sound waves forced their way beneath his skin and made his hairs stand on end. His testicles drew closer to his body and his nipples hardened.

He climbed higher still.

When his face was before the Menhir the power it emitted made Glenn's eyes roll back. His heartbeat accelerated and he instantly climaxed in his pants. It was not just his irises that went red but the surface of the eye entirely, leaving only the trace of a thin, black circle where the irises had been. He felt sunburned and frozen at once, the song of screams rattling his eardrums, his mind throbbing with the black influx of knowledge. And though the blood of innocents had cloaked the Menhir, now it all had been boiled down to red steam, and the combined forces of the stone and the Koyote overpowered the remaining holy mist.

The chamber burst.

*

Byrne's jaw fell.

Glenn Amarok was floating, the Menhir in his hands, glowing blackly as the statue of Christ began to crumble, the crucifix falling to rot and rust and sailing to the floor. A noose of darkness garroted the Savior, beheading Him, and the tubes popped free from the torso as it collapsed into itself.

Glenn's back was turned but shooting him would be useless. He was at the peak of his powers now—wolfen turned warlock, a dark prince. Byrne crouched in the shadows, knowing he was no match. He was failing. They all were. Glenn had the key—now he only needed a gate. Byrne had to form a plan. More than that, he needed the strength and cunning to make it successful. Ducking behind a temple of candles, he watched as the head Koyote became so much more, so much worse. He spotted Sister Mable then, dripping with gore but alive. The other members of the church had not fared as well. Their guts and flesh were thrown about like ornaments.

Glenn descended.

His fur shimmered, black as his skin had turned, a man carved of onyx and brimstone. He landed gracefully, hugging the Menhir to his chest, and when Byrne saw his eyes he skipped a breath and wrapped his arms around himself. His chin trembled. Glenn was bound to sense him—unless he was too overwhelmed and distracted by his newfound power. Byrne felt suddenly lost, as abandoned as he'd been as a child. Closing his eyes tight, he crouched into a ball just as Mable had and tucked his head, praying for the first time since he'd fled from the orphanage.

*

Hiram stood at the foot of the stairs.

Beside him, Jasper's bones lay defeated. At least now the First Koyote could rest.

Even with both pistols drawn, he found he lacked the nerve to walk down the stairs into the underground church. His jaw jutted and he bit his upper lip. Lights of unnatural color shimmered from the hole at the bottom of the stairwell and a haunting song filled the shaft. The wolf within him urged to sing along but he could not make a sound.

He'd thought he'd been ready for this.

He'd thought wrong.

Though he was a man of sadistic cruelty and had gorged himself on the most lavish evils, the energy thrumming below caused him to pale. A sick fear hollowed him, leaving less of a man, and he moved back, away from the stairwell, pistols shaking useless in his hands.

*

"Oscar!"

He was on his belly in the snow, his head turned to one side, eyes closed. Delia ran around the fence and into the garden, seeing the shape of another body among the rows of bushes but unable to tell whom it was. Beside her, Grace Cowlin toted the purse of medical supplies. Slung over her other shoulder was the marshal's rifle, the one they'd taken from Reinhold, his possession of it an ominous implication.

Oscar moaned. Delia never thought she'd be so happy to hear a man in pain. It meant he was still alive. They managed to turn him over. He'd been shot in the hip and across his breast. Grace unbuttoned his shirt.

Delia stood. "Tend to him but keep your eyes open. I'm going inside."

Grace opened her mouth to object but Delia was already running. She clutched her repeater as she dodged between tall shrubbery and the stacked poles and rope cradling dead tomato vines. She hopped over the snow bank at the garden's end and found herself behind the Koyote's cart. Kasa lay lifeless, in a woman's form but still spouting the snout of a grizzly. Sitting before her like some grotesque tombstone was the ghoulish man-spider, his head hung as if he were asleep, muttering gibberish.

Sitting in a slush puddle was Webster Tipton.

The foul and wretched beast was in a meditative state, eyes closed and breathing deep. Blood was all around him. He was drenched in it. Delia walked on the balls of her feet, cautious of the snow so her heels would not crunch it. Moving across this patch of dirt, she came behind Web and the musk of his body titillated her nostrils. Her belly swelled with emptiness. She salivated. Raising the rifle, she aimed at the back of his skull.

No.

This is too good for him.

She put the repeater down and leaned it against the cart. Her hand went to the sheath at her side, fingers tight upon the handle of her deer-skinning knife. She figured it would do just as well on a man.

"Hello, Web."

The man turned his neck and it clearly pained him to do so. His eyes were watering, red snot bubbles in one nostril whenever he breathed. Blood trickled from the corner of his mouth. When she stepped to his side, Delia saw he was holding in his guts. He'd been nearly eviscerated by Kasa and was hanging on, hoping to heal, praying to whatever horrible god he worshipped.

"Want to live another day?" she asked. "So you can rape and torture and kill? So you can tear families apart and eat little babies?"

He looked her in the eyes but showed no sign of recognition. A lifetime of heartlessness had left a long line of victims behind. It seemed their faces had all blurred together. Delia was just another babe in the woods to him.

"I aim to kill you, Webster Tipton. Not just for what you did to me. This is justice for everyone you've wronged throughout your miserable life. You chose a path of cruelty and it dead ends here, with me."

He turned away from her, watching the snow tumble from a stonewashed sky. The blizzard had not fully passed but it mellowed to gentler, holiday flakes.

"Any last words, Tipton?"

He didn't reply.

Delia drew the knife. Now he looked at her.

"Your eyes," he said.

But that was all. He'd begun coughing blood.

Later, Delia would understand the man's final words, but right now they failed to matter. She grabbed his hair, pulled his head back, and dragged the blade across his neck. The sight of the blood gushing from his arteries drew her in. Her teeth ached and when she tongued her canines they were rising spikes, the gums bleeding. Her skin rippled. Her belly groaned. She sawed the knife back and forth, pulling the head back the whole time, and Web's eyes rolled as his stump offered a red waterfall. By the time he was fully decapitated, Delia was barking with excitement. The pack of wolves made a circle around her, raised their snouts to the sky, and howled in celebration of their new sister.

*

It was like looking through milk. The snow was not what obscured his vision. Vern was finally dying. Though his thoughts were failing to connect as the dementia set in, he could still comprehend his encroaching demise. The black magic only lasted so long. His stars were going out, his farm paid in full. He chuckled at the notion. After a life spent in the worship of death, he was still unprepared for it. He found himself waiting for his life to flash before his eyes, but all he saw was that milky, pus-filled blur, and when he tried to think of fond memories there were no glimpses of his mother or the too few women he'd loved, nor of the smell of grass in spring or good meals had by a warm fire. Instead all he conjured up were unearthed graves, corpses embalmed with arsenic for preservation, the illegal selling of human parts, and all the little, dead girls he'd defiled.

The undertaker died smiling.

*

The roof of the chapel opened. The last of the ravens flew. Darkness swarmed. Inside, the eerie blue light dissipated, swallowed by blackness that smoked through the floorboards.

Glenn Amarok appeared in the stairway. Climbing the steps, he

351

carried the glittering Menhir as if it were his firstborn child. He was neither man nor beast nor any shape in between. He was a wolfen warlock of the highest crown, a creature of pure malevolence come to leave only ashes of an earth forged of the bodies of ancient, fallen gods.

The walls of the chapel collapsed outward, the building opening like a puzzle box, its holiness dead and forgotten. Glenn drifted rather than walked, his feet just a quarter of an inch off the ground, his muscular body now light as a ghost. Passing by Hiram, he clucked his tongue and his second-in-command came to his side like an obedient pup, and the Koyotes emerged from the rubble of the church house and into the vast, open oblivion of destiny.

CHAPTER XXXXV

IN THE UNDERGROUND CHURCH, BYRNE went to Sister Mable, but there remained a glaze upon her that forced him to step back.

"Come on," he said. "We have to get out of here."

She looked up. "Luther?"

"Yeah, it's me. Now get off your setter and move."

She reached out for him to help her up but he pulled away his hands.

"Can't touch you yet," he said. "I'll vomit and my fingers will probably burn."

Mable got her feet. The walls of the subterranean church were shuddering, the ground beneath them breaking out in rivers of cracks. She looked about with bloodshot eyes.

"He didn't kill us," Byrne said. "Don't know why, but he didn't. Maybe he didn't sense us hiding."

"He knew. But we're insignificant now." She gazed into space. "He has the Menhir. What could we possibly matter? The Menhir has bigger plans for him, ones that will see us suffer or die anyway, along with everyone else."

Byrne headed for the stairs, waving her to follow, and the nun snapped out of her daze and joined him on his ascension, following what little light was left in the wake of Glenn the Dreadful. They rose up the shaft cautiously, Byrne clenching his iron. He peered over the next floor. Glenn and Hiram were climbing back into their saddles. All he could do was lay low until the Koyotes were out of sight.

*

It was Delia who found him.

With Oscar there'd been a question. There was no question here.

Henry Russell was dead.

The marshal lay beneath the smoldering, blown-out boards of the chapel in a large, red pool, facedown in the snow. His legs were crossed awkwardly, one arm bent behind him. He'd been shot in the back, the kill shot of a cowardly assassin.

The posse reconvened at the schoolhouse, wounded in body and spirit, many of them covered in blood not their own. Byrne carried Russell's body inside, placed him upon the floor behind Grace's desk, and covered him with the blanket the teacher used for picnics. Now there were two corpses in the building.

Grace fled to the watering room to be alone but her cries were too intense to be muffled.

Sister Mable was wrapped in Byrne's overcoat to hide her nudity. Her hair was matted with crusting blood, half-hiding her face. The bullet in Byrne's rotator cuff had popped out but the wound was still gaping, healing too slowly for comfort. But he was better off than Oscar Shies. The schoolmarm had done what she could, but he'd been shot twice and struggled to move around, limping with labored breath.

Delia almost felt guilty for escaping the battle unscathed. She'd been nicked by Reinhold's bullet, but it was merely a flesh wound, tended to with only a bandage.

But she wasn't well. The first urges of her condition had come and she'd been unable to control the rage of the beast within. She'd at least forced herself to get away from Web's body so not to eat it. Lord knows she'd wanted to. It had taken every last shred of self-control to fight off that disgusting impulse. Her fangs had receded, and though she was not aware, the red glow left her eyes.

She came beside Byrne. "We should bring the others inside too."

"Actually, I was thinking of taking the marshal and that Reinhold fellow and hauling them out back for burial. Might as well take the others there too."

She gave him an incredulous look. "You want to dig holes *now?*"

He hung his head and put his hands on his hips.

"Kid," he said, "I don't know what in the hell to do no more."

"We have to go after them."

"You and me alone? You must be off your rocker."

Another voice came from behind them. "You won't be alone."

Shies was using his Whitworth as a cane. Even in this weakened state the man looked so strong, as if fueled by some irrefutable, masculine force.

Byrne shook his head. "You are a man with grit, I give you that. But them wounds are numb right now and you can't feel them. Come tomorrow you'll be with fever and so in pain you'll beg for a death that will not come."

"That's then. This is now."

"Mr. Shies," Delia said. "You're all shot up mighty dreadful. Why, you can hardly walk."

"I've been worse off than this and still did not bow out of combat. You want to go after the Koyotes and I agree with you. We can't let them win this. It'll be the end. Of everything. So if I must go after them in a limp, then that's what I'll do. Them boys won't have Oscar Shies off their tails until either they or I are six feet in the ground."

There was silence then, thick and heavy.

"Okay," Delia said. "Then I say we ride."

Byrne glowered. "Ride a trail that ends in death."

"If we don't, we'll die anyway."

*

Mable sat beside the lawman's carcass. She sighed. Here the marshal had a hole in his heart, and yet the holes he left in the hearts of others was larger. He was their leader, their hope beacon in a choppy sea of violence. Now the last remaining possemen were gearing up again to ride into the throat of Hell with no leadership. They were crippled and spent, burdened by the near certainty of their deaths.

The poor marshal, already dead, had not even been able to receive the last rites. It seemed a sin upon itself to deny him this, so Sister Mable said prayers for his soul and placed her hand upon his chest.

Warmth surged through her.

She gasped and opened her eyes. Incandescence was coiling around her outstretched arm, wavering like slivers torn from the sky. The light rippled across the marshal's chest, slithering into his armpits and up around his neck. Another prayer came to her.

"Lord Jesus Christ," she began, "by Thy patience in suffering You hallowed earthly pain and gave us the example of obedience to Your Father's will. Be near this man in his time of weakness and pain."

She hung her head, thinking of the children and all she'd done to them. The cemetery up on the mountain had been filled with the church's victims. She'd killed sickly children for their innocent blood, the latest including a mongoloid boy and a two-headed girl brought to the nuns by Oscar Shies. Mable told herself they were mercy killings but still they made her furious with herself. She thought of the hatred she'd felt toward God as He'd failed to deliver them from evil. But anger did not constitute disbelief, and even the Fifth Commandment could be forgiven if one confessed and offered their allegiance to the Lord.

"Though I find myself unworthy in my terrible sin," she said, "sustain me with Thy grace, so that my power shall not fail. Heal this man according to Thy will, and help me to believe what I have done is worthy of Thy pardon if You hold me in eternal life, my Lord and God. Amen."

The dried blood on her arm grew moist again and the droplets ran toward the dead man below. Her hair dripped onto his face. She tore open his shirt, exposing his bare chest and the gaping exit wound, and then took off her coat and pressed her naked body upon his, breast to breast and belly to belly, and when the holy blood touched him it was absorbed through his skin. His wound shimmered with white magic. The fleshy hole grew smaller and when she took his wrist there was a pulse.

"Praise God…"

Mable turned to the three walking toward the door. "Wait!"

*

The others were huddled around him. Delia, Byrne, Shies and Sister Mable. Her nudity shocked him. So did all that blood. There was a smoky, blue aurora dancing between him and them, creating a sort of dream world.

"Have we gone on?" he asked. "Did we all die?"

Delia took his hand in hers. Her red hair and freckles made her an angelic vision, a reflection of youth and innocence, of long summer days filled with butterflies, of flowers in full bloom being suckled by fat, fluffy bees.

"You're back," she said.

"From where?"

The girl turned away and the others would not look him in the eye when he asked again.

Byrne crouched down beside him. "We haven't gone on. But you did. You've come back from the other side."

Russell stared at the man. He chuckled and started getting to his feet. He was wobbly, but when he braced himself with the schoolmarm's desk he was able to get straight.

"Luther, you're talking nonsense."

"Why would I? Hell, Henry, after all you've experienced you can't accept resurrection?"

"I must've been knocked unconscious. That's all."

The others remained silent.

Mable came to him and placed her hand upon his chest. The spot was tender. He looked down and saw the still-healing hole. There was no denying it was an exit wound. He'd been shot through the upper chest.

"Jesus," he said. "I'm… I'm undead…"

"You're a miracle," the nun said. "You'd be dead but by God's grace. He let me bring you back."

The marshal blinked. "Witchcraft?"

"Of a sort," Byrne said. "Magic ain't always black. There's some witchery for good. This blue light you see all about you is the very spirit of it."

Russell stared off. "Jesus…"

Mable gave him a smile but her eyes were tearing up.

"Yes," she said. "Jesus rescued you."

He put his hands on the desk and leaned over, feeling isolated though surrounded by friends. Byrne put his coat around Mable's shoulders and she drew it closed. Delia went to the back room.

"It isn't over," Shies said, attaching a lariat to his side.

Somehow Russell had already guessed that.

A voice cried, "Henry!"

He turned just as Grace Cowlin came to him with open arms. She hugged him tight, warming his soul, and he wrapped his arms around her. When she drew back to look him in the eyes he kissed her, a deep and passionate kiss, unashamed. She tasted of hope, both of them surging with the radiant rivers of newfound love. He wished they would never unlock.

When at last they did Grace beamed at him, cheeks rosy, and she took his hands in hers, squeezing them tight as if to prove to herself he was really there and make sure not to let him slip away.

"How?" she asked.

He smiled. "Heck if I know."

CHAPTER XXXXVI

THE HORSES THUNDERED UP THE bluff, snow flying from their hooves as the Koyotes cracked the reins. Glenn's horse, Belial, had long been an iniquitous beast of Satan, and now the roan Hiram had stolen was imbued with similar wickedness, the power of the Menhir having transformed it into a demonic steed. Between its ears a row of bone-thorns had sprouted. Its nostrils snorted dark fire as a litany of symbols were burned into the hide by invisible irons, as if being branded by the kings of Hell. An inverted star appeared between the roan's shoulders, glowing and weeping blood.

Hiram tightened his legs on the horse's sides, nervous of being bucked. But the roan never broke from its gallop, keeping alongside Belial. Glenn was tall in the saddle. He'd developed new muscle that added weight to him. His midnight hair was even longer than before and it fluttered behind him like a cape. He was in an in-between state, jaws out and muttonchops burly, but mostly in human form.

Hiram thought of Web. He'd been little more than pieces in the snow, probably too far-gone to be resurrected even by Glenn's new powers. But Glenn hadn't even tried. It seemed wrong to Hiram to leave their brother like that. They could have at least gathered him up to bury later on. But he dared not mention it. The Koyotes had thinned to only two members. He would just have to accept that. There were always more outlaws they could initiate into the gang, but was the gang even going to matter anymore? Now that Glenn was becoming a prince, what use would there be for the old company? The two of them were bound for greater things.

A covering of stratus churned overhead and there was a rumble of thunder snow. A sky-wide flash shook the heavens and the earth trembled, a deafening thunderclap echoing like a distant war, scaring off the remaining ravens. This electricity was a revival for Hiram. A weight was freed from his chest as adrenaline rushed through him. What fear he'd felt back at the chapel was now a faded illusion. The ecstasy of evil had returned to him in full and his mouth watered and his loins stirred. His eyes burned like hot coals and a wide smile stretched his wolf chops.

The O'Conner farm appeared on the horizon.

*

The posse leapt into the fray, joined by the wolf pack. Byrne followed the scent of the Koyotes. Shies and the Van Vracken girl rode behind him while Russell kept his horse beside Byrne's. Clutching Byrne's back was Sister Mable, who'd insisted on coming along. With much of the white magic used to bring back Russell, she and Byrne could now touch, as long as they did not graze each other's flesh. She'd rubbed at Shies' wounds with what little blue glow remained. It did not heal them completely, but it helped. Byrne hated to admit it, but there was no doubt her witchery would prove useful. His disdain for her had not waned, but she was needed, so he would protect her.

Delia had left her pony at the stationhouse, choosing instead the stronger, faster horse Brazzo had ridden into Hope's Hill. Russell wanted Grace Cowlin to stay behind but she refused, riding Kasa's mustang out of the schoolyard, somewhat uneasy in the saddle.

Byrne was glad to have a medic in her, for he knew there would be blood. They could use every hand in the oncoming battle. Taking the streets out of town, Byrne tried not to look at the slain bodies the Koyotes had left behind. Hope's Hill was practically becoming a mass grave. But when they bypassed The Rusty Nail two men were standing on the porch, waving the posse down.

Russell said, "It's Zeke Ottoman."

Byrne recognized the saloonkeeper, but not the young man with him. He was hardly more than a boy and had hair as fiery as Delia's. When they slowed their horses the schoolteacher identified him.

"Cillian O'Conner," she said.

His face was grave. "Howdy, ma'am."

"We saw those outlaws heading back toward them hills," Zeke said. "I've got me a rifle and a six-shooter for the boy here."

Russell said, "Now hold on. Cillian's just a boy and—"

"We're coming with," Cillian told him.

"Your family has suffered great loss, son. Think of your wee brothers and sisters."

"I am, sir. If my Pa hadn't gone to perdition, he'd have rode with you men too. I'm filling in his shoes in every which way I can. If we don't fight, what remains of my family will go the way of Ma and Pa."

The possemen looked to one another.

"Well then," Byrne said, "best get a wiggle on."

Zeke glanced at the wolves and gave Byrne a questioning look but didn't object to them. He fetched his horse and Cillian took one that had been left at the hitching post by a man now dead. They saddled up, giving the posse greater numbers as they galloped up the trail toward Black Mountain, chasing the lightning and breathing the bitter air, their hearts like locomotives as they pursued the greatest evil they would ever know.

CHAPTER XXXXVII

STANDING IN THE RUINS OF the O'Conner house, Glenn raised the Menhir to the fury of the coming storm. The clouds were the color of ink. Electric veins raked the firmament. Staring straight ahead, Glenn watched a pinhole of pure blackness appear in the air, hovering six feet above ground. Around the circle was a ring of warped light that bent the image of the horizon beyond like heat rays on desert plains. And though this hole was minuscule its vacuum was evident. It pulled at space, bending the visual world to its whims.

The Menhir smoked in his hands but his palms had the coarse pads of the werewolf, too tough to burn. Every drop of holy blood had cooked and turned to vapor, and now the Menhir shone clean, its power cascading in beams of impenetrable darkness. The cries of all the orphans who had died in vain rose from the Menhir's crannies, memories of horror adding kindling to its hellfire. The beams came out in a terrible rainbow of gray and black that pulled light rather than offered it, stealing from the realm of man and feeding it to the swirling hole, and with every captured atom the circle widened until it was a yonic perforation in space. It was the size of an apple, then a horse's head, and then a small tree. It rippled as it drained color from the world around it, casting the land in gray sepia.

Glenn stood in awe.

This was it—the power to pull the sun from the sky, to cast the world into eternal night, perpetually starless for the rolling cloak of storm clouds. He would unleash Hell—not in the form of fire and brimstone but in a suffocating absence of all that gave life, leaving humanity in a winter without end where nothing could grow or prosper.

The slow death of all mankind. The ultimate human sacrifice.

"Open," he whispered.

The slit widened and Glenn peered into the gateway. First there was only the emptiness of a starving void. It pulled the air around him and his hat blew from his head and disappeared into the vortex. When he leaned forward he heard the guttural sound of the abyss. The glow of his eyes illuminated it, and in those depths the blackness stirred like magma, alive with red eyes of its own. There was the sharp stench of sulfur, of burning flesh and steaming feces and expunged guts. The void sang to him with a billion screams of anguish, of infinite misery and the furious battle cry of demonic war machines.

And in the center of it all was an array of monoliths. They were pulsing, crimson pillars, riddled with holes where chunks had been torn free. About these stones smaller stones orbited like planets around a sun, Menhirs circling, awaiting a warlock or witch worthy of possessing them.

As Glenn drew back out of the void, the edges of the entryway in space became visible. They were curtains of gray, spoiled meat, like a wound in a goliath's side or the decaying genitalia of a female giant. Curtains of rot opened and closed as if breathing.

He clutched the Menhir to his breast and his flesh gave way. The skin and muscle painlessly tore in half and his ribcage opened like a cabinet, revealing a heart even larger and blacker than Jasper's, swollen with satanic sorcery. He pushed the Menhir inside of him and veins rushing blood to his heart reached for the glowing stone, ventricles convulsing as the Menhir adhered to the throbbing muscle. Ichor flowed out of his opening like a babbling brook and with every beat of his heart came incantations whispered from the beyond. The vortex rose and stretched, the ancient dimension slowly revealed.

It swarmed with a legion of demons.

*

"God in Heaven..."

Reality had been torn in two. Delia gasped at the sight. The O'Conner farm was drained of what little color it had left. A choir made a melody of misery, anger, and lust, calling to them from a cave of festering flesh. The ground crackled and the mustang stirred beneath her. The posse came to a stop.

"Mr. Byrne? What... what is that?"

His face was hard and gray. "Hell. The very door to Hell."

"I thought Hell would be different."

"Everyone does. Hell's not so much a place bad men go when they die. It's another universe entirely—a dimension of horror."

She exhaled. "What do we do?"

He snapped the reins and charged among the ashen cornstalks, Sister Mable clinging to him half-naked and blood-encrusted and calling out an endless stream of prayers. The corn and rye bent toward the vacuum, dead husks sailing like bats into the witch's wind. Delia touched the repeater in the scabbard, feeling the collection of flat metals and animal bones and feathers pinned to the leather. There was a saddlebag there, some sort of long pipes inside. Before she could look into it, Zeke rode on and Cillian followed, and Oscar Shies came after Byrne, kicking his horse, his Colt drawn and his eyes full of murder.

Russell looked to the women. "Are you ladies sure about this?"

Delia clacked the reins.

Dust devils spun, sending twigs and leaves and gray snow into the wind. Her red hair whipped like battle flags. Brazzo's horse obeyed, neighing with hooves the pounding hammers of gods as they raced into the deadening, Russell and Grace coming fast at her tail. Delia's jaw tightened as small fangs pushed their way out. The backs of her hands quivered with hair. And as the battalion came into the clearing the remains of the farmhouse shook and the singed boards stood on end, jutting out of the earth like spears, two topped with human skulls and a smaller, infant's skull impaled upon an adult femur.

Before the void stood Glenn Amarok, barely recognizable. The image of his enormous, black body was warped by the vapors all about him, but Delia could see he was more than a hybrid of man and beast. The heart of Jasper Thurston pulsed at Glenn's arm, a bulbous membrane, and as he'd changed his clothes had torn to ribbons and fell away, burgundy thorns rising from his shoulders and out of his thighs. Reflecting the glow of his eyes were the silvery ram horns curling from his forehead, drizzling blood as they split the skin. His wolf snout puffed smoke and every tooth was a yellow fang with more rows behind it, the mouth of a shark. His chest was open, revealing a pulsing mass that emitted heat and pushed her back with magnetic energy. Glenn raised his arms in welcome, and as the riders came forward shapes moved behind him, creatures clawing their way into the world of man, dragging the black flames of Hell behind them.

*

Hiram rode out from behind the cover of the surrounding thicket, the roan running with the increased power of the four additional legs it had spouted. He dropped the reins and charged toward the posse with both pistols drawn and when Byrne came into view he fired at the man's horse, sending it crashing into the ground and hurling Byrne and the nun off its back. Hiram raced for them but was intercepted by another man on horseback who returned fire with a rifle. Hiram recognized him as the saloonkeeper. A round struck Hiram but he felt little pain and he emptied chamber after chamber in a haze of gun smoke and the saloonkeeper twitched in the saddle as he was peppered with bullets, his shirt blossoming red. He fell out of the saddle and Hiram's roan ran right over him, crushing his legs and hips before pulverizing his skull. His head popped like a melon.

More bullets ripped past and Hiram turned to see a teenage boy struggling to aim a revolver as his spooked horse shuffled. Hiram pulled the trigger and would have killed the boy dead had he not already run out of bullets. He tried the other gun. It too had run dry. There was a flash of lightning and the thunderclap caused the boy's horse to rise on its hind legs and he fell out of the saddle and scampered to his feet. He stared—not at Hiram, but at something behind Hiram. He screamed and dived into the maze of corn.

Hiram look back.

Behind him lay a nightmare galaxy.

The demons writhed and loped. Some ran but others crawled like babies and slithered like earthworms. Others flapped broken limbs and snapped with mouths dripping acid. A humanoid form came out of the shadows, snakes at the sides of his head where his ears should have been, their fangs sunk into his nipples, draining black milk while his eyes rolled back in delight. A centaur covered in thousands of weeping cuts strode out, his face torn off and eyes pulled from his skull and dangling upon his cheeks like skinned scrotums. Ghouls and imps emerged, screaming like newborns as they were forced into the natural world on roiling rivulets of lightning, their limbs weeping pus and gastric juices spilling from the human mouths that served as their genitals and anuses. Other monstrosities dropped through tornadic air, gliding on wings forged of vivisected human lungs and the latissimus dorsi muscles of dead men's hairy backs. And emerging from the black hole came a horrible form that chilled even Hiram.

*

Byrne froze when he saw it.

A single, humongous creature, the top of which was comprised of the upper bodies of hundreds of men and women, all of them sentient beings with white eyes and obsidian flesh. The base of the big creature's body was comprised of an assemblage of black tentacles thick as redwood roots and its midsection was encased in a locked ring of armor like a giant chastity belt, the upper parts of the tentacles clothed with rotting hides linked together by a belt of flensed skulls and hair. The suckers of the feelers were the mouths of human children. The assembly of demon-people at its top wielded crude swords and axes forged from bones and maces of mortar and spurs, all wet with blood that glowed black. Some carried bayoneted rifles, others pistols that had adhered to their hands, the barrels wet with flesh that hung in festoons.

At the creature's sides were two hellhounds, their bodies like phlegm-slick jellyfish with the legs of hyenas. Their dog heads had no eyes, only drooling jaws and snouts that inhaled in search of prey.

Though Bo had been his best and only friend for many years, Byrne would have to mourn the horse another day. He reached for Sister Mable. She was pale and sweaty, her eyes wide with fright. He

365

had to pull her up and their skin contact made him queasy. As they retreated, the rest of the posse entered the clearing. He heard some of them scream. Then the demons came and Glenn climbed atop his horse to lead the horde.

The pack of wolves came to Byrne's side, barking at the demons, and their presence made his spine arch. Hair curled out of his pores and his bottom paws tore through the toes of his boots.

He let himself go.

The beast within was in charge now.

CHAPTER XXXXVII

A SMALL, RED PTERODACTYL SWOOPED down and Russell took aim with his Colt and blasted it out of the sky. It hit the ground, broken wing twitching, and Russell shot it in the head and it went still.

"So these things *can* die."

Shies took up his rifle. The man with snakes for ears came at them and Shies put a bullet through his skull. The demon dropped dead but still the snakes hissed, dripping venom.

A tentacle came through the rye and wrapped around Mable's waist. She beat at it with her fists but it only tightened like an anaconda. Its feelers flashed with hundreds of child teeth and they tore the coat and latched onto her skin.

As I walk through the valley of the shadow of death I shall fear no evil, for Thou art with—

Byrne pulled her to his chest, placed the barrel of his iron against the tentacle, and fired. The appendage writhed and Byrne pulled her free. Dots of flesh were torn from her body as the suckers came loose and she fell into Byrne's arms.

"Deliver us, oh Lord!" she cried. "Turn back the evil upon my foes, and in Your faithfulness destroy them!"

As her fear turned to anger, these emotions manifested in the form of a sheer haze that coated her skin, the remainder of the dried blood taking effect. Her flesh faded to a frostbitten blue and Byrne stepped away so not to be scalded. He was fully transformed now. His clothes were mostly intact and he could still hold a gun, but he was a lumbering werewolf, and though he'd just saved her life she still feared him. Here was the little boy she'd taken into her orphanage to teach him he was not a dog but a human being. But the spirit of his canine mother had never left him, and seeing him now Mable realized it never could.

They turned at the sound of corn stalks being snapped in two, falling in rows, shadowy figures storming across the field. Byrne handed her the pistol and she gripped it with both hands, as if she knew what she were doing, and he pounced into a fighting stance, legs spread and arms wide, claws out for the slaughter.

*

Many of the demons that stepped through the portal keeled over as they entered the world of man. They recoiled and were pushed backward as if by some invisible battering ram.

White-knuckled, Delia gripped the reins.

It's like a foreign object in the body, she thought. *They don't belong here and our world is forcing them out.*

But not all of them.

Staring up at the beast of many bodies, she felt suddenly helpless, hopeless. Her limbs were shaking and her breaths burst in and out. The behemoth swung its weapons as it slithered across the land, and though the horse had been in many of Brazzo's battles it backed away with the same level of fear as its rider.

But Oscar Shies showed no fear at all.

He charged at the behemoth with his rifle in one hand and a pistol in the other, both blazing, holding the reins in his teeth as he massacred the lesser demons swarming about in a hail. The pack of wolves chased down the wounded creatures and pulled them apart, their faces turning pink with gore. Bullets flew from out of the corn and Delia spotted Cillian, his iron clutched in both hands. Russell rode circles around the attacking horde, struggling to keep them back, but Grace covered him, repeater blasting.

The centaur galloped in Delia's direction, a mutilated monstrosity bearing a horseman's lance, a long pole lined with arrowheads and ending in a cone-shaped point. The point puffed the same black fire the centaur breathed. Delia drew the Smith and Wesson and fired upon this creature as it charged, and though chunks of its flesh went sailing into the air still the centaur came for her. She galloped away, murmuring prayers as she gained ground, and when she halted the horse she rushed to reload the six chambers and just as the centaur came upon her she let off three rounds into its face and one of its dislodged eyes snapped from the connective tissue as the bullets entered its brain. The centaur crashed onto its forelegs and slid in the slush and Delia fired again to make sure it was dead, planting one in its back. The centaur moved no more, but worms and ticks began to rise out of its many open cuts and when its mouth came open a swarm of horseflies escaped.

The ground trembled. The behemoth was slithering toward the cornfield, toward Shies and Russell trying to keep it away, the wolves biting into the tentacles only to be batted away like gnats. One wolf was ensnared and crushed. Another broke its neck when it was slammed into the ground.

The behemoth's mass of bodies fired bullets and arrows and as the possemen attacked its bottom half squatted so the bodies could swing their maces and launch their spears and swipe with medieval swords. Delia swallowed hard and rushed back into the deadening and unloaded upon the behemoth, taking out some of the bodies as they came at Shies, Russell, and Grace. The bodies fell limp with death but still the others raged on, the behemoth far from dead.

*

A tentacle slammed into his horse and Shies flew out of the saddle, landing on top of the tentacle. He clutched it with both legs and grabbed a hunk of gelatinous tissue and clutched on, flashing back to his days breaking mean horses, holding fast as the appendage bucked with full force. He kept one arm in the air, leaning in the opposite direction the tentacle dipped, and when he saw his chance he reached for the iron at his hip and put all six shots into the wiggling mass. He holstered the weapon and drew his Bowie knife and began hacking at the tentacle's bullet wounds, holding tight with one hand and slashing with the other until the meat was split. He reached in and pried the tentacle in two. It broke free from the behemoth but still it writhed and Shies gripped the stump and pulled it upward, and like a horse the tentacle obeyed the pull and Shies rode it away from the behemoth as the mass of bodies chucked spears at him. The tentacle undulated beneath him but carried on, and when he reached the cornfield he tossed himself from the dying append- age and rolled to cover as spears stuck into the ground behind him, their sticks vibrating from the force.

Cillian O'Conner came to him. The kid was shaking.

"I'm out of bullets, sir."

Shies sat up and reached into his coat for ammo and they re- loaded their handguns. He stood, put his arm around the boy's shoulders, and ran them into the maze of stalks.

*

They were in a mist of gore.

Werewolf Byrne slashed open demon bellies and tore apart their throats with his fangs as they stabbed at him with crooked daggers. A snake with three heads latched onto his leg but the head wolf of the remaining pack pulled it free and bit off all the heads. Behind him, Sister Mable was the color of violets, and when she moaned rays of light streamed out of her mouth, vaporizing any demon that fell before the ray. Two more wolves warred alongside Byrne as the monstrosities came in a stampede, hauling black fire in footsteps that set the stalks ablaze, clearing a path for Glenn the Dreadful as he bounded into the rows, his mustang braying with a forked tongue.

Byrne turned to Mable. His voice was gravel in this state. "Run!"

Mable's face pinched. "To where?"

The demons were all around them. But Glenn Amarok—the worst demon of all—was riding toward them in a slow gait, as if to mock them. The Menhir thrummed in his chest cavity.

"Run!" Byrne shouted.

Mable fled through the stalks, the shredded coat blowing in rib- bons, her bloody hair whipping in all directions as the wind ripped through the field. When Glenn reached Byrne he clicked his tongue and the lesser demons scurried away like roaches. He leapt out of the saddle, squatting on his hind legs, and he pointed at Byrne, mal- ice swirling in his eyes.

"We could have burned this earth together," Glenn said.

Byrne barreled toward his old brother and the Koyotes collided, the light of the Menhir pulsing as they converged. Byrne tore at Glenn but he only laughed, Byrne's claws only freeing a dust of skin, unable to break through the flesh, like pawing at leather five inches thick. Glenn throttled Byrne and swung him into the air and when he fell back to earth something in his back popped when he hit the ground. When he looked up, Glenn had his arms outstretched, calling more lightning into the sky. Jasper's heart pulsed in his forearm as a sphere of decayed meat lined with jutting spikes rose out of it like a popping zit, the tips of the spikes lit like candles with black flames.

The wolves barked and ducked into the corn. The pack leader bit at Byrne's ankle, telling him to run.

He did.

*

Her ammo box was empty now, so Delia dug into the saddlebag, hoping Brazzo carried extra bullets in it. She felt the tubes inside but found no rounds for her rifle or the Smith & Wesson. She pulled out one of the cylinders. It was almost as long as her forearm. A wick was at its head.

Dynamite.

In the clearing ahead, the army of the behemoth's upper mass was being stretched out, the torsos attached to other, smaller tentacles. They moved in serpentine dances, arched like cobras ready to strike, and the behemoth came toward Russell and Grace as they rode their horses in circles just to get away from the lesser demons, shooting them out of the sky and bashing at their heads with the butts of their rifles when the monsters launched at their horses. The behemoth slithered across the farmland, crushing the rye, its writhing humanoid forms screaming and flailing, hatchets swinging through the air and swords chucked like spears and the balls of maces spinning from their chains. An axe tumbled head-over-tail and sank into the chest of Grace's horse and it bounced on its hooves, not knowing where to run for they were surrounded by the hordes of hell.

Delia found the matchbox in the saddlebag, next to Brazzo's chewed cigars. She lit a stick of dynamite and rode toward the clearing before the behemoth could get too close to her friends. The sparkling fuse gave a small sphere of light and she outstretched her arm so it may guide her way through the gun smoke. It gave color to a world that had been robbed of it, and she praised The Father, The Son, and The Holy Spirit as she charged through the deadening, past the oscillating void as it vomited more horrible forms, and just as the fuse sizzled to the cylinder she reared back and threw the dynamite into the crowd of bodies atop the behemoth.

*

The detonation drew Glenn's attention.

He turned just as the bodies of the behemoth burst. Flaming carrion and dismembered limbs filled the air in a mushroom cloud of burning gore and weapons flew from severed hands as great plumes of flame devoured the behemoth's upper body.

Glenn clacked the reins and Belial rode out of the maze, both of them howling in a rage, furious at the failure of this army. He'd freed these creatures from the abyss after centuries of suffering— surely they should be able to destroy a posse of mere mortals! As he reached the clearing he caught sight of another stick of dynamite thrown in an arc, and he grit his teeth as the behemoth's lower body exploded. Flames ate its dead skin loincloth and its body armor glowed red-hot and singed its flesh. Tentacles ruptured in flaming chunks and the behemoth caved into itself like an imploding star and the earth quaked as it hit the ground, spraying puss and sparks and emitting waves of smoke.

A horse galloped away. Atop its back was a young girl with red hair.

Glenn recognized her.

*

When the behemoth first emerged from the void, Hiram had retreated back into the thicket on the edge of the clearing. The sight of the creature made something go cold in his chest, for the horrors Glenn had pulled out of this depraved dimension made Hiram sick with dread. He'd never dreamed there could be such paragon demons, even in Hell.

When the behemoth fell dead, a weight left Hiram and he headed back into the farm, hoping Glenn had not seen him ride off scared. He had to get back into the battle or he too would face his leader's wrath and be sent screaming into a dimension of pure, endless pain. He galloped toward the corn where he'd seen the black man flee with the boy. One of them had a familiar scent but he was not sure which one. He'd have to get closer. They seemed easy enough prey.

As the rain faded Hiram reloaded his pistols, climbed off the roan, and entered the maze, pushing through dead stalks. He tested the air again. Even through the gunpowder and blood he picked up their scent and sprinted through the rows. There was a rustle. Getting into a crouch, he peered through the stalks. The boy had his back to Hiram so he cocked the hammers of his pistols, grinning, aroused. If there were more time he'd like to assure the kid he was a lawman, guide him to one of the bluffs surrounding the farm, and give him a false sense of security before pulling him apart.

There'd be other boys, he told himself—all the children of the earth would soon bow at his feet, begging for food and mercy, worshipping at the altar of him, hoping to find his favor by begging to be sodomized and fellating him on command. He was the sidekick to a new prince of Hell. He and Glenn would take the world and poison it to the edge of dying but keep it alive for their own sadistic hedonism.

He steadied his aim.

*

"What do we do now, Mr. Shie—"

Cillian's head snapped forward as a bullet entered the back of his skull and exited through his mouth, splintering teeth and blowing out the tongue. Ten feet away, Shies turned from the parting in the corn where he'd been watching for pursuing demons. As the young man collapsed Shies felt as if his stomach were rising to his gullet.

He would have gone to the boy, but there was nothing left to give him. So instead Shies fired into the corn, shooting all over and screaming at the horror of it all. Someone fired back and when he saw the curls of gun smoke he honed in on the barrel of the pistol and shot at the hand holding it as it poked between the stalks. The pistol flew from the assassin's grasp along with one finger.

"Son of a whore!" the man yelled.

Now that he'd disarmed him, Shies ran through the rows, but as

373

he reached the man a second gun appeared as his other hand came out of hiding and Shies caught a bullet to the head.

*

Grace tried not to look at the vortex of flesh but the sheer horror of it demanded attention. It pulled not physical matter so much as the energy of the living world, swallowing the air and draining all color and light, as if it were devouring the very fabric of existence. She forced herself to look away so not to be drawn into it too.

A child with legs for arms came at her in a headstand and the madness of it was nearly enough to crack her. Skinned bats flapped overhead, gnashing with smiling, crocodile mouths. They called her dirty names and cackled. They were too close to shoot, so all she could do was swing at them and put her horse into a run. She entered the haze rising from the smoldering behemoth and the bats lost their way, but still the mutant child pursued and when it jumped it landed upon the rear of the wounded horse and swung its leg-arms, hitting her in the back of the head until she fell from the wobbling mustang and landed in the warm ooze of tentacles.

"Grace!"

Russell appeared, reaching down from his horse. She stretched, they joined hands, and Grace climbed up and wrapped her arms around his waist. The screaming-mad child rode off, laughing and flailing its limbs in the air as the mustang struggled to support him. Grace realized she'd lost her rifle. The void was expanding and Russell's horse struggled against the vacuum.

Grace said, "Don't look at it, Henry."

Russell closed his eyes and leaned to his horse's ear. "Don't look, Fury. Come on now, you can do it, ol' boy."

Though the horse gave it his all its legs began to buckle. Russell kicked its sides and snapped the reins but Fury continued to collapse.

The marshal turned back to Grace. "Climb off him."

They dismounted as the horse lowered to the ground, and once it was no longer burdened with their weight it started to rise. Russell fired his rifle into the air to send it running away from the vortex. He and Grace averted their gaze and broke into a run of their own, Russell firing at ghouls and hellhounds when they got close, but only some of the demons even seemed interested in the humans.

Now they seemed ecstatic just to be free, dancing and leaping across the farmland, as if celebrating bringing their special blend of horror to the world.

*

Shies opened his eyes.

His head was pounding and his vision was blurred, but he could make out the shape standing over him. He blinked the blood from his eyes and the white man's face came into view, a rat-like mug with thick whiskers. Shies reached to his hip but there was no iron, only the lariat looped in a ring. He pawed the ground for his revolver.

The assassin sneered. "Don't even bother."

Shies rose onto his elbows, thinking of the knife hidden within his coat. The Koyote leaned over and took a whiff of him.

"Now I recognize that stink," he said. "Not just the regular stink of a nigger, but the very specific stink of your bloodline. I know that bloodline well, seeing as I severed it."

Shies narrowed his eyes. "So it was you."

"Naturally. Hiram Zeindler, at your service." He snickered. "My brothers had a gay romp with your little, red bride. Not a bad looker for a filthy savage."

Shies shot up but the Koyote was quick and kicked him in the head, filling it with stars. He fell back onto his elbows, struggling to regain his senses.

"I want you to know I didn't have anything to do with her," Hiram said. "Know why?"

Shies bared his teeth but said nothing.

Hiram grinned. "Was too busy with my *delight*. Would you like to know what your little boy said when I held him down and buggered him? Want to guess whose name he called, who he was crying out for?"

Again Shies tried to lunge but Hiram kicked him in the stomach and he turned over in the snow.

"Papa!" Hiram yelled in a child's voice. "Papa, help! Where are you? Please, help us!"

Still on his side, Shies reached into his coat while the Koyote was howling with laughter.

"He was still alive you know," Hiram said, "when I ripped his

375

liver out he was still calling for you. Tasted pretty good, especially considering he was a dirty half-breed."

In one quick swoop Shies pulled the Bowie knife free and slammed it down through Hiram's foot. The Koyote screamed. Shies grabbed Hiram's wrist and twisted it until it snapped and the pistol fell into Shies' lap. He shot Hiram in the belly and the Koyote hissed a spurt of blood. Though still dizzy, Shies got to his feet and pistol-whipped Hiram to the ground, straddled him, and twisted the Bowie knife in the man's foot, making him squeal before yanking it out. Hiram's eyes flashed with panic.

"Wait!" Hiram said. "Just hold on a minute!"

Shies stabbed the knife where the man had been gut-shot. The blade entered the hole and he plunged it in and out, sending the bullet deeper as he dug in search of his prize. Hiram begged with a mouth bubbling blood.

"I can... give you anything... please..."

With a turn of the blade Shies pushed his way in, his hand sinking into the wound. He punctured the Koyote's spleen, tore open the stomach in a splatter of bile, and then sent the knife upward and impaled the liver. Hiram writhed and screeched and Shies relished this suffering even more than he relished the liver when he took his first bite.

*

Mable stood before the ruins.

She had caught a glimpse of the portal's presence once before, when the O'Conners were cursed by unknown forces and the blackness had first appeared. It seemed a lifetime ago.

She watched the vortex breathe. It was devastating and macrophagous. The folds of flesh wept plasma, strange insects scurrying through the seepage, and when a ghoul with a body turned inside out climbed from the abyss Mable opened her mouth, releasing a ray that knocked it back into the void. Demons frolicking through the farmland gave her a wide berth, spooked by her glimmering aura and sensing her witchery. Gazing upon the gateway, she thought of the Good Book and how it had foretold Armageddon.

I watched while he ripped off the sixth seal...

She let the coat fall off her shoulders and curl about her feet. Her nude body was caked in divine blood—to hide it from sight was to lessen its effect. When touched by the winter air the dried flakes began to rehydrate, glowing in blue beads as if they'd never left the children's veins.

And then the pandemonium, everyone and his dog running for cover....

Her skeleton vibrated. Tears ran down her cheeks.

Hide us from the One Seated on the Throne and the wrath of the Lamb. The great day of Their wrath has come—who can stand it?

Was that what lay within the void? Was Jesus Christ returning with angels to initiate the foretold war with Lucifer? Would the good ascend in rapture and the rest of humanity burn and scream as Judgment Day arrived?

The four angels were released, who had been held ready for the hour, the day, the month, and the year, to kill a third of humankind.... And in those days shall men seek death, and shall not find it: and shall desire to die, and death shall free from them.

Was the opening of the void part of the divine plan? Was it His will? And if so, was it a sin to try and close it? What truly lay within this black dimension? Could it perhaps be God Himself?

She swallowed hard and clenched her fists. Peals of thunder rose from the shadows and the vortex poured rivers of anti-light, the blackness coming in full, deep and rich and suffocating.

The fifth angel poured out his vial upon the throne of the beast, and its kingdom was plunged into darkness.

"Who am I to question Thee?" she asked.

The void replied with the familiar screams of children.

CHAPTER XXXXVIII

DELIA SPOTTED SHIES STUMBLING OUT of the corn-field. He seemed dazed. His mouth, chin, and neck were slick with blood. She trotted her horse, calling his name, but he did not notice her and she wondered if he'd gone half-deaf from all the gunshots. She came closer and waved, catching his attention. His face was slack, eyes like those of a dead man, but as she drew closer to the corn his expression suddenly changed, eyes and mouth going wide. He pointed behind her.

"Look out!"

There was a loud crack as the first fireball soared by her head.

It was the size of a howitzer round, a sphere of meat and spiked metal surging with black flame. It flew off toward the hillside and exploded into a rocky bluff that gave way to a small avalanche. When she looked back she saw the towering nightmare of Glenn the Dreadful. His arm was outstretched and birthing out of Jasper's attached heart came another black ball, growing larger as it split the muscle. She clacked the reins, charging across the deadening, snow rising from the earth around her horse, her breath caught in her thudding chest as she galloped toward Shies. He fired at the Koyote chasing her, struggling to keep his aim steady.

Another fireball flew by, snapping like thunder and just missing her as she galloped over the fallen bodies of mutilated demons and wolves and the crushed corpse of Zeke the saloonkeeper. The horse hurdled over another horse's bloody carcass and she raced along the corn as the stalks bent and clacked in the tornadic wind, her horse slick with sweat, the heat of another fireball rising at their backs.

This one blew past Shies and the hot air around it knocked him back. Delia came to him and he made a crazed leap and grabbed onto the charging horse, holding tight, dangling from its side as it bounded into great plumes of smoke wafting from the burning behemoth, scores of winged demons surging past, shrieking and hissing gore against the pall. Shies pulled himself up behind the saddle and wrapped one arm around Delia's waist and fired upon the coming spheres. When he hit some the bullets knocked them off course. She kicked her heels and they raced across the clearing to dodge Glenn's onslaught, a fireball zooming ahead of them so the horse had to leap into the air, the ball ripping just under its belly and singing its hair. The fireballs came quicker, two passing overhead, and Delia ducked low, pushing the horse to its full power, the black orbs all around her now—behind her, beside her, before her— detonating in the earth in volcanic eruptions, demons bursting in the crossfire as they danced and brayed and rioted, and the chaos of Hell made Delia scream.

Her horse burst.

The fireball went through its body and out the other side. Delia and Shies were thrown into the air as the horse split in two and steaming innards spewed within the rising flames. Delia's skin blistered. She fell back to earth and mewled when she hit the ground. Her shaking hands were now covered in red fur. Shies came out of the mist. She noticed his left ear was gone, the side of his head torn open, likely by a bullet. He helped her up and when she saw the smoldering saddle she went to it despite Shies' objections and removed the last stick, realizing it was actually two cylinders of dynamite tied together by twine. She bit into the string, pried them apart, and shoved them into her coat.

Something in the farmhouse ruins caught her eye.

"Look yonder!"

They ran toward the blue light.

*

379

This was his only chance.

Byrne ran on all fours, chasing Glenn's mustang with lycan-thropic skill and gaining ground. Glenn was hurling hell-spheres and had not noticed Byrne behind him. He dodged the flaming hoof prints, his mouth foaming, and when he was upon the horse's tail he lunged and sunk his fangs into its upper leg, tearing the muscle, and the horse tumbled and Glenn started to slide. Byrne bounced away as the horse collapsed.

Had Glenn been human, he would have been crushed. But in this other form he shoved the mustang off and struggled to his feet, limping slightly. His roar was deafening and followed by a display of his warlock aptitude. Byrne braced himself as the ground quaked, cracking into a ring of fire that surrounded the very last of the Koyotes. They stared at each other with claws twitching, fangs gleaming like topaz.

Glenn moved slow, loping along the edge of the circle, watching. Byrne remained where he stood, waiting for his opponent to make the first move, but Glenn only tested the air and licked his chops as if savoring the anticipation. The tumor of Jasper's heart dribbled ooze and the Menhir thrummed within Glenn's deformed chest.

Neither man wavered in his stare.

"I won't kill you now," Glenn said. "Instead I'll throw you screaming into the void. You'll be trapped there, crying for all eter-nity in a pit of pain beyond anything you could imagine, not even in your blackest dream. You'll be—"

"Can't be worse than listening to you jabber on."

Glenn's eyes narrowed. "Why'd you turn on us, Luther?"

"If'n you can't figure out the obvious, I guess you'll just have to die wondering."

Glenn gave a small laugh. "Ready?"

The Koyotes howled.

*

Demons were everywhere.

As he ran, Russell continued shooting, but he only had so many rounds left in his coat pocket, some for the Henry rifle and some for the Colt at his hip. If they didn't find cover, they'd run out all the quicker.

"There!" Grace called.

He followed her to the bluff. The stone formation made a cliff out of the side of the hill and covered a small dip in the land like an awning. They slinked backward into the bunker of rock and Russell fired at anything that came close until the horde retreated out of sight. But they had not gone far. He could hear them screeching and running circles around the bluff like Indians awaiting the chance to strike.

Russell sighed. They'd been surrounded. Now they were cornered.

If we hadn't ducked in here we'd be dead already, he told himself.

Then he thought: *You already are, Henry. You already are.*

His joints were feeling stiff and his skin bore a slight gray sheen. Whatever magic had brought him back to life would fade. He tucked his hands so Grace would not see when he checked his pulse. It was still going, but the pumps were far between. Grace leaned into him, gasping to catch her breath, and when she placed her head on his shoulder her forehead touched his cheek.

She gasped. "Henry! You're so cold."

Something scurried past. A chucked spear landed on the sandy rise before them. Russell fired and the creature rolled into the mud. It did not get up.

"You need to make a run for it," he told Grace.

"What? No—"

"I'll give you my six-shooter. It'll be better close range. I'll cover you with the rifle. Fury is a good horse and he won't have traveled far without me. You get to him and get on outta here."

"Not without you."

"Can't save a life that's already gone."

"Don't talk that way."

"What other way is there? I'm undead and not long for this world. Whether my time runs out or one of those monsters gets me, I'm dead either way. You've got to flee from here, Grace. Get to safety."

"What safety is there in a world gone mad?"

He took her hand in his and though he knew his were like ice she gripped him tenderly.

"Hell's broke loose," Russell said, "but that don't mean its gonna stay this way. We've still got a shot at beating this thing. But I want you away from here. I can no longer stand to see you in danger."

Another demon moved past the bluff, an amorphous thing with stripes of teeth and toenails covering it like porcupine quills. Russell shot it down. The blob vanished, a raindrop hitting stone, and the teeth and nails sprouted insectile legs and scurried in all directions.

"You say we can beat this thing," Grace said. "I believe you. But we do it together."

When he looked into those lovely eyes he saw a strength there he hadn't noticed before though it had been there all along. She would make a good wife and even better mother, he thought. Somewhere there was a man who would recognize gold when he saw it, and he would make Grace Cowlin his bride. She would be happy then. In these final hours, Russell found he wanted that most of all.

"Stay behind me," he said.

They crawled out of the bunker.

*

Mable was arms-deep into the vortex. The monoliths were spraying crimson ash and hail, awakened by the severing of the seal, offering up maiden voyage Menhirs to enter the natural world.

She reached deeper. She owed it to the children crying in those shadows. They had passed on to this dimension. If she could give them her light, would the blueness give them a sky to gaze upon, seeing shapes in the clouds, the very sort of childhood she'd tried to give them on those sunny picnics by the creek?

Those were warmer days. Her arms were covered in ice now, the flesh turned purple in the arctic void. But its freezing felt so tender, making her skin go to goose bumps and her nipples harden. The darkness rippled when she ran her hands through it, as if she were standing beneath a waterfall, and the rejuvenated, holy blood began to pull away from her to be swallowed by the vortex, the coat of blue incandescence going with it. Would the blood return to the orphans? Would it give them a second baptism, enabling them to ascend from this purgatory? She didn't know. She didn't have to know. All she had to do was *feel*—feel and follow the glory of God.

*

"What is she doing?" Delia said.

They'd followed the light radiating off the nun, hoping her white magic would shield or empower them. Instead it seemed Sister Mable was feeding it to the void. It swirled off of her in electric wisps and was pulled into the black hole. Delia growled and Shies looked to her, seeing now how the girl had changed. Her red eyes shimmered, canine teeth rising from her jaw and over her upper lip.

"Delia…. you're *changing*."

She turned away. "Don't look at me."

"You are wolfen?"

The girl hung her head. A single tear ran down her cheek where the peach fuzz had gone thick, looking like the beginnings of a teenage boy's beard. He wondered how it had happened, if this was a new development or if she'd always been this way. Right now it didn't matter. He was having trouble standing, his many wounds joining together to make one solid throb of pain.

Hiram had shot his ear off. Had the bullet landed just an inch inward, he'd have been dead. Shies knew he'd stolen time from the reaper. Despite how crippled he was, he aimed to make the most of whatever remained.

"We have to stop her," he said. "I don't rightly know what that blue light is but it's the only good magic I've seen. We lose it, we lose everything else."

Delia wiped her eyes. They went into the ruins of the house now, climbing over the jutting boards and the skulls of the O'Conners.

Shies shouted. "Sister Mable!"

But the nun did not turn around.

He limped toward her, calling her name, but still she did not respond. Delia ran at her but the darkness swarmed, pushing her back, and she rolled and tumbled through the wreckage. Beholding the vortex, Shies felt suddenly enamored by it and had to shake the strange feeling out of his head.

Is this what happened to Mable? Is the vortex deceiving her?

The coating of holy blood was stripped from the nun now and she was doing a slow dance before the gathering veil, dipping her upper body in and out of the void. Tenebrous tendrils embraced her. They slithered around her back, snaked her thighs, and glided across the crevices of her buttocks and her sex.

Shies freed the lariat from his hip. He swung the rope overhead, building momentum, and flung it. He lassoed Sister Mable as if she

383

were a horse he intended to break. She flew out of the void and he dragged her through the snow while she struggled and kicked, rambling Scripture. Delia came to her side, leaned in, and sniffed her up and down.

"Hardly a trace," she said. "That holy blood… it's all gone."

The nun shuddered. Her frozen arms were pinned to her sides by the rope. Her face, breasts, and belly were horribly frostbitten, the flesh raw and purple. There were ice burns everywhere the tendrils had touched her.

"I have kissed Him," she said. "I have kissed the lips of Christ."

Shies shook his head. *The poor woman has gone mad. Who can blame her?*

There was a low rumbling, almost like thunder.

Shies tensed when he realized the sound was coming from Delia.

*

He was losing.

Even before he'd pounced he'd known Glenn was going to defeat him. The head Koyote was too powerful now, too infused with the sorcery. It wouldn't be the first time Byrne had lost something. He'd been failing all his life. There'd been a time when he tended to assign blame to others for his own bankruptcy, but as he'd grown older he realized he wasn't the only one who'd been dealt a handful of shit from the get-go. It was possible for even the most abused and beaten-down soul to rise from the rubble of their misfortunes. Luther Byrne had chosen not to. Instead he'd taken to the life of wicked wolfen and welcomed his branding as the thirteenth Koyote, a mark he'd carried the rest of his life, a taint on his very soul. In a way, it seemed only right the leader of the pack he'd betrayed should kill him. There was an amusing poetry to it, like a sad punchline.

Still he fought, ripping at Glenn with teeth and claw, coming away with satisfying hunks of skin. But Glenn was twice as fast and three times as mean, imbued by all the evil of the netherworld he'd unlocked. As it turned out, there was a world even more horrible than this one Byrne was trying to rescue—if human beings were worth saving at all. He tried to conjure up reasons mankind deserved to go on but kept coming up empty. So much injustice, so much inhumanity. In his time on this planet he'd witnessed an endless carousel of needless suffering. Worst of all, he'd contributed to it. Luther Byrne was an outlaw—robber, rapist, killer, cannibal. If Glenn was to send him to Hell, he figured he had it coming.

But even as Glenn closed his jaws upon his shoulder, Byrne counterattacked. Turning his head, he was just able to reach Glenn's ear and nearly ripped it free with his fangs. Glenn came off him, clutching the flapping lobe, and Byrne struggled to his feet. His knees grinded and his lower back pinged. He was getting weaker. His body seemed to be counting down to an inevitable cessation of all functions. Stumbling forward like a weary pugilist, Byrne put up his paws, head tucked behind them for cover. Blood bubbled in his nostrils and seeped from his perforated eye socket. His wounds were failing to heal now. For years his body had regenerated, bouncing back from an injury in a matter of hours. He barely even aged. Now Byrne realized he'd been stealing from the devil and he'd just gotten caught. Being a Koyote meant a life dedicated to corruption and depravity. Such an existence came with a high price tag.

Time to pay up.

He barely dodged Glenn's blow and stumbled to the ground anyway, and when the second blow came he had nothing left to defend himself with, not even the smallest love for life to carry him on.

*

Glenn would keep his promise. He felt he owed Luther Byrne that much. They'd been brothers once, but were estranged to say the least. There would be no mercy for the betrayer, and though Byrne's death would make Glenn the last of his kind the notion brought him no hesitation. He'd sensed Hiram's death. The Koyotes were extinct. Only the last one standing had evolved.

Dragging Byrne by the ankle, Glenn made his way back to the ruins. He beheld the surging spectacle of the void, marveling at the unparalleled beauty. All the joys this life had given him were based in the suffering of others. Even when he'd found out he'd slaughtered his parents to win the favor of a false goddess, he never regretted it because the cult had championed him for his cruelties. That moment had defined him. From then on he was always chasing the next sin, for sin and pleasure were twins. He never felt tempted by evil, only instructed, guided, bestowed. He'd been taught to whip slaves and locked them in tiny vivariums to swelter and starve and suffocate until they came to him on their knees and pledged obedience. He raped girls as young as nine and devoured mothers in front of their children and committed mass murders while pillaging. He allowed hate to engulf him, and every vile, nefarious action caused him greater delight, guiding him to his leadership of the most heinous band of outlaws the west had ever seen, and in that kinghood he'd tasted the foremost ecstasy of evil. Now he was a warlock in the presence of the great void, his life's work culminated, and he found his density to be beautiful, even serene.

Glenn hauled his barely-conscious brother through the bloody ice and slush of bodies, through horse guts and the torn limbs of demons and the pulverized carcass of the saloonkeeper, covering him in gore so the void would be all the more enticed when it came time to take him.

CHAPTER XXXXIX

"AMAROK IS COMING."

When Sister Mable heard Shies speak, her eyes fluttered open. They'd turned white with cataracts, but though she was nearly blind she was graced by other visions, ones that told her more than mere sight ever could.

Father Blackwell is gone, she thought. *There is only I. There is but one keeper of the Menhir.*

She couldn't allow that keeper to be Glenn the Dreadful. With the preacher dead, the visions were passed on to her now, the ability gifted to her, perhaps by God, in her hour of greatest need. Mable felt unworthy of it, of any of His kindnesses. The void had deceived her so easily, scrambling her mind and convincing her something so godless might be the face of God Himself. She knew now the lost orphans had not been lost to the void. Devils had performed their trickery on her, twisting her sins against her.

I am a murderer.

I am unworthy.

But perhaps that did not matter now. God so loved the world that He gave His only begotten Son so that we would not perish, but have everlasting light. Maybe the same applied here. The Lord had not given her the gift of vision the instant Reverend Blackwell had died, because she was indeed a sinner, and therefore unworthy. But God so loved the world He granted her the power to save it. She was not a perfect woman, but she had always been His servant, her entire life dedicated—*sacrificed*—so that she may spread His love and glory.

The shapes of the others were blurs, but she recognized the girl by her red hair. When she reached out to touch her hand Mable felt fur. Her breath caught in her throat, thinking she'd been mistaken, that a Koyote was about to tear her apart. But then she heard the girl speak.

"Why did you do it?" Delia asked.

She chose to be honest. "I don't know."

The shadow of Shies came before her. "Sister, do you have any other source of that white magic?"

"I fear the void took it all away."

Delia 's voice quivered. "Without the innocent blood, we don't stand a chance."

Mable shivered—not from the frost covering her body, but from the sudden revelation. The thought came to her in a flash across, an epiphany so profound she knew it could not be her own. She'd been touched by the angels. She was cradled in the arms of Christ once again.

"It doesn't have to be innocent blood," she said. "It just has to be holy."

Mable took the girl by her lapel and drew her close. Delia was fanged and the end of her nose was black and slick. Her eyes were the same color as her hair, burning not with the black flames of the beyond but with the pure, orange flickers of the natural world—*their* world.

"Take me," Mable said.

"What do you mean?"

But she knew the girl understood. She just didn't want to accept the idea, even if it was their last hope.

"I am not innocent," Mable said. "But I have dedicated my life to being a bride of Christ our Lord. All the years of my life were spent on my knees before the cross. What blood could be holier than that of a nun?"

When she looked into the girl's wolfen eyes she saw another tiny flicker inside, a spark that assured Mable she had chosen wisely.

The flicker was blue.

*

Even half transformed into a werewolf, Delia knew right from wrong. Once she was fully changed into one, she'd be a slave to her curse for a night, but right now she was still cognizant and maintained control of herself.

She knew it was wrong to take the nun's blood. A few drops would not be enough to recreate the power the children's blood possessed. They needed pints, perhaps every last drop. They would have to kill her. Sister Mable knew this but, incredibly, she was still asking Delia to do it.

"Take me," the nun said. "Take my life so that my sacrifice may benefit all the world."

"Sister—"

"I have learned the importance of sacrifice from Christ the Savior."

"I'll be swearing to a life of sin if I take a woman of God."

Delia looked to Shies. His face was cast iron, hardened by war and loss. His inner torment was so great she could *smell* it.

"Mr. Shies?" she asked, but had no follow up.

He nodded. "I'll do it."

Shies drew his Bowie knife. It was tacky with blood and he spat onto the blade to refresh it so it could be wiped away on his pant leg. Delia understood. Whoever's blood it was, it had come from either a wicked man or some demon from the netherworld. Bad blood might contaminate the nun's and diminish its power.

"Hurry," Sister Mable said. "He is fast approaching."

Shies placed the blade to the nun's throat and she swallowed hard, bracing for her jugular to be slit, but Shies hesitated.

"What are we going to gather it with?" he asked.

Delia didn't know. There was no time to go back to the dead horses to search the saddles for a canteen. She made a cup out of her hands. Shies took a deep breath, put the knife at an angle, and just as he was about to make the incision a ball of fire slammed into him and sent him soaring, his coat engulfed in flames as he crashed into a snow bank several yards away.

Delia screamed after him.

Glenn the Dreadful was nearly upon her, the Menhir in his open

389

chest glowing like Mars in a night sky. The smell of his wolfen musk made her tingle. His cycle was far greater than hers, and her stomach cramped with hunger as she was willed by his magnetism. She began to shapeshift further, her face elongating, whiskers taking root, and her shoulders crackled with expansion. She leaned over to better smell the nun. Her flesh had the scent of a warm meal, of steaks cooked to perfection. Delia could smell the very heat of Mable's blood pulsing through her veins. The urge germinated until it was all she could feel.

"Take me now, Delia!"

But the nun no longer had to ask.

Delia sunk her teeth into Sister Mable's neck, and when she pulled a strip of flesh away she could not stop herself from swallowing it whole. She'd never tasted anything so delicious, for she had never felt so starved as she did right now. But she was still cognizant. She forced herself to back away. She slashed the nun's neck until she severed both carotid arteries and jets of gore splattered.

Glenn stopped. His eyebrows rose and he laughed as she ripped her way into Sister Mable's torso, slathering her arms.

*

"How wonderful," Glenn said. "You came for me with a heart full of vengeance, but now all you want is belly full of human flesh."

The girl kept digging into the nun's body. A mist of blood decorated her fur.

"You've found something greater than revenge, girl. You've found the glory of the wolfen." He smiled. "So eat up. This is your virgin voyage. I envy you—all the dark delights that lay ahead. *This* is your new path. *This* is your *destiny*."

He took a deep breath, savoring the sight. He was in middle state now, only slightly less wolf in form than she. Covered in so many wounds, his lycanthropy retreated to shift his power to healing. The cuts and bites were rapidly closing, drawing over with new, tougher flesh.

"I knew there was something about you, girl. You should join—
"

He fell silent. The nun's blood was turning blue. The girl's fur glimmered with azure stars. This wasn't just a meal. This was a plan.

"You little bitch!"

Glenn let go of Byrne's leg and came at her. They rolled into the blood-spattered snow, tearing at each other and snapping their teeth. She was stronger than Byrne. The younger the wolfen, the more strength they possessed, and she was at the peak of her lycanthropic abilities. This would prove more of a challenge, especially now that she was empowered by the holy blood. Jasper's heart pounded at his arm and the Menhir shifted in his separated ribs. The veins of Glenn's own heart drew tighter around the stone, suckling at it, taking every sliver of sorcery he could endure.

He catapulted toward the she-wolf. The turquoise aurora made wraiths about her and he recoiled but then spun and powered through the nausea, using the energy of the Menhir to combat the holy blood's effects. The girl was certainly young and motivated, but Glenn had the edge of experience and the brute force of a lifetime of meanness, and as he dove into her he hacked at her belly, driving her away, and he lacerated the meat of her arm when she blocked his next attack.

She has power, but doesn't know how to use it.

He had let her live the last time. He'd learned from his mistake.

She managed to get in a few good slashes before he tackled her to the ground, shredding away braids of his skin and severing tendons as he went into a counter frenzy, biting into her shoulder and whipping his head back and forth in an effort to dislocate it. He wanted to tear the arm from her body completely, and might have succeeded had the bullets not bombarded him.

*

Ducked behind an assortment of small boulders, Russell fired his Henry rifle at the huge, black werewolf as it towered over the smaller one. The sight of the wolfen with the red fur had shocked him and Grace, for they recognized Delia's clothes, and when the girl turned they saw her face, recognizing her despite the canine features. She was taking on Glenn Amarok with phosphorescence covering her like a cloak, the same sort of powder blue magic Sister Mable had possessed when she was alive.

They'd not seen her die, but from the look of her carcass it was clearly a brutal death. Just beyond her body lay Luther Byrne in human form, but it was impossible to tell if he were alive or not. Oscars Shies was nowhere in sight. Russell steadied his aim, making sure to hit Glenn instead of Delia.

Beside him, Grace popped off the six-shooter. Together they peppered the werewolf with rounds that made him twist and mewl, allowing Delia to get out from under him. She lunged and when she hit Glenn there was the sound of snapping bones. Russell smiled, but it didn't last. His tongue glided across his teeth. Some of them loosened. He tongued one again and it fell from his gums and he spit it out. At least Grace hadn't noticed. She was too busy trying to save the young girl she'd come to care for, maternal instinct giving her the fury of a mother bear.

The wolfen continued their war, Delia overpowering her opponent, her entire body surging with light. The magic seemed fueled by her fury. Glenn grabbed her and they rolled into a low dip of rocks on the edge of the cornfield, out of sight. Russell pulled the Henry's lever action, ejecting the spent cartridge and instating the next, closing the breech. There were seven spent cartridges at his feet, which meant he had nine left inside the rifle.

"I'm going after them," he said.

Grace was already reloading. "And so am I."

*

Shies drifted into consciousness. The one thing he was painfully aware of was the numbness in his left leg. The hole of his missing ear had gone deaf and the blood dribbling from his forehead blurred his vision. Patches of skin had singed from the fireball. The snow had put out the flames on his clothes and he lay there steaming in the ice, unsure if he was really alive. He managed to sit up, but when he looked down at his body, he knew he would not stand.

*

Delia grabbed Glenn by the hair and bashed his skull into the rock. His body quaked beneath her like a beached fish and she slammed his face again, black blood spraying. They were both wounded enough to have returned to nearly human form, but she still retained her incredible strength whereas Glenn had weakened, torn and chewed and riddled with bullets.

Delia turned him over and straddled him. She dug her nails into the membrane of Jasper's heart and started peeling it from Glenn's forearm. It hissed as she gripped it, bubbling into a tarry slime that sizzled when it hit the ground, and one final ball of ichor hellfire dropped with a clunk and set a patch of dead leaves awash in black flame. She crushed Jasper's heart, neutralizing it with the remnants of white magic, the founder of the Koyotes finally at rest.

Glenn's heart shook with internal thunder. The Menhir shifted, as if trying to hide in the folds of his tissue. A warmth filled Delia's throat and when she opened her mouth a brilliant ray shot out, enveloping the Koyote's torso.

She reached for the Menhir.

When her fingertips touched it, her mind rattled with sudden thoughts of cruelty, not just toward Glenn Amarok, but toward anyone, everyone. She desired blood to wet her fangs and flesh to gather beneath her fingernails. She wanted others to suffer the way her family had suffered, for happy homes to be ripped asunder in orgies of carnage, for any young man she chose to be forced to mate with her, for mothers to be torn screaming from their children so that Delia might feast upon their sweet innards and—

She snapped her hand away, trembling. The Menhir turned inside Glenn's chest, wrapping tighter the ventricles and sinew. Glenn's eyes came open and he hissed. He grabbed her.

"You feel it," he said with a cough of blood. "The Menhir… it feeds your primal, wolfen instincts. Come, girl. Give yourself over to the beast within."

He pulled her closer, staring into her eyes, one of which he'd whipped nearly to ruin before making Delia eat her mother. She returned his stare as if she were considering what he'd said, distracting him as she pulled the stick of dynamite from her coat.

"My only instinct," she said, "is to kill you."

She placed her hand over his face. Digging her nails into his scalp and cheeks, she raked skin from his skull. As he shut tight his eyes, shrieking as his face was torn off, Delia put the fuse to the patch of black flames the fireball had made. It sparkled as she shoved the dynamite into his chest cavity, driving it like a stake into the dark heart of Glenn Amarok and securing it next to the Menhir. Glenn's arms fell limp at his sides and his eyes rolled back in his skull—but still he shuddered, alive but not for long.

Delia ran back, never taking her eyes off of him.

CHAPTER L

THE DETONATION SHOOK THE EARTH. Glenn burst in a webbing of black blood and blacker light, his body making a noise like one final howl as his torso exploded, arms snapping free, muscles disintegrating, his legs cracking like twigs, sending bone fragments into the surrounding thicket where they stuck in trees like arrowheads. Giblets of hot fat hung from branches overhead. Decapitated by the blast, his head spun into the snow, his shredded face charred and his muttonchops taken by fire.

Delia was drenched in the melting gore of her enemy. It soaked her shredded clothes and ran down her face. When a nugget of flesh dripped out of her hair, she snatched it up and popped in her mouth, chewing the remains of Glenn the Dreadful, the last of the men who had destroyed her family, her life. But though she'd longed for this moment—had lain in bed promising herself she would make it so—now that her quest of vengeance was complete she found no real joy in it. There was satisfaction and a sense of justice served, but the road to getting here had been a pathway to perdition.

She wasn't a girl anymore—wasn't a woman either. She was something else.

Something vicious stirred inside her now. It wouldn't be long before it overtook her on nights when the moon was full and Mars burned with crimson dust.

The sound of gunfire made her turn toward the ruins of the farmhouse. Russell and Grace were sprinting through the drear, assassinating squirreling demons. Behind them, the vortex was even more massive than before. Delia despaired. Somehow she'd expected it to close upon Glenn's death.

She crouched beside his smoldering remains. There amongst the carnage lay Glenn's heart, fused to the Menhir, churning blackness. She looked to the vortex again, realizing the Menhir-heart was a smaller, mirror image of the void—the gateway and the key.

Delia stepped forward carefully. When the first evil thoughts came to her she retreated and wrung her hands in frustration. There had to be a way, even if the blue aurora was fading.

Glenn's heart beat, mocking her even in death.

*

Byrne limped toward the edge of the thicket. He had the rope slung over his shoulder and was dragging the corpse of Sister Mable through the slush. There was still an azure gleam about her. He'd seen what Delia had done, what value remained in Sister Mable. To think the bitch could have used her own blood for that stupid Jesus statue instead of the children's, instead of his own.

He pulled harder, thighs burning from exertion, his decimated shoulders grinding and popping as he hauled the dead nun toward the tree line, and when he rounded the cornfield he saw Delia, in human form just as he was, drenched in the blood of Glenn Amarok. She was wounded but those gashes and holes would seal over. He'd been that young once, but now his wounds were more stubborn when it came to healing. Many of these new injuries would be permanent.

Delia looked to him, then down at the nun.

"Mr. Byrne. What are you doing with the Sister?"

"Thought we might need her."

Delia shook her head. "She was a goodly Christian. She deserves better than what all I did to her."

"You *had* to do it, kid."

"I could've shot her first. Let her go easy."

"It's hard to think about things like that when you're clouded by wolfen urges. Besides, you had to act fast. You did right." He looked at the smoldering body parts and when he saw Glenn's severed head he went over to it and spat. "See you in Hell, brother."

"It's not over," Delia said. "The portal—it's still open."

She nodded her head toward a black shape on the ground. Byrne leaned forward, realizing what it was.

"That thing," she said. "It's tied to the portal somehow. I don't think it'll close until we destroy the stone and Glenn's heart. I tired to blow them up, but—"

"They won't burn."

"I can't even *pick it* up. When I do, it pulls at something in me, tempting me with dark thoughts. I'm afraid if I hold it in my hands the beast within will take me over."

"It will at that."

"Silly question but… can you pick it up?"

"Reckon if I do, I'll be on the same path as ol' Glenn was. The Menhir is ancient evil shrunk down to its purest form. No wolfen, no matter how pure of heart, can resist its call. It stains your mind and that beast within you speak of, well… it takes over for good."

Delia leaned against a tree, wrought with the exhaustion of war and weighted by the crippling burden of protecting the world. All she'd wanted was to kill the men who'd killed her kin, a noble enough cause in Byrne's mind. Now the poor kid was a defender of all mankind, one hell of a task for a teen girl to be saddled with.

"When they buried Jasper's heart," Byrne said, "the sisters made a special amulet to put it in and they blessed it, otherwise they would not be able to touch it without being poisoned and turned into the living dead, like that doctor was. And the Menhir they kept inside a holy symbol—the statue of Christ—and it was sealed in a chamber always filled with the blood of the innocent, blood made into a sort of holy water to keep the stone's power contained, to hide it from men like the Koyotes."

"So… we need an amulet? A Christian symbol to carry it in, so it doesn't turn us into…"

"Into wolfen no better than the one you just killed."

She sighed. "Where are we gonna get an amulet? There's no time to go back to the chapel and—"

"I reckon the amulet ain't the thing. It ain't the chamber itself—its what purifies it."

The girl's eyebrows drew closer together. She stared at him and followed his gaze when he looked down at Sister's Mable's bound carcass.

Delia shifted. "You think…"

Byrne squatted beside the nun.

Delia had not left much of Mable's neck. All that kept her head on was the splintered link of vertebra and a few slivers of flesh at the back. He pushed two fingers into her dead, white eyes, digging them into the sockets. Delia gasped and looked away. He put his thumb into Mable's mouth, put his other hand on the vertebra, and pulled up, cracking the skull free. It glowed in his hands and the light made him queasy, but if it burned his skin he was too numb from other wounds to feel it.

He would have to move fast with the Menhir-heart. If he held it too long his mind would never return from the thrall of its malevolence. He reached for the Menhir and bit down on his tongue so the pain would distract him from the thoughts the stone put in his head. His mind convulsed in a seizure of sadistic desires. Visions of human slaughter exploded across his mind's eye, bodies being stretched on racks, toddlers being cooked alive, his victims' skins stuffed into his mouth while they screamed and writhed, women raped by his massive, werewolf body until they were hobbled and died from shock.

Byrne pushed the Menhir-heart under the dead nun's jaw and up into the concavity of her severed head, then turned the skull upside down, cradling the heart and stone inside it. The Menhir-heart pulsed but its blackness was engulfed by waves of blessed, blue blood, muting the stone's influence. His mind was released, as was the breath he'd been holding.

"Tear her open," he said.

Delia looked at him. "Do what?"

"I'm too weak to do it now. Besides, I have to hold this darned thing. You go on and rip into the sister's belly. We needed to lather up this skull with her, keep the Menhir covered in holy blood and guts."

The girl closed her eyes.

"Feel bad later, kid."

CHAPTER LI

THE SIGHT OF THEM MADE Grace gasp.

Delia and Byrne were caked in blood and ash, in gunpowder, dirt, and slush. Byrne was holding a sphere of some kind. It glowed a heavenly blue and Grace sighed with relief just seeing this sign of white magic.

Then she realized what the sphere was.

She gagged and took Russell's arm. Even through his coat sleeve she could feel how cold he was.

The four approached each other. The pandemonium had settled, at least for now, but still the vortex churned with the symphony of Hell. The clicking vocals of demons echoed across the field, their forms hidden by smoke and festering rye as they fled to the hillside.

Byrne held the decapitated head close to him. Around his neck and shoulders was a length of intestine the color of blueberries. His arms were shaking and he looked only a few feet from death's door. Grace pitied the poor man. The curse had afflicted him in more ways than she could ever imagine. It pained her to know Delia was now infected. Would she too choose the crooked path of the Koyotes? Grace found it hard to believe the heart of a mere girl-child could spoil so, but Delia had come into their lives on the

398

blades of vengeance. Such a journey would toxify even the purest of women, even without the curse of the wolf.

They didn't ask about the nun's severed head. The madness all around them no longer warranted explanations. They could come later. The horror took precedent.

The group gazed upon the vortex.

Russell said, "What now, Luther?"

Byrne gazed down at the Menhir and when he turned his neck Grace saw the branded number thirteen there, bloody below the webbing of his whiskers.

"What have we got?" he asked.

They looked to one another, lost.

"Weapons wise," Byrne said.

Russell held up his rifle. "Five shots left."

Grace popped the revolver's chamber. "Three."

"Okay," Byrne said. "How about you, kid?"

Delia reached into coat, withdrawing one final stick of dynamite. Byrne took it and she handed him the matches.

"Grace and Henry," Byrne said, "I got a feeling them demons on that hill yonder will be coming back right quick when I get close."

"Close to what?" Russell asked.

Byrne nodded toward the vortex.

Russell squinted. "What are you aiming to do?"

"Close her up, if'n I can."

Delia shook her head. "Dynamite couldn't even blow up the Menhir. You think it'll blow up the portal?"

"Not the dynamite alone, but with Mable's blood and the Menhir contained, maybe…"

He trailed off.

Delia said, "Maybe what?"

Byrne put his hand on her good shoulder. Their eyes locked, both holding a faded, red glow.

"We can't just throw it in there and hope for the best. We need to be sure."

She furrowed her brow but said nothing.

"Kid, you'll learn to trust your wolfen instincts, just as I trust mine."

"But, Mr. Byrne—"

"It'll be hard for a while, being what you are. You will kill others—innocents. There ain't no avoiding that. But if'n you keep your heart pure you can overcome the call of your curse and use the pull of Mars to your advantage. Follow your wolfen instincts and you can take possession of the beast. You can satisfy the urge without giving in to the worst of it. Just steer clear of bad packs. Be a lone wolf, kid. Instead of following a path, make your own."

He went to Russell and extended his hand. The men shook.

"Never thought I'd respect a lawman, but here I am."

Russell nodded. "You are a man worth his salt, Luther Byrne."

Grace furrowed her brow, unsure what was happening.

"I'd ask you a favor," Byrne told the marshal, "but I don't think you're up for it."

Grace took Russell's hand, hoping he would not volunteer for whatever it was, wanting him to come home with her so he might heal and conquer his deterioration. She wanted to believe that. She *had* to believe it.

Byrne turned to Delia before Russell could offer.

"Kid. I want you to make me two promises."

He leaned into the girl then, whispering something Grace could not hear over the roar of the vortex and the dust devils that tossed dead leaves all about them. The sky rumbled with heavy clouds but pink rays had appeared upon the horizon, the color of her world shining as a beacon in this anarchic west.

Byrne stepped away from Delia and she nodded in agreement to whatever he'd requested, and he walked over the rubble of the farmhouse and up to the stairway of rotting meat that led into the void.

*

He lit the fuse.

The blackness enveloped him like a hail of locusts, frightened into frenzy as the blue gore of Sister Mable dribbled upon the fleshy platform. Byrne forced the stick of dynamite into the skull's mouth and clutched it in both hands, raising it before him like a shield. The vortex bellowed, calling the escaped demons to their home to protect the monoliths. Byrne realized now that there was no devil, no fallen angel. The true king of Hell was the evil itself, combined negative forces born of all cruelty, an accumulation of eons of deviant brutality.

The posse fired their weapons, covering him as the demons returned from the hillside, but there were only so many bullets left and soon the remaining creatures were charging through the ruins, squealing and gnashing as they came for him.

It didn't matter. The fuse was almost spent.

Byrne stepped into the vortex and turned around, his blue glow filling the darkness, making it recede into the tunnel of the void. Tears came to his eyes as the creatures crawled upon him, but there was a wide smile on his face. After a life of wickedness, he was finally doing something good—one last, beautiful thing. And as the claws of demons tore into the Thirteenth Koyote his smile never wavered for his heart was black no more.

Even white magic accepts a sacrifice.

*

He exploded in a geyser of flaming, blue gore. The nun's skull burst, sending the Menhir and Glenn Amarok's heart hurtling backward into the void, lost to the pull of a collapsing dimension. The holy droplets of blood transmogrified into crystalline prisms that sent rainbows of various blues beaming in and out of the seal, thrumming with ferocity.

The others ducked but Delia stayed standing, watching the dimension implode in a cyclone of azure flame. Both forms of sorcery called to her, the white and the black. They would do so as long as she lived.

Many of the demons that swarmed over Byrne had been obliterated. Others fell into the void. But some scurried off into the cornfield and rye and deep into the surrounding woodland. The void shrank to the size of one of Glenn's fireballs and burned with the same black fire, and then all its light bent into the laceration in space from which it had appeared, and with a great thunderclap the portal to Hell closed.

The dead bodies of demons began to disintegrate and the remains of the slain behemoth turned to black puddles to be absorbed into the earth. The void's meat sizzled in the snow, decaying rapidly until it was only ash that drifted on the wind. The storm clouds began to separate then, revealing a swirl of reds and yellows in the western sky. The sunlight was dying, but only for the day, not for the eternity the void had promised, and Delia turned her face to its glow, her whiskers fluttering with those same colors.

CHAPTER LII

GRACE HUGGED DELIA FROM BEHIND and kissed her cheek despite the muttonchops. Delia kissed her back and had to pull away, smelling the schoolmarm's sweet flesh. Her stomach pinched in hunger and she salivated, her canines inching up as she heard Grace's blood pump at her throat. She closed her eyes against the urge, stifling it for now. But night was falling. And some night soon there would be full moonlight and the great call of Mars.

"I best be moving on now," she said.

Grace blinked. "Moving on? What do you mean?"

"Just what I said, ma'am. I thank you for your hospitality, but it's time I be leaving Hope's Hill."

Grace looked to Russell, but he had nothing to say. He'd gone pale, his lips an alarming purple and his neck sprinkled with small spider-webs of protruding veins.

"But where will you go?" Grace asked.

Delia stared into the horizon, the golden light making the pinpoints of red glimmer in her pupils.

"I reckon I'll forge my own path," she said. "Goodbye, Ms. Cowlin. Goodbye, Marshal. I'll carry you with me always."

She left them behind, Russell leaning on Grace for support. The schoolteacher watched as Delia disappeared into the woodland where she'd conquered the man who'd killed her family. Standing before Glenn's smoking remains was his gray mustang, black horns protruding from its head and neck. The wound in its hind leg would have made a normal horse lame, but it was healing rapidly, the hide already turned to scar tissue. Delia came up beside it slowly, giving the horse a better look at her. She patted his neck and ran her fingers through its black mane.

Belial neighed and nuzzled into her, drawn by her wolfen scent.

She gathered only what she felt she needed. She lifted her leg over the saddle's cantle and sat the horse. The clouds had sunk backward into the crevices of the mountain, darkening the jagged rocks and white willows that twisted through the crags like the unearthed bones of the dead, reaching toward the first spattering of stars in welcome of the coming of night. The moon had appeared in the gloaming, a huge sphere swelled red by the setting sun, hovering like the baneful, watching eye of a wolfen God.

Delia clacked reins made of her own hair.

Tied by his hair to the saddle horn, Glenn's severed head bounced at her side as she rode toward the moon.

CHAPTER LIII

THEY'D FOUND HIS HORSE, BUT Russell wouldn't leave until he found Shies, even if the man were dead. When they found him he was still breathing, but they had to act quickly. He'd surely die before they could make it back to Hope's Hill.

His leg had been shredded, the foot gone and the shin burned down to just fat and bone. Shies had torn his sleeve off and wrapped it tight around the thigh as a tourniquet, slowing the blood flow from the exposed arteries. His breaths were shallow, eyelids fluttering. Grace turned to Russell, her eyes saying more than words ever could. He went to the scattered swords left by the behemoth, came back with one with a serrated blade, and started sawing.

*

He awoke in pain, surprised to have awoken at all.

Shies did not know where he was, but he was alive and that was enough for now. He got up on his elbows. He was on a feather mattress. To his right was a window. A yellow curtain blew in the breeze. It was a warm day for winter, the air reminding him of autumn, his favorite season. It made him think of Nizhoni and days they'd spent picking apples from trees with foliage bright as fireworks against an October sky. Their love was young back then. In his mind it would stay that way forever.

He sat up and drew the blanket back. The stump was wrapped in heavy bandages, his leg cut off at the knee. He stared down at it, but there was no more room for loss in his heart. Looking to the bedside table, he saw the small bottle of purple elixir and took a long pull on the laudanum. Relief was instantaneous. The opiates not only soothed the physical pain but also clouded his grief, making him feel warm and safe, blessed by numbness.

Maybe I've died after all. Maybe this is as good as heaven gets.

The door to the room came open and a grayed woman poked her head inside.

"Mr. Shies?" she asked.

"The very same, ma'am."

He tried to rise but couldn't. "Forgive me for not standing."

"Oh, come now, sir." She entered but left the door open. "My name is Joyce Abercrombie. This is my rooming house."

"Where?"

"In Hope's Hill, of course. Or what's left of it, I should say."

Shies rubbed his eyes. "How long have I been sleeping?"

"You've been in and out a few days now with the fever. Marshal Russell brought you here and got a doctor to come in from Battlecreek to treat you for blood poisoning. Doc Southington's his name. A fine man, come here with the brigade. He's been tending to lots of folks in town."

"Brigade?"

"Our good marshal brought in the Calvary. Lawmen, carpenters, and volunteers come to clean up the mess those outlaws left behind. That no account coward Murphy Hyers up and abandoned us, but the council's invested too much in Hope's Hill to give up on us. It troubles me to see what all those bad men have done to our little town, but like folks say, there's still hope in Hope's Hill."

When he tried to sit all the way up the housemother came to his side and eased him back, propping a pillow behind his shoulders.

"Easy now, Mr. Shies."

He rubbed the bridge of his nose, blinking against the blur of the laudanum.

"The others…" he said. "Where are they?"

"You must rest. When you're feeling better, the doctor has

crutches for you. You'll be able to move around soon enough, and then you can see whomever you wish."

It came to Shies like a punch to the stomach—he was an invalid. He'd spend the rest of his life braced on a crutch. He leaned back at the housemother's insistence, hoping the laudanum would take his sadness away, but he would soon learn he had no reason to mourn his lost limb. In the days to come, his biggest problem would be hiding that the leg was growing back.

*

The marshal stood before her like the ghost of a man. He was wan and pale, waxen against the daylight that fell into the room, the mark of death clear upon his face.

And yet she loved him.

The snow was falling gently, barely coating the ground behind Russell's house. The evergreens were a reminder of long ago Christmases. Grace wasn't sure what day it was today, if this year's holiday season had passed or not. She liked the idea of spending Christmas Eve sitting before the fireplace she sat in front of now, wrapped in Henry Russell's arms, watching the embers crackle and spark, sipping tea as they snuggled into one another, warm and cozy and wonderful. Grace sighed. Some things, no matter how important or desired or deserved, had a way of simply not working out. She held his hands in hers. They were so cold they made her ache but still she would not let them go.

"There has to be some way," she said. "After all the things we've witnessed, surely there is some form of magic that can bring you back in full."

"Reckon this is as back as a man can be."

Her eyes flooded. "You ought to be rewarded for your bravery. Instead you're punished. It's not fair."

He stroked the tear from her cheek. "Someone once told me I saw justice and meaning in a world that lacks both."

"Henry, I…"

"There may not always be justice, but there is meaning. This I know with my full heart. For when I look into your lovely eyes I see the meaning behind all mankind. Therein I see the humanity, the mercy, and the faith, everything that gives life its magic—not some witchcraft good or bad, but the simple, everyday magic of being alive. And of them all I can think of no magic as great as love."

Her kissed her then, held her and kissed her with the lips of a man who would never kiss again, and though he was cold to the touch Grace felt only warmth, for while Henry Russell was a man of great courage and grit, in his arms she felt not only safe but also cherished. Here she could dream, if for but a moment, of a small cottage on a hillside and a summer breeze, of children chasing one another in the tall grass, their father retired from the U.S. Marshals and watching them play as he lay beside her on the picnic blanket. Her husband would hold her hand and they would kiss just like this, long and deep, and in those kisses all the humanity and mercy and faith he spoke of would flourish into something stronger every time.

Instead, the kiss ended. When Russell pulled back, she saw the thin, black crow's feet at his eyes and the dark purple of his smile.

"Grace," he said, "your name certainly suits you."

He stepped to the coat rack for his hat.

CHAPTER LIV

THEY PULLED INTO THE STATION at noon, right on time. The conductor stood at the rear of the walkway as the other ticketholders made their exit, and once they were gone he came to the man in the heavy coat sitting low with his hat down, covering his face.

"We're here, mister. Fort Channer, Texas."

The man looked at him, the brim of his hat rising, revealing the bandages wrapped around his face. The conductor thought of the mummies he'd read about in the Galveston Daily News, the ones that had been shipped overseas to America to be used in the study of mummia and the making of bituminous medicines. The strange man had given the conductor a whopping twenty dollars just to tend to him, so he wasn't going to let his spooky appearance worry him. He helped the man up, careful not touch his bandages, keeping his hands on the coat just in case he had some sort of contagious disease. The man walked on unsteady legs and his breaths made strained wheezing noises. The conductor could only assume he'd made the long trip south to see some kind of specialist, but he didn't pry, thinking it'd be rude to bring up anything involving the man's condition, whatever it may be.

When the boxcar was set before the loading chute, the conductor guided the man's horse down and over to the watering trough. It was a fine stallion, coal-black and muscly. He helped the man over the saddle's cantle.

The conductor tipped his cap. "Reckon this here horse'll get you where you need to be right quick."

"I am obliged to you for all your assistance."

"I've been well compensated for my time."

The man gazed at the massive windmill at the edge of the station, which provided water to the otherwise barren soil and churned gallons upon gallons for locomotive steam.

The man said, "The railroads have done much for Texas."

The conductor nodded, taking a pre-rolled cigarette from a silver billfold.

"You a settler?" the conductor asked. "This land's filling up with more farmers every day it seems. Maybe one day I'll quit riding all over this country, find myself a prairillon to stake claim. But I've yet to find a place I wish to call home."

"Yeah," the man said. "I thought the same thing once."

*

He reached Lonely Bell early the next morning.

It was much warmer here than it was up in Hope's Hill. Hell, it was always warm in Texas, but Russell pulled his coat tighter around him, both to cover his ghastliness and keep his bones from rattling. It was hard to stay warm with translucent flesh.

The town was no different than when he had left it, but somehow it looked faded, an old sepia photograph as foggy as the memories it tried to preserve. He made no stops, not wanting to be seen. He drew a few stares from children wondering why a man would be so heavily covered in wraps, but made his way down the pebbled streets without incident, riding until the main road turned to dirt.

The marshal journeyed across the plains, the Texas sun rising in a cloudless sky.

The perfect day.

He followed the wagon trail across the sandy terrain, taking a break to watch the pronghorns amongst the bald cypress and bur oaks. A single painted bunting flew low, giving him a glimpse of its rainbow of feathers.

409

"It's good to be home."

When he reached the low basin where the oak tree stood reaching to heaven, he gazed to the east and there was the house he'd built all those years ago. Shirts and a yellow dress fluttered on the clothesline. When he'd been ready to leave home he'd sold the place to a family of five. Russell hoped they were living well, that they were happier there than he had turned out to be. He hoped Grace Cowlin would be happy in her life too, and that Delia Van Vracken would find peace, and that Oscar Shies would learn to live with his deformity. It had been a long trip back to town, Shies draped over the horse Cillian O'Conner had rode in on, Russell and Grace sharing his horse. But they'd made it back alive, or alive for the time being, at least.

He trotted Fury down to the tree and there in the dead grass was the wooden slab, still standing up straight. He dismounted and read the words he'd carved into it, using the same knife he'd once used to put their initials in the tree, back when they were first courting.

Here lies Caldonia Russell, a goodly wife. Never was one more beloved. May she rest in peace.

Removing his hat, Russell sat down beside his wife's grave and watched the clouds the way they once had. He sat there for a long time. When he tried to stand up he couldn't do it on his own, so he called Fury over and the horse lowered his neck so Russell could pull himself to his feet.

There was a barn at the old house and the family had horses and a mule. Fury would be bound to wander over there when this was over. He was a good horse and deserved a loving family. Let him enjoy that life for the both of them.

U.S. Marshal Henry Russell climbed back into the saddle, using the last of his strength to do so, and guided the horse beneath the oak tree. He took the rope from around the saddle horn, tied the knot, and slung the noose over the branch. He tied the end of the rope into another knot to secure it to the tree, put his head through the loop, and got Fury into position. He thought about saying a final prayer, but none came to mind. Just as well. He had little use for such things anyway.

CHAPTER LV

STEELBRANCH WAS A FARMING TOWN not much different from her own hometown of Cottonwood, but it had a much livelier main street. Revelers were gallivanting on the porches of the saloon, jovial as if it were a holiday. In a way, Delia felt like celebrating too. So far she'd been lucky. While riding lonesome on the prairie, a duo of robbers crossed her path, leaping from the bushes to sabotage her. They'd waived their pistols like boys playing chase and the ugly one had licked his rotting teeth while looking her up and down, cursing and spitting. Knowing their intentions, Delia had felt no guilt in killing them and satiated her hunger for two days with pieces of the men she carried in her saddlebag. Keeping her belly full of human flesh made it easier to control her urges, but she had not yet been forced to transform in full. But the pull of Mars was even stronger tonight, and soon the moon would be at its zenith.

Delia rolled her shoulders. Tomorrow night would bring her first full moon as a lycanthrope. She would shed innocent blood, take innocent lives. The thought of blacking out in her werewolf state made her mouth go dry. Of all her troubles, her first transformation lay heaviest on her mind. She'd never been a drinker, but felt she could use a stiff one, though that was not what had led her to the dance hall.

She'd made a promise and her word was her bond.

She tied Belial to the hitching post and an old drunk blinked at the sight of the strange-looking horse. Though it had adjusted to its new owner, the mustang was still devilish in appearance, though not as devilish as the creatures who had escaped the dark dimension during that final battle, the ones Delia would continue to hunt, town by town, world by world.

She went inside and paid the seventy-five cent cover charge and took up a stool at the bar. She ordered up a whiskey, her daddy's favorite, and turned around to face the dance floor. A skinny man was playing a honky-tonk piano while a dwarf did a jig upon the stage, clinging cymbals at his heels in perfect rhythm. A pair of stooped-over fiddlers riled up the crowd, everyone singing and cheering with cheeks rosy with booze. Cowboys twirled cherub sa-loon girls like glass ballerinas on a jewelry box and the girls seemed to glow with an alien beauty, bright bursts of color fluttering like butterflies among the drab, gray dust of men.

She sipped her drink, scanning the crowd for a girl who fit the description Byrne had given her. A lithe blonde was spinning about. Delia watched her flow and bob, her curls like gold being spun. When the song was over, the saloon girl came to the bar for a rest, dabbing at her brow with a kerchief. Her ruffled skirt rode up as she sat, showing off her bright petticoat.

Delia walked over. The saloon girl looked at her.

"Oh, p'shaw," the girl said. "Don't tell me you want a dance. I'm open-minded but the men 'round these parts don't take kindly to women being, you know, *funny*."

Delia shook her head. "No, I'm here on behalf of a friend."

"Saw the handbill, did you?" She looked her up and down. "Yeah, I'll bet the owner will like you, being young and having that fiery hair and all. Forgive me for saying so, honey, but you've got a little of that hair on your cheeks there. We can take care of that, though. We got us a barber 'round back."

"Ain't looking for a job. I come here looking for Sorrow."

The salon girl sat up straight. "Well, you found her. Of what do I owe the pleasure?"

"Like I said, I'm here on behalf of a friend. His name was Luther Byrne."

She expected the girl to raise her eyebrows or even gasp when

Delia said his name *was* Luther Byrne instead of *is*. Instead Sorrow's face was blank. She leaned forward, as if expecting more.

"And?" Sorrow asked. "What about him? Pray tell."

"You don't know that name?"

"I can't says that I do."

"He came in here not too long ago, spent a night dancing with you. I guess your time together made quite an impression, at least on him."

Sorrow gave her a small smile. "Sorry, darlin'. Really, I am. But your friend matches the description of every cowpoke who comes in here."

"He was tall and dark-skinned—a half-breed." Delia pushed back her hair, revealing the sideburns growing longer down her jaw each day. "Whiskers like these."

Sorrow put her chin in her hand. "You know, I do recollect a half-Indian with tough whiskers. They were *really* tough, like metal shavings."

Delia took Sorrow's hand and touched it to her whiskers. The saloon girl's eyes went wide.

"Lordy," she said. "You don't look like him but you must be his kin."

"In a way. So you remember him?"

"Well, I surely remember them whiskers. So yes, I do believe I recollect the man. He was a scary-looking thing, but a gentleman." Her eyes lit. "Wait. He said something, something queer. It just came to mind."

"What's that?"

"He said the rules of Hell would surprise me. Something like that. It was odd, but it didn't seem like a threat, not the way he said it. He kind of laughed when he said it, like it was a joke. I didn't understand it, but I always laugh at a paying customer's jokes anyhow. Know what I mean?"

"I reckon so."

"Well... what do you think he meant, about the rules of Hell?"

"I'm not sure," Delia said, "but I've many moons to find out."

Sorrow gave her a quizzical look. She stood up, giving Delia the pretty, polite smile again. "Well, honey, it's been nice chatting, but I've got work to do—got to pull in the pieces, as they say. I am sorry about your friend. You talk like he's gone on."

"He has at that."

"Well, you do have my condolences. I'm sure he's in a better place."

Delia thought of Byrne's tears of joy as he was blown into a black dimension.

"Yeah," she said, leaving it at that. "But see, before he died he asked me two favors. One of them was to come here and tell you you're the last woman he ever danced with. You were his final dance. Those were his exact words—*Sorrow, you were my final dance.* He wanted me to tell you that."

Sorrow's face matched her namesake then. "Your friend... he liked to speak in riddles, didn't he?"

"Sometimes. But if you think about this one just a while, you'll see it's pretty straightforward." She tipped her hat and put a coin on the bar and slid it to the saloon girl. "Have yourself a good life, ma'am."

As Delia stepped away, Sorrow called out to her. "What was the other promise?"

"To remember him," Delia said. "To just remember him."

She walked through the haze of cigar smoke, grateful for it to drown out the smell of all that sweaty human flesh. A sign at the back told of the barber Sorrow spoke of, so Delia made her way to through the throng of patrons and entered the small backroom. The walls were lined with hand-drawn pictures of bears and swallows, of flags and the smiling faces of children. An old man with whirly, gray hair was sitting in the chair, reading a penny dreadful. When Delia entered he stood and brushed the loose hairs from his slacks. A pair of scissors and two pencils stuck out of his shirt pocket.

"Evenin', young miss. Needin' a trimmin' are you?"

"No. I'm growing it long."

"You've a fine shock of red hair. It'd look good longer."

"I always thought it did. Wasn't too happy when it was cut off."

He rubbed his hands together. "So what'll it be then? I also pull teeth, if one is ailing you."

"How about tattoos?"

The old man smiled, rubbing his hands more vigorously.

"Oh, miss, you have come to the right place!" He rolled up one sleeve and came closer, showing off a faded horseshoe tattoo. "Did this one myself, many years ago. It was for luck, though I don't see it's brought me much. Never did get a piece of pudding. But I can draw, see?" He gestured to the artwork tacked to the walls. "You name it, I can tattoo it."

Delia sat in the chair and leaned back. She removed the beaded Kiowa necklace.

"I don't need anything fancy," she said. "Just a simple number, to remember a friend by."

"A tattoo is a fine tribute. What number would you like?"

A red glimmer filled her scarred eye.

"Thirteen," she said.

ACKNOWLEDGEMENTS

Thanks to Wile E. Young, Justin Coons, Aron Beauregard, John Wayne Comunale, Ryan Harding, Josh Doherty, Brian Keene, Gregg Kirby, CV Hunt, Bryan Smith, and Jack Ketchum.

And special thanks to Tom Mumme—always.

Kristopher Triana is the Splatterpunk Award-winning author of *Full Brutal, Gone to See the River Man, They All Died Screaming* and many other terrifying books. He is also the author of the crime thrillers *The Ruin Season* and *Shepherd of the Black Sheep*. His work has been published in multiple languages and has drawn praise from the likes of *Publisher's Weekly, Rue Morgue Magazine, Cemetery Dance, Scream Magazine, The Horror Fiction Review* and many more.

He lives somewhere in New England.

Get signed books and more at: TRIANAHORROR.COM

Visit him at:
Kristophertriana.com
Twitter: Koyotekris
Facebook: Kristopher Triana
Instagram: Kristopher_Triana

Made in United States
Troutdale, OR
12/11/2024

26254092R10260